DARK EXODUS

THE ORDER OF VAMPIRES 2

LYDIA MICHAELS

DARK EXODUS
THE ORDER OF VAMPIRES 2
Copyright © 2021 Lydia Michaels Books, LLC

BAILEY BROWN PUBLISHING
Paranormal Romance

First Editor: Lindsay Guthrie
Final Editor: Loren Brake
Cover Design: Lydia Michaels

WORLD RIGHTS
USA | CANADA | SPAIN | EUROPE | NEW ZEALAND |
AUSTRALIA | ASIA

DEDICATION

For my beautiful readers.

CHAPTER 1

Dane Foster leaned forward in his chair. The tattered shoelaces of his dusty Converse dragged through the sandy dirt where soot and ash drifted like black snow. He prodded the snapping fire with the poker when a marshmallow pegged him in the temple.

He scowled over his shoulder to glare at the culprit, doing his best to look severe. But her laughing gaze, peeping out from beneath her cockeyed wool cap, made true irritation impossible. Cybil's eyes had been Dane's kryptonite since the first time he looked into them when their parents brought her home from the hospital. Liquid brown and so inno-cent, she could easily get away with murder.

With her face bundled up to the nose in a bright yellow scarf and that ridiculous wool hat on her head, she blinked innocently again. Then she tipped her head, crossed those majestic eyes, and made a zombie-like groan as soggy marshmallows fell from her overstuffed mouth. She laughed before her cheeks were empty and nearly choked on the last one.

"You're wasting them," Dane scolded, but his voice trembled with the urge to giggle. "You're such a child."

"*You're such a child,*" Cybil mimicked. She stuffed a marshmallow partially up her nose, plugged the other nostril with her finger, and shot the white ball at his knee.

"Grow up."

She giggled and sat back. The collapsible legs of her nylon camp chair whined under her slight weight.

Dane plunged the poker into the ground and reached for another marshmallow. He examined the sweet puff and, after blowing off a few speckles of dirt, popped it into his mouth.

"Ew!" Cybil squealed in a piercing shrill only little girls could manage. "Was that the one from my nose?"

He secretly hoped not. "So?" He shrugged,

too cool to show concern. "We're camping. Gotta eat a pound of dirt before we die."

"Mom, Dane's eating boogers!" she yelled, knowing their mom was too far from camp to hear. She left them alone so she could search for kindling, but since their mom hadn't asked for help meant she likely had to go to the bathroom.

He opened his mouth wide to offer his sister one last vulgar display of the squishy treat. He laughed at her repulsion and swallowed, then picked up two skewers. "Here, give me the bag. I'll set you up so you can roast one."

She tossed the light bag to him. "Boys are so gross."

"Yup."

"Shouldn't you be a little more mature for sixteen? That's probably why Gwen dumped you."

His eyes narrowed. The sting from his recent breakup still smarted. "Shouldn't you be a little taller for ten?"

She stuck out her tongue and snatched the skewered marshmallow out of his hands. They sat in silence, waiting for their mom to return. The fire crackled in a hypnotic rhythm as crisp autumn leaves whispered through the dry branches above.

The temperature dropped as the sun disappeared. The buzzing insects clocked out as nocturnal creatures started their shift. The opening act always belonged to the owls.

"Why's Mommy taking so long?"

"She probably had to pee."

"She didn't bring toilet paper." Cybil pointed to the supplies by the tent where a roll of toilet paper sat.

Dane shrugged. "Maybe it was an emergency. She'll be back in a few minutes. Your marshmallow's gonna catch fire if you hold it that close to the flame."

"I like it burnt."

Camping became a tradition after their father and grandfather had passed away. Every October they would retreat to the tall hills of northern Pennsylvania and reconnect as a family. No television, no Wi-Fi, no gaming systems. Just family. The only difference this year compared to the last several years was that their Nanna wasn't with them.

As if reading his thoughts, Cybil quietly asked, "Do you think last year was the last time Nanna will ever camp with us?"

Adjusting his skewer over the flame, eyes

transfixed on the dancing yellow tongues, his mind numbed at the memory of so much loss. They buried half their family all at once. And he couldn't handle how quickly grief aged their grandmother as if her broken heart had left her weak and susceptible to other things.

"I don't know. Maybe." He knew Nanna would never venture on another camping trip with them again. He heard his mom and Nanna whispering at night. The cancer was back, and his grandmother was all out of fight. But saying it out loud somehow made it all too real.

"How do the doctors know how long a person can live? They could come out with a cure for Nanna."

"There is a cure, Cybil. It's called chemo. Nanna doesn't want it."

"Why not?" his sister demanded.

Her outrage was confused sadness at the idea of losing her grandmother, losing yet another family member. He was sad, too, but he was a teenage boy. It wouldn't be right for him to fall apart because his Nanna was dying.

"You were too young to remember the last time she went through treatment. Chemo makes you really sick. She got really weak, vomited constantly, and lost all her hair. It's painful. Nanna's already in pain. She doesn't want any more."

"She doesn't look like she's in pain. She doesn't even look sick."

"She is. Just because people don't talk about things doesn't mean they don't feel them."

"She's just giving up!"

"We all die, Cybil. If Nanna wants to die peacefully, that's her choice. She's had a full life. She had no control over losing Grandpa. Let her at least have control over her own destiny."

His sister swung the skewer and her crispy, puffed marshmallow flung off the tip and plunged into the flames. She watched dispassionately as it caught fire and burned into blackened ash.

Her big eyes glazed with unshed tears, catching the flickering reflection of the flare, and he suffered her sorrow as if it were his own. Her ivory skin was so youthful it looked translucent around her features, and when she stared like that, parts of her looked made of glass.

He held his breath, silently begging a god he didn't believe in not to let one tear fall. He was tired of watching his mother, sister, and grandmother cry because there was nothing he could do to ease their pain, and he hated feeling so damn useless. His dad always could make them laugh, but now he was gone, and Dane didn't have a clue how to repair the ache his absence brought.

His mother was barely keeping it together since they arrived here. He continuously caught her swiping the rims of her eyes until they grew red and puffy with irritation. That was the problem with small families. When you lost a member, you lost a notable chunk of the group.

Soon, his grandmother will pass. Probably sometime within the next few months. Then it would be only him, Cybil, and their mom. And all the tears.

His stomach knotted as his anxiety spiked. He set his skewer against the hot metal rim of the firepit. The marshmallow melted off the tip and oozed into the flames. Why bother saving it?

His sister bolted out of her chair and tossed the skewer in the sand. "I'm going to look for Mom."

Dane stood. "I'll come with you."

Her unspoken relief welcomed him.

It was getting dark. Dane regretted not grabbing a flashlight before they left their site. The crunch of newly fallen leaves muffled the snap of twigs under their feet, and with each breath a cloud of mist filled the air before them. He wouldn't be surprised if the temperatures dropped into the forties once the stars came out.

"How far would she go to collect sticks?" Since losing their father, Cybil had developed a pattern of constant griping whenever she worried, but Dane read into her negativity and saw it stemmed from the worries that often clouded her mind.

"I told you, she probably had to pee."

"There are sticks all over the place. She could have just walked around our tent and found enough to keep the fire going all night."

Cybil was always one of those kids who needed to fill the air with meaningless words as if silence was simply unbearable. But recent events had hiked up her anxiety and shifted her regular commentary toward pessimism.

"Maybe she just wanted some air." He sensed his mom wasn't looking for sticks but rather a quiet place to hide and cry.

"We're outside, doofus. There's air

everywhere."

A loud crack broke the silence and a small creature skittered across the bed of fallen leaves. The shadows had grown and it was getting too dark to tell if it was a chipmunk or something less adorable, like a skunk. "Watch your step. There are night critters underfoot." Dane warned.

"They're called nocturnal—" A crash echoed through the woods, stealing their attention in a split second. "What was that?"

"A branch must have fallen." Dane squinted into the darkening forest. "Be careful. These trees are old and some are rotted."

It grew impossibly dark under the shelter of the trees. He glanced back to make sure he could still see the glow from their fire, not wanting to get lost.

Another creak of wood. Then a louder snap. This time rattling the leaves and hitting other trees as it fell.

"What's doing that?" Cybil's voice shook, and she stepped closer to his side. "Are there bears in these woods?"

"There are bears all over Pennsylvania, Cyb. It was probably just a big branch falling. Or a tree. Watch your step."

"Maybe we should go back."

Dane agreed, but he couldn't remember if his mom took a flashlight either. What if she was lost? He wondered if he should go back to the site to grab one of the halogen lanterns then return to find her.

"Let's call for Mom."

They both cupped their hands around their mouths and yelled, "Mom!"

"Mommy?"

"Mom, are you out here?"

"Where are you?"

They took turns yelling but heard no response. The further they walked into the woods the less Dane could see the fire's glow.

As he searched the shadows for his mother, he became disoriented and his sense of direction grew less trustworthy. "Okay, on the count of three. Ready? One, two, three…*Mom!*"

They paused, listening for any sound in the distance. Dane shut his eyes to focus on his hearing and fear tickled up his spine.

He reached for Cybil's small hand, a protective gesture as much as a comforting one. She had stopped chattering, which meant she was more than anxious. She was scared. The darker her thoughts became, the harder she was to read.

They hiked over dead leaves and knotted tree roots as the brush thickened and the forest grew dense. When Cybil lost her footing in a dip on the nonexistent path, he steadied her. The woods silenced, their breathing the only whisper of sound.

Something was off. Where was the hum of insects and the skitters of night critters? Usually, there was the rattle of cicadas and the chortle of owls. He heard nothing but their panting.

"Something's out there." He squinted into the inky shadows. "Maybe a bear." Only a predator would scare away all the smaller creatures.

Cybil's breath hitched. "Let's go back." She jerked her hand out of his and turned, but he grabbed the back of her sweatshirt.

"Don't! You never run from a predator."

"You're scaring me, Dane. I wanna go back to the site. Mommy's probably looking for us."

He dropped his voice to a whisper. "If something's out there and you run, it might chase us. We have to be quiet. Stay by my side."

He circled slowly, straining to see into every shadow. The hair on the back of his neck spiked as a gust of wind raced past their backs and he pivoted.

Nothing. But he swore he heard something. It was too fast to be a bear. Did Pennsylvania have cougars?

Another gust of wind funneled through the trees and something sped behind them. He spun around. This time he saw the ruffle of pine needle branches and the up-kick of dried leaves twirling off the ground. Whatever it was, it was taunting them.

"What is it? And *do not* say a bear." Cybil's hand clamped tight around his.

"That was too fast for a bear. It was probably just a cat or a fox or something."

It sounded too large to be a fox. "I want Mommy," Cybil whimpered.

He sniffed the air and his nose scrunched at the putrid stench. "Do you smell that?"

She barely sniffed. "No. I think we should walk back."

The rotting scent filled his lungs. "Whatever is out there, it stinks."

"All I smell is the fire." She tugged out of his grip and started walking back the way they came.

"Hey, I said stay by my side."

"I wanna go back, Dane."

Sleeping birds scattered from the trees above, and they both looked up with wide eyes. Cybil whimpered, standing stock-still, and Dane's heart dropped to the pit of his stomach. Whatever it was stood behind her, its glowing eyes cutting through the darkness as a low growl rumbled.

"Cybil, don't move."

A cloud of silver mist puffed behind her. It was tall—twice her height.

"Cybil—"

What is it? A thousand splinters of fear shot through Dane's heart.

"Don't look at it," the words left him in a silent whisper. His sister spun, her mouth opening in a soundless cry as she staggered back, stumbling into Dane's arms and belting out a blood-curdling scream.

The creature bellowed and bolted toward the trees.

Panicking, Dane let out a scream of his own. "Let's go!"

"It touched me!" She scurried into Dane's arms, climbing up his body. "What was it?"

It all happened so fast. Dane trembled with the urge to protect her, desperate to run but fearful of the creature. A sharp snarl, like a bobcat, ripped through the air, and they both silenced and stilled as it returned.

Eyes, unnatural, red-glowing eyes, watched them from only a few feet away. Dane's heart hammered against his ribs.

"What do we do?"

It was no animal. It was a man, but also not a man. Standing slightly hunched, the beast had matted hair, knotted and tangled with leaves and twigs.

Mud caked onto his bare flesh, and his naked body twisted with thickly corded sinew. It was unnatural. Fangs dripped with drool as the moonlight caught the sharp angles of its face. Definitely male, and it stared directly at Cybil as it stepped closer.

In one second, Dane sucked in a hundred useless breaths. The beast held something limp and lifeless in his arms. His heart plummeted as he recognized his mother's hair.

Cybil's scream cut through the night with enough force to pierce the moon. The animal dropped their mother's limp body onto the earth and sprung twenty feet into the trees.

His sister collapsed to the ground and crawled to their mother, but it was too late. A whimpered, "No…" was the last thing he heard his sister say.

CHAPTER 2

$\mathcal{L}$arissa bounced impatiently behind the curtain as her body thrummed with adrenaline and her pulse raced faster than the music vibrating Club Silhouettes. It was Halloween. When her boss laid out a selection of provocative costumes for the girls to choose from, she eagerly selected a dainty black lace ensemble with soft black fur trim, a feathered tail, and two tiny kitten ears.

She loved clothes. She loved the many colors and decadent fabrics, and she loved the freedom English women had in choosing their garments.

It was a world of indulgence outside the farm where she had lived her forty-nine years. Of course, due to the advantages of her species, she didn't look a day older than twenty-five.

She was half a century old, a woman in her own right, yet she had the autonomy of a child—exactly why she fled her oppressive Amish roots and risked everything to find happiness.

She regretted nothing since running away. Sure, she missed her parents. But after The Elders *gave* her to her husband, Silus, like an auctioneer passes a horse to a rancher, she had seen her mother and father, less and less. And what a terrible husband Silus Hostetler proved to be.

She tried not to think of her younger sister, Grace. Larissa did miss Gracie, as well as her brothers, Adam and Cain. Her one blessing was that Cain had found her. He had given her some money and helped her find a place to live while he, too, took some time away from the farm. But he was a male and did not have an overbearing husband to answer to.

Larissa trusted Cain more than anyone in the world to protect her freedom and not tell anyone back at the farm of her whereabouts. He was her only link to the family she left behind, but he understood why she could never return. Not to the farm, not to their sheltered way of life, and most of all, not to Silus.

A low, soft whistle sounded behind her. It was a sound she came to recognize as praise and approval from English men. She smiled at Vito.

"You approve?" She curtsied in front of her rotund friend. Vito was a soft-hearted man who protected the ladies at the club and guarded the door.

"Well, will you look at you." He took her hand and slowly twirled her for inspection. "Prettiest kitty I've ever seen."

Her cheeks heated, a smile cresting her lips as her gaze demurely dropped to the floor. "You're sweet, Vito."

He pulled a cigarette out of its pack with his teeth but didn't light it. "You up next?"

"Yes."

He flipped the lid of his metal lighter open and closed with his thumb. "What are you dancing to?"

"'I'm a Slave 4 U' by Britney Spears."

He nodded, lighting the cigarette tip until it glowed cherry red. "Good choice."

Larissa readjusted her cat-ear headband as

he blew out a cloud of smoke. "Is my tail on straight?"

Vito cleared his throat. "Ah … yeah … just…" He adjusted the black-feathered tail hanging from her lace panties. Cool fingers briefly touched the flesh of her bottom and she reflexively rose up on her toes. "Looks good."

She smiled, trusting his honesty. "Thank you."

"No problem. Candy's song is ending. You better get ready to go out there."

She nodded and shifted to peek out the curtain. Candy ended her routine in a flourished press across the stage floor that reminded Larissa of a mermaid pulling herself out of water. Larissa took a deep, calming breath.

She recently discovered a love for dance. The fact that she found a job that paid her to do just that was a blessing.

With one last look to make sure her high, shiny, black boots were zipped tight, she stepped out and waited for the lights to hit her. The spotlights made it so simple to lose herself on stage. They emphasized her every move for the audience yet also provided her privacy. So long as the lights were on her, she couldn't see another soul.

She felt blissfully alone on the stage, dancing out every emotion her body could feel and draw from the music. She was finally learning to embrace and love her femininity rather than fear what trouble it might invite. Here, unlike home, she was stronger than any male who tried to touch her.

The drumming base of the song rattled from the speakers and the lights flipped on. Smoke billowed from a machine hidden in the shadows, and she rotated her shoulders and hips to the beat of the music.

As Britney Spears's voice softly mewed, Larissa traipsed to the edge of the stage where a pole protruded. Prowling around the silver beam like a cat stalking its prey, she marched in her high, spiked boots with her feathered tail swishing and tickling the exposed flesh of her thighs.

Grasping the pole with one hand clad in a long-netted glove, she lifted her weight off the stage with feline-like agility and twirled her body around the sleek metal. Whistles erupted with approval from the males sitting in the darkness.

The other girls said she was an amazing

dancer. Apparently, it was a struggle for a mortal to hold their body weight in precarious positions for extended amounts of time. Larissa, an immortal, suffered no such strain.

Dropping her knees to the floor, she held the pole with both hands and arched her spine back to lower her shoulders to the stage. She peeked at the audience through thick lashes, her long, dark hair dragging freely across the floor.

She reveled in her exposed vanity, careless of her newfound conceit. There were no more tight braids or sharp pins or bonnets in this new world. And she was never returning to her old, oppressive ways.

She swung her head up, and with a flip of her hair, she rolled to her stomach, arching and crawling back to the pole as her legs twisted and her toes pointed. Extending her tapered arms above her head so her breasts lifted, she then cocked her hips to the beat of the music.

Dollar bills accumulated at her feet. It still struck her as surreal that she could get paid for displaying a body the Amish demanded she hide.

Taking one last stroll across the front of the stage, she bent at the waist to scoop up the scattered money. Vito assured her she was safe. Men were not allowed to touch the dancers unless they had purchased the privilege beforehand.

If anyone touched without permission, the bouncer hauled them out of the bar. Vito was a mountain of a man, even next to Larissa's five-feet-nine-inch frame. He displayed impressive strength for a mortal, and she appreciated his protective nature because he always treated her and the other females respectfully.

When the song ended, the crowd applauded. The lights dimmed, and Larissa quickly collected the rest of her money. She passed the next dancer to take the stage and went to her locker to drop off the crisp dollars she held between her palms. Dabbing her damp skin with a towel, she took a sip of water from a bottle.

Some of the girls had warned her about not locking up her belongings, but Larissa just figured old habits die hard. Amish rarely used locks. If someone wanted to take her money, they must have needed it more than her.

She passed Vito on her way out to the main floor. "Nice job, Larissa."

"Thanks."

Over the next few hours, she earned tips by serving beverages to the customers. Her job, when not performing, was to smile and treat the customers kindly. The only time she had difficulty smiling was when one gentleman asked her for a favor.

Some of the girls danced privately for certain customers. There were different types of dancing the men could pay for. Larissa had yet to do any private dances, but that was supposed to change tonight.

Steve, her boss, had said she needed to start offering at least a "Level One" lap dance. That was where the dancer remained clothed and provided a patron with a few minutes of swaying, but the customer could not touch the dancer.

There were ten levels. Some involved touching. Others required the men to lie down or get tied up. Some were done in the privacy of the back rooms, and for almost all levels, the girls displayed their breasts.

Larissa never showed such private body parts to anyone but her husband. And even that made her uncomfortable.

Her lack of experience and Amish background made the exposed hair on her head even seem scandalous. The thought of going topless might cause her blush to catch fire.

She was the only girl who remained modestly covered by English standards while working the club. It just felt wrong to share those parts of herself with strangers, but Steve said it was a job requirement and she needed to leave her modesty at the door.

Tonight, she was expected to perform her first lap dance. Vito had promised her he would be close to make sure the customer did not touch her in any way. The touch of a man was the only thing she feared more than showing her breasts. It was something she simply could not abide, something she so deeply loathed, taking her top off felt inconsequential in comparison.

She loved her job. She loved being able to dance to her heart's content. But she just hoped she could handle the close proximity.

When her break came, she found Vito lingering by the stage. He was a friend and a comfort, and they often *shared a meal.* He followed her into the employee lounge.

"You making good tips, Larissa?" She perched on the arm of a worn, black leather couch.

"Yes."

"Good." He ripped open a foil bag and tossed a chip into his mouth. His brows drew together as he chewed. "Hey, you okay? Someone bother you out there?"

"Yes, I mean no, no one bothered me. I'm fine. Just nervous."

"Nervous 'bout what?"

"I have to do that lap dance after my break."

His smile lifted his cheeks so much his eyes squinted as he nodded knowingly. "You'll be fine. I told you, I won't let anyone touch you."

"I know, it's just, I don't do well with … with being close to others. I'm afraid I'll freeze up."

"Did you practice on a chair like I suggested?"

"Yes, but I don't have an issue being close to wooden objects. I have an issue getting too close to males."

He tossed the last chip into his mouth and crumpled the bag in his fist. "You could practice on me."

Larissa hesitated. A wave of guilt wafted from him, and she did not understand why such a suggestion might fill him with shame. They were friends.

"Never mind. That was a stupid idea."

"No. Not stupid. That might actually help me. I trust you, Vito. If you wouldn't mind me practicing with you, I would really appreciate it."

His cheeks flushed and his Adam's apple bobbed as he swallowed. "I'll shut the door."

Oddly giddy for his assistance, Larissa stood.

"Do you want me on the couch or the chair?"

"The chair, I think."

He hefted the wooden seat into the center of the room. The wood whined under the bulk of his weight as he sat.

"If the girls don't want to be touched, I instruct the guys to keep their hands at their sides, so I'll just..." He lowered his hands so they hung by the back legs of the chair.

Vito was tall, but so was she. She stood before him, his eyes practically level with her own. She twisted her lips, considering their positioning one last time. "Ready?"

"What about music?"

The music from the club filtered through the lounge walls, but it was muffled and the lack of sound made the act all the more awkward. "Your phone?"

He reached in his pocket and withdrew the device. Making a quick selection, he said, "This should work." He tossed the phone on the couch and returned his arms to his side.

Larissa recognized the song playing, which helped her formulate her movements. She prowled around the perimeter of the chair, placing a delicate finger on his broad shoulder and tracing it across his back.

She had watched several lap dances, so she had an idea of what to do. As she circled him, he kept his eyes on her. Her body stayed in constant motion, rolling and undulating, twisting and pivoting. Her nose teased close to his chest. His skin smelled of soap and tobacco with a trace of barbecue from the chips he had eaten.

As his pulse kicked up, she could hear the blood pumping through his veins. His heartbeat quickened as she stepped over his knee and placed a hand on his shoulder. She lowered her body but did not make contact with his lap.

Hunger slammed through her. It was challenging to meet her needs under the watchful eyes of modern civilization, and she spent many hours fighting off her body's demand to feed.

Had it been two days? Three? She remembered hunting down a small rabbit but had only taken a few sips of its blood, enough to stave off the hunger pains and leave the creature unharmed.

The longer she danced, the louder Vito's heartbeat pounded until it was all she could hear. His face flushed with color, hot, thick blood rising to the surface. She could scent it pumping under his inviting flesh.

She ground her body into his thigh, needing to get closer to the smell. His head fell back and he groaned.

"Fuck, Larissa, you're better at this than you think."

Her gaze zeroed in on the flutter of his pulse. Her gums ached and her belly tightened. The punch of her extending fangs had her lips parting and her breath panting. She licked over the swell of her open mouth, watching him like a starved lioness eyeing her prey.

"Jesus. I'm going to have to break skulls to keep the guys' hands off you. You sure you never did this before?"

His body stretched and hardened. She could scent his growing arousal. "This is okay?"

"Yeah, this is fuckin' okay. It's so okay that I think maybe we should stop."

"The song's only half over."

He groaned again as if in pain. "You have no idea what you do to a man, do you?"

Her lips twisted, remembering how powerless she was against her husband. "Where I come from, I can do nothing to a man. It's the men who handle all the doing."

"We should stop."

She frowned, her mind distracted as she focused on his throat. "Just a sip."

"What?"

Her fingers forked through his hair, angling his head back with a hard yank. She dropped her weight into his lap and wrapped her legs around his hips, pinning him to the chair. Her tongue licked over the stubble on his throat, tracing the flutter of his pulse, then she snapped her fangs apart, sinking deep into his flesh.

Vito grunted, his body stiffened as his erection ground against her. The first rush of hot, human blood coating her lips and tongue.

She opened her jaw wide to draw in a full sip and moaned as the flavor slipped down her throat. "Be still."

His body froze as she found the puncture,

sealing her lips tightly around his open flesh and feeding hungrily from the source. His jaw slackened and his pupils dilated.

She had never fed from a mortal while living on the farm, only her immortal mother as a child and her husband as an adult. Typically, her kind was taught to survive on animal blood and protein.

Vito's blood always tasted different, sweeter than an immortal's, lacking potency, but making up for it in smoothness. However, there was always an aftertaste of guilt. He was her friend, and she shouldn't use him in such ways. Every night, she promised she wouldn't feed from him, but her willpower weakened more with every shift until she found herself stealing his blood.

She shut her eyes at the memories of Silus feeding from her. He was never gentle and often left her anemic and weak. He took *everything* he wanted from her, always making sure his every hunger and need was met.

She shivered and took a few more sips before carefully closing the puncture at Vito's neck with her healing saliva. She delicately wiped her mouth with her fingers and sucked away any trace of blood. He blinked several times, a mix of fear and awe in his eyes.

She slid off his lap and held his stare. "We only danced. I never touched you." She pressed a kiss to his cheek, and he blinked rapidly.

"That was…" His eyes looked down and to the left, searching for the right words. "That was amazing. I think you'll do fine out there."

She offered him a forlorn smile, already disgusted with herself for taking advantage of her friend. Sometimes she hated what she was. Her needs were satisfied, but at what cost? Her principles had been betrayed.

"Thank you, Vito."

LARISSA CLIMBED the steps of her dark, odorous apartment complex, still feeling guilty about Vito. Stepping into her private dwelling, she tossed her bag onto a chair.

"You really should lock your door, Larissa."

Screeching with alarm, she sprung to the wall to flip on the light. "For the love of God, Cain! You scared me out of my skin."

"How was work, dear sister? Still dangling your bits for all the English world to see?"

She gave him a mocking smile. "No Englishman has seen my *bits*." Steve had been kind tonight, allowing her the option to keep her top on. But tomorrow night would be different.

"Silus would be so proud."

"You're in a mood." She disappeared into her bedroom to change into a nightgown. Emerging from the room, she breezed past her brother into the kitchen. "What are you doing here?" Filling a glass of water, she fed her houseplant.

Cain plopped onto her couch and picked up a book from her side table. He fingered the pages of the romance novel, landing on a random one. His eyebrows lifted as he read a passage. "I came to see if you wanted to go hunting with me."

"Thank you, but I've already fed." She stuffed down her lingering guilt from earlier.

He tossed the book back onto the table. "You really do need to start locking the door."

She rolled her eyes and came to sit next to him. "I'm an immortal female, Cain. Nothing can hurt me here."

"Nothing mortal."

She stilled. "Has Silus left the farm?"

Fear inched up her spine until her shoulders locked. She mentally forced herself to relax.

He wouldn't find her. They weren't true mates. After years of living together he knew her scent, but they were not bonded like called mates were, and her blood would have long since left his system by now. Called mates could sense their other half from opposing sides of the earth, but Silus would never be her mate.

Cain had found her only because he'd been injured on the night she left, and she gave him her blood to help him feed. Her actions broke their laws and sent her husband into a violent rage.

"Last I heard, Bishop King refused to let him off on some wild goose chase, so you're safe for now. But that was several weeks ago. You should at least scan for emotions before you enter."

"I assure you, I can protect myself from the English."

"I'm not speaking of the English. There are others like us out there, Larissa. Not every immortal was raised with Amish values. Some are wild, and they could sense a female nearby."

Her hand lifted protectively to her throat.

The males of her race were much stronger than the females. At only fifty years old, she was still quite young for her species. An elder could also possess gifts and would dominate her in strength.

However, she couldn't allow her brother's paranoia to intrude on her newfound peace. "Silus doesn't know where I am, and if he's on the farm, I'm safe enough."

"I think the bishop is searching for you."

"The bishop? Why?" How absurd for a man of his power to trouble himself with her whereabouts.

"Apparently, when Silus requested permission to retrieve his disobedient wife—" he smirked with brotherly pride, "the bishop thought himself better suited for the task."

"Why would that crabby old male care where I am? I'm not the first female to escape."

"You're the first one in some time. My guess is because you abandoned your duty. He was one of The Elders who approved Silus's request to marry you. Perhaps he's invested."

She let out an unladylike snort. "My *duty*? If Silus had his way, I'd live a millennium as nothing more than an object to serve him.

No, I think not. I'm happy here. I'll never go back. Not for Silus, not for the bishop, not even for our family."

"Your true mate's still out there, Larissa. You won't be free forever."

She understood that, but she was free for now. "*If* that time ever comes, it will be different."

Marriage was child's play in comparison to the bond shared between called mates. Marriages were contracts by choice, and usually only the male's choice. Being bonded was a calling from God. There was no breaking a bond between true mates. It was sewn into one's soul at creation.

"The Elders showed little care about my destined mate when they married me off to Silus, so why should I concern myself with his whereabouts now?" Bitterness tightened her mouth into a frown.

"I think, should you find your mate, you will want to be with him."

She knew he was right. No matter how liberated or undomesticated she desired to be, surrender remained an innate part of her makeup whenever she fantasized about finding her true mate. Only one other soul could perfectly match hers.

Her heart pinched for her brother. After everything he'd suffered from Adam and Annalise's mating, he had changed. He no longer smiled as easily or appeared as the carefree brother she had always known.

"Anyway, it was your suggestion I leave." She plopped beside him on the sofa and gave his shoulder a nudge, attempting to lighten the mood. "I prefer to think of my situation as self-inflicted excommunication."

Cain chuckled. "If Bishop King finds you, you'll have a tough time."

"That wretched old man doesn't frighten me."

Cain's eyes darkened. "He should. I've experienced his anger, and it isn't pleasant."

She studied him in silence for a long moment. "What did he do to you down in that cell?"

He shook his head. "It's best for everyone if we never speak of that night again."

That day was horrific. There had been so much blood, and the sound of her mother's screams would haunt her for all of her eternal life. Perhaps he was right; some events were best left in the past.

"Well, then I simply won't be found."

"Good luck with that." He stood and the mood finally lightened. "I need to feed."

Her mind returned to Bishop King. The miserable elder was at least five hundred years older than her. If he wanted to find her, he would.

She didn't want to live like a nomad. She simply wanted peace and her freedom. He would steal both from her if he delivered her back to Silus. Therefore, he was another enemy.

Wanting to escape such terrifying thoughts, she asked, "How is Father?"

Cain sighed, and his usually jovial expression faltered under the weight of his honest concern. "Annalise tells me he's worsening every day, growing weaker and more withdrawn from Mother."

Annalise was married to their brother, Adam, yet she and Cain shared a special bond. Perhaps because he and Adam were twins. No one had a reliable explanation for such a phenomenon.

"He's losing weight," Cain continued. "He's been horribly lethargic, yet Mother claims he refuses to sleep for anything longer than a few minutes here and there."

"What do The Elders say?"

"Perhaps Father is developing some sort of allergy. The world is not what it was, and the pollution from the English drifts over our land. While we heal fast, we're still vulnerable to illness. I'm sure he'll recover eventually."

Larissa frowned. Their kind rarely fell ill. Allergies were something mortals dealt with, not their species. "Will you go to him soon?"

She wanted to check on him but could not. If she ever returned to her home, she would never escape again. Silus would see to it.

"If he needs me, I will go. You know I would do anything for any of you."

That was true. Although Cain appeared the most careless member of the family, he was as loyal a brother as one could find.

She squeezed his hand. "I know you would, Cain. So do the others. That is why I thank God every day that you are still a part of my life." She shivered to think that she almost lost him a not too long ago.

"Enough of this melancholy discussion. If you're not hungry, then I better be off. Perhaps I'll hunt for some company as well."

"Cain, wait." He glanced back and she fidgeted, her guilt returning. "Have you ever… Have you ever fed from a mortal?"

He laughed and she flushed, unsure what was so funny. "What do you think I'm doing when I take women back to my bed?"

A vision of Silus and their bedroom popped into her mind and she cringed. "I know what men and women do. Do not forget I'm married."

"And I suspect your husband did more than *speak* to you wrong. There are a lot of females who enjoy the comfort of a man."

"Yes, well, I'm not asking about … that. I'm asking about feeding."

"My darling sister, they are one and the same. When a male feeds from a female, it's incredibly erotic. Did you not even have that with that bastard husband of yours?"

Her back stiffened. "Do not pity me, Cain Hartzler. He may have been a bastard, but I escaped him. He does not get to mistreat me and keep me." She considered his description all the same. *Erotic* was a term she'd never apply to her experiences in the marriage bed. "Perhaps it's only that way for males."

He shook his head. "No, females experience it as well. I've been intimate with enough females of our kind to know."

"You're a whore," she teased.

"Perhaps, but I'm a well-satisfied whore who's never hungry."

"You really should try to be a little less proud, Cain."

"This, from the Amish stripper?"

"I do not strip! I *dance*."

"Tomato, *toe-mah-tow*."

"There's a difference."

"Whatever. But if you're feeding from mortals in that skanky little club, make sure you remove the memory. And don't take too much. Their blood's stronger than most animals'. Actually, if the bishop *is* searching for you, it may not be a bad idea to find yourself a mortal to feed from, to keep up your strength."

Her guilt washed away. "You're right."

"Perhaps, you could bed one as well. Erase all those tragic memories of Silus." He stuck out his tongue and gagged.

"I will not! No matter how awful Silus was, he was my husband. I believe a female should only share such intimacies with her husband or called mate."

"Awfully prudish for a stripper."

She swatted at him.

"My apologies! *Dancer*."

"You're an evil brother."

"Yes, and Adam is an angel. What is a boy to do with such an incongruent existence? Seems it will only ever be sex and sin for me. Pity."

"You're incorrigible."

"I know. But I must be going. It's getting late, and I've much to hunt. Lock the door behind me, sister. Sleep well."

She closed the door and flipped the deadbolt. Only then did she notice a curtain slightly out of place. Had Cain moved that?

A chill chased up her spine as she crossed the room to adjust the drapes. Her fingers twisted the window latch, making sure it was locked.

Wonderful, now she was paranoid. Rolling her eyes at her silly fear, she shut off the lights and went to bed. But before she made it to her room, she glanced at another window. It was open.

CHAPTER 3

Jonas pressed his forehead on the cool plaster wall of the safe house where he'd been pacing just outside Council Hall. His palms were trembling against the chipped surface, body quaking with pain, as he tried to collect himself.

Agony radiated through his bones. It seized his intestines, tying them into knots, stabbing every nerve ending along his spine, and vibrating his skull until he could barely hold a single rational thought.

His breath hissed through his clenched teeth as his eyes pinched shut, trapping his tears. Not now. He could not suffer another spell at this moment.

The voices of The Elders and the other

males gathering in The Council room muffled under the onslaught of pain. There are only a few more minutes until the meeting begins.

He needed to get control of himself. There was no way he could slip in unnoticed. Today, he was being questioned on his daughter Larissa's whereabouts. He knew not where his eldest daughter was. Only that she had fled the farm the evening of his son Adam's wedding—the same evening the dreams had started.

Another excruciating hunger pain knifed through his gut. He grunted against the sharp stab and flinched as agony reverberated through his body, causing even his shoulders to tremble. He could not let the others see him like this.

Oh God, his poor Abilene. How much longer could he pretend that everything was all right? That everything was how it had always been? He was fighting a losing battle.

It had been two months. Two months since those godforsaken dreams had begun. Their kind did not dream. Dreams were sacred and saved for those called upon by God. Yet, he suffered such torment every evening for more than sixty nights. The visions were growing more frequent and intense. He deprived himself of sleep as long as possible, but his clumsy exhaustion was killing him. He wouldn't last much longer.

The first night he saw his mate in his dreams, he knew he would not be able to outwit God's will. He was called, and the fate of the *unanswered* was no better than the inevitable surrender to his destiny. Neither would save or protect his sweet Abilene. He hated himself for the pain this would bring. She was all he needed and the only one he wanted. So, why was God smiting him?

One hundred and forty-one years on this earth without even a whisper from the Almighty and now this. He refused to accept his fate. He refused to hurt his Abilene.

The mortal's name was Clara. Even her name seemed too intimate a detail, especially as it flitted through his mind before and behind every waking thought. Her hair was the color of snow and as delicate as spun silk. With eyes greener than cut emeralds, she often watched him in his dreams.

Treachery. His fist curled into a ball and pounded on the wall. He could not willingly betray his beloved Abilene.

His darling wife had only been eighteen when they fell in love. That was sixty years ago. She was a baby in the eyes of immortals.

He fell in love with every inch of her. Mesmerized by any strand of fawn-colored hair that escaped her bonnet and fixated with the doe-like shape of her eyes. She was pure femininity and gentleness.

Many advised against marrying a female that was not one's true mate, but Jonas could not let her go. She was his, and he needed to claim her in every sense of the word.

Abilene gave him four beautiful children. Their family had not been an easy achievement. She suffered through several miscarriages, despite how rare such complications are to their kind. Others suspected God was punishing them. Perhaps they were right, but all the loss in the world was still not enough to diminish his love for her.

He fought the calling with every ounce of strength he had. He loved his wife, but nothing was more powerful than the will of God.

As Jonas grew weaker, Abilene grew more suspicious. Beyond the pain was the ever-present hunger that left him thirsting for only the blood of his mate. Nothing satisfied his craving. He was ravenous. He drunk a calf to death to try to stave off the ache and delirium. Never in his long existence had he killed a creature of God, but he was losing control.

If he didn't do something soon, he would do something inapprehensible, something irredeemable. The longer he waited and fought the inevitable, the more dangerous he became to others.

Existing in agony, complete pain encompassed every inch of flesh, every organ, every nerve, every limb, and every motion for every moment of the day. Yes, he was an immortal of substantial strength and impeccable health, but with each circle of the moon, his strength waned and his health faltered.

He was dying. Survival called, but he couldn't accept this as his only option. He couldn't bear the thought of hurting his wife.

Pressing his cheek now along the cool wall as he fought the urge to weep. So tired. He shut his eyes for a moment and slumber gripped him. Clara's green eyes watched him, and he jerked awake. He stumbled back from the wall, disoriented and startled. The hall was empty.

He could barely hold on to a complete thought anymore. The dizzy spells, light sensitivity, relentless hunger, and endless exhaustion were too much to outsmart. Soon, if he didn't find his mate and bond, he would turn *feeish.*

The remaining layers of his humanity would be stripped away until nothing merciful remained—only a rabid beast needing to be put down. An ignored blessing became a curse. An unanswered immortal only had one fate. They became *vampire.*

A blood-tinged tear slipped past his entwined lashes, mixing with the chilled sweat on his skin. If he could not grant her *eawichkeit*—eternity—he will not go on. His heart only belonged to one female, and her name was Abilene.

"Father?"

He didn't hear Adam approach. Jonas pressed his eyes tight and wiped his face clean. "Adam, I was just coming to join the others. Has the meeting begun?"

"The Elders are settling in now." His son studied him and frowned. "Are you ill? Is it another attack? I can request we postpone."

Jonas straightened his posture, ignoring the tremble in his bones and the ache in his joints. "No, that won't be necessary. I shall not put off my duty another day. I was merely taking a moment to pray."

Adam appeared to want to argue with his father's desire to proceed as scheduled, but Jonas did not give him the opportunity. Walking toward the door, Jonas kept his steps moving and his focus resolute. "Come. Let us do what is asked of us. No doubt Silus has already paced a divot in the floor."

They traveled in silence to the old doors at the end of the long corridor that connected the safe house to the bishop's home. Adriel Schrock, the oldest female on the farm, waited on a wooden bench outside Council Hall as usual.

The female was almost five hundred years old, two hundred years older than some of The Elders on The Council, but she was a female and, therefore, not invited to attend council meetings. However, she never missed a summit, even if she could only attend from the outer side of a closed door.

Eavesdropping was her way of staying abreast of The Order's political business. Although she was on the outside, she was an extremely powerful immortal. Jonas had no doubt she heard every whispered word from within the hall.

"Good evening, Adriel." He nodded as he passed.

"Jonas." Her shrewd gaze followed him, and he resisted the urge to twitch under her scrutiny. Adriel had been around for a long time and would be able to spot any subtle changes.

Holding the door for his son, Jonas stepped inside and let the heavy oak creek shut with an echoing thud. His stare immediately found his father, Ezekiel, on The Elders' bench. The bishop's empty seat did not go unnoticed.

"Welcome, Brother Jonas. Brother Adam," Abraham Gerig, the eldest male member of The Council, greeted. He would be presiding over the meeting in the bishop's stead.

"Good evening, gentlemen," Jonas replied, taking a seat on one of the many pews that faced The Council.

"We ask that you join us up here, Brother Jonas." Abraham gestured to an isolated chair set before The Council. "We would like to get started straight away. There is much to discuss this evening."

There was a tiredness in Abraham's eyes that marked his time on this earth. However, the Gerig family was not a long lineage. After losing his mate on the ship over from Europe three centuries back, the Gerig clan had ceased to grow.

"Of course." Jonas casually moved toward the designated chair, disguising his pain and blanking his mind from curious eavesdroppers nearby. He kept his expression friendly and greeted Abraham, "Good day, brother. May I ask of your family? I assume Abigail is well."

It was only Abraham and his daughter Abigail living in the Gerig house. The girl had become a source of pity for most members of The Order. At two hundred and seventy-some years, she had the autonomy of a child. Abraham rarely let his daughter out of his sight. He was old, alone, and eternally set in his ways. Jonas briefly regretted that the bishop would not be questioning him this night.

"No need for niceties. Let us move this along," Abraham grumbled.

Jonas took the seat at the front end of the room to face the others and removed his hat.

"Let the record state that on this second Tuesday of November, The Council is questioning Jonas Hartzler, son of Council Elder Ezekiel Hartzler, on the whereabouts of his daughter Larissa Hartzler Hostetler, wife of

Silus Hostetler." Abraham folded his hands and set his stare to Jonas. "Questioning will begin with Council Elder Damascus Hostetler, father of Silus Hostetler. Do you object, Brother Jonas?"

"No, sir." There was no doubt in Jonas's mind that Silus had instructed his father on precisely what to ask.

"Very well. You may begin, Brother Damascus."

Damascus Hostetler faced Jonas, his chair creaking in the quiet room. "Jonas, when was the last time you saw your daughter Larissa?"

"The evening of my son Adam's wedding."

"And when was that exactly?"

"The last Tuesday of this past August."

"Was that the same day that your other son, Cain, left the farm?"

"Yes, but I believe Cain and Larissa did not leave together. Cain had been injured, and Silus removed Larissa from the situation and took her home immediately. That was the last I saw her."

"Are there any other witnesses to Cain's presence post-Larissa's absence?"

"Yes. Bishop Eleazar King can vouch for my son's presence at the farm late that evening. He was retaining Cain in a cell."

"Let the record show that the bishop is not present to concur."

Ezekiel interjected on his family's behalf. "Let the record also show that Bishop King's personal log will note that while my grandson was in his custody, he was also released that same evening. I beg your pardon, early the following morning, after my granddaughter was declared missing by her husband, Brother Silus Hostetler."

"Very well," Damascus stated, turning back to Jonas. "Did your daughter speak to you or your wife about possibly running away?"

"No."

"You seem awfully certain of that. Perhaps you should take a moment before speaking for your wife with such conviction."

"I do not need a moment to think. I know my wife. She keeps no secrets from me. Neither she nor I had any knowledge of Larissa's intentions to leave the farm."

"Is it true that the evening of her disappearance, the vehicle from your son Adam's journey into the suburbs also disappeared?"

"Yes."

"Have you noticed Larissa in the presence of other males while in the care of your family?"

"I'm not sure I understand."

"My son attends many meetings. He tells me that he trusts his wife in your family's care when he cannot chaperone her. Has there ever been males, aside from your two sons, present during those times?"

"We have many visitors. I could not be sure. As you know, I, too, attend the same meetings as Silus."

"Perhaps we should call your other daughter Grace in for questioning. Or perhaps Abilene."

Jonas growled and bared his teeth. "There will be no reason to call in my wife or daughter. I would see it as a personal insult if they were bothered with such questioning. It's under Family Law that such business remains that of a wife and her husband. I suggest you take such a private matter up with your son."

"True. However, it becomes a council matter if a mated female is placed in jeopardy when under the protection of other relatives."

"That's enough," Ezekiel interrupted calmly. "I will remind you, Brother Damascus, that Larissa and your son are not called mates. Simply husband and wife. Furthermore, I will not tolerate the moral fiber of my kin being called into question. Perhaps you would prefer to call your son up for questioning to obtain the personal information you seek."

Damascus did not seem pleased by Jonas's father's suggestion but relented nonetheless. "Is it true that your daughter-in-law Annalise, wife of Adam, can communicate with Cain through dreams?"

A wash of whispers flowed from the males sitting in the pews. It was common knowledge only true mates shared dreams. "That is correct."

"Yet she also shared dreams with her husband, Adam."

"True, though I'm unsure if that's changed since the mating."

"Is Annalise aware of Cain's whereabouts?"

"I don't know." A splitting headache produced a steady pounding in Jonas's head, and he wanted nothing more than to shut his eyes.

Damascus looked at Adam, "Would you be able to speak on your wife's behalf?"

Adam stood. "I will speak on my *mate's* behalf." He enunciated the title so there would be no confusion about Annalise's position in his life. "When Anna dreams of Cain, it's often set in a location they both know. It must be a familiar place they can each imagine. She tells me she mostly sees him in her dreams right here on the farm, more specifically on the western side of our family's barn where the sun sets. Cain tells her he is spending his time away exploring. He moves around often, and his sole purpose in maintaining a link with my mate is to keep informed of the family."

"And you find this acceptable?"

"That is not your concern," Adam growled. "While you may be my elder, she is my mate, and you will not question our private affairs."

The elder's thin lips twitched at Adam's arrogance, but Adam was correct. No male, elder or not, had any right to interfere with Family Law as decided by the head of each household. Marriages were navigated privately. As long as they were not breaking any higher laws, it was forbidden for others to interfere or question a husband's rule over his wife.

Ezekiel cleared his throat. "While I can understand your desire to locate my granddaughter, I cannot see the purpose in questioning my family to this degree. This line of questioning has run its course, and I move to close the issue for today."

As the other members of The Council seconded Ezekiel's movement, Damascus hesitantly agreed. There was no mistaking the displeasure on the elder's face.

Abraham stood. "I excuse Jonas and call Silus Hostetler, son of Council Elder Damascus Hostetler, to the bench."

Jonas was never fond of his son-in-law, and any remaining respect had withered faster than the decaying autumn leaves trespassing at every door. He wished there was a fast solution to sweep this trouble away. Silus stood, his paunch pressing hard against his suspenders, his arched spine a result of him puffing up his chest with nothing but wind. His beady eyes narrowed behind the lenses of his specs as he walked to The Council bench without once acknowledging Jonas or Adam.

"Brother Silus, you may speak your issue."

"Thank you, Brother Abraham." Silus faced both The Elders on The Council bench and the males of The Order filling the pews. "It has been nine weeks since my wife's disappearance. Bishop King wasted eight of those weeks claiming to be searching for her while he attended other private matters. I have always been a male to honor the laws of The Order, but I grow weary waiting for news. My wife is weak.

She is uneducated in the ways of the English."

Jonas's jaw clenched at the attack on his daughter's intelligence, but he knew better than to object. Arguing would only escalate the controversy today, and he wanted the issue of his runaway daughter put to rest, at least for a while. If Larissa was in danger, he trusted his son, Cain, would find and protect her.

Silus continued his verbal rant. "Her sheltered existence here on the farm has not prepared her for the evils that lurk outside of our sanctuary. While she is immortal, I fear she may be pulled into the claws of temptation. She needs protection and a firm hand. Loose morals could confuse and corrupt her. I do not want my wife returned to me *damaged*. I beg to overrule the bishop's decision that I should remain on the farm. I must search for my wife. Her morality is at stake."

Abraham shut his eyes and collected his thoughts. "While I understand your concern, Brother Silus, and I sympathize with your plight, I cannot overrule a direct order from the bishop—"

"But she is *my* wife!"

"Hold your tongue, boy. While I sympathize with you, you will not address me disrespectfully. You will remember yourself while in the presence of The Council or you will find yourself on the other side of the door. As I was saying, the bishop's direct command cannot simply be overruled because an Order member is losing patience. It has been eight weeks. Bishop King is the eldest of all The Order. It's foolish of you to question his ability to find your wife. His abilities are unmatched. If God has intended for her to be found, Bishop Eleazar King will find her."

The tight bulk of Silus's bunched shoulders proved he wanted to argue. "I have suspicions that her brother, Cain, is assisting her in hiding."

Jonas shook his head. This was turning into a sideshow. Larissa was a bit sheltered, but she was not so naive that she would jeopardize her morality. She was a smart woman, and Jonas had complete faith in all his children to survive any challenge without sacrificing their principles. He had four good children and trusted God to protect them in all matters.

"What exactly would your wife be hiding from, Brother Silus?" Abraham asked.

There was a substantial difference between the way Jonas and Adam treated Abilene and Anna and how Silus treated Larissa. However, the same Family Law that protected them from others interfering in their marriage protected Silus.

Silus did not come to Jonas when he had asked for Larissa's hand, an error Jonas had struggled with forgiving. Instead, the boy had gone directly to The Council to ask permission to marry his daughter. With Silus's father, grandfather, and great-grandfather all sitting members of the Elder's Council, he could get his wish. Holding a link to the Hostetler, Zehra, and Rocke family lines, Silus was a young male with unquestionable influence over matters of The Order.

Aside from Abilene and Jonas's fathers' objections to the union, the remaining four elders favored helping their lineage. No doubt experiencing pressure from the direction of three of the founding families. Jonas had been outnumbered and forced to give his eldest daughter to a man he did not trust.

"Larissa sometimes suffers bouts of delirium and confusion," Silus claimed.

"That is a lie!" Adam stood and scowled. "Larissa is one of the sanest and most level-headed females I have ever come across. She does not give in to rash decisions, nor does she shy away from responsibility. She's strong, capable, and kind. I will not stand idly by while you make a mockery of her reputation in her absence. You may be my brother by law, but she is my sister by blood, and I advise you to think long and hard before you utter one more lie about her."

"Do you see how prideful their family can be?" Silus accused.

"That's enough, Adam," Ezekiel admonished his grandson. "Silus, you've said enough. While I want to see my granddaughter returned home as swiftly as possible, I will not tolerate such lies about her character. Yes, you are her husband and have every right to be concerned. But until we have all the facts, we cannot make any assumptions. For as much as we know about the Almighty's intentions, she may have been called to leave the farm."

"Inconceivable!" Silus barked.

"Is it?" Ezekiel snapped back, silencing the younger male and leaning forward on his fisted knuckles. "You are not her mate. You have yet to father children with her. Do not disregard the power of God, thinking you are wiser than He. You may have laid claim to my granddaughter and been granted her virtue, but you are no more entitled to her than any other male who is not her true called mate. A smidge of temperance now may save you a pound of humiliation in the end. You blame everyone but yourself for my granddaughter's disappearance. And you prowl around hurling accusations like a man in a glass house with a fist full of stones, careless of what you break."

"She is my *wife*. I could break her neck for running and face no consequence."

Ezekiel's eyes narrowed. "I'm *sure* you wish to see Larissa returned safely, as does her family. We love her and will do anything in our power to protect her, brother. *Anything*."

A prideful smirk crept over Jonas's lips as his father put Silus in his place.

"I believe we've heard enough on the topic of Larissa Hostetler today," Abraham announced. "Brother Silus, you may return to your seat. Let the record show that no new evidence in the girl's whereabouts has been brought to light, and the command given by Bishop King remains in effect. Let us move on to the next matter."

As Silus returned to his seat, he glared at

Adam and Jonas. While the men in their family were innately kind, they were also loyal. No one would speak ill of Larissa without consequence. Not even her husband.

For all that Jonas missed his daughter, with the way things appeared, it might be best if she never returned.

CHAPTER 4

The stench of human waste lingered in the air. It was supper time for most mortals, the time when they settled into their homes for the night. However, Bishop Eleazar King would not be settling into his home because he was *still* tracking the Hartzler female.

He was disgusted. Humans were a withering species. In all his five hundred and twenty-six years he had never seen such a display of waste, rudeness, and utter disregard for morality.

Repulsed by the ideals held by the self-proclaimed most intelligent species, Eleazar did not want to spend another moment in this godforsaken place. The women ran around with little to no clothing covering their flesh. They, as well as the men, swilled their minds with alcohol and drugs. Babes were transferred from mothers' breasts to strangers' arms so that the females could run amuck in the overzealous capitalism.

Identities were not defined by character but rather by material and money. Elders were ignored and disrespected. Children were arrogant and vulgar. And the noise—when would it quiet? There was never a moment of silence among the English.

Eleazar was prepared to return home empty-handed. He would have never volunteered to track the sour brat, but it became apparent that Silus would severely punish her for running away, and Eleazar could not let that happen.

Eleazar reached for his overcooked meat sandwich and thought better of it. Pushing the paper-wrapped meal away, he stood to leave the establishment where he had hoped to find something resembling nourishment.

A female smiled at him, her thoughts unclean. What happened to the world since he last entered it?

Trying to be polite, he gave a tight-lipped grin and tensed when the female stood. She crossed the brightly-colored eatery and brazenly approached his table.

"Hey."

Without altering his expression, he picked through the mortal's mind. Twenty years old. An orgy of past intimacies littering her mind and a desolate sense of hollowness drowning her emotions. Disgraceful. The result of living a life without integrity or purpose.

"You want to go grab a drink and talk?"

Her words suggested conversation, but her mind played a carousel of lewd images of the two of them. Not used to seeing his likeness in such compromising positions, he drew back, appalled.

"Look at me."

He held her gaze. Her overdone eyes were unfocused.

"Go home and dispose of all your clothing that does not cover your skin in a way your great-great-grandmother would find proper. Then wash that makeup off your face and pray for God's mercy. And *never* approach a strange man in such a manner again."

The child blinked at him, a little confused but under his compulsion nonetheless. She quickly left to do as he suggested. Eleazar mentally scoffed. As if he had time to save all the souls of this English nightmare.

He had only one soul he needed to save and that was Larissa Hartzler's. If he didn't find her soon, this journey would be labeled a failure, and he'd never forgive her.

Abandoning the restaurant, he left the city and traveled along a deeply wooded forest. Even the woodlands were not natural here. There was not an acre of earth left untouched by the English.

He passed small kiosks and podiums that declared the woods to be a state park as he hunted. Too many screaming children nearby made it difficult to find other forms of life. Standing still, he shut his eyes and searched nature's vibration for a quick pulse.

His mind locked on a deer. Its quick-leaping instincts giving its variety away. Yes, a white-tail. Eleazar latched onto the animal's cognitive process and compelled it to find him. Seconds later, the doe was licking his fingertips.

"Good girl." Crouching down, he stroked the animal and stared into her soft brown eyes. "Calm. Very good."

Tipping the animal's muzzle back, he located the thick cord of its carotid artery and sank his fangs into its flesh. Its spindly hind leg twitched, but it didn't bolt. He soothed the animal as he fed, not wanting to cause any harm. When he finished, his body was somewhat satisfied, yet his mind was not.

The blood of animals could no longer sustain him. He spent his days lethargic and more exhausted than he had ever been in his entire life, unable to remember the last time he awoke refreshed.

Worst of all, his sleep was often interrupted by the dreams. He did not enjoy this altogether disorienting experience; it led to more restless nights. The sooner he found her, the sooner these symptoms would stop.

How have more than two hundred and seventy years passed since he ventured this far from the farm? The river upon which their ship had docked in Philadelphia was now unrecognizable. The memory of debarking from their vessel, *The Charming Nancy,* was nothing like what presently occupied the area.

Dirt roads were now paved. The asphalt pocked with sinkholes and grates that reeked of sewage. Buildings crammed tightly together to cover what was once open space.

Litter tickled every surface like flies scratch over rotting flesh.

The overwhelming scent of desperation and poverty reminded him of Europe during the age of the plague. Although the streets were not filled with rotting bodies, they were crawling with mortals whose conscience had died long ago.

Every mind he touched had been scheming in one way or another. Rarely did he pick up a thought about God. When he did, it was usually followed by a silent request for some frivolous favor, like winning the *Pick 6*, whatever that was.

He considered the called mates brought to their farm over the past century. How was it that those mates, who were of good moral fiber, for the most part, had come from such a grim place? It was a wonder mortals were not breaking into the Amish communities in droves, trying to escape this evil.

He did not think of himself as overly cantankerous. Sure, he had a way of doing things and saw no need in adjusting, but it was not as if he had grown into an unbendable grump. He could be a bit pious, but he was the bishop. It was his duty to maintain a level of religious honor among The Order.

Who was he kidding? He was turning into a sour old man. Every dawn he faced with more and more cynical views.

Half a millennia was a long time. Perhaps he should step down as bishop and allow one of the others to fill his seat on The Council's bench. He could maybe return to his birthplace in Spain. But would Spain today be anything like it was in the sixteenth century? Most likely not.

He traveled all over Europe, but Lancaster was the only place he called home. He did not want to leave, but it could be his time to go.

He left the woods to meander along a suburban sidewalk lit by electric lamp posts. Letting down his guard, he allowed the voices of the mortals to seep into his mind—the normally intolerable roar of English citizens quieting to a low hum. And still no sign of Larissa Hartzler.

Discouraged, he slowed and paused outside of a brick home. For once, he allowed all the emotions of love and loyalty to wash over him. A good family lived within those four walls, a male and female with three young sons.

The woman's affection for the man struck him like a foreign language. More than five centuries old, and Eleazar still didn't know what it meant to make love, what it felt like to be loved, or if his heart was even capable of loving another.

After so many centuries of living life completely alone, he doubted he would make a decent partner, which fueled his hesitation to claim his mate. Perhaps he was worrying over nothing. Many around him had been called, but his existence, up until recently, had been destined to be a solitary one.

Meaningless. Endless. Empty.

No wonder he'd become such a miserable son of a bitch.

CHAPTER 5

$\mathcal{A}$bilene watched the light from the blue moon sneak through a tiny crack in the window covering and blossom into a pool of silver over her bed. She lay still beneath the weight of her wedding quilt, waiting for her husband to come home to her.

Supper was quiet. Silence swallowed their home since the night of Adam's wedding.

While Gracie, their youngest at only twenty-one years, was still living under their roof, the rest had left the nest. It had all happened so suddenly that Abilene was still acclimating to the hush that filled her home. She was not sure she would ever come to terms with its oppressing presence. Homes should be filled with children, laughter, and love. Instead, hers was turning into nothing more than a hollow building.

She did not blame her children. They were her babies. To love them meant letting them go. They needed to fly into the world and spread their own wings.

She loved all four of them with her every breath, nurtured them well past adulthood, and armed them with wisdom, morals, and enough love to extend well past her children's children's children. So why did she appear so downtrodden, so sad? She couldn't shake the sense that she'd somehow failed.

Perhaps if she had more babies, she would not feel so alone. But God had not blessed her with children since Gracie, and that was her greatest failure of all.

She wondered if she would ever hold a babe with Jonas's ice-blue eyes and her straight nose in her arms again. Beyond the grace of God, a distance invaded her marriage.

Did no one want her anymore? Had she served her purpose? Like a jar of jam set on a shelf for winter, she was forced into a dark season of her life, despite sensing it was too soon. Only seventy-eight years and a frost was creeping in.

She was more than happy for Adam and Annalise. They were true mates, and come spring they would be giving birth to her first grandchild. Anna was a beautiful woman with an even more enchanting soul. She was good for her Adam.

The way her son looked at his mate reminded Abilene of how Jonas had always looked at her. Jonas saw her as a precious gift, one he would battle a thousand men to protect. He often referred to Abilene as his breath and, sometimes, the music to his soul.

How long had it been since he said such sweet words to her? She did not imagine this distance between them. It was growing into a great yawning void neither of them could seem to reach across.

Abilene's skin chilled. Pulling the quilt up to her shoulders, she stared into the empty bedroom filled with silver puddles of moonlight. The black fingers of shadows choked her like the silence.

She shut her eyes and fought her tears. She would not break. Whatever her husband was going through, she would be there for him when he was ready to accept her help. He was her one and only true love.

After sixty years of love, honor, trust, and obedience without a single moment of hesitating, she still believed he was a remarkable male. He loved her with every cell of his being. She had never doubted his devotion to their children, so why was she questioning it now?

An idle mind was the devil's playground, she thought, ashamed of where her thoughts had taken her. It was this godforsaken silence!

She considered waking Gracie to get her mind off this morose path of thinking. Gracie was always a wonderful distraction with her naturally charming optimism. She was so different from her older daughter, Larissa.

Larissa was a woman of duty. Their stoic daughter never voiced any objections when The Elders approached them with Silus's request to wed, and once the marriage took place, Abilene saw her eldest daughter less and less.

Though it was against their laws to question such intimate things, Abilene worried what Larissa had suffered to make her believe running away was her only option. Silus had used nepotism to gain The Council's permission to wed her daughter. He was an incredibly private man. And while Abilene had raised her children to be obedient in the eyes of God, she had also raised them to be shepherds rather than sheep. It pleased some indispensable feminine part of her to know that Larissa was perhaps now finding her own way.

The sound of the front door clicking shut had Abilene's thoughts of her children scattering. Jonas was home. Would he come to her? Finally sleep in their bed beside her again? She turned as his shadow filled the door to their bedroom.

"You're awake."

Abilene looked at her husband, still taken aback by his handsomeness at times. He was a large man, bold and strong, yet kind and always gentle. Like his father, he had long, dark hair, blacker than pitch, that made his ice-blue eyes appear even more piercing. His broad shoulders and trim, muscled body filled the doorway.

Her gaze dropped to his hands. Hands that had cradled their children, hands that held her through countless times of sadness, caressed her through moments of great passion, and supported her when she did not know how to move on. He was her everything. And she wanted—more than anything—him to hold her now and promise her that they were going to get through whatever this was.

"I waited up for you." She always had, but he never left her waiting as much as he'd been lately. "How was the meeting?"

He did not move to join her as he filled the doorway, watching her. "It was fine. They're waiting for word from the bishop before making any new decisions. Silus isn't happy about the ruling. He'll likely try again."

If her daughter ran, there was a reason.

Silence stretched. She moved to sit up, folding back the quilt in invitation, but he halted her movements with a staying hand.

"I have other business to tend to."

His rejection stung, layering directly over the fresh rejection from the night before. He stepped toward the hall, and she called his name, "Jonas?"

Her marriage was becoming a scattered line of disjointed dismissals. He waited patiently for what she needed to ask him. But what could she say?

Why don't you touch me anymore?

Why does it seem to pain you to even look into my eyes?

How are you surviving this ache between us?

"I ... I need to feed." It was a pitiful attempt at contact, but one he would be duty-bound to oblige. She was starved for the warmth, the connection, the evidence that she still owned some part of him.

In sixty years of marriage, he never put her in the position to ask for his affection. He always gave it freely, yet recently she had to beg for him to simply hold her hand.

"I think I would sleep better if my belly were full."

He hesitated, his mouth opening slightly, but his voice choked by more silence. "I'll fetch you another glass." He left before she could argue.

A tightness seized her chest. Dismissed again.

Being insignificant to her husband was too much to bear in this godforsaken silence. Her fist clenched in the bedding as she fought a rage building inside of her. She wanted to pierce his reserve with cries of injustice. This never-ending quiet was suffocating her. She was trapped in her head, screaming into the hollow abyss overtaking their marriage, yet her lips remained obediently closed.

The heft of his returning footsteps caused her to shut her eyes. She would not turn to face him. He would have to step past more than just their doorway. Let him see her displeasure in his solution to her hunger. Let him know that his disregard for her has gone too far and force him to face what his neglect has wrought.

He should see that his endless rejection hurt her. The Jonas she married would never abide her heartache. He would cross any distance to reach her. So who was this man approaching her now with such timidness in his eyes?

She waited for him to apologize for neglecting her so. She was his wife, not a jar of jam to be ignored on a shelf.

Shutting her eyes, she waited for his fingers' press or his palm's caress across her cheek. She waited for any sign that he saw her pain and desired to make amends. There was no doubt he could sense her sadness.

The sound of a pewter goblet touching down on the nightstand interrupted the silence. She sensed him watching her.

"I'll see you in the morning."

She winced, choking back a sob and pressing her eyes tight to keep the tears from seeping free. At the click of the door closing, her mouth gaped open in a soundless wail. Cold air tripped into her lungs, and she shivered uncontrollably. Why was he doing this to her?

The pressure in her chest was too tight. There was no room to breathe.

Turning, she pressed her face into the pillows and released a guttural cry. Nothing should hurt this much. What had she done? Why was he punishing her away with such indifference?

A dam had broken. She cried until her energy depleted. Her tears waned into shuddering whimpers. Body numb, eyes unblinking, she watched as the silver moonlight tinged to shades of gold.

Dawn arrived, and he had not returned to her. The goblet of blood remained untouched. Too exhausted to sleep, she stared through the endless silence.

When she heard Gracie emerge from the room down the hall and heard pots heating over the stove, her treacherous mind snidely questioned if she should rise. *For what?* Would anyone really miss her if she did not attend breakfast?

Gracie would spend her mornings tending to the baby calves in the barn. Jonas barely touched his food anymore, so she doubted he'd attend breakfast.

Abilene thought of the grief after her miscarriages and how her sorrow caused her appetite to lag. Was Jonas depressed?

After she heard Gracie leave for the morning, Abilene finally dressed. Methodically pulling on her shift, she pinned her apron extra snug, needing *something* to hold her tight. She braided her hair until it pinched her scalp, hoping the pain would distract her from the ache in her heart. As she reached for her lace bonnet, she noticed her fingers trembling.

Shutting her eyes, she willed her body to settle. She would be a good wife and patiently wait for her husband to seek her company once again. Even if it took a century, she would abide by the pain and loneliness because she had complete faith in Jonas's love.

But when she spotted that pewter goblet still sitting beside the bed, a cold substitute for her husband's care, she snapped. The back of her trembling hand lashed out, smacking the goblet off the nightstand. The heavy pewter cup crashed against the plaster wall, spewing its crimson contents over the surface and clattering heavily to the floor. She stilled, horrified, as rivulets of red crawled down her clean walls and onto the floor.

Distant sounds filled the floor below as someone entered the house. Abilene couldn't move. Struck dumb and deaf at the hypnotic way the blood seeped into the plaster's pores and ran tiny streams over the cracks of the wood-planked floor. Like a poison seeping into her life, she watched silently as the liquid collected into a small puddle and slowly crept to her toes peeking out from beneath her dress.

"Abilene?" The sound of Annalise's voice had her eyes jerking to the door.

What had she done? Galvanized into action by her daughter-in-law's approaching footsteps, she pulled the water pitcher from her dresser and doused the wall where the cup had crashed.

Realizing the stupidity of her solution before the arc of water even touched the plaster wall, she watched in helpless horror as crimson faded into pink, spreading into a bigger mess. Her lace apron became speckled with dots of diluted blood. She was utterly hopeless, and in a matter of seconds, her state would be humiliatingly exposed.

She wanted to run and hide. Seventy-eight years old and she actually considered hiding under her bed. What was happening to her? Was she losing her mind?

"Mom?" A soft scratch opened the door. "Abilene?"

She stood motionless as Annalise stepped in.

Her daughter-in-law grinned. "There you are. I wanted to see if you—oh no. What happened?"

Abilene shook her head. "I…" Tears prickled her eyes and her body quaked as reality suddenly became too much, the silence of her life finally too heavy to bear. "I've made a mess of everything." Her face pressed into her palms.

Annalise rushed to wrap her in her arms, but Abilene collapsed to the bloodied floor. A sob ripped from her throat.

"Oh, Mom, no. Don't do this to yourself. Whatever it is, whatever has happened, we'll fix it."

Abilene sobbed like a babe into Anna's elbow. Her white apron slowly turning pink as the puddle seeped into the fibers of her gown. Anna continued to hold her and whisper soothing words.

She felt atrocious, selfish, and too weak to remain silent. It was as if she could witness herself breaking, fragmenting into tiny pieces she could not collect.

CHAPTER 6

*B*lackness flickered, waking Cain's subconscious. Anna's voice pulling him into a dream. "Cain?"

His mind searched for the frequency where they connected as if there was one specific plane of existence that belonged only to them.

First appeared the expansive grass, then the satisfying sense of nostalgia that overcame him whenever he returned to the farm. Trees took shape, building a private world around them. There was a glimmer of light, the scent of fresh air, and the always-present honeysuckle fragrance that accompanied Annalise.

And there she was. Always beautiful, with her fiery-golden hair and soft, loving smile.

His brother was a lucky male to have the love of such a loyal woman.

He glanced toward her belly. The child in her womb was growing and this pleased him to no end. He smiled. "How is my brother, beautiful Anna? No doubt he is prouder than the proudest cock on the farm at the sight of you swelling with his seed."

When she did not immediately laugh at his teasing, Cain looked into her eyes. Something was wrong.

"What is it? What happened? Is it Father?"

Her concern snapped through him. "No, not Jonas. It's your mom."

Cain sucked in a breath at the thought of trouble befalling his gentle mother. Although fiercely maternal, his mother was one of the most delicate females he knew. He loved and adored her as completely as only a child could, and he would protect her with his last breath.

"What is it?" He prayed she had not conceived again and lost another babe. "Has she gotten with child? Has she…"

"No." Anna shook her head, lips pressing tight.

Impatience rolled through him like thunder. "Spit it out, Anna. If something happened, I need to know."

"Your mother's sick, Cain."

"Sick? Our kind does not get sick." There seemed a curse on his childhood home. "Are her symptoms like Father's?"

"Not that kind of sick."

"What other kind is there?"

"I think she suffered a nervous breakdown."

"I don't understand. What's a *nervous breakdown?*"

"Your father's illness, not knowing what's causing him to withdraw, has taken a toll on all of us. We're concerned but do not want to alert the others until we know more. Your mother won't tell me exactly what happened between her and your dad, but I walked in on her falling apart. I'm worried for her mental health."

"What do you mean? My mother does not give in to emotional fits."

"It's more than crying. She was hysterical when I found her today. I couldn't seem to calm her down. She seems to believe whatever's happening with your father is somehow her fault."

"What does my father have to say about this?"

"I'm not sure that he cares!" Anna snapped. "I'm sorry, but I'm on your mother's side with this one."

Cain drew back. "There are no sides. They're married. And, I assure you, my father cares. He loves her above all else, above The Order, above his children, and perhaps even above his God."

"Then why the hell isn't he doing something? Your mother isn't well. This is no joke! Adam refuses to interfere in their business because it's against Family Law."

Cain held up his hands, not wishing to upset her. "Tell me what you think I should do."

She looked up, desperate concern filling her eyes with unshed tears. "I don't know if there is anything you can do. She's just so sad. It's heartbreaking to see her this way."

"Should I return home?"

Anna's mouth moved, but her voice silenced.

"Anna? Speak up. I can't hear you."

She frowned and continued to talk, but her voice remained muted.

Cain couldn't make out her words. Perhaps there was an interruption in their frequency. "Anna?" His vision wavered and an unfamiliar voice intruded their dream.

"Bodies drained of blood... Waiting for autopsy reports..."

Cain scowled, irritably searching for the unknown speaker. "Anna, is that you?"

No sound came from his sister-in-law's mouth, yet he read the frustration in her eyes. Holding her hands wide, she mouthed, *Is what me?*

"Did you hear that?"

Hear what? Her lips firmed impatiently.

"Unidentified female victim..." the annoying voice spoke again.

"What the hell is going on?" he snapped.

Anna's image faltered, dancing in and out of his vision.

A small, dark-haired woman suddenly appeared, and Cain jumped at the interference. "Who the hell are you?"

Anna followed his gaze but didn't seem to see the female. Her image flickered again, fading and losing shape and dimension. The intruding woman remained.

"Who are you?" he demanded, but the female didn't seem to hear him.

She held something in her hand.

"Cain…" He faintly heard Anna's distant voice yell for him, yet her call was nothing more than a whisper by the time it reached his ears. Her image completely vanished.

"Who are you?" he shouted again at the woman standing before him.

She looked through him. "…following the death of Sharon Foster, leaving her two children Dane Foster, age sixteen, and daughter, Cybil Foster, age ten, in the custody of the victim's mother and last surviving relative, Clara Barnes."

"What?" Cain's frustration shifted to pure fury. This had never happened before. Although his ability to share dreams with his brother's mate was a phenomenon among their people, he had never dreamt of another being. Who was this woman, and what was she doing in his and Anna's dream?

Angry, he yelled, "Get out of here!"

The world faded to black. The strange woman's curvy figure fading with it. He scowled, finding himself in an unfamiliar bedroom with no link back to Anna.

The back of his head thumped into the pillow, stirring the unconscious blonde woman draped over him. He moved a curtain of curly hair off the female's face. Definitely not the intruder of his dreams.

"Experts are questioning local zoos to see if there have been any animal outbreaks."

Cain jolted upright. The sound streaming from the television and an exact match to the woman's voice in his dream. It was her.

He recognized her olive skin and dark, corkscrew hair. Her curves were full and generous, and his body responded with approval. The woman on his lap flopped to her back and muttered some indecisive complaint in her sleep.

He had the urge to burry himself in a female's heat but glanced disinterestedly at his bed companion. Her pale breasts were soft. Cain momentarily considered licking them into flushed pink peaks like he had the night before, but his desire hardly reached impartiality. She suddenly struck him as a mediocre substitute—a fast-food burger when his gut desired a thick, juicy steak.

His gaze returned to the television. His lusty thoughts quickly dispelled the moment the report penetrated his half-sleeping brain, and he was suddenly fully awake.

The woman from his dream occupied half

of the screen while a man sitting at a desk occupied the other half.

"Is there any word on whether or not this will interfere with the upcoming hunting season, Destiny?"

Cain scowled. *Who was this putz?*

"From what I can gather, Mike, the local hunters are eager to hit the woods in search of what could be the next Bigfoot." She winked, and Cain's scowl deepened.

Her full lips wore a deep, unnatural shade of red. Black curls wildly contoured her heart-shaped face. Who was she, and how had she broken into his dream? It must have been the sound of the television interfering with his sleep.

"Our hearts go out to the Foster family," the man said.

A solemn expression stole over the female reporter's face. "This is the sixth case this year of a female victim found in these woods. Police suspect they may have a serial killer on their hands. Whether a Jane Doe or identified female, each victim has borne the same twin telltale markings along the neck. Whatever is attacking these women, be it man or beast, is draining their blood. The DA has yet to release any reports of sexual assault."

The screen switched to another male, this one standing on the steps of a building Cain assumed to be a police station. The reporter, Destiny, was there as well but dressed in different clothing. "District Attorney Schwartz," she pressed a microphone in the direction of the other man. "Can you comment on whether any of these women have suffered any other signs of assault prior to their deaths?"

The man appeared rather serious and sternly replied, "I'm not at liberty to comment. However, I would like to state, for the record, these are women of our community. They are mothers, daughters, wives, and sisters. Many of them have left families and friends behind. Most of these women were reportedly camping in what has always been a favorable environment for such recreation. I want to make this perfectly clear. Until whatever is out there is caught, these woods are not safe. Whatever is killing these women is strong and large. Don't be foolish and tempt fate. I would also like to advise those who plan to participate in the upcoming hunting season. Don't try to be a hero. If you see an animal approaching, use your head. Get to safety, or better yet, get out of there."

The screen switched back to a split-screenshot of Destiny and the man at the desk. "Tragic," the man at the desk declared.

"It is, Mike. Families throughout the community are struggling with the loss of loved ones. We'll keep the victims like Dane and Cybil Foster in our thoughts and hope that we can soon bring whatever or whoever is out there wreaking such havoc to justice. This is Destiny Santos, reporting live from Jim Thorpe, Channel Six News."

The screen cut away and the female was gone. Cain thought for a moment. Bodies drained of blood. Six victims. All women.

He had a lot to do. He needed to check on Larissa and then head home to see what was happening with his mother. Perhaps he should have a quick look in the woods surrounding Jim Thorpe before he returned to the farm. But first, he would enjoy the luscious blonde sharing his bed one last time.

*E*leazar prowled in the shadows of the trees just off the highway's shoulder. As the autumn chill approached, greens burst into vibrant hues of plum, sienna, and gold. He had always found fall to be life's most radiant bow before surrendering to winter's cold. Yet, there was no sense of beauty where he stood now, only a sense of depravity lurking nearby.

Upon rising that evening, he suffered an undeniable pull to come to this exact place. He recognized it, perhaps from one of his dreams.

Cars rushed by in the dark, speeding past with fleeting impressions of mortal thoughts tickling his mind. The establishment across the freeway was a nondescript building with several vehicles occupying the lot—Club Silhouettes.

He frowned, confused how such a place could relate to his purpose. He should move on, yet his instincts insisted he get closer.

On a sigh, he crossed the road, hopped the median, and slipped into the lot between two parked cars. He heard a pulsing, rhythmic beat pumping from deep within what a mortal would declare soundproof walls. His ears prickled at a muffled moan. His black eyes sought out where the sound was coming from.

There, inside a shiny black car, was a woman leaning over a man's lap. The man's expression was enraptured by what the woman was doing to him.

The desire to return to his morally-rich home surged through him at the sight of such a public display. The English were hopeless.

Running a hand down his crisp, white shirt, Eleazar moved toward the door of the facility. The brown paint of the heavy metal door was chipped, showing patches of battleship gray underneath. Opening the door, the scent of human lust assaulted him.

What was this house of sin?

A low red light illuminated the small entry room. The dark, stained carpet cushioned his steps. There were two doors ahead of him. Music pulsed through the walls loud enough to vibrate the soles of his feet.

A large man entered the foyer. Eleazar sized up the other male. He was overweight. A trickle of sweat rolled over the coarse stubble covering his flushed neck. The man adjusted his belt and pressed a few fingers into the waist of his pants, wedging his black t-shirt inside past his paunch.

"Sorry, man, I had a taco earlier that didn't agree with me."

He gave the mortal a tight-lipped smile and probed his mind, seeking a name. *Vito*. He waited for the man to continue, finding silence often lent itself to authority.

Brushing his hands together, Vito asked, "Are you with either of the bachelor parties?"

"I'm not."

"Okay, then it's gonna be an eight-dollar cover, and there are two-dollar drafts 'til midnight. You got ID?"

"ID?" Eleazar echoed.

"Yeah, a license. Can't go in if you are underage."

"I assure you I'm certainly not 'underage,'"

Eleazar said, giving the mortal a gentle push to let him pass.

The man stepped aside and hesitated. "Wait," Vito said, eyes still slightly glazed from the bishop's compulsion. "You need a stamp to get in."

Eleazar looked at the device the man held in his hand. Another probe into his mind and he understood. He extended his arm and waited as Vito pressed a red-ink silhouette of a female's profile into the tan flesh of his wrist.

Eleazar frowned at the mark, anxious to find a washroom to wash it off.

"One more thing," Vito said as he swung the door open. "No touching the girls unless you pay for it."

The bishop scowled at such an implication.

Loud music reverberated through all the walls. A robotic voice chanted, followed by a raspy female voice singing about sex, chains, and whips. The intensified emotions throbbing from the mortals in the room could bring a lesser immortal to his knees.

Only males gathered on the floor, each staring desperately at the stage where a female undulated in a scant strip of lace.

Crowds milled around a bar. Tables filled the dim room. Men of all ages occupied the seats; some dressed in street clothes and others in formal attire.

Lust. The stench of the emotion was suffocating.

A blue-lit stage, wide in the rear and shaping forward like a T, extended between the tables of men. There was a pole running from the platform to the ceiling. A bare-breasted woman dangled from the pole. Mortified by her lack of modesty, Eleazar looked away.

His stare then caught on another topless woman in sharp, shiny, red boots. Her legs were spread, her rear pressed into a seated man's face. The woman's white hair appeared blue in the light reflecting from the stage. She wore some sort of string contraption between her hindquarters. There were dollar bills laced throughout the string and a wad of more sweaty bills in the male's hand.

There was no logic behind his presence here. He needed to leave. He maneuvered his way through the crowds, using compulsion to deter the woman serving drinks from approaching him and slowing his exit.

The song playing thankfully ended but

was then replaced by the bleat of a horn pumping over a woman's erotic moans and sighs. A voice chimed in over the music. "Next up, the lovely Larissa, dancing to Janet Jackson's 'Throb.'"

Eleazar stilled.

He moved in slow motion toward the stage. All was dark.

The pole was mysteriously gone, and a wooden chair sat in its place.

Breathy moans chanted to an erotic beat, increasing in tempo as a tall female wearing a man's white dress shirt and necktie strutted into the glow of the central spotlight. It couldn't be.

Her smooth, bare legs caught the light at every shapely slope of toned muscle. High shoes caused her calves to flex as if amid a climax. Those shoes had been created to tempt a male. Those shoes were the embodiment of sin.

He still wasn't convinced it was her. Perhaps an English woman with the same name.

A wide-brimmed, masculine hat shadowed her face. He could not quite make out the color of the female's hair, as it was tucked within the fedora.

When she reached the chair, she stood behind it, facing the audience, and grasped the high back with her hand, spinning the wooden seat around to face her. She made to straddle the seat but instead hovered over the wood, legs spread, her pelvis undulating slowly. Eleazar locked his jaw and swallowed.

The music was not music at all, but rather a collection of fast beats accompanied by sighs a woman would make in the throes of passion. The eroticism of the song was so blatant it almost had him blushing. More than five centuries old and *blushing!*

When she finally did lower her bottom onto the seat, Eleazar also found himself sitting but had no recollection of locating a chair. His mouth had gone dry at the sight of her dainty hands gripping the wood.

Never in his long life had he reacted to a female in this way. He noticed the loosely cuffed sleeves of the shirt draping over her petite wrists. He wanted to find the man whose shirt she wore and rip his throat out.

She stood again, twisting the chair as she did so. She glided around the piece of furniture as if she walked on air, straddling the chair again, now with her back to the audience.

Eleazar quickly scanned the crowd, a

growl slowly building in his chest as the other men in the audience admired her.

Arching back, her head tipped and the hat fell. Long, black hair cascaded to the stage floor like a waterfall. He recognized her hair, knew it better than he had any right to. It smelled of mixed berries and was softer than silk. It was thick enough to fill his fist. He saw his fingers running through the raven-colored strands and knew the soft weight of it upon his palms. A punch of fury hit him as she shared her luxurious hair with such depraved mortal men.

There, dancing like a common harlot upon this stage of ill repute, was his mate.

He stood so fast his chair crashed backward to the floor. His jaw clenched and his nostrils flared. Barely containing his rage, he growled at the men in the bar and sent out a mental command. At once, every patron lowered their eyes and tilted their heads away from the stage.

Apparently undeterred by her audience's sudden lack of interest, Larissa continued. Could she not see the crowd that watched her so avidly, with eyes full of lust and minds full of dishonorable thoughts?

She danced. Her hips swaying, mimicking

the intimate motions that should be shared only by man and wife. He was mortified for her.

Her fingers tugged the knot of the tie. Her left hand stroked up and down the narrow strip of fabric. Her actions somehow stimulated an image of his very own anatomy—her hands working his flesh until he swelled to the point of pain that would be eased only by plunging into her warmth.

Dear God, she had to be stopped. Looking back one last time at the practically sleeping crowd, satisfied no eyes were on her, he sprung to the stage, but not before buttons went pinging and her breasts were exposed.

Larissa stumbled back into her chair with a startled scream. Staring up at him, pie-eyed with fear, she gasped. "Bishop King!"

Fury spun through him, hot and hungry for a hunt. He wanted a reason to punish her. His lip curled as he sneered. "Go ahead, Larissa, run."

CHAPTER 8

*L*arissa's fear ricocheted off Eleazar. She bolted to the door at the back of the stage with immortal speed. He reached it first. His chest swelled at the rush of adrenaline. Some deep-seated instinct wanted to chase her.

His heart pounded with the rush of blood and a long-forgotten emotion pumping through his veins. Arousal.

She stood before him, dark hair tousled around her oval face, eyes wide, and lips parted as she caught her breath. Her shirt, no longer in possession of buttons, gaped open, exposing the valley between her full breasts, the length of her long, trim torso, and her narrow hips. He resented her nudity, but not as much as he resented the scrap of black silk covering the V between her thighs.

Glaring into her eyes, he suffered a jolt of disorienting déjà vu but shoved it away. "Your family has been worried about you." A twitch of irritation groused at the thought of her bothersome husband, Silus Hostetler. Soon, he would be a non-issue. "It's time to return home and honor your duties."

"I'm not going with you."

Her impudence was expected, based on everything he'd heard of the willful female. He reached forward, drawing the edges of her shirt together. "You've had your fun with the English. Now, it's time to come home."

"I'll only leave again. I will not live out my eternity as Silus Hostetler's oppressed wife."

She had, at least, one detail correct. "Be that as it may, I have a duty to return you to your family and rightful place. The English world is dangerous. You're not safe here."

"I don't care. I'll… I'll learn to be stronger."

She was trembling. Her fear of him would be another inconvenience. He was quickly losing patience. "Enough. Your situation is not up for debate."

"It's *my* life!"

"Come with me now, and you won't be in too much trouble when you return."

Her chin quivered. "And if I refuse?"

"We both know your objections will only take you so far. You're no match for me, and you don't belong here in the English world. You certainly do not belong here on this stage. If you fight me, it will only double my determination. Come with me easily, and you can atone quickly, putting all of this behind you."

Regardless of Eleazar's position, he technically would have no authority over another male's wife. A female's husband decided which methods of discipline suited their marriage. There seemed a sensible order to resolving the complication of Larissa's unhappiness, but her stubbornness was confusing matters, and he wasn't prepared to show a vulnerable side just yet.

Silus saw his wife's disappearance as public humiliation and a direct insult to him. Her absence implied something lacking in Silus's character, and the male openly planned to punish her. Eleazar suspected he'd beat her until his bruised ego fully healed.

He would never let that happen. But

Eleazar also would never tolerate such loose English behavior from a mate.

"I'll only run again. I'm never going back to that life."

Regardless, he was her bishop and she would be wise to obey him before overly complicating an already complicated matter. "And what of your family? Do you plan on living out your immortal existence and never seeing your parents or brothers or little Grace again?"

"I see my brother now."

He pressed his lips together. "Yes, Cain would be the one to find you and turn his back on his Order by not informing them of your whereabouts."

Her eyes narrowed and her chest lifted, distracting him with a glimpse of flawless flesh. "Cain is loyal to his family before all else."

"How noble." He pressed his lips tight, unimpressed, and grabbed her thin wrist in an unbreakable grip. "Now, if you'll come with me, we can be on our way."

"No!" She jerked her arm and dug her bare feet into the ground.

He stilled, eyebrows slowly rising at her endless stubbornness. "No?"

"No."

He shook his head. He'd thought to help her, but now she was simply behaving like a brat. "How disappointing. Very well."

Eleazar shoved into her thoughts, intending to force her mind into an unconscious state. But the compulsion ricocheted and he staggered back, grunting at the force of energy pulsing between them.

His brow creased as he shook off the jab. A female her age should not have the power to block him. He had centuries over her.

He shoved into her mind again, forcing a command that she sleep, and she bared her teeth. "I said *no!*"

The compulsion to sleep catapulted back at him. A sudden fog of peace settled over him, cloaking all sound. A startled look of shock overtook Larissa's face, and he reached for her with a sluggish hand, but she stepped out of his grip.

The world tilted off its axis and gravity pulled him down. His vision blurred and everything went dark.

Eleazar awoke as the doorman hauled him off the stage. Grunting, he jerked his arm free of the other man's grip. "Take your hands off me."

The large Englishman scoffed. "You're out of here, bro—"

Before he could grab him again, Eleazar compelled the man to be silent. Eleazar's head was ringing like a gong and the pressure was nauseating. He erased all memories of his presence from the man called Vito and shuffled out of the dingey club.

Sniffing his palm, he tracked Larissa's scent into the night. She was nearby, but the overpopulated streets and housing complexes made her difficult to find—an infuriating and disobedient needle buried in a haystack of sin.

Hours later, he stood—irritatingly aroused —at the foot of Larissa's bed, watching her sleep. His body was a mix of disapproval and desire. The hunt was over, but there would be no spoils. His disappointment surprised him, because, physically, she was not disappointing at all, and he couldn't recall the last time his body responded to a female in such a manner.

Raven-colored hair fanned over the pillows. Her lithe body was tall for a female but still small in comparison to his size. Her scent filled him like an obsession, needling his soul and imprinting into his memory.

He pulled back the quilt draped over her body, revealing one inch of naked flesh at a time. Her breasts were full, her nipples the exact pink of her lush lips. While one arm curved up toward her face, the other gently rested over her narrow torso. He swallowed at the sight of her small belly button.

The quilt slithered lower, revealing the soft swell of her hips. She was built as a woman should be and would have good, healthy pregnancies.

A soft dusting of black hair covered the apex of her thighs. She shifted restlessly. A sigh escaped her lips, and he stilled.

Her lashes fluttered just above the high arch of her cheekbones and her eyes flashed open. A cold, ice-blue stare locking on him.

"What are you doing here?" Her voice was husky from sleep. She didn't try to hide her body or jolt out of bed. She simply held his stare, cemented by her infuriating stubbornness.

"I told you I'd find you."

"I'll run again."

"And I'll find you again. There will be no escaping me, Larissa. I'm more powerful than you, more powerful than any male of The Order. And I'm used to getting what I want."

"And what is it you want, Bishop?"

He released the quilt, letting it fall to the floor. Her beauty enraged him. "Your family misses you."

"I'm not going back to Silus."

On that, they agreed. "You're not staying here."

Slowly, she stretched before him. She was magnificent. Her arms extended above her head, lifting her breasts. Then, realizing he was watching her, her gaze shifted and any sense of warmth disappeared, replaced with an icy stare of contempt and deliberate disrespect.

"Do you think that look will work on me?" He snatched the sheet. His fingers curled around the delicate bones of her ankle, preventing her escape. Enough with the facades. "You've broken the rules, Larissa."

The more she struggled to break his hold, the more she aroused him. Her body was a work of art and a dangerous distraction. His fingers itched to caress every secret inch of her flesh, despite her husband's claim.

Rumpled and angry, she shot forward,

overpowered by his unbreakable grip of her ankle. "I'm English now! There are no rules!"

"You are *not* English. You're simply behaving like a belligerent child. You belong with The Order."

She reared back and flashed her fangs. "How dare you call me such a name, you gnarled old crow!"

His eyes bulged. He was not gnarled.

"I will not allow you to disregard our hard-earned values and traditions to bear your breasts to a room full of animals."

"Animals? Funny, not one of those animals broke into my home and mistreated me like you're doing now."

"Yes, animals. I read their vile thoughts. Why don't you explain to me how you were able to reject my compulsion earlier?"

Her brow kinked and she momentarily stopped struggling. "I don't know."

"You must know."

"I don't. I just… did it."

"And what was it you did?"

"All I did was say no."

"Not a word I enjoy." Especially from her.

Her eyes narrowed as she blew a hank of hair out of her face. "I'll tell you no again and again whether you like it or not. I'm *not* going with you."

He chuckled softly. "You will. I have ways of getting you to comply."

"Like taking away my free will? How noble and progressive of you, not at all primitive or barbaric."

"Brat."

"Bastard."

He arched an eyebrow, tired of her insolence, and her eyes widened.

"No!" she shouted, launching her body toward the pillows attempting to get away and bearing her backside to him in the process. Too little, too late.

He jerked her back to pin her body beneath his weight, bearing his fangs and hissing into her ear. "What did I tell you about telling me no?"

Her breath hitched, and she stopped fighting. His body hardened at her well-earned surrender. Then she whimpered, and he sensed her absolute fear.

"Larissa?"

"Get off of me."

He couldn't let her go, not without a promise that she would obey. "Give me your word you'll do as I say—"

"I said no!" Her objection plowed through him like a bolt of lightning. It hurled his body off of her with such force that he slammed hard against the wall.

His teeth clacked and his skull rattled as all went black. *Again.*

CHAPTER 9

"Oh no, oh no, oh no, oh no! Not again!" Larissa paced around the bishop's limp body in a full panic. This was the second time she knocked him out, and she had no idea how.

Why was he here? And why was he following her? Silus couldn't possibly have so much power within The Order that the bishop would run an errand for him? Did he?

Maybe she severely underestimated her husband. There was no way she could outrun a male the age of Eleazar King. She was done. Now that he knew where she lived and worked, there would be no escaping him.

"This is not good." She couldn't give up. Wrapping the sheet around her body, she quickly returned to the bishop and nudged him with her toe. Nothing.

She chewed her lip and glanced at the door. Where was Cain when she could use help? How much time did she have before the bishop woke?

"Okay, Fabio, it's time for you to go."

She grabbed his foot and tugged his weight toward the door. His shoe slipped off when she stumbled and tripped into the far wall. "Damn it."

She tossed the shoe aside and grabbed his foot in a tighter grip, grunting as she dragged him across her apartment floor. He didn't rouse, not even when she shoved him through the front door and accidentally hit his head on the corner.

It was late, so the halls were dark. A quick probe into her neighbor's apartments confirmed everyone close by was deep asleep. She sent out a strong compulsion for them to stay sleeping as she hauled the bishop's long body off the floor.

"My goodness, you're heavy." His body was lean but dense with muscle.

The sheet around her slipped and she panicked, modesty taking priority. She released her hold of him and caught the material before it could fall to the floor. The bishop, however, was not so lucky. He landed with a heavy thud, and she winced.

"Oops." She hoisted him back up and shuffled his weight across the hall to the trash chute.

The trap door whined open with a scrape of metal. It was going to be a tight fit.

Leveraging his weight into the opening, she first guided his feet into the opening. It took some finagling, but once she worked his hips into the chute, the rest of his body followed easily. She meant to send him off gently, but at the last moment, she lost her grip, and his body went sailing down the chute with a loud clatter and the metal door snapped shut.

Larissa blinked, jaw hanging wide. Did she really just throw the bishop into a dumpster?

Her gaze skittered to the shadows, assuring herself no one witnessed such behavior.

She ran into her apartment, grabbed his shoe, and chucked it down the chute as well. "Sorry." She bit her lip. "Maybe I am a brat, but no means no." When the trap door slammed closed, she winced.

SOMEONE WAS GOING TO DIE.

Eleazar's fangs punched through his gums. He pushed himself up from the plastic cushion and sniffed the putrid air. Garbage. He was lying in a pit of garbage.

Shocked by how weak his limbs were and dizzy from what could only have been a blow to the head, he fought back a woozy sensation and the urge to empty his stomach. He hadn't suffered such a sense of illness since he was a young boy.

She did this to him.

His jaw locked as he clamored his way out of the dumpster. He grunted as he pulled his body fully upright and his spine popped into alignment. His tongue tasted blood.

Reeking of human refuse, he marched around her building and found the front entrance. Adjusting his soiled clothing, he twisted and cracked his neck, shaking off the lingering aches and pain. The brat was going to pay.

His dirty hand closed over the knob, and he stilled. Someone was in his mind. He immediately threw up a wall and guarded his thoughts.

He mentally shoved back at the intruder, and they surrendered under the pressure of his compulsion. He followed the cognitive bond, probing the intruder's mind until they revealed their identity.

Adriel. He relaxed, recognizing the familiar presence of his friend.

Eleazar? You seem...off. Is everything all right?

I'm fine. He allowed his friend to enter the surface of his mind, just enough to communicate over such distance but never granting her full access to his thoughts. *Do you need something?*

Rarely could any immortal cross his mental guard, but Adriel had been his friend for four hundred years. She was only a few decades his minor, so she possessed a great deal of her own power.

A strong tonic might help. I'll have a headache for the next hour, thanks to the jab you just drilled into my mind. Why are you so guarded? You feel ... hostile.

I'm out of my element. To say the least. He flicked what looked like lettuce off his cuff. *I'm in the middle of something and I only have a moment to spare.* He glared up at Larissa's window. *I'll be out of reach soon, so share whatever news you have.*

I thought you would be interested to know that there's been talk of Isaiah Hartzler.

Isaiah Hartzler might have disappeared long ago, but his reputation remained. If anything, rumors of his extinction helped to enforce the younger generation's obedience.

Why would that interest me?

Because Isaiah's kin, the young Hartzler twin, has just returned to the farm with suspicions that his great-uncle is still alive.

She had his full attention now. *Impossible,* he thought back to her. *The male turned rogue over eighty years ago. He would not have survived this long without a mate.*

The boy, Cain, disagrees. He approached Ezekiel upon his return. The elder called a council meeting directly after he received the news.

Eleazar was not convinced.

Isaiah was Ezekiel's brother. It's natural for him to believe the rumors. His heart wants to find hope where there is none.

In the early 1900s, Isaiah Hartzler, patriarch and council elder of the Hartzler line, had been called. He displayed the common symptoms: sensitivity to the sun, lack of appetite, vertigo, increased hunger for the blood of his specific mate, and, eventually, a loss of humanity.

Left unanswered, Isaiah Hartzler became more animal than a rational-thinking man. His mind quickly fragmented from bloodlust, but the blood of other creatures could no longer sustain him. He was lost without the blood of his true mate.

Once he turned *feeish,* a nocturnal beast awoke from within, bearing fangs and claws and randomly selecting victims. When a *feeish* immortal drank the blood of anyone but their true mate, they fell into a rage and sometimes went on a killing spree.

Having realized his own calling shortly after agreeing to Silus's marriage, Eleazar questioned his fate. But Silus had kept his wife so secluded, the bishop hardly suffered any symptoms at all. That all changed the night he saw Silus strike Larissa.

Eleazar did not want to turn *feeish,* nor did he want to reveal his situation until he had matters under his control. But when he saw Silus strike Larissa, a murderous rage woke within him and he knew he was out of time. Then she ran.

He did not want to lose her in the wide-open English world. He had no choice but to hunt and claim his mate or risk eternally damning his soul.

The carnage and loss of innocent lives over the centuries bred legends of monsters. One lost soul was a burden for all to bear. Once words like *vampire* surfaced within communities, there was no choice but to act and end the life of one of their own.

Years ago, they hunted Isaiah and found him in a bloody rage. After weeks of feeding from mortals, his strength had multiplied. Ezekiel delivered what should have been a final death blow, but he hesitated a moment too long, and Isaiah slit his brother's throat so deep it almost severed Ezekiel's head.

There had never been another sighting of Isaiah after that. The Council had assumed him long dead, most likely driven to the point of insanity too deep to survive.

He could have survived, Eleazar, Adriel said, pulling him back from his memories.

Doubtful.

I think you should return home and hear the evidence for yourself.

What evidence? Hearsay and rumors are not concrete facts.

The boy said there have been reports of six murders. Females, all of them.

How does he know this? I do not trust Cain Hartzler. Perhaps he killed these women.

Perhaps, but why would he return home and draw The Council's attention to the act? He says the deaths are all over the English news. He claims he found markings in the woods, impressions that only a male, traveling at immortal speeds, could make in the earth.

Eleazar was growing tired of this conversation. *This is only speculation. The Council laid the issue of Isaiah Hartzler to rest long ago. I assure you, Isaiah Hartzler is dead. It's far past the time to bury rumors of his return.*

But Eleazar, the women—

I must go, Adriel. I have work to do. He couldn't waste any more time on such nonsense.

Before their connection cut off, Adriel rushed out, *Each victim was drained of blood!*

Eleazar stilled. Drained of blood? Impossible. Why now?

He glanced up at Larissa's window one last time, then spun in the opposite direction and ran, not stopping until he located a corner store. The bell chimed as he shoved into the small shop reeking of gasoline and overheated pork products. A metal rack of newspapers sat beside the door.

He rummaged through the pages, searching for any reports of females drained of blood. Inked articles fluttered to the floor, and he only then realized he was missing a shoe. He was going to throttle his mate when he got his hands on her again.

"Sir, you have to buy that if you're going to read it," the clerk at the counter said.

"*Quiet!*" he barked, giving the clerk a mental push to mind his own business.

Finally, he found what he was seeking. Under a picture of a young boy and an even younger girl, both appearing consumed by grief, was the headline, BEAST LEAVES CHILDREN ORPHANED.

The article recapped the events of the past year. Adriel was right. The murders all happened in the town of Jim Thorpe, not far from their farm.

Words jumped out at Eleazar as he read. BLOODLESS. DRAINED. FEMALES. SEXUALLY ASSAULTED. MAN. EYEWITNESSES. CARNAGE. PUNCTURE MARKS AT THE CAROTID ARTERY.

Eleazar slammed the crumpled paper into the bin and left the store. If this was, in fact, Isaiah Hartzler returned and running rogue, he would need to be hunted and destroyed.

This time, no other Hartzler would accompany the men on the hunt and there would be no mistakes.

He needed to retrieve his disobedient mate and return home, but something stopped him from doing so. Some inexplicable emotion that refused him to go to her in a fit of rage—and that only aggravated him more.

He could easily retrieve her from her apartment and drag her back to the farm. He simply had to keep his mental block in place.

But he wasn't ready. He wanted time. Time to punish her. Time to torment her. Time to understand her. And time to claim her. The Silus situation could wait.

Selfishly, Eleazar decided he would deal with the Isaiah Hartzler threat after he dealt with his mate—another Hartzler. Why was this family always complicating his life?

On his way back to Larissa's dwelling, he reconnected with Adriel.

Rude, she scoffed in greeting.

Adriel kept up-to-date on council business because she listened from a bench just outside the Council Hall doors. A bench he had placed there specifically for her. She never missed a meeting, but she had never once been granted entrance because she was female. Yet, she heard every word from her place in the hallway.

Cain Hartzler is right. There's news of something murdering English women in the woods, he confirmed.

Do you think it's Isaiah?

Despite her earlier concern, he sensed her reluctance to accept such an unfathomable possibility. Isaiah was dead.

Doubtful. We're not the only immortals in existence. There are plenty of lawless others. Do you have any other news?

As a matter of fact, I do. Jonas Hartzler.

The mention of his mate's father captured his interest. *Go on.*

He and Abilene are fighting. Jonas hasn't been sharing his wife's bed.

And you know this how?

When under stress, immortals rarely guard their thoughts. I plucked it right from his mind.

Eleazar shook his head and chuckled. *Such a busybody.*

Do not judge me, Eleazar. Snooping is the only way a female can learn anything around here. Change the laws, and I'll consider changing my ways.

I doubt it.

Adriel snickered. *You know me too well. Anyway, I suspect Jonas has been called.*

Eleazar stopped walking. *You cannot be serious.*

A calling is always serious.

He frowned. How could that be? First Adam, then Cain, sooner or later Larissa would realize, and now Jonas? It was unheard of. *You gained all of this from him simply passing by?*

Don't underestimate my abilities, Eleazar. I can hold onto a male's thoughts beyond some silly door.

We have to stop approving these marital unions. When an immortal is meant to mate, God will decide. That's two annulments I'll have to oversee.

Too late, he realized his slip. Adriel's shock registered with a sharp ping of interest, and he closed off his thoughts.

Dear God, Eleazar, is it true? How long have you known and does anyone else know?

He grit his teeth. *No one. And I wish to keep it that way.*

You've always kept my secrets, so I will keep yours. But promise me, when it comes time to tell Silus, you'll make sure I'm around. He'll be mad as a hatter and as helpless as a kitten.

A growl ripped from his throat. *He will never touch Larissa again.*

She laughed. *Well, listen to you... I never imagined a female not even half a century old would be the one to bring you to your knees.*

I have to go.

Oh, I'm sure, she teased. *Just one last word of warning, my friend,* her tone sobered, *Silus Hostetler may be a male who comes from a long line of elders, but he's not as honorable as he pretends. Females talk, and when they do, I listen. Larissa is a sweet girl. Why you jackasses approved a union between her and Silus, I'll never understand. He's spoiled by nepotism, and he can be especially cruel when given the upper hand.*

What are you saying?

I'm saying I know what it's like to be married to a bastard. My husband killed parts of me that will never heal. Don't be surprised if there are consequences to your choices. A few short years with a monster can pass like an eternity.

Regret stabbed him, and he questioned if she'd ever forgive him for such an oversight. *You've been in her mind?*

Enough to know that she deserves someone who is kind to her. Do not let your emotions or your ego get the better of you. And be patient with her. I have a feeling she's a fighter.

That much, he was sure of.

CHAPTER 10

$\mathcal{J}$onas wondered why he was there again.

The ground of the mortal graveyard turned out with soft soil where a coffin covered in yellow roses lowered into the earth.

He had this dream a dozen times in the past few weeks. Always with the woman he recognized as his called mate, always with the crying children he didn't know, always the middle-aged man holding the Bible. It was as if the dark dream haunted him. Or perhaps his mate was, and she managed to project these images into his subconscious.

Clara looked right at him this time. Her

snowy hair was pulled into a bun at the nape of her neck, a few wisps escaping in the breeze and caressing her plain face. Dressed in all black except for a bulky, gray sweater that covered her, she looked chilled to the bone by something other than the cold.

He battled the urge to comfort her. A deep instinct driving him closer so that he might relieve her of such agony.

The children, a boy of about fifteen or sixteen years and a girl several years younger, stood to Clara's right with their heads bowed. The boy's arm clung to the girl's shoulders as they both stared at the grave. There were no tears, only expressions of disbelief as if the passing of this loved one was simply inconceivable.

Clara's weathered hands clenched at her afghan sweater as the blustery wind whistled over the vacant cemetery. She appeared smaller and thinner than how he remembered her being from his last dream.

He studied her as he always did, but he never spoke directly to her. Speaking to Clara would make his presence and their situation too real. He would not allow it.

Yet, when Clara looked directly at him, he

feared his loyalties to Abilene would disappear.

Clara had a plainness that spoke to him. Bare of makeup, her skin wore age gracefully. Although creases encased her sharp eyes, time had not diminished her attractiveness. She was small and frail, but there was strength in those wise eyes.

Judging a mortal's age wasn't easy. He could tell her life had been long by the thinness of her hair, the transparency of her skin, and the delicate structure of her bones. In immortal terms, Clara was still a baby. But as a mortal, she was vintage.

Why now? Where was she sixty years ago, before he'd given his heart to Abilene?

The man with the Bible continued to speak softly over the grave. The children continued to stare motionlessly at the casket. And Clara continued to stare at him.

"Why are you here?" Her voice traveled like windchimes through a breeze, echoing in the air with an effervescent quality.

She never spoke directly to him before, a sign that their bond was progressing against his will. The others did not hear her or notice his presence, most likely because it was not their dream. She was the only one who saw him, and she did not appear pleased.

"Are you the angel of death?" Her tone snapped with accusation. "Have you come to finish this? Why must you torture them so?"

Her words were clipped and resolute, but Jonas saw the slight trembling of her chin and the uncertainty and vulnerability of her eyes. If he *were* the angel of death, she certainly wouldn't beg for more time. No, his mate was too proud for that.

"I'm no angel of death or angel otherwise," Jonas assured her, and some of the tension noticeably left her shoulders.

"Then who are you? Did you know Sharon?"

"Sharon?"

"Yes, my daughter. Dane and Cybil's mother," she replied, jerking her chin to the plot.

"I did not."

"Then what business do you have here? This is my memory, my nightmare. I've seen you here many times, yet I have no idea who you are."

"I'm Jonas."

"And what does that mean to me, Jonas?"

Apparently nothing. Mortals knew nothing of their kind and even less about fate and the power of God's call.

"Eventually, I will come to you, Clara." At the use of her name, she stiffened. Her sharp, blue eyes staring into his.

He should have welcomed her curious stare with hope and affection, but the ominous speed of time left him pressed. Now that he'd connected with her, there would be no keeping him away. His soul had already begun the hunt and it wouldn't relent until it claimed its other half.

It was best to prepare her. The outcome, for them both, was inevitable.

"When I come to you, I will offer you the gift of eternal life. You will offer me salvation."

She laughed in a way that lacked humor. "Another liar. I don't need one more person selling me promises with no guarantees. You can't promise me eternal life any more than I can promise my grandchildren a home that will still be here next year."

He frowned at the children and followed their gazes to the grave. "You're all they have left?"

"Yes. Isn't God thoughtful? He's given two children a guardian at the end of her life to watch over them." Her words dripped with sarcasm.

"I also take issue with our Lord's decisions as of late."

"Have you lost someone?"

"No, but I will soon." His heart jerked from the punch of pain as the thought of losing his sweet Abilene knocked the wind out of him.

Her mouth firmed into a thin line. "Perhaps death is the reward. I find life more and more punishing the longer it goes on."

"Perhaps." He still considered refusing the call and ending his life. It seemed a kinder fate than one that required him to betray the female he loved. "I may also die very soon."

"The doctors tell me I have only a few months left."

"How can any man decide such a thing?"

"Science," she stated concisely. "I find it rather inconvenient to know such things. I would prefer ignorance. At least if I were ignorant, I would be able to enjoy my grandchildren in these last moments rather than be in a constant state of distraction, burdened with worry over what will become of them."

"And what will become of them?"

"The state will get custody. If they're lucky, they'll remain together, but the chances of that are unlikely."

Her attention shifted to the boy when he started to cry. She let him work through the moment then returned her stare to Jonas. "It's been six weeks since Sharon was killed, and Cybil hasn't spoken a single word since. I used to call her my little jabber box."

"Was she there when it happened?"

"They both were," Clara's eyes closed as she drew in a slow breath. "Dane seems to understand what she needs, so who knows what will happen to her if he is taken away from her. Psychologists will label her, and she'll have to contend with carrying this trauma alone for the rest of her life."

"What if you could stay with them? What if neither of us had to die?"

She laughed, the sound dry and brittle, triggering a cough. "Why would I want to stay in a life that is marked by suffering? I can't bear to lose another person I love. If I lived forever, I'd lose everyone eventually." She shook her head. "I love them dearly, but I'm tired. I'm all out of fight."

"I could take away your tiredness."

"For a young man, you sure do have an issue with your hearing. My time here is ending. I'm beyond bargaining."

"I assure you, I'm no young man."

"Not a young man. Not an angel. So what are you?"

"I don't know. I thought I was a good man, but perhaps I'm not."

Clara coughed again, this time the hacking rattle shook her entire body and the image of trees and grass wavered. The children no longer seemed alive but rather two-dimensional figures frozen in time, as did the man with the Bible. The drizzle no longer fell from the sky, it shimmered, suspended in midair.

"What's happening?" He sensed himself slipping away.

"This is one of my paintings. I've painted this day a hundred times. Don't worry, it will fade. In the end, I always wash it away."

Just as she said it would, the gray clouds bled into the dissolving blue sky. Browns formed as the smudges from the sky blended with the autumn leaves. Like puddles of mud, the children melted away.

The casket covered in yellow roses swirled into a whirlpool of black where all the colors smeared into the center of the page. Clara stood before him covered in paint, no longer dressed in black or wrapped in a sweater, but wearing a stained, oversized artist's smock.

"You see, Jonas, nothing lasts forever. Beauty fades, as do our memories. The only thing that continues on in this world is pain."

Could she somehow relieve him of his heartache? The pain had been suffocating him. He couldn't bear to look into his sweet Abilene's eyes anymore, knowing that he was living a lie—lying to her.

"It's a shame you're not the angel I suspected." She pivoted and walked away.

"Wait!" The vision smeared and blackness swallowed her silhouette. "Come back!"

When he opened his eyes and found himself at home in his den, he noticed the fire had burned low and was due for another log. Then he glanced at the woodpile and found his wife watching him, tears streaming from her eyes.

Abilene stood stock-still, her expression one of utter disbelief. Her face drained of blood. "You were dreaming."

Unable to speak, unable to form a lie, at least not to his undeserving wife, he simply stared back at her, hoping she saw the agony he suffered at such treachery.

"Answer me!"

He swallowed, not ready to destroy them. Grief strangled his voice into a mere rasp. He rose to his feet. "Yes—"

"How long?" she interrupted. "How long have you kept this from me?"

Of course, she would be more upset that he had kept a secret from her. "Two months."

She faced away from him.

"I didn't want to hurt you, Abilene."

"And yet, I can't remember the last time I experienced happiness, Jonas. Since this secret came between us, you've done nothing but hurt me."

"That wasn't my intention. I was trying to protect you."

"You can't! You know better! There is no avoiding a calling from God!" Her voice cracked as she battled back a sob. "You brought lies into our home, our bedroom, and our marriage." Her words quivered with emotion, and she swiped at her fallen tears. "If we had any time to spare, you've wasted it."

Her sorrow crippled him. "I won't go away. I'll refuse the call," he insisted, his voice thick with tears.

"Then you shall die as your uncle did.

There's no way to ignore a calling, Jonas. You, of all immortals, should know that."

"I cannot accept that this is our fate."

"Then you're a fool."

He took a step toward her only to have her step back. He deserved her rejection. So many days and nights he forced distance between them when she so obviously needed him. Still, her withdrawal gutted him.

"I need to hold you, Abilene. I need to hold you in my arms, right now in this moment. Please, no more distance."

"I can't touch you when you've been dreaming of someone else. A call is sacred." Her lips trembled and twin tears fell. "I have no right to you, and I won't let you follow your uncle's fate."

"Abilene, do not walk away from me!"

She stilled at the door but did not turn to face him. "Was I not a good wife to you, Jonas? An obedient wife?"

"You are the best wife a male could ask for."

Her head nodded, ripples of unbraided hair trailing down her back. "At least I can rest easy knowing I did my job well."

"We're not through. Not yet anyway." A

vise locked around his heart. "I need you. Don't turn your back on me, Abilene!"

She left the room.

Tears blurred his vision as she walked away from him. It was the first time in sixty years she denied him anything. Death would be merciful after living through this.

CHAPTER 11

Cain watched his brother shove another burnt biscuit into his mouth and frowned. "I don't know how you can eat that," he whispered to Adam while Annalise was busy basting a roast in the oven.

"What? I like my wife's cooking."

Cain reexamined his blackened roll and chucked the inedible briquette onto his plate. It landed with the subtlety of a paperweight. "I suppose that's love."

"The roast should be done in about five minutes," Annalise said as she returned to the table. She sat down and let out a long sigh, rubbing her slightly protruding belly. Her long, copper hair hung loose and glimmered in the glow from the lamp behind her.

"Greaaaat," Cain commented with as much enthusiasm as he could muster for his sister-in-law's cooking.

"Anna, why don't you find your bonnet. We have company."

She scrunched her nose. "Cain's not company. He's family."

Cain had no doubt that his brother's empathic gifts were perceptive enough to sense him admiring his wife's beauty.

"Annalise."

She pouted. "My feet hurt—"

"Fine." Adam stood. "I'll get it."

As soon as Adam left the kitchen, Cain snickered, "You've got him wrapped around your pretty little finger."

"Hardly. Let him try wearing that stupid bonnet all day."

"Well, it's good that you've taught him to fetch so early. Some mates are hard to train."

She flicked a blackened chip of bread at him. "You're going to get me in trouble. Tell me more about the meeting."

"There isn't much more to tell. The Council didn't seem too concerned."

Cain struggled to understand how the situation in the woods wasn't a top priority. The Order protected privacy above all else. A rogue, *feeish* vampire on the loose was not just a danger to mortals. It threatened the very essence of their immortal existence.

"That's so weird. If there's a wild vampire on the loose—"

"Or several."

"—Right. If there's an army of crazed immortals out there, running around, murdering innocent civilians, it's our responsibility to do something."

"You would think. Seriously, how are you eating that? It can't be good for the baby."

She looked at that charred biscuit and shrugged, taking another bite and mumbling, "I'm hungry."

Adam returned with the cap and frowned the moment he sensed a shift in the energy in the room. "*Ainsicht,* you shouldn't be discussing Order business. You'll get yourself worked up. It could upset the baby."

Cain rolled his eyes. "You know she's going to have to go through labor to pop that kid out, right? You can't protect her from everything, Adam."

Anna waved away her husband's concerns. "I guess it could just be a bear or something."

"It wasn't a bear."

"What makes you so sure?"

Cain recalled the markings in the woods. Beyond the strands of human-like hair snagged in the branches and the footprints pressed into the mud, there was something else. "I could smell whatever it was. It was not the scent an animal leaves behind."

The front door opened and a petite figure, cloaked in black, stepped inside. A chilled gust of November wind following. Small hands reached out from below the heavy fabric and pulled back the hood, revealing their sister Gracie's smiling face. "Can you believe how chilly it's for November?" Her ivory cheeks wore a rosy flush. "I dread to see what sort of weather this winter will bring."

Anna used her napkin to fan the cool air onto her shiny face. "I haven't stopped sweating."

Gracie hung her cloak on a hook by the door and laughed. "That's because you're baking a baby in your oven."

Briskly rubbing her hands together, she approached the table and pressed her palms on top of Anna's apron, cupping her protruding belly. Gracie's gift to overhear thoughts helped Adam and Anna check the baby's condition regularly.

After witnessing their parents suffer so

many miscarriages, every positive update was a welcomed one. Anna and Adam's baby was a blessing for their whole family, a long, overdue symbol of hope and healing.

Until these last few months, no one in the Hartzler line had been called for several decades. Uncle Isaiah had been the last, and his notorious behavior left a mark on the family that The Order would never forget. It was time to turn the page, and a new marriage and a new baby could possibly get things moving.

"He's active tonight."

"He?" Cain asked with a look of pure skepticism.

Gracie faced him with her usual smile. "Yes, the baby's a boy. Did they not tell you?" She clucked her tongue. "Well, that's what you get for never being around."

"You act as though I was off doing nothing of importance. I'll have you know, if not for me, The Council would be clueless about the recent events that could greatly affect The Order."

Gracie pulled out a chair and sat. "And exactly how does you fornicating with mortals affect The Order, brother?"

"Well, the fornication was for my own

personal research. I'm speaking of the latest news of Uncle Isaiah."

"Bite your tongue," she gasped, suddenly serious.

"You haven't heard?" Before he finished his question, Grace was rummaging around in his thoughts. "Out!"

"Tell me," his sister demanded, instantly withdrawing from his mind.

Telepathy among immortals was a skill that took centuries to hone. Grace had been born with the gift. While most immortals could pluck a thought from an unguarded mortal's mind or plant one for survival purposes, immortal brains were much more complex and challenging to penetrate.

She had a natural ability to overhear the thoughts of other immortals on the farm. Cain knew of only one other female in possession of such a refined skill, but she was much older and, therefore, her ability was likely the result of age. Gracie was still in her twenties, and her capabilities were that of a mature immortal.

"Cain thinks Uncle Isaiah's still alive, possibly living in the nearby woods," Adam explained.

Gracie stood and naturally took over the

cooking from Annalise. She removed the roast from the oven, slicing the meat with practiced ease. "How nearby?"

"There have been reports in the English news of six murders in the forests surrounding Jim Thorpe."

His sister's hand stilled, the knife slightly trembling. "Females?"

Cain nodded. "Mortals. The bodies were all…" He opened his mind and Gracie gasped.

"The last woman had children?"

"Two."

"The Council has to do something. They can't let this go on."

For the next hour, Cain told his siblings everything he found in the woods and all his theories. Unlike the stuffy, old Council, his family actually believed him.

Anna's eyes widened. "Do you think there will be more before they catch him?"

If it was an immortal out there, catching it was out of the question. For the safety of The Order, the creature needed to be destroyed.

"I think there have already been more," Cain said, remembering the traces of human hair and strange prints he found. "I don't have much faith in English law. Their tracking skills are too dependent on technology. That won't work when hunting a wild animal. And, if it's really Uncle Isaiah, he's been out there for eighty years, he knows how to survive, and he's been killing the entire time."

"How could The Council ignore this?" Gracie asked, offended. "Grandfather has to demand some form of action. What if the English catch him and discover what he is?"

"Grandfather's outnumbered. None of The Elders appeared overly concerned. Sad to say, but Larissa's absence has taken up more of their attention lately than anything else."

"That's ridiculous. They should leave Larissa alone. Dumb, old Silus needs to find someone else to boss around."

"Grace," Adam warned. "Do not involve yourself in their marital business."

"And why not? She's our sister, Adam. She ran away for a reason. Silus is a grumpy old toad who never smiles or laughs. I'm not even sure he has teeth."

"It's not your business, and it's against Family Law to involve yourself in another's marriage."

"I hate that law," Annalise commented, shoveling a bite into her mouth.

"That law protects you, *ainsicht.*"

"No, Adam, that law protects men who are

bad husbands from having to answer for their actions. It's irresponsible and should be revised."

"And how would you feel if The Council was allowed to decide such rules for us? Would that make you feel safer? I assure you, they'd object to the way I allow you to run around with your hair uncovered and the music I permit in this house."

"*Allow*? Really, Adam?"

Cain laughed. "Now you've done it, brother. Always so smooth with the ladies."

He scowled at Cain and turned back to his wife. "Yes, *allow*. I'm your husband and, therefore, the head of this family. My word is law. You agreed to that when you married me."

"Let's not talk about promises we made at our wedding." She pointed a fork at him. "You're still on thin ice. Any authority you have, you have because *I* allow you to have it. Abuse that authority, and I'll disappear faster than Larissa. Never forget that I'm here by choice, Adam. *My* choice."

Cain chuckled, but Adam couldn't let it go.

"Annalise, as your husband, I—"

Gracie let her fork clatter to the table. "Goodness, Adam, let it go! If you could hear your wife's thoughts right now, you would know that silence is the wisest move. We all get it. You are the man of the house and we are *merely women*. Now, can we please move on to a different topic and enjoy our dinner?"

His brother valued Amish tradition far more than the rest of them. Grace always preferred a simple life, but even she kept an open mind as she waited for her calling.

Cain, on the other hand, found life on the farm far too restrictive. Their laws had nearly killed him, and The Elder Council consisted of so many ancient males, he saw no way of amending the patriarchal decrees that determined the laws of The Order, despite how outdated their beliefs became.

It was no wonder Larissa ran. He couldn't imagine living his life as another person's property, which was basically the way Silus viewed her. Family Law protected his treatment and authority. But what laws protected their sister?

Cain waited until everyone finished their dessert to ask, "Why has Mother been staying at Aunt Rebecca's?"

"She and Father had a fight," Gracie explained.

Anna looked up at him, her brows

drawing together. "I told you they've been fighting a lot."

Adam pushed back his chair. "This is none of our business—"

"Are you kidding?"

"Give it up!"

"It's our business!"

The three of them snapped at Adam, frustrated with endless propriety.

"We're talking about Mom and Dad," Cain reminded. "It isn't gossip if we're trying to help."

Adam's disapproving scowl clearly showed his disagreement, but his brother was outnumbered. Anna and Gracie leaned into the conversation, tossing out probable causes for the recent tension.

"Perhaps it has to do with Mother's fear of losing another pregnancy?"

"Or Father's unwillingness to put her through another possible miscarriage."

Both possibilities made sense, but neither was enough cause for their parents to fight. In all of his thirty-seven years, Cain had never known his mother and father to argue. They might disagree, but they never went to bed angry or let a quarrel outlast the day.

The room fell silent. There was only one

unsolvable problem he could think of, but his mind rejected it. For that to be the case…

It would be horrible. He couldn't imagine how things would change and how much damage such a predicament would do.

"One of us has to say it out loud," Gracie whispered. "We all suspect it. We're all thinking it."

"It can't be," Cain argued, shaking his head.

Adam shifted in obvious discomfort. "We always knew it was a possibility."

Gracie's face pinched and her arms closed protectively around her body as if she suffered a chill. "Poor Mother."

"How do you know it's Father?" Adam asked. "What if it's Mother—"

"It's Father. He's showing too many symptoms," Cain said. "We can't go on denying the reality of the situation."

"But he's been sleeping," Gracie argued.

"He has to." A knot formed in Cain's gut. "It's the only way he can dream."

They all wore the same haunted expression. "How much time do you think they have?" Anna asked.

Cain looked at his brother and shrugged. "It depends when the symptoms started."

Once they voiced the fear, there was no taking it back. Silence consumed them. No words could fix this. No action could outmaneuver God's call. If anyone knew that, Cain did.

Every single day he lived with the pain of his sacrifice, secretly suspecting his loss would eventually kill him. The delicate bond he shared with Anna might be the only thing sustaining him, but no one knew how temporary such a hold could last.

The Elders were useless when it came to their unique situation. There had never been a twin calling like his and Adam's before. He hoped no immortal ever suffered such a fate again.

Perhaps that was why he needed to find whatever was in the woods. What if he and the creature shared a similar fate? He needed to know if the stories were true. He needed to hunt it and see for himself if an unanswered immortal had no other fate than to become *vampire.*

Anna glanced in his direction and gave a sympathetic smile as if guessing the path of his thoughts. Adam wouldn't look his way; he possibly still questioned if he had acted fairly in their situation. But, in the end, it had been

Cain's decision, one he was still processing and might never fully come to terms with.

His body itched to escape, and his muscles bounced with the urge to run. This place used to be a sanctuary, but lately it was as dangerous as the outside world. The longer he stayed, the more the walls closed in on him.

Adam's hand closed over Anna's. Envy and bitterness spiked inside of Cain, alerting him that it was time to go.

Cain stood and set his napkin on his plate. "Thank you for dinner, Anna." He knew better than to touch his brother's wife. "I'll talk to you soon."

"Wait," Gracie wore a look of concern. "Where are you going?"

He looked back at his siblings, so content to simply stay on the farm. Even Annalise had adapted to their primitive life. But the longer he lived, the more restless he grew, desperate to find a greater purpose and certain he would never find it here.

"I'm going back to the woods. I'm going to hunt down whatever's out there and deal with it before it hurts anyone else." He planned to then disappear for a long time.

CHAPTER 12

*J*onas's heart froze the moment he heard her footsteps, and the bedroom door opened. The relief he felt at seeing his beautiful wife standing in their home after days of avoidance could have dropped him to his knees.

"Abilene." Her name was a plea, a cry for mercy.

"I wanted to come home." She stepped into the room and shut the door with a quiet snick.

This was the closest they had been in months. The closed-off room became a sanctuary the moment she stepped inside: shut away from the rest of the world, safe from the dreams, guarded against the pain, deaf to consequence.

"Abilene, I never—"

She held up her hand, silencing him. "Don't speak, Jonas. There's nothing either of us can say to change this."

She unpinned her bonnet and carefully placed it on her dresser, where it had sat every evening for the past sixty years. He could not imagine a life that did not include her belongings sprinkled throughout.

He watched, mesmerized, as she slowly unwove her braids. Her small hands worked easily over her soft, brown hair, twisting and unraveling the strands into long, wavy locks. That was his prize. No other male had ever seen his Abilene's hair. That was his privilege as her husband.

A sob lodged in his chest and his body buckled forward to smother it down. Once this was done, she would eventually move on. Eternity was too long to live alone, and Abilene was a female made for love. He should love her enough to selflessly hope she found happiness with another, but he couldn't bear the thought of any other male touching her.

Once her hair hung loose, she pushed it behind her narrow shoulders and removed the pins of her apron. Her hair protested the action and fell back over her shoulder, framing her beautiful face.

She was still as lovely and timid as the night he made her his bride. She had only ever known his lips, his touch, his body. She had given herself freely to him and loved him beyond measure.

Memories of their wedding night, of that first time he took her, caused him to harden. He was starved for the taste of her skin.

Stripped down to only her shift, she faced him. Her breasts tightened beneath the delicate fabric, nipples darkening at the tips.

"My beautiful wife." He could stare at her for centuries. "Will you come to bed?"

She crossed the room slowly, always his sweet, submissive wife when they were alone, but as a mother, she was a lioness.

Rising to sit on the edge of the bed, he parted his knees, drawing her into his space. As he lifted his hands to frame her trim waist, his fingers were trembling.

His thumbs rubbed softly over her tummy, where she had carried so many of his children. He leaned forward and pressed his face to her ribs as a tear trickled down his cheek.

She was there with him now, offering herself, yet the void between them remained. They would, in time, be severed apart.

He couldn't stand the ache such distance had caused, couldn't fathom a life without her. "I need to be absolved of my sins." He pulled her close, weeping into her shift and breathing her familiar scent deep into his lungs. "Forgive me, Abilene. I beg you."

Her delicate touch ran through his hair, and he dropped to his knees to the floor, wrapping his arms around her hips and refusing to let go.

"I can't bear the thought of what this will do to you, to us, to the children."

She lowered to the floor, kneeling before him as she cupped his face and pressed a soft kiss on his tear-dampened lips. "Jonas, you have always been a man of worth. Anything you have ever done, you have done out of love. For sixty years, you loved me fiercely. I'm grateful to have had at least that."

Her touch was his undoing. His shoulders shook with the emotion he tried to contain. "I'll never love another with the depth I love you, Abilene."

"You lie to yourself, Jonas, but you can't lie to me. Loving your mate will not be a chore. You must accept that."

"I can't." For as sturdy and powerful as he was in all his maleness, this tiny woman was his strength. He hugged her tightly to him, never wanting to let her go.

She pressed a soft kiss over his heart and looked up at him with those familiar big, brown eyes causing the ache in his chest to explode into a million shards of glass. Unable to wait another moment, he lifted her into his arms and placed her on their bed.

Kissing her deeply, her body quivered beneath his touch as he trembled with pent-up passion. He anointed every bared inch of her flesh with his mouth, pouring his heart and soul into every caress.

Their bodies became one, rolling and intertwining, knotted so tightly together, nothing could ever separate them.

"I love you, Jonas," she cried as he entered her. "I'll always love you, even when I know I shouldn't."

"Never stop," he begged selfishly. "Never stop loving me, Abilene, and I swear I'll do the same. You're in my veins. Our children were made from our love and bones. You're the breath in my lungs." Losing her love would be an excruciating death he could never survive.

"I won't stop," she promised. "I can't stop. Loving you is all I know."

He pressed into her, wearing his agony clearly on his face. "*You* are the other half of my soul, Abilene. *You!*"

When the stars burned out and the moon no longer shined, his soul would still hold the imprint of her heart. Her love would forever be a part of him, and he could not accept a future that took such an integral piece of him away.

Her head tilted back into the pillows as he drove deeper, wishful that she might never escape him. He bathed in her scent as it filled the air around them. He memorized every feature as he kissed her eyes, the sharp bones of her cheeks, her delicate ears, and the corners of her mouth.

Together, they wrung every drop of pleasure from each other. Cradling her onto his lap, he held her securely. Sifting his fingers through her thick hair, he turned her head into his shoulder, nuzzling her throat and causing her pulse to leap.

"I've needed you."

"Please," she begged. "I'm nothing without your need of me."

That wasn't true. She was everything.

Eventually, she'd learn that and he would become the forgotten piece.

He drew her closer, licking over her pulse, and sank his fangs into her flesh. Hot, life-saving blood coated his tongue and he groaned at her familiar flavor. Her body arched in his arms as muscles tightened and she climaxed.

Adrenaline laced every sip, but as her passion faded, the flavor settled like ash on his tongue. His soul did not recognize her as his mate, and for that he cursed God.

Rage tunneled through him. He drank deeply from her vein, pulling with bruising force, insistent that she be *the one*. Her weak moan teased his fraying sanity, but his greedy, masculine grunts muffled her gentle cries.

"Jonas…"

He pinned her beneath him. More. He needed more. If he drank enough of her, he'd find what he was after.

A gluttonous animal awoke inside of him and he growled, anchoring her petite body to the bed and rutting into her with brute force, but he still wasn't satisfied. Sinking his fangs deeper, he tore at her gentle flesh, thrusting hard and forcing himself into her soul.

"Jonas!" Her plea couldn't penetrate his resolve.

He was determined to find what he needed in her. Her hands broke free of his hold and slapped at his shoulders, but he dwarfed her with his strength.

"You're hurting me!" Her cry hardly registered until sharp claws scored his flesh.

Blood—his own—blurred his vision as she clawed her way free and sprung to her feet.

Naked and panting, she stood before him, unruly hair forming a halo around her pale face, blood trickling from her throat, down her narrow shoulders and past her breast, as she hissed at him, bearing her fangs.

She looked at him as if he were a stranger, as if she didn't recognize him. Glancing down at his crimson-stained flesh and throbbing body, he hardly recognized himself.

What's happening to me?

He staggered back from the bed, forcing himself to the other side of the room. All he wanted was for her to be *the one*, but his instincts knew better. The beast inside was not clouded by emotion, and there would be no reasoning with the beast once it was fully in control.

How much time did they have left?

Unable to risk her safety another second, he unlatched the door and fled, racing as fast as he could to the distant forest where animals belonged.

CHAPTER 13

"Thanks for coming over," Larissa said as she opened her apartment door to let Vito in. Before shutting it, she quickly scanned the hall for any signs of the bishop.

"Any time, babe. That's what friends are for."

It had been days since the incident with the bishop, and he hadn't returned. Perhaps he gave up his ridiculous quest to find and return her and decided to let her choose her own fate—Silus be damned.

She hoped so because the bishop was a strong and dangerous man. Unsure if he was truly gone, she'd been hiding in her apartment, consequently starving. She tried to hunt close by, but every slight rustling of leaves on the ground had her jumping and worrying that the bishop had found her. She was as skittish as a rabbit.

"Would you like something to drink? I have popcorn to eat during our show, but I wasn't sure how to cook it." She held up the compact little bag filled with kernels and smelling deliciously like butter.

"I'll take a beer if you got one."

"Sure. I have beer. I bought some last week."

She loved the convenience of English grocery stores, loved the ability to buy anything without the inconvenience of readying a horse or waiting for her overbearing husband's permission. The bishop was just another male inflicting on her freedom.

Opening the electric refrigerator, she pulled one of the glass bottles from the handy little carrier holding six beers. "Here you go."

Vito frowned at the bottle. "What the hell is that, Larissa?"

She looked at the beer and her momentary pride deflated. "It's a beer." Had she purchased the wrong kind? "The guy at the counter said it was a popular flavor."

"It's a friggen' wine cooler, Larissa. Peach,

no less! I'm a two-hundred-fifty-pound man. I can't drink that shit."

"Oh." She lowered her hand.

"Christ, give it to me. I don't want to hurt your feelings. Thank you for the... *beer*."

He cracked open the cap and a whisp of cool mist hissed from the opening of the bottle. She watched anxiously as he took a sip. "How is it?"

He pulled the bottle away from his lips, frowned at the label, and shrugged. "It's actually not that bad."

Larissa's smile returned. "Oh, good! Now..." She shook the envelope of kernels. "Do you have any idea how to bake this?"

He laughed. "You don't know how to microwave popcorn?"

"We don't have microwaves where I'm from."

"Right," he said slowly, then took the bag of kernels into the kitchen.

She followed him, watching closely as he tore off the plastic packaging with his teeth and tossed the pouch into the tiny electrical box. He slammed the door and punched a knuckle into a button, and the box hummed to life.

"That's it?"

"Yup. Electrons absorb into the food and vibrate, producing heat."

Something popped and then popped again. The bag twirled on a rotating plate, expanding as the popping continued.

Impressed, she grinned at her friend. "You're so smart, Vito."

He shrugged and chugged his peach beer. "I watch a lot of *Discovery*." Chucking the empty bottle into the trash, he retrieved a new one from the fridge. "What movie do you want to watch?"

"You can pick."

Once the popcorn was ready—in under three minutes—she transferred it into a bowl and settled on the sofa beside Vito. He was very good at using the remote control and quickly found a movie with racing cars and explosions. Sometimes television overwhelmed her and made her heart race, but tonight she was hardly watching the screen.

Her attention lingered on her guest as she leaned into his warm side. She sensed his tension every time she moved closer, but eventually he smiled and put his arm around her. The scent of blood pumping under his skin called to her.

Vito reminded her of a big grizzly bear.

He was all gruff and growls on the outside, but a big softy on the inside. She nuzzled her nose along his throat and he stiffened.

"Larissa, what are you doing?"

She shut her eyes and scooted closer. "Just getting comfortable."

"Um, I didn't know we… did that."

"Did what?"

"You know… We're friends."

"Close friends." Her fangs punched through her gums and her stomach cramped with need. Her hunger pangs were so sharp recently. She dragged her lips over the stubble of his throat and he caught her shoulders.

"Whoa! Hold on."

"What's the matter?"

"Nothing. It's just… Uh, I'm not really sure what you're expecting here."

She pressed into his mind, giving him a gentle command. "Shh, just relax. I won't hurt you." She ran her lips over his pulse and—

"Screw it." Catching her off guard, Vito changed positions, rolling her to her back and moving his body over hers.

Startled, she opened her mouth to protest, but his lips met hers before her words could form. Her eyes widened at the first swipe of his tongue, and she squeaked in shock when his knee wedged between her thighs.

Preparing to push him off, she gripped his shoulders, but before she could apply force, something hurled his weight off of her. Vito crashed into the other side of the room. Larissa sprung to her feet as a feral growl filled her apartment, and the bishop appeared, enraged and ready to kill her only friend.

"What did you do?" she yelled, her first concern for Vito.

She rushed to his side, but the bishop got to him first. He wrenched Vito's head back, exposed a mouth of sharp fangs, and bit into her friend's throat.

"*No!*"

Vito's legs twitched and she screamed, shoving the bishop back, but her meager strength was no match for an immortal of his age. She was too distraught to attempt any sort of mental push, and his mind seemed especially guarded tonight.

"*Stop!*" she screamed. "You're killing him!" Hysterical, she pulled at his limbs but it was no use. "I'll go with you! I'll do anything you ask, just let him go." A sob belted out of her as she watched the color of Vito's face fade. "Please, Bishop King, don't hurt him!"

Everything stilled, and she looked up at the bishop with tears in her eyes as she kneeled before him. Something potent fizzed in the air between them, and she had the sudden urge to run, but she couldn't leave her friend there to die.

The bishop sneered at her with a dark look of disapproval. "You let this man touch you."

Her eyes closed as regret swallowed her. She had a husband, a duty to honor. The limitations of her choices tightened like a noose around her neck until she could hardly breathe.

Dropping her weight to her heels, she pressed her face to her hands and wept. "I'll go home. Just let my friend go."

The fear of Silus's anger was nothing in comparison to the fear for Vito's life. She'd never forgive herself if he died because of her.

The bishop closed a fist in her friend's hair and wrenched back his head. "What are you to her?"

"Just a friend," Vito wheezed, his eyes wide with horror.

"Your thoughts reek of lust. How dare you lay a hand on Larissa?"

He pronounced her name *Lar-ees-ah.*

"That was the first time I kissed her! I swear, man, I was a Boy Scout up until thirty seconds ago! She started it!"

Bishop King growled, his glare snapping back to her.

"Feeding, Bishop King. I was only going to feed. My hunger pains… they're… frequent."

The bishop released Vito. "Get up."

Despite his coughing and notable weakness, Vito was compelled to obey. He stood on shaky legs.

"You will leave this place with no recollection that you were here. You will forget meeting Larissa. You will forget me. Any memories of tonight are only leftover pieces of a dream. Do you understand?"

"Yes."

"Get out."

Vito shuffled toward the door only to pause when he noticed Larissa sitting on the floor, tears streaming down her face in a state of obvious distress. "Miss, are you okay?"

"Do not speak to her!"

Larissa flinched at the lash of the bishop's voice and silently wept as Vito left. She would never see him again.

Her sniffles and sighs broke the silence.

The bishop reached for her, speaking in a soft voice. "Come off the floor, child."

She recoiled. "Don't touch me."

"Larissa—"

"I did not give you permission to use my first name."

"Fine," he said through gritted teeth, "Sister Hartzler—"

Ice formed over her heart, frigid and solid. She glared up at him with cold disdain. "My *name* is Sister Hostetler. It's the name you and the rest of The Elders sentenced me to use, the name of the brute you married me to and are so determined to return me to." She stood, without assistance, and raised her trembling chin. "I'm ready whenever you are."

He studied her for a long moment. "Do you fear Silus?"

"Fear is useless."

His brow pinched. "I want to help you."

"Help me?" The man was her absolute enemy. "Do not pretend that we are friends when all you want to do is return me to misery. I'll be lucky if I have all of my fingers by the end of the week. So, excuse me, Bishop, when I see you on the farm and do not wave."

He drew back as if she slapped him. "I

don't intend to make your return a miserable one."

"You just attacked my only friend and erased every memory he had of me."

Something close to regret flashed in his eyes but then his jaw hardened. "That man harbored lustful thoughts of you, and you left me flailing in human waste two days ago."

"What you did was worse." She moved to walk past him toward the door and he caught her arm.

"You need to feed. Your hunger is beating at me."

"I'm fine." She couldn't bear his presence. Her arm tingled where he touched her, so she yanked it free of his grip. "I want to leave."

"You will feed now."

"I can't."

"You can."

She glared at him. "Silus would take issue with my feeding from another male of The Order."

"So let him." His eyes narrowed. "Silus does not worry me. Your hunger does."

She scoffed. "Don't pretend to suddenly care about my wellbeing."

He caught her arm again, a stunned look taking over his face. "I care very much."

Her lips firmed. She supposed it was a bishop's job to worry, but she wasn't convinced he considered anyone else's concerns when making decisions. Besides, if he insisted on taking her back to the farm, Silus would detect another male's blood in her system the moment he scented her. "I prefer to wait."

"Your pain is unacceptable to me," he snapped. "As your bishop, I order you to feed."

His command infuriated her. As if she had not been stripped of her independence enough.

A scream built in her mind and she wanted to let it out. *I should hit you, you arrogant male! I'd like to rail at you until I'm all out of strength and then you will truly know how empty your orders have left me.*

"Then do it," he said, apparently overhearing her thoughts. "Strike me if you wish. My actions earned it. But first, you'll feed."

She frowned as he looked away from her. "What's wrong with you?"

He appeared rather frustrated with himself. "I don't know how to communicate with you."

"It would help if you stopped ordering me around."

His jaw ticked. "Your willfulness is infuriating, yet I find myself wanting to compromise, wanting to do something to soften your dislike for me."

"Why?" It should make no difference to him if she liked him or not.

Rather than answer her, he asked, "Would it help if I allowed you another night?"

"What?"

He refused to look at her. "Perhaps another twenty-four hours here would make your return to the farm more bearable."

Was he negotiating with her? "I don't understand."

When he faced her, he wore lines of stress around his eyes. "One more day of freedom, but you have to feed now."

It had to be a trick. She didn't trust him. He just wanted her to feed, then he would force her to go home, and she'd be punished even more for drinking from another male.

But maybe it would be better if she had her strength. She dreaded seeing Silus. Unlike the bishop, her husband wouldn't care about her discomfort. He'd use her hunger as a punishment, on top of whatever else he had planned.

Still, the thought of feeding from the bishop... She shivered, never having shared such an intimate act with a male other than her husband before. "Couldn't we just go for a hunt?"

"My blood is the strongest source available to you. It will do you well."

She drew back as understanding dawned. "You want me to take your blood so you can track me."

It made sense since she'd already run once. She had to starve herself before escaping the farm, ensuring Silus's blood had completely left her system. If she drank from the bishop now, she'd never get away from him.

"That's one reason."

"Are there more?"

"Yes, but my reasons are private. I'll share them with you once you start cooperating."

"You mean obeying."

"I mean compromising. Are you always this infuriating?"

"Are you always this calculating?"

"Is feeding from me so repulsive to you that you would sacrifice your own comfort?"

What comfort? He was set on stealing away the only comfort she'd found.

Weakened by an inescapable sense of defeat, she no longer cared if she fed from the bishop or starved to death. Her weight dropped onto the couch as she numbly stared at the floor.

"It doesn't matter. Whether I feed from you now or Silus later, I'm just a puppet tied to another man's strings."

Sit up, Larissa.

Do not argue, Larissa.

Wear the maroon dress, Larissa.

Lay still, Larissa.

A tear rolled from her eye. "What a tragic existence my life has become."

The bishop silently watched her for a long moment. When he finally spoke, he softened his tone. "You're still quite young. Your life has hardly begun."

"Then why does it feel like it's already over?" She dashed away another tear.

"You must keep an open mind so your soul can recognize your mate."

"And what mate is that? The mate that you and The Elders assigned to me?"

"I'm speaking of your *true* mate."

"Sentenced to one, promised to another." She shook her head. "Only a male god could come up with such incongruent laws of nature."

"God loves you, child."

"Do not speak to me about love. If God

loved me, then why has he forsaken me?" Where was God the first time Silus forced himself inside of her, or the first time he raised a hand to her in anger? Where was He the night her husband locked her in the closet and left her there for days without light or water?

"God does not punish."

"Maybe not, but my husband does. I've looked into his mind, Bishop, and, like many males in The Order, he likes to pretend he's a god. You've certainly given him the power of one."

"He'll never mistreat you again," he vowed through clenched teeth.

"Even you don't have that sort of authority over him. I'm his wife—his property. Family Law states—"

"He will *never* mistreat you again."

The certainty in his voice stole the argument from her lungs like a shift of the wind steals the strength of sails. A tickle traveled along her scalp and her spine softened, her body relaxing into the sofa. She was suddenly too exhausted to keep her eyes fully open.

He lowered onto the cushion beside her, and she watched him through a tranquil haze.

There was something strangely familiar about him that made her frown.

He slowly rolled up his sleeve. "Larissa, you're hungry and must feed now."

"Yes," she murmured, barely opening her mouth for the word and finding it impossible to lift her head.

"Will you be a good girl and do as you are told?"

"Yes."

"Very good, *little mouse.*"

She frowned and blinked at him, but her motions were subdued as if she were moving through water. Did he just call her a mouse? She wasn't a mouse, or at least she didn't want to be, not anymore at least.

He tipped up her chin and looked into her eyes. "Are you ready to feed?"

She nodded. Somehow detached from the present, she watched the bishop slowly open his crisp, black shirt, exposing a wall of sculpted muscle. A gentle hand slid under her hair and her head relaxed in his hold.

"Very good." He shifted, pulling her closer and angling her mouth toward his throat. His scent was intoxicating, and her fangs lengthened as her ears focused on the quick beat of his pulse. "Drink now, little mouse."

Her jaw opened and her teeth pierced his flesh. The warm, potent tang of his aged, immortal blood shocked her system. It burst over her tongue, awaking a desperate need to feed. Moaning at the delicious flavor, she angled her body for better access and slipped her fingers through his hair, holding him to her.

She had been hungrier than she realized, and the nourishment he supplied satisfied her on an indescribable level. It was the best-tasting blood she'd ever sampled and she drank ravenously from his vein.

Gluttonous, she fed greedily, unsure if her hunger would ever be sated. He pulled her onto his lap and settled her body over his. She shut her eyes as his palm gently coaxed her up and down.

"That's it, Larissa, take everything you need."

She needed friction. Her body slowly rocked as other sensations unraveled. Something tugged inside of her, and a new hunger developed in her core. She desired pressure—something to bring some sort of relief.

"Yes, sweet Larissa," he groaned, his hands pressing along her back and guiding her rocking motions.

She moaned against his throat and pulled harder at his vein. Her hips swayed.

The tickle of his soft hair teased her into a sort of frenzy. She licked at his throat, no longer simply feeding but slaking a darker hunger. Warm lips, softer than flower petals, traced over her skin, teasing softly at her pulse. He coaxed her head back and dragged the edge of his nose from her pulse to the curve of her shoulder. She arched before him, her spine bending as her pelvis fit perfectly against his.

Something was happening. Pressure coiled inside of her, building and stretching. His hands held her, guiding her rolling hips, pulling her hard against his arousal. A little longer and—

Larissa stilled.

Suddenly aware of what she was doing, she flew off the bishop's lap, flipping the coffee table on its side and covering her face with her hands. Mortified, she pressed her back into the far wall. What had she done?

"Larissa, you did nothing wrong."

Trembling fingers traced her lips, where she could still taste his potent blood. His rich scent clung to her skin. "You *compelled* me!"

"You needed to feed."

"You made me do it! How could you take away my choice?"

"I only did what was necessary. You were emotional and suffering from sharp hunger pains."

She shook her head. That didn't justify his actions. "How could you?"

"It was for your own good, Larissa."

"For my own good? *My* own good? *My own good!*" Her body carried the lingering tells of his contact. The muscles of her sex clamped with need, finding only emptiness. Her body was unwittingly aroused. Fury spilled into outrage. "*Get out of my apartment!*"

"Larissa—"

"I said leave!" The front door flung open. "You got your wish, now get out. I want my last day alone."

"That wasn't the agreement."

"You took advantage of me! You compelled me!"

"You threw me down a garbage chute. I dare to say we're even."

Except feeding from him wasn't garbage. It was divine, and that knowledge enraged her all the more. For nearly two years, she'd been feeding off the sewage in her husband's veins.

She wiped her mouth on the back of her hand, resisting the urge to spit. "I'm a married female!"

"You don't love him and he doesn't love you!" he bellowed with such startling ferocity his roar echoed off the rafters.

"Thank you, Bishop," she said with no emotion. "Thank you for reminding me just how empty my marriage is and, once again, valuing me as worthless as a sow at an auction. Now, get out."

"I'm not leaving—"

"You're awful!" she screamed, at her wit's end. "Haven't you done enough? I just want to be left the hell alone to mourn my last day of freedom!"

Something tickled along her scalp again as she recognized the slight sensation of an intruder probing the surface of her mind. Appalled, she slammed a lid on her private thoughts and redirected his telepathic energy back at the source.

He gripped his head and shouted, staggering back several steps. "Enough!"

They both panted and glared at each other.

His eyes narrowed and a broken blood vessel flooded his eye. "How did you do that?"

She wasn't entirely sure. She merely threw his command back at him. "Serves you right." She was glad she hurt him. "How does it feel to have your own powers used against you?"

"That was more than my power. You intensified it by at least a thousand percent."

"I did not."

She couldn't have. Her sister was telepathic and her brother was an empath, but she had no such gifts. Even Cain was discovering ways to control the weather, but Larissa had always been the plain and boring one. Perhaps she built up a strong defense from rejecting Grace's intrusions over the last two decades.

The whites of his eyes slowly returned. "Do not do it again."

She crossed her arms over her chest. "Don't compel me again."

He growled and angrily adjusted his shirt. Maybe he was finally leaving.

His hair was sticking up on end, and she liked seeing him disheveled. "Tomorrow will be a long and tedious day. I suggest you get some rest."

The nerve of him. "If you stay here, I won't sleep."

"I told you, I'm not leaving—"

"Please, Bishop King," she begged, openly sharing her own insecurities in an attempt for mercy. "I'm uncomfortable in your presence, and I do need to rest if we're to return tomorrow. So please let me at least have my privacy for one last night."

He studied her for a long moment and then looked away. She wasn't sure what he perceived when he looked at her so intensely, but it worked in her favor. "Very well, Larissa. I'll return in the morning. Do not make me regret this."

She couldn't escape him even if she wanted to, not with his potent blood now racing through her veins.

CHAPTER 14

*J*onas entered his home after midnight only to be greeted with an uncomfortable foreboding. Abilene, Gracie, Adam, and Annalise sat at the kitchen table in silence, waiting for him.

"What is it?" he asked, reluctant to fully enter the room.

"Why don't you sit down, Father," Adam suggested.

"Thank you, but I'd rather stand."

Abilene looked up at him with glassy eyes. "The children know, Jonas."

His jaw ticked. He wasn't ready to face the inevitable. "Know what?"

"We know you are being called, Father,"

Grace said softly, sympathy pinching her features. "Mother did not betray your trust. We figured it out on our own."

"And you are all waiting here for what, exactly?" He braced for anger and blame.

"We want to know who she is." His daughter studied him but, respectfully, stayed out of his personal thoughts. Her desire to understand him, only when he was ready to share, slayed the last of his reserve.

Only a monster would hurt them. "She is of no consequence. Who she is, matters not. You will never know her."

"Father—"

"I'm sorry, Grace. I'm sorry to all of you. I never chose for this to happen, and I have no control over the situation, but I will not simply turn away from my family because God suddenly decrees another female is intended for me. This is my home. You are my family. I do not need nor want another. Now, if you will excuse me—"

Adam stood. "Father, you cannot just ignore this."

"I can and I will!" he thundered with shocking determination.

Abilene looked away and tears gathered in Grace's eyes.

"I do not mean to shout, but this discussion is over." He turned to leave.

"Jonas, stop."

He could not ignore the command in his wife's voice, yet he lacked the strength to face them.

"This is happening to *all* of us," Abilene said. "You will either go to her or you will die. Neither outcome is what any of us want, but you have to choose one."

He looked toward the dark hallway and whispered, "then I choose to die."

A collective gasp stole the air.

A chair scraped along the floor, and when his wife spoke again, she stood only inches behind him. "Then I will follow you."

He spun to face her. "You will not. I forbid it!"

"You did not teach me to be an obedient wife, Jonas. Everything I've given you, I gave of my own free will. You have no such authority over me, and I'm too old to change my ways now. We've always shared a partnership grounded in mutual respect. If you want to keep me safe, you will protect yourself. If you can't do that, then I'm afraid there's nothing more to say."

"Don't threaten me, Abilene."

"Jonas," she said his name with cold certainty, "I will treat you as you treat me. I always have. I always will. Take away your threat, and I'll retract mine."

He swallowed. Was she really suggesting he go to another female? His head bowed, "You ask too much of me."

"God only gives us what we can handle, my love. I ask nothing more than He has already asked of you."

He was desperate to alter his fate and save his marriage, his family. "I can't willingly leave you."

"I *will not* watch you die," she vowed. "I will leave this world long before my only option is to watch you suffer. Do you understand me?"

A boulder of emotion formed in his throat, blocking his voice and words. He nodded tightly, taking his wife's hands in his and pulling her fingers to his lips. He kissed her cold skin and shook under the weight of her love. "I'm so sorry—"

"Clara!" Gracie jumped to her feet and all eyes directed toward his daughter.

They tricked him. They distracted him and manipulated his emotions so he would lower his guard. Stunned, he staggered back. A line had been drawn between them and him. "Grace, do not do this. I'm your father. I forbid it."

But she had already stolen all the information she needed, and he was too weak to stop her.

"I'm sorry, Father." She faced the others. "Her name is Clara Barnes. She has hair the color of snow. She lives in a yellow house with clay pots stacked all over the porch. I think we can find her."

"You had no right," he choked.

"We're only trying to help," Anna said.

He no longer belonged there. Family was based on trust, and they had broken his.

***

ANNALISE CONTACTED Cain that night through a dream. He hadn't expected to hear from her so soon and feared something was wrong. When she explained about the intervention with his father, he had no choice but to get involved.

"What is the woman's name?"

"Clara Barnes."

Why did that name seem so familiar? "I know that name."

Surprised, Anna asked, "How?"

"The English news. The reporter following the murders. Clara Barnes was the mother of the most recent victim."

"Wait, you're saying your father's called mate is somehow connected to a victim from the Jim Thorpe murders? You think your uncle might have killed her daughter?"

Even to his own ears it sounded too full of coincidences. "We don't know enough about mortals when they are called. Did you have any symptoms, aside from the dreams?"

"Um, I was hungry. And sometimes men complained that I had… an odor. But my girlfriends couldn't smell it."

"An odor? They didn't like the smell?"

Anna blushed. "No, it sort of repelled them."

Cain considered this. "Adam could have put his scent on you." Knowing his brother and how territorial he was of his wife, that was probably the case.

"What are you thinking?"

"I'm wondering if a called mortal might attract a *feeish* immortal. Maybe that's what brought this thing to our area."

She drew back. "Is that possible?"

"I don't know." But if something happened to his father's mate, there would be no saving him. "We have to destroy whatever is out there."

"What about Clara? Your dad refuses to go to her."

"He'll go. Sooner or later, he won't have a choice. His loyalty to my mom won't withstand the call of his true mate."

"But what if she's in danger?"

They needed to at least figure out where this Clara Barnes lived. "Gracie said she saw the woman's house?"

"Yes, but she couldn't make out any landmarks. She said the visions in your father's head were more like paintings."

They were running out of time. "I have an idea. I think I know how we can find her."

"How?"

He grinned, but his smile was anything but kind. "The reporter. She'll know where the victims' families live."

"Cain, you can't get close to anyone following the murders. What if they suspect you're involved."

He waved off her concern. "You underestimate me, Annalise. I can get the information I need and erase her mind. She's just a mortal woman."

"Hey, watch it! I used to be *just a mortal woman*."

He chuckled. "We all go through awkward stages."

CHAPTER 15

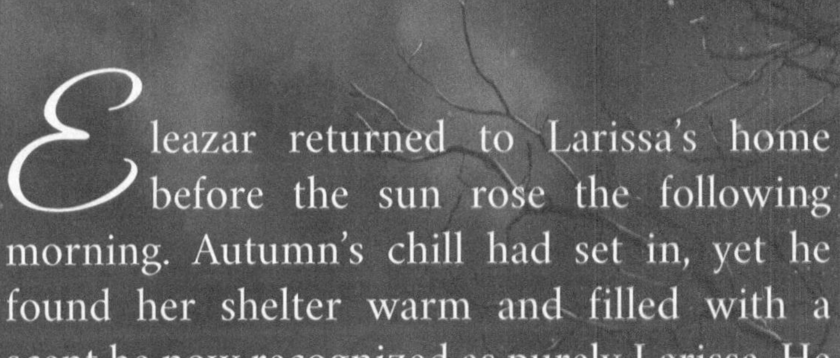

$\mathcal{E}$leazar returned to Larissa's home before the sun rose the following morning. Autumn's chill had set in, yet he found her shelter warm and filled with a scent he now recognized as purely Larissa. He explored her apartment while she still slept, searching for clues about his mate.

Finding a worn Bible tucked neatly beside the couch brought him comfort. Larissa had not forsaken all of her values on her journey to the English suburbs, and this filled him with a hope he had not anticipated finding here.

Her apartment was sparse. Not quite to the degree of their Amish homes, but still less decorated than a born-and-bred English woman's might be.

Unsure how the day would play out, he found himself navigating several nervous jolts of energy. He wasn't typically an anxious male, so this was new territory for him.

Small bits of dreams returned to him last night. It was still surreal, after five hundred years, to suddenly find himself blessed with a calling. He'd always expected it would come more… effortlessly. Nothing about his situation was effortless. If anything, Larissa required an exhausting amount of effort and, even after trying his best, there was no guarantee that she would like him.

Love wasn't even a consideration at this point.

Larissa didn't seem aware of the calling they shared. Aside from her ravenous hunger yesterday, he didn't know if she suffered any other symptoms. And who knew if her hunger was the result of starvation or a need for her mate? This would be much easier if she felt something other than hatred for him.

But could he blame her? He should have paid closer attention to her when The Council questioned her. She was clearly entering a loveless marriage.

Such information should please him, as her lack of love for Silus Hostetler uncomplicated matters. But it did not please him. Six short months after her wedding, his symptoms had begun.

He had given her away, his most precious gift. And the male responsible for her care at the time had abused and mistreated her. Had he known what was happening in their marriage, he would have interfered sooner, but his anger at himself got in his way.

He knew nothing about the young female and figured they would have even less than nothing in common. Every time he asked Silus about her, the male commented on what a nuisance she was. Eleazer had been a gullible fool.

The way Larissa spoke of her husband concerned him. He thought of Adriel's warnings, and for the first time in his life, he took issue with Family Law.

Family Law was intended to give each couple autonomy, but it had done the opposite in Larissa's case. How many other females viewed marriage as imprisonment?

He did not enjoy thinking of his mate belonging to another male. Detangling her life from Silus would be a minor irritant, and he would act swiftly. But first, he needed Larissa to accept him as her mate.

He found himself watching over her as she slept. She looked so peaceful when she wasn't shouting at him. An exquisite female.

He finally had a chance to look at her and envision her as his mate. He sighed. She was so young.

Of course, fifty years old would not be considered young to a mortal, but to Eleazar… He sighed again. He could still recall paying his respects to the Hartzlers the evening of her birth. A precious newborn bundle, and yet, here she was, almost fifty years later, fully grown, no longer a babe, but a woman—his mate.

Why had it taken so long to receive his calling? Why would God allow him to sit idly by and watch his mate be handed off to another male? Normally, he was not one to question the Almighty.

Yesterday, he told Larissa God did not punish. If that were true, why did he suspect they had both been punished? Larissa suffered a loveless marriage, and he would always suffer the shame of knowing he put her there.

He wondered if mates could survive such

an early betrayal? Even if it was an unintentional one, he accepted the blame. If only he'd insisted Silus wait a few years...

But there was no going back now. The innocence she once had was now gone—wisdom in its place.

Time would heal. Eleazar simply had to be patient, patient with her and patient with himself.

Larissa was strong. One simple male should not have been able to break her spirit. She had gifts Eleazar still did not fully understand. Perhaps she did not comprehend the extent of her gifts either.

That would make sense because he couldn't understand how she could outmaneuver him, yet she grew as skittish as a field mouse when it came to her husband. Once trust was established, they could share their gifts, and she would never have to worry about irrelevant little pests like Silus again.

Trust. Such a small word to carry such a big meaning. Trust became his first goal. He would do whatever he could to earn Larissa's trust, and then everything else would naturally follow.

Eleazar's mate was a riddle to him in so many ways. He watched her now, curled under the covers of her small bed. Her raven-colored hair fanned over her white pillow, creating a beautiful contrast. Her angelic features mesmerized him from the soft, purple shadows from her dark lashes that crested her high cheekbones to her delicate little toes.

Long and lithe, her body curved and swelled with natural perfection. She was tall, taller than most females, which suited him well.

His predatory, male scent filled the room as he observed her. Her lashes fluttered, and he casually stepped back.

Unaccustomed to his body's baser urges, he swallowed a groan and shut his eyes as a kaleidoscope of images wheeled through his mind, each one more arousing than the last. He wanted her.

"What are you doing here?"

His eyes flashed open to find her sitting up, bare breasts exposed, as the sheet gathered at her full hips.

Her downy-soft curves stole the breath right from his lungs. An offended growl filled the silence, and Eleazar pried his gaze from her beautiful breasts to meet her stare. "I told you I would return in the morning."

"Do you not possess the ability to knock?"

When has social graces become so tedious? "I know how to knock."

She jerked the sheet up to her chest. "Get out!"

"Larissa—"

"Now!"

He grew tired of her defensiveness. "We have to talk." He decided it was time to give her the full truth.

He was not prepared for the lone tear that trickled down her cheek.

"Why are you crying?" Everything inside of him demanded he soothe her, but when he took a step forward, her breath hitched with fear and she drew back.

"Why are you doing this?" Her voice was small and her shoulders curled forward protectively. She was terrified.

Alarmed that he could frighten her so, he gentled his voice and gave her space. "You don't need to fear me, Larissa. I will never hurt you."

"I'm married. Your presence here is unforgivable. You, of all immortals, should know better."

Her loyalty to a man she did not love infuriated him. As his mate, there should be no distance between them. They owned each other's soul. Her body was his. She was his mate.

"We must talk."

"I have nothing to say to you." Spine stiff and chin lifted, one could choke on such thick arrogance. From a timid field mouse to a haughty duchess. He much preferred her confident side, even if it made her more of a challenge.

"Very well. I'll speak and you can listen." He paced at the foot of the bed, ignoring the way she scowled at him. "You're angry. I understand that. However, I hoped we could each employ a level of diplomacy and have a mature discussion—as equals."

"You and I both know I'm not entitled to speak as your equal, nor will I ever be."

"I permit you to speak to me as such."

Her eyes narrowed beneath a tumble of dark, raven hair. "Ah, but if we were true equals, I wouldn't need your permission."

"Clever mouse."

"I'm no mouse, but I'm clever enough to know better than to address you as an equal, only to be punished for my words later once your edict expires."

"I give you my word, I will not punish you for anything you say to me. I only want truth between us, and I want us to speak as equals."

She raised a brow. "Fine. I find you to be a self-righteous, intrusive, pious pain." She smirked. "There, was that equal and truthful enough for you?"

"No. I find your tone disrespectful, where mine was not."

"As if you are the epitome of manners and propriety, breaking into my private quarters and allowing your filthy thoughts to wake me from sleep."

He would not apologize for wanting her. "Are you typically a light sleeper, Larissa?"

"I have not slept soundly since I became Silus's property."

"You are not his property."

"No? Try telling him that."

He was beginning to hate Silus Hostetler's existence and his link to Larissa's life. "No individual, male or female, is the *property* of another. Even mates do not own one another, they merely make one complete soul. If Silus informed you otherwise, he lied."

"And how exactly does one contest the lie of a husband under the bounds of Family Law, Bishop?"

His jaw clenched so tightly the muscles

popped. "The law was created to protect members of The Order, not infringe on their rights as individuals."

"Well, the road to hell is paved with good intentions."

"This is getting us nowhere."

"Nor will it ever."

They both scowled. His stare shifted only at the moment the sheet slipped down the slope of her creamy shoulder.

She followed his gaze and scoffed. "Get out!"

Needing to clear his head, he stormed out.

After several minutes of pacing the den, she finally emerged from the bedroom fully clothed in an Amish shift and apron.

All moisture left his throat. Despite her simple clothing, there was nothing plain about her. Long, ebony hair, still slightly tousled from sleep, tumbled in loose waves down her back.

"I see no reason for us drawing out our return. If you don't mind, I would like to be on our way." She moved to the chair in the den and picked up the rose-colored sweater draped over the back of it.

He wasn't ready to leave yet. They had privacy here. Once they returned to the farm, things would become chaotic.

She slipped her feet into plain black boots and stood. "Are you ready?"

He lost the ability to blink.

She flicked her long hair over her shoulder impatiently. "Bishop King?"

"Call me Eleazar," he rasped. His fingers twitched with the desire to touch her.

She frowned. "Excuse me?"

"I want you to call me Eleazar."

"No."

"Please." His gravelly voice was unrecognizable to his own ears. "Say my name, Larissa."

"Bishop—"

"Eleazar. Say it."

She drew back and scowled. "Fine, *Eleazar*, can we go?"

Her tongue stroked over his name like a caress. "No."

She tilted her head at him in concern. "Are you all right?"

"No."

"Is there something you need?"

"Patience. I need patience."

Her brow creased even more. "Bishop—"

"Eleazar."

She shook her head. "Eleazar, perhaps you should sit."

Perhaps she was right.

"Larissa," he whispered, lowering to the sofa.

Wringing her hands, she cautiously approached. "Yes, Bishop?"

He swallowed, his control slipping. "I need…" She smelled incredible. He couldn't think. "I need…" He shook his head as if he could not save her from the truth. *"You."*

She darted back a step, spine ramrod straight.

Suddenly on his feet, his animal instincts excited at the idea of a chase, he stepped forward. She rushed back but he followed her every retreating step with a pursuant one of his own.

Her hand lifted as if she could stay him with such a meager gesture. "Bishop, stop. What are you doing?"

"I asked you to call me by my name."

"I'm not comfortable with that."

"I suggest you become comfortable with it."

She took another step back, and her shoulders pressed into the wall. He had her now.

"I think it's best if we use our formal titles, Bishop King."

"There will be no formalities between us. Only raw honesty and trust."

"Have you lost your senses?"

He crowded her body, caging her in with his size. "No, but I've found the other half of my soul."

Her expression fell as the blood rushed from her face. "You're mistaken."

His hand swept under her hair, cupping the side of her throat possessively and running his thumb along her jaw. "I've never been more certain of anything."

Shallow breaths panted past her lips. "I haven't dreamed."

"Because you don't sleep."

"I sleep."

"But never soundly." He looked into her eyes, daring her to deny this strange connection they shared. "Larissa, you are my mate."

He closed the distance, but she angled her face away, squeezing her eyes shut. "Please don't do this, Bishop."

He stilled, breathing in her unmistakable terror. Was it him or the thought of intimacy?

Reining in his control, he whispered against her ear, "I'll never hurt you, Larissa.

This will be nothing like your past experiences."

"What do you know of my experiences?" More tears fell. "You know nothing about what I've done."

He twisted away from her, and she slid down the wall. Her soft whimpers gutted him, and he ran a hand over the back of his neck, pinching the developing tension, unsure what to do.

He wanted to be in her head, to see what she was thinking, but she would not appreciate the intrusion. On some level, she had to trust him. He needed to get close enough to prove he was not a threat to her.

Her confused sobs gutted him. "This can't be happening. Not with you."

He had no choice but to force his nearness if he ever hoped to bridge this distance. Crouching at her side, he carefully slipped his arms under her shoulders and knees and pulled her to his chest. She stiffened, but he lifted her anyway. "I am not as cruel as you believe me to be."

"You were there. You married me to him. How long did you know?"

Was it the idea of being mated to him that caused her to weep, or the misconception that he might have known she was his mate when he performed her wedding ceremony? "I didn't know then. I swear it."

She shook her head. "How can you even look at me, knowing that… that…"

"None of that matters." He hugged her close. "The only thing that matters is where we go from here. You're safe with me, Larissa. I'll never let another male touch you again."

Like a child, unable to cope under so many confusing emotions, she shattered in his arms. Each sob tore through him like a freight train, but he refused to let her go.

He rocked her as she cried, stroking her hair and whispering promises that he would never hurt her, and eventually—blissfully— she fell asleep in his arms.

CHAPTER 16

Cain's arm swept in front of him in a practiced motion, fingers spread like a fan, causing a gust of wind to clear the newly fallen leaves from the wooded area. He was careful not to disturb the decaying body lying on the ground.

Another female victim, another attack by whatever was haunting in the woods. Cain was now certain the predator was vampire.

The victim's body was desecrated and bloodless, left alone in the forest like a for-gotten rag doll. From what he could deduce, the mortal woman had been hiking. It was never wise to hike alone in these steep hills. To Cain's thinking, it was plain stupid to do so with a predator on the loose. Still, he sympathized with the victim and any family she may have left behind.

The police would open an investigation once she was reported missing. If she did have loved ones waiting for her, they deserved closure, so he left her body where it would be easily found.

The footprints proved the attacker was shoeless, but the imprints were much smaller than the last set he came across, smaller than any full-grown male's foot. They pressed lightly into the claylike ground, further proving the attacker was of a small build. The compression showed that the attacker was slight in weight, but the trajectory of the markings showed impressive speed.

While he initially feared this was the work of his uncle at play, he now thought differently. Claw marks on a nearby tree trunk also appeared an unnatural height for a male's reach. So how had the victim been sexually violated if the attacker was not male?

Examining the scene, he gently moved debris with a long stick. The body stunk like a male predator.

"There it is." To the left of the victim's leg

was a handprint larger than her own, larger than any female. As he now feared, more than one predator was lurking in the woods.

Careful not to leave any trail of evidence leading the police closer to the truth, he retraced his steps and covered any hint of his presence with a light rain.

English technologies relied on DNA and fingerprints. An immortal's fingerprints were different from mortals because they did not age and rapidly healed, so their skin did not wrinkle.

But as he looked around, noting the various markings and mentally comparing them to the last crime scene, he noted one crucial difference. The attacker—or attackers—were getting sloppy.

He could not leave any evidence of his kind, even if they were his foe. He had an obligation to The Order and a duty to protect those he loved. That meant keeping their species hidden at all cost.

Random drops pelted the dry leaves of the trees until a rushing spray of rain showered down. Cain stood silently, watching as the clay ground softened and water rose over its surface. Imprints faded and puddles filled gullies. Underground creatures burrowed deeper below the earth, where it was dry.

Cain commanded the rain to wash away all evidence and by the time he left the woods, his clothing was soaked through. The storm followed his progress, removing any traces of him being there. Once he reached the bottom of the mountain, it was dawn.

He walked to a visitors' pavilion where a few vending machines stood and a small kiosk held brochures. Helping himself to one of the tourists' guides, he sat on a bench where the sun would first shine and waited. It wouldn't be long. If he stayed put, she would eventually show.

A few hours later, his clothing had dried to nothing more than a slight dampness that clung to parts of his skin. He fixed his shirttail and adjusted his belt. Long gone were his Amish suspenders and hat. He much pre-ferred the lackadaisical dress of the English.

At the sound of the news van approaching, he moved over to the kiosk and pretended to examine his brochure. The large vehicle, with some sort of towering satellite peeking from the roof, parked close to the pavilion. The sliding door swished.

"Todd, I want to get the shot over here to-day. I think the light will be better."

Bingo. Just as he predicted, she showed up, bloodthirsty for a story and lacking any sign of compassion for the lives that had been lost or that another corpse lay only a hundred yards away.

The reporter and the cameraman moved to the optimal area for the shot. While the man readied the equipment, the reporter looked over some notes and then applied a red gloss to her lips. She was much smaller in person than she appeared on television.

Once the camera was set up, she stood in front of it, holding her microphone and waited. She touched her ear, and Cain real-ized she must have some sort of device in there that allowed her to communicate with someone unseen.

The light on the camera switched from red to white. With a final nod, she straight-ened and blanked her expression.

"Thank you, Michael. We are here again in the mountains of Jim Thorpe where another victim has been reported missing after ven-turing into the woods three days ago for some recreational hiking. While the trails of Jim

Thorpe are known for their beautiful fall foliage and ideal peaks for bird-watching, the local police department has issued a press release advising all visitors to travel in groups and be extremely cautious while visiting the sights.

"Local merchants are not enthusiastic about the negative press their town is receiving. They claim a notable dip in retail trends in comparison to last fall's records. Unfortunately, there is nothing to be done to alter the circumstances so long as whatever is preying on these once-welcoming hills remains at large.

"Police are asking that if anyone has seen or heard from a Ms. Kate Lynn Hobs to please contact the number at the bottom of the screen. Ms. Hobs is twenty-eight, average height, approximately a hundred and twenty pounds, with medium-blonde hair and brown eyes. She has been missing for three days and was last seen purchasing some last-minute items at a convenience store four miles from here."

The body in the woods matched the woman's description. It somehow made it worse knowing the female's name. He needed to find the creature in the woods and destroy it before another person went missing.

Remaining in the shadows, Cain watched as the woman finished her report. As the light on the camera returned to red, she touched her ear as if listening for something, then said, "That's a wrap."

She passed the microphone to the cameraman as he carried the equipment back to the van. The reporter retrieved a water bottle from the ground. As she sipped from the bottle, she casually looked around.

He gave her a mental push to come and talk to him and waited as she screwed the cap back on her water bottle and slowly walked toward him.

"Hello," she said, pausing a few feet away. "Are you planning on hiking the trails today?"

Cain casually tucked his brochure under his arm and faced her. "Perhaps. You're that reporter, Destiny Santos, right?"

"That's right. You just missed my story. I could've gotten you an interview on camera."

He gave a tight-lipped smile that didn't reach his eyes. "Pity."

She glanced over his clothing. "You're awfully dressed up for being in the woods."

"I'm here on business."

"What kind of business? Are you a detective?"

She was a pushy little thing. "My business doesn't concern you."

"Are you a reporter?"

Relentless.

"Who I am is of no consequence to you."

"Did the DA send you? If so, I'd like to get an interview." Turning toward her van, she yelled for her cameraman. "Todd, we need the camera again."

He sighed. "That won't be necessary."

She flipped open a compact mirror and checked her teeth. "The public has a right to know if there have been any leads in the case."

"I'm sure that's your first concern."

She bristled. "Hey, I'm just doing my job."

"And what job is that exactly? Tell me, Destiny Santos, how does chasing down two orphaned children in the middle of their mother's funeral fall under any noble job description?"

Her posture grew defensive. "You're talking about the Foster children, Dane and Cybil? They were eyewitnesses. They could have seen something to help catch this guy."

"They're children. Children who lost both parents. Children who were standing over turned-up dirt that hadn't even buried their dead mother yet, and you thought nothing of shoving a microphone into their faces. You should be ashamed of yourself."

She at least had the decency to flush. "I don't make the rules. The network does."

"Then work for a better network. Or are they paying you enough to buy your self-respect?"

"Fuck you, mister." When her temper spiked, she spoke with her whole body. "I live around here. The people of this community deserve to know what's out there. I'm doing my part."

So were her hips. "Which part is that, stirring pandemonium or harassing orphans?"

"I don't need to stand here and listen to this shit."

As she stormed back to the van, he grinned at the full-figured view. Then, realizing his mistake, he winced.

"Wait!" He jogged after her. "I need to know where the children live."

"I'm not helping—"

Before he got distracted by her hot-blooded temper again, he gave her a mental push and a hard order. "Give me an address."

Her eyes glazed. "Clara Barnes. Twenty-two Fors—" She made a face as if tasting something bitter. Then, shaking her head, she cleared her throat. "I'm sorry, I missed what you asked."

He somehow released her mind a second too soon. He made a mental reach for her mind again, but she stepped back as if she were physically avoiding his grasp.

He reached again, but, for some reason, he couldn't get ahold of her mind. He had no choice but to fish for the information. "I need Clara Barnes's address."

"What? I can't tell you that."

"Yes, you can." It wasn't like she was a woman of great scruples.

"Why are you here?"

No longer amused, his jaw ticked. "Tell me where she lives."

She laughed in his face. "Um, no."

Locking his molars, he shoved hard at her mind but hit a wall. "How are you doing that?" Thunder rolled in the distance.

"Doing what? Look, I've been following this case since last year and this is the first I've seen you around." Her eyes narrowed and she withdrew a phone. "Actually…" She snapped his picture.

"Hey! You can't take my photograph?"

"Why?" she asked, her tone ripe with attitude. "Are you Amish?"

As a matter of fact... No, that would only complicate matters.

He opted for the fastest solution and snatched her phone.

"Hey! Give me my phone, asshole!"

The feisty little strumpet jumped for her device, but he held it out of reach. "Give me Clara's address!"

"I don't share my notes with assholes."

This unexpected aggressive side of her intrigued him, but he was determined to dislike her on principle. He laughed as she strained for her phone, her body practically climbing up his until she grabbed it.

She yanked it out of his hand and scowled at him. "I should have you arrested." She inspected her phone as if it were the most precious thing she owned. Walking away, she glared over her shoulder and yelled, "I'll be sure to send your picture to the cops, prick."

He cursed. This had gone the opposite of what he had planned. He once again jogged after her. "Destiny, wait, perhaps we got off on the wrong foot. Can we please start again?"

"Bite me."

"Gladly." He stilled the second the word

left his mouth. *Gladly?* Where the hell had that come from?

The van door slammed shut and the engine started.

"Wait!" He was too late. The van took off, leaving him in a cloud of dust.

CHAPTER 17

*E*leazar held Larissa's sleeping body until the blue sky faded to dim shades of red and orange as dusk approached. She appeared to sleep soundly for once, and he hated to disturb her, but they had a long journey ahead and much to discuss.

Gently, he dragged a knuckle across her cheek. "Little mouse, you must wake."

Her lashes fluttered and he braced for another explosive fight. But when she opened her eyes, she simply stared at him.

She broke eye contact and glanced away with a sigh but made no move to leave his hold. "I saw you."

The thrill that jolted through his veins was unmatched. "You dreamt?"

"I suppose that's what it was. I never had a dream before."

"It's a gift reserved for called mates."

Another sigh.

"Larissa, a calling is a blessing."

"It doesn't feel like one."

"You're focused on the complications. Let me worry about that."

She shook her head. "You'll be disappointed."

"Impossible."

She looked at him again. "You don't understand. I'm broken." A tear slid from her eye. She shed the drop as if its presence did not affect her, as if she were simply resigned to be sad.

He forced her to sit up and face him. Looking directly into her eyes, he said, "This bruised perception you have of yourself will heal. But you have to be patient with yourself and also with me. We're both in new territory, and we have a lot to learn about each other. Tolerance can go a long way, but there's one thing I will *never* tolerate from you."

Her mouth formed a stubborn line. "I figured as much."

"I will not allow you to degrade yourself."

Surprise flashed in her eyes before she

lowered her head, hiding her face from his view.

Hooking a finger under her chin, he lifted her face. "Why does that make you cry?"

She sniffed and shook her head. "I can't be your mate."

"It's not something you choose, Larissa. It's something that simply is."

"You don't understand. I can't…" She drew in a jagged breath. "I can't bear the touch of a male."

His heart sank. Images of the only other man who had intimate knowledge of her flashed through his mind, his imagination painting a cruel picture. "Why?"

"Because he broke me."

A cold stone settled in the pit of his stomach. "How did he break you? Show me."

She held his stare for a moment, and then her mind opened to him. He witnessed her memories from a first-hand perspective. Every sense and emotion was fresh and tangible.

Her father, Jonas, speaking to her about Silus's request. She harbored so much curiosity and hope as a young, single female wishing only to find a partner in a big, lonesome world.

Their courtship was brief but pleasant. Picnics and after supper walks. Sometimes Larissa would visit him in the field, racing out to greet him with a cool glass of homemade lemonade.

Like in many Amish sects, Silus was eventually granted bundling privileges. Eleazar shifted uncomfortably at the vision of another male entering the childhood bedroom of his mate. But bundling was a long-standing tradition among the Amish.

Swallowing tightly, he pressed through the memory, watching Silus enter her room where she waited in only her underclothes beneath the sheets. His jaw locked and his mind jerked out of her memories, startling both of them.

Larissa looked up at him, her eyes wide with concern. "I'm sorry. I shouldn't have shown you that."

He cleared his throat, forcing back his displeasure to fully understand what she experienced. Silus had done nothing outside of typical tradition.

Silus waited until the house was dark to enter her room. Approaching her bed, fully clothed, he exercised his granted right to explore Larissa's body within reason, so long as he did not look at her or penetrate her.

Eleazar took issue with the act, and that shared sensation of another man touching his mate filled him with a murderous rage. He drew in a steadying breath but found it impossible to relax the tension now knotting his shoulders.

"We should keep going."

Curious of her response to the other man, he suffered through the memories. He made her nervous and failed to arouse her, which pleased Eleazar to no end. In Larissa's mind, the entire bundling was most comparable to being sized for garments or an inspection conducted by a healer. But as the courtship carried on, Silus's sense of entitlement grew.

Eleazar watched recollections of her mother explaining the difference between a bundling bed and a marriage bed and suffered Larissa's internal debate about confessing too much. But, in the end, she kept her silence, and Silus took advantage of her innocence.

Eleazar pushed forward in her memories, grinding his molars and, once again, wanting to slaughter the other man. He suffered through the clumsy petting and Silus's slippery fumbling, truly comprehending how awful some of these practices must be for females. The selfish male never considered Larissa's comfort when seeking his own.

Then he saw a memory he recognized— her wedding. Eleazar had performed the ceremony, and it was difficult to see himself through her eyes. She didn't think much of him.

He would work on that.

He recalled the ceremony, but it looked different from her point of view. The reception was held at her home, but the bride and groom hadn't stayed long.

Anxiety spiked when he found her recollection of the carriage ride to her new home. Silus had been in a rush to bed his new bride. Taking Larissa's arm in a firm grip, Silus led her up the stairs to the master bedroom, where he quickly undressed her.

Eleazar recoiled at the memory of her fear and trepidation, experiencing everything from the sting of tears in her throat to the cold press of Silus's hand, lowering her to her stomach as he bent her over the bed.

These memories were no one else's business, but they were hers and she was his mate. If Larissa had borne the reality, he could bear the memory.

The echo of her sharp cry cut through him, and his arms tightened reflexively as if he could somehow save her from such a past. She had expected the pain but not the humiliation.

A reoccurring thought played through her head as her husband rutted into her like an animal. She hadn't even had a chance to unpin the braids in her hair. In the end, what hurt her most was her husband's absolute disregard for her feelings.

He suffered with her through the memory of her wedding night, feeling every apprehension, down to the chill in the air when that selfish bastard left her wearing a mix of virgin blood and semen. She was confused and worried. Her fear that the man she expected to love her might actually hate her mingled with her unbreakable desire to try still to please him.

In the weeks and months that followed, she tried everything to earn her husband's approval and praise. But when Silus wasn't crushing her body, he crushed her spirit with snide comments until he altogether pulverized Larissa's hopes of forming a connection.

He kept her from her family, monitored her every chore, and criticized her housekeeping. The emotional neglect was endless, unbearable when he experienced it from her perspective and saw how much she genuinely wanted to please her husband.

Then the mental abuse started and Eleazar had heard enough. "He didn't deserve you." Silus wasn't worthy of a single minute of her day, and Eleazar had put her with that monster. Then, lowering his head in shame, he rasped, "You should never forgive me."

"Now you see."

He had seen more than he ever wanted to see, and those memories would haunt him for the rest of eternity. "I'm so sorry, Larissa. If I had known that was happening…"

"You would have done nothing." Her smile was anything but pleased. "That's the grim truth about Family Law."

Unwittingly, a glimpse of another memory assaulted him and he flinched. She followed it with another, and another, each one a bullet through his heart.

"I understand," he choked. It never got better for her. Every time Silus touched her, he treated her worse.

"Do you? Do you truly understand what I mean when I tell you I'm broken? He broke me, Bishop. I'm afraid even God's too late. Those firsts can never be undone."

Eleazar could take no more. Through gritted teeth, he snarled, "It's not you who is broken, it's the barbarian that married you."

"Perhaps we both are."

He could not pressure her, yet there was no escaping the urgent need to complete their bond. "I would never take from you the way he did."

"Every man takes. It's the nature of the beast."

"It will not be so between us."

"I shared my pain, but you can't understand my scars."

Offended by her naivety, he set her down and paced. "And I could say the same for you, Larissa. I've survived five centuries on my own. Do you think your half a century of loneliness can compare? I've suffered incredible loss, watched loved ones fall to plagues, and suffer through famine. You do not have the world cornered when it comes to hardships.

"I understand that he hurt you, but that's over now. He will never come near you again. As your mate, you have my word and my protection. But I will not let you give up. Your life has only begun. You should be thanking God for this gift He's given us. Instead, you're refusing something others wait an eternity to find. Happiness isn't luck, Larissa, it's a choice. You have to choose to be happy and do the work."

Her chin trembled. "I shared my most intimate secrets with you—"

"And I sympathized with you. But now, this is where we are. What do you choose? Do you want to live in the past or move forward?" He softened his voice. "I promised you honesty, Larissa, and that's what I've given you. I desperately want your trust and I'm willing to be patient, but in *this* we only have so much time before we risk losing our humanity."

"So, you're saying I have no choice."

"You have a choice. Right now, you can choose our future together."

"But that's it! That's the only option!"

"Would you rather suffer? Would you rather become a danger to others? Another Hartzler lost to *feeishness?* You know what the right choice is. Why won't you make it?"

"Because I can't do it! I can't bear to be touched!"

"You have to trust that it will be different

between us." He pressed his lips to hers, and she drew back.

"Don't."

"You know the risks of ignoring the call. The outcome is inevitable. This is your chance to decide for yourself."

He kissed her again, hard and demanding. She jerked her mouth away, dragging the back of her hand against her lips. "What are you doing?"

"Give in, little mouse."

"I'm not a mouse."

"Prove it. Not because you have to, but because you want to. Take charge. Be a lioness. I'll hand over control. I know you sense our chemistry. You can't fool me into thinking you're cold, not when I can scent the heat pooling between your thighs."

Her eyes widened, completely dilated, and her skin flushed. "Stop it!"

He toppled her to her back, caging her with his aroused body. "I'm not ashamed and you shouldn't be either."

She shoved at his chest, but he only settled his body more firmly over hers. "Look at me, Larissa. I'm not hurting you. We're barely touching. Let the weight of my body sink in.

Eventually, you'll be as familiar with it as you are with your own."

"I don't want that."

"*Liar*," he hissed, breathing deep. "Your scent fills the air and your eyes give you away. Are you afraid you might like it?"

She stiffened. "You swore you wouldn't hurt me."

"And I'm not. You're in control."

"It doesn't feel that way."

"Kiss me. You will see."

When she didn't move, he lowered his mouth and initiated. This time, rather than pull away, she pushed back.

She nipped at his lips with her sharp, little fangs, and he grinned when he tasted blood. "There's that lioness."

He leaned down and licked the fullness of her lower lip, and a low purr hummed from deep within her throat. Her scent thickened, threatening to snap the fine thread of control he still held. He rocked into her and she moaned, her body softening beneath his and her thighs falling open. That was his cue.

With a final, teasing kiss, he licked over her luscious mouth and stood. Startled by his retreat, she gasped and stared up at him with a look of confusion.

"Like I said, I'll leave the choice up to you. You can be a tame little mouse or a proud and powerful lioness. I can be patient while you find your courage. But try not to make us wait too long. I'll make no secret of wanting you." He eyed his groin then sent her a pointed look. "What would be the point when the proof's clear to see?"

CHAPTER 18

As night fell, the temperature continued to drop. Cain moved farther into the forest. He purchased some items in town—enough to stage a vulnerable campsite and lure whatever lurked in the woods out of hiding.

He lit a fire, but its heat did nothing to warm him as he was several yards away in the shadows. The area was purposefully littered with mortal items, from food packages to women's perfume. He even purchased women's clothing from a thrift store because the lingering scent of a mortal remained in the fibers. He waited silently for hours and was convinced he would be there the following night because nothing had happened yet.

Then a branch snapped in the distance, bringing his body to full attention. The slight crunch of leaves caught his ear. A rush of fast movement circling the faux camp, and his muscles bunched with anticipation.

Finally, it was here.

His limbs loosened in preparation for whatever was out there. His hands flexed and curled, claws extending.

The forest grew eerily quiet, a sign that a predator was near. Cain scanned the nearby shadows for any unnatural movement. To his left, another branch snapped. He was not alone.

A low growl rumbled. Cain grinned and growled back at the intruder. The rumble grew in volume and intensity, rushing past him with a gust of wind. Shutting his eyes, he sniffed the air.

Pungent and unmistakably male.

Cain dropped lower, prepared to battle the bloodthirsty killer to the death. No doubt his opponent was out for his life as well. The creature enjoyed the game of cat and mouse; only it remained undetermined who was the predator and who was the prey.

Cain remained alert, braced in the center of what they determined to be the arena, and allowed the other male to have his fun. The beast hissed, circling Cain too fast for him to set eyes on, but the scent was unmistakable. *Vampire.*

High above in the canopy of dried branches and withering autumn leaves, a limb creaked. Cain whirled toward the sound. There, about a hundred feet up, was his prey.

The animal stood upon a fat, winding branch of a sycamore while grasping another limb in his hands. His legs were spread wide and his posture resembled more that of a wild animal than that of a man.

Cain tracked and branches rustled as it leaped from one tree to another. Its comfort with the elements was evident in its agility.

Growing tired of the production, Cain sighed. "Are you trying to slaughter me or dance with me?"

More tree limbs jostled above and the beast plunged twenty feet through the canopy, landing in a crouch directly in front of Cain. "Dance it is."

The creature sprung to its feet. It was no male, yet it wore the stink of a male's scent.

Dark eyes, almost black, acted as mirrors

in the dark, glowing with reflected moonlight and the red hue of the campfire. Cain couldn't tell where her irises ended and her pupils began.

Her flesh was filthy, without a stitch of clothing, and her hair was long and matted with dried clumps of mud and debris. A repellant odor poured off of her soiled skin.

"Who are you?"

"Who are you?" the female echoed, mimicking the inflection of his accent. Her voice was not feminine but shredded as if her words passed over shards of glass.

"How did you come here?"

"How did you come here?" she parodied again with a glimpse of rotted teeth. Sharp fangs showed she was, in fact, immortal. Her lack of civility confirmed she'd long ago became vampire.

"Are you the one killing all the women?"

"Are you the one killing all the women?"

Cain rolled his eyes. Great. A looker *and* smart. Did she speak English? "*Sprichst du Englisch?*"

"*Sprichst du Englisch?*" She spoke slowly, her filthy lips wrapping deliberately over every unfamiliar word.

Then Cain noticed something that gave him pause. A mark on her hip. A tattoo.

Immortals couldn't get tattoos. Well, they could, but they would fade and heal, disappearing in a matter of days.

He squinted, trying to read the scrolling print under the layer of grime that coated her skin. *Ricky*.

His head cocked as she prowled about. "You're a transition."

"You're a transition." Reminding him of the excitable orangutan he'd once seen caged at a zoo exhibit, she flung her limbs and bobbed about, circling in a way that translated a low intellect.

Transitions were different from bonded mates who were once mortal. They were... *unique* and not in a good way.

The longer she gyrated and cackled about, the more his discouragement grew. Wonderful. He had stumbled across a deranged parakeet. "Who is your sire?"

"Who is your sire?"

Cain pinched the bridge of his nose. This could go on forever.

Perhaps he should capture the girl and bring her back to his farm to hand over to The Council. Of course, they hadn't been too concerned about the presence of a rogue. Why would he assume anything had changed?

Or perhaps this was *his* purpose in this life, to protect those who needed protection from wild creatures of his own kind. The idea of becoming a celebrated hunter and hero of The Order appealed to him, but the thought of destroying this unstable female did not suit him. Females were soft, gentle creatures meant to be loved and caressed.

"Look, if we could just talk, you could possibly come out of this situation alive."

"Alive."

Dear God, this would never end. "How did you come here?" he shouted, as if she had a hearing problem rather than a processing one.

"How did you come here? How did you come here? How did you come here!"

She cackled, lowering to her haunches, exposing herself to him and rocking back and forth. He looked away from the gruesome, unwashed view.

That could scar a man.

She stilled, causing a tangible shift in energy. Peeking over his shoulder, he frowned at the hunched way she crouched as if she were sad he no longer wanted to play with her. Big black eyes stared up at him and she pouted.

"Oh, come on. Look, I'm just not into—"

She hissed and lunged. Claws scraped over his chest, slicing through his clothing and scoring his flesh. The burn of torn skin instantly stung as the heat of spilled blood gathered over his flayed skin.

Flinging her off of him, he bared his fangs with a feral growl, then crouched to face off. Playtime was over. He no longer saw her as female, only the enemy. "Game on, bitch."

ANNALISE ENTERED the house and called for Abilene. She was supposed to meet her at the barn so that they could take a buggy to town, but her mother-in-law had not shown up. "Mom?" she called as she walked through the kitchen. "Abilene? Gracie? Jonas?"

A floorboard creaked and Anna stilled, scenting the air. A soft, distant whimper broke the silence, and Anna rushed up the stairs.

"Abilene?" Her mother-in-law lay curled up on her side, weeping.

As Annalise crossed the threshold, she

stumbled, the other woman's hunger hitting her like a sucker punch to the gut. "Jesus, Abilene, you're starving. When's the last time you fed?"

She made no attempt to answer, she only lay motionless, staring at the wall through teary eyes, trembling. Was she trying to beat her husband to the grave?

Gently settling on the bed, Annalise pulled Abilene's head onto her lap against her swollen stomach. "You can't go on like this." She bit into her wrist and held it to her mother-in-law's lips. "Drink, Mother."

Abilene's fangs reflexively shot out at the scent of warm blood, but she turned away. "The baby—"

"The baby needs a grandmother. Now, drink."

Slowly, Abilene's mouth closed over Annalise's wrist and she gently suckled. Annalise smoothed back Abilene's hair with tender strokes from her fingers as her color slowly returned.

"No more of this, Abilene. You have to take care of yourself. We need you here, with us."

Abilene shut her eyes, licked Anna's wrist to close the wound, and nodded. "I'm sorry."

She helped her sit up. "Let's talk." Pulling her legs under her skirt, she waited for Abilene to explain.

Her head hung low in defeat. "I couldn't bring myself to drink any more distilled blood."

Anna nodded with understanding. "You could have come to us—"

"No, Anna. It's forbidden. This can't happen again. It's against our laws. Your blood is for your mate and your children."

Annalise waved away her words. "I don't care about those silly laws. And Adam would have done the same thing."

Tears welled in her eyes. She reached for Anna's hand and squeezed affectionately. "You are a blessing to this family, Annalise."

"Thank—*ahhh*—" Searing pain blazed across Anna's torso, and she grabbed her stomach protectively.

"Anna, what's wrong?" Abilene sprung to her feet, eyes wide with panic.

Annalise screamed as another lash of bursting, burning heat scored down her body. Her back bowed and she collapsed onto the bed, angling away from the invisible enemy and crying for help. "Get Adam!"

Heat coated her hand and she lifted her

palm, her body shaking in horror at the sight of thick, fresh blood.

"What's happening?" Abilene screamed.

Another blow of searing pain knocked Anna's head back and she tasted blood. Her spine arched and she gasped, cradling her belly, desperate to protect her unborn child. Her saliva thickened as she fought the urge to vomit from the unending sting.

She curled to her side with an agonizing moan and wheezed, "Get Adam. Run."

CAIN SPRUNG at the little she-witch, claws bared, fangs snapping, and flayed her flesh wide. She hissed and rolled across the ground, escaping what would have been a deathblow. He lunged and they stumbled through the dry leaves, sharp rocks bruising his spine. She plowed her fists into his side and bit a hunk of flesh off his shoulder.

"*Ah!*" He shoved her hard, throwing her several feet, but she was fast and wild, coming back at him with doubled determination and going for his eyes.

Cain flinched and struggled as her dirty thumbs pressed into his sockets. Fetid breath snarled in his face as she latched onto his body. He clawed at her hair, trying to rip her off of him, but she bit him. He backhanded her and she took a chunk of his flesh with her when her head snapped back.

Scrabbling to his feet, he hissed and put his back to a tree. The female stayed low, crawling like a crab along the ground, eyes wild, claws clicking as they needled over the ground. She was not a natural creation of God's. It became clear, perhaps more than he initially grasped, that she needed to be destroyed.

She snapped her jaw and charged. He dodged, wanting information before he ended this once and for all. "Who is your sire? And *do not* repeat me!"

Blood dripped down his chest and torso, burning with the infectious filth she embedded in her claws.

She laughed, her dry cackle echoing off the trees. "You no strong 'nough fer 'im."

He paused. It was the first time she hadn't repeated his words. "Who?"

His skin burned where she bit him as if she carried some sort of venom. The wound needed to heal and fast.

Another cackle as her hips undulated in a

gross display. "He bigger than yooooou," she sang in that horrible voice.

"Hate to inform you, but size isn't everything." Reaching into the back of his belt, he wrapped his finders around cold steel. As soon as he got the information he needed from her, she was dead.

"There too many of us. Hun'reds."

Cain froze. "There are more?"

Her black-toothed smile mocked him. "We his mates."

"You're all women?"

A hiss came from the shadows like locusts screaming from the trees. "Maaaaatessss."

His eyes widened.

Dropping her head between her shoulders, she swayed toward him, thrusting her hips and emitting a call that echoed from the wood. He had the sense he was outnumbered and needed to move fast.

"What's his name?"

"What's his name?"

Back to this again? "Answer me!"

Her jaw unhinged like a python and he braced. Whatever came next was going to hurt.

"GET MORE RAGS!" Adam shouted as he gripped his wife's trembling hand.

An agonizing scream belted from her lungs as her back bowed against the mattress.

"Another opening started!" Gracie tossed away yet another sopping red towel.

"Anna, stay with me. I need you to stay with me." He pressed his lips to her damp skin. "Check the baby, Grace."

"I just did. This wound needs a suture—"

"Now!" Adam ordered.

His sister's hands went to Anna's swollen stomach.

"Adam, what's happening to me?" Anna's cry ripped through his heart.

"The baby's stressed, but his heart's beating."

"Tell me what you need, *ainsicht*."

"Sleep, Adam, I need to sleep. The pain—" Another scream ripped through her, and he winced.

As soon as one wound healed, another two opened. His mother rushed in with a stack of towels. They couldn't keep up with the blood.

"She's losing too much, Adam," Gracie said, her eyes wide with panic.

He tore into his wrist, opening his flesh,

and shoved his vein to her lips. "Drink, Anna." She was so weak. "Do it!"

The flutter of her mouth was barely detectable. She sipped only to jerk back and grab her skull, screaming hysterically. "My eyes! It's crushing me!"

"What is it?" He was on his feet, helpless. "Anna, talk to me!"

A chunk of her skin ripped away, exposing the raw, pink pulp of her inner flesh. Bruises took shape as he stared in horror.

"Make it stop! Please!" A jagged gouge scored her arm and she coughed up blood.

"For God's sake, go get the healer!"

CAIN GRUNTED and spat a mouthful of blood onto the ground, his limbs trembling and muscles pleading for this to end. This was no ordinary female. Her strength wouldn't wane.

He screamed as she tackled him to the ground, claws ripping open his throat and teeth tearing at his back. The sick gurgle filling his lungs and the taste of fresh blood on his tongue was alarming as he wrestled her off in a frantic attempt to escape.

The scores of claw marks running over his

back burned down to the nerve. Sticky blood caked around his eyes and dirt coated his sweaty flesh. His clothing hung like ribbons off his bleeding limbs.

This had gone on long enough.

He kicked out his legs and threw her off of him, hearing her land somewhere twenty feet away.

Panting and grunting, he staggered to his feet and froze. His eyes searched the shadows. Where was she?

The unexpected weight crashed onto his shoulders, knocking him to his knees with an excruciating crunch of bone. She screeched, ripping back his hair and biting into his throat as if planning to gnaw his head clean off his shoulders.

***

ANNA'S SCREAMS beat against the walls as she arched off the bed. Her muscles clenched and her limbs flailed. She clawed at an invisible enemy, doing more damage to herself.

The bedding wore a crimson stain so thick it dripped to the wood floor. Her spine bore lacerations too deep to close. The horrific sight of his wife's tortured body stole his breath. If he lost her, he'd have nothing to live for.

"Anna, breathe with me."

"Adam," her voice was weak, a mere tremble beneath the pain.

"Give me your pain. Let me—"

One glimpse of the agony she suffered and he jerked hard, his knees buckling as a grunt robbed him of the air in his lungs. How was she surviving this?

The healer, who had been sopping up the blood with soiled rags, staggered back, head shaking as if running out of hope.

"*Do something!*" Adam raged.

"Please, Adam," Anna rasped, red with busted blood vessels. "Please, let me sleep. I want to be numb."

Selfishly, he didn't want to lose their connection. "No, *ainsicht,* you need to stay awake."

"Perhaps it would be better if she slept. Less traumatic for the baby," the healer suggested.

Adam looked at Gracie, who held Anna's belly with shaking, blood-soaked hands. She nodded, which could only mean that her concern for their unborn child had grown.

Adam pressed a kiss to his wife's damp

hair, his breath rushing past his lips, and he fought the urge to cry. "I'll be right here, my love. Come back to me." He gave the mental command for her to sleep and the tension in her body loosened, her weight sinking life-lessly into the blood-soaked bed.

CAIN DREW BACK HIS ARM, prepared to strike when his vision flickered. The edges of his peripheral field darkened with black shadows and he blinked, fighting to see through the dim woods. A sharp tug at the back of his mind threw his balance and his enemy winked out of view.

Had he lost too much blood? If he passed out, she'd kill him.

"Tell me who your maker is!" Breath soughed in and out of his lungs like fire fed by bellows.

Laughter rung with a haunting echo from the canopy above. Another tug, hard at the back of his mind, and he staggered.

Grabbing his head, he tried to shake away whatever the sensation was. Vertigo ripped through him and he stumbled into a tree. What was happening?

His vision swirled out of focus and he relied on his hearing to track his enemy, fearful this might be the end. Weak beyond expectation, he stumbled and collapsed, his face smacking hard against the sandy ground as blood eclipsed his vision.

Breath panted past his lips as he lay prone and vulnerable. He listened to the cackling, but the shrieks wavered, and he didn't trust his perception. He was losing consciousness and only had a few seconds—

He blinked, his muscles heavy and motor skills slow. The farm. He recognized the barn and the scent of hay mixing with honeysuckle. Animals brayed and bleated in the distance. Why was he there?

A flash of darkness jolted his head back, pulling him somewhere else. He grunted and found it impossible to move. Paralyzed.

With each flash of light came silence and the sweet scent of home. Then came the darkness followed by the incessant cackling above. Silence. Cackle. Silence. Cackle. Silence—no. Wait. Screaming.

His body tensed. He recognized that voice. "Anna?"

He struggled to move but could barely twitch a finger. His visions jumbled—black night—blue sky—black night—blue sky—it was too much at once.

"Cain!"

"Annalise!" He couldn't find her. "Where are you?"

"Help me!"

Growling, he forced his body to move, but his heavy limbs only dragged. This was no dream. He was trapped in a nightmare. "Anna, I'm coming!"

"Cain, make it stop!" Her scream ripped over the field, cutting into the woods and trees as his vision flashed to black and something sliced up his leg. He roared and struggled to go back to the dream to get to Anna.

Pain consumed him, and he wheezed, "Anna?"

Her cry pleaded from a distance in a broken sob, "Cain…"

Then he saw her, covered in rags, soaked in blood, her crimson hands cradling her pregnant belly. "Am I dying?"

The blood rushed from his veins and his jaw hung in horror. "Anna!" He struggled to go to her but couldn't move. "Who did this to you?"

Her face contorted with another sob. "I don't know."

His eyes counted every laceration, struggling to see the true wounds through the spattered blood. There was so much blood.

Her injuries matched his own. Mark for mark. Bite for bite. Dear God, he was killing her.

"Cain, make it stop…" She sobbed. "I don't want to lose my baby."

Shafts of ice cut through his veins. What had he done?

She suffered his pain. Was that possible? Of course, it was. He'd experienced her transition, he'd known how close she was to death before. He'd never forgive himself if his actions…

"Don't move. I can end this!"

He roared and tightened every muscle, forcing his mind away. The moment he awoke on the forest floor, the pain came back to him tenfold. The she-bitch crouched in the distance, hissing when she saw him move, and then she barreled toward him, faster than a speeding horse.

He leaped to his feet and opened his claws, *"Come at me, you fucking bitch!"*

He jumped and they lunged through the air, colliding in a clatter of flesh and bone. Possessed by his beast within, he held nothing back. He grabbed hold of her head and yanked hard and fast until an inhuman crack snapped inside her throat.

He landed in a crouch. The enemy's body collapsing to the ground in a pile of boney limbs. Finally, silent.

Her finger twitched, and he dragged himself to his full height. Lurching closer to the heap of broken bones, he glared down at her black eyes and sank his booted foot onto her broken neck. Gravel crunched under the weight of his other foot as he grabbed a fistful of her snarled hair.

Blood trickled from his scalp into his eyes as he stared dispassionately at her mangled body. "Tell me who your sire is."

A restricted wheeze escaped her chest. *"I-say-ahhhhhhh..."*

With a snap of his arm, he further broke her neck then plunged his fist into her chest, closing fingers around the beating tissue and yanking hard, leaving nothing but an empty cavity behind. Then, raising his blood-soaked arm to the moon, he let out a battle cry and squeezed the dead heart.

The corpse at his feet rotted to dust as the wasted heart in his fist crumbled like sand.

Lightning lit the sky and rain pelted his skin, washing away the blood.

Cain shut his eyes and caught his breath as the wind howled through the trees scattering the ash away.

CHAPTER 19

The floorboard creaked and Adam spun, a feral glint in his eye as his brother stood in the doorway of the room. "Get out."

Cain's heart lurched at the gruesome sight of the bloodstained floor, the ominous sense that something horrific had transpired there, and the palpable heat of his brother's fury. His stare searched the motionless form on the bed, and he held up his bloodied hands in surrender. "Is she—"

"I said *get out!*" His brother shoved him back and growled.

"Adam, don't." Anna's plea was weak and small. "Cain…" She held out a hand, her eyes hardly open. "It's okay. Come here."

Watching Adam through a defensive glare, he dropped to his knees at the side of the bed and pulled Anna's fingers to his forehead. "Is the baby…?"

"The baby's fine. What about you?"

He looked at her through glassy eyes and shook his head. "I don't know how this happened."

She smiled, but it cost her and she shut her eyes. "I guess we're more connected than we realized." She let out a pained breath. "Cain, you need to feed. I think your hunger is what's slowing me from healing."

He hadn't done anything but rush to the farm the moment he learned she was in danger. His eyes pleaded as he looked up at his brother. "Adam, can you…?"

His brother scoffed and left the room. He returned a moment later with a glass of distilled sheep blood. Cain drank it down greedily, and Anna sighed at the same time as him.

The ache in his bones eased and the throbbing in his skull subsided. It was as if they could feel each other getting well, and since they'd never been able to share more than dreams or pain, he found the sense of her relief the closest he'd ever get to knowing her pleasure.

"What did this to you?" Her gaze roamed over the dried blood and fading bruises on his body.

"Something like us but much worse. I don't have a name for it, but there are more and they're all dangerous."

Over the next hour, he told them of what he'd found in the woods and how his suspicions of Isaiah were most likely correct.

"Will you tell The Council?"

He frowned at his dutiful brother. "What for? I already tried and no one believed me."

"This is different, Cain. One of those things came after *you*."

He shook his head, still processing what he found in the woods. "I'll think about it. Right now, my mind's on other things."

He stood, unable to suffer their presence much longer. He loved Anna and his brother, but he could only tolerate their love for each other for so long. He glanced back at Anna, wishing he could hold her for just a moment. "I'm sorry I did this to you."

"I'm okay, Cain. It wasn't your fault."

He nodded, trying hard to swallow her forgiveness but finding it difficult. "I'll be more careful from now on."

"You better," Adam growled.

He didn't blame him for his protectiveness of his mate. Leaving the bedroom, he grazed a hand over his brother's tight shoulder. "Take care of her."

"I always do."

Cain nodded and left the way he came in.

CHAPTER 20

$\mathscr{B}$ubbles gathered around Larissa as she sat in the bathtub, her brow wearing a perpetual frown. Her twenty-four hours had expired. Yet, here she sat, in her lovely, modern apartment, the bishop waiting in the wings with not a single idea of what to do.

He was her mate. Not Silus, but Eleazar, the bishop.

When she last walked off the farm, she swore she'd never return. To say this news was unexpected would be the understatement of the century.

If she returned—and that was a big if—she would not return to living out her miserable existence as Silus Hostetler's obedient wife.

The dreams were clear earlier when she slept. Each time she drifted to sleep the bishop was there. At first, his presence bothered her but now she was growing used to him. So fast.

She hadn't expected her emotions to invest this quickly and, while her brain warned against falling for yet another immortal more powerful than she, the bishop was always kind in her dreams. When he touched her—a gentle caress here or a trace of his fingers there—it gave her an unexpected thrill. The experience was altogether odd and somewhat unsettling.

Some dreams were sensual, while others were simple comforts in casual settings. The last dream had left her flushed and aching in ways she wasn't ready to acknowledge. The bishop had trailed a ruby-colored ribbon over her naked breasts until the flesh tightened and goose bumps covered her soft skin.

There was no shame in the dream. She suffered no modesty or instinct to cover herself. She simply allowed his touch as if it were as natural and entitled to her body as her own hands.

When he smiled at her, she smiled back. The expression was new to her, something she'd never seen the bishop do in person, so she liked glimpsing into that softer side of him when she slept. He was quite beautiful when he wasn't scowling.

A knock on the door had her gasping and jerking her gaze to the lock.

"Larissa?"

"Yes?"

The knob jiggled. "The door's locked."

As it should be. "Did you need something?"

A click and the door opened. Panicked, she scooted under the water as far as her long legs would permit. Her knees sloshed above the surface, and she scooted bubbles along the surface to cover the parts she didn't want him to see.

"Do you mind?"

"Not at all."

The audacity of this man! Her arms crossed over her breasts. "Get out!"

"You need not be shy around me, little mouse."

He poked at her with that silly pet name and she hated it. But he was right. She *was* a mouse, unsure if she'd ever find the courage to face off with such a potent male. Her disappointment in herself was perhaps the hardest truth to swallow.

His gaze traced over the suds floating on the water as if he could will them away for a better view. Her heart raced and she slid lower in the tub, wishing the water was a touch warmer.

"Please go."

With a sigh, he said, "I've decided we'll leave tomorrow. I don't want to rush. We have some issues to iron out."

"Fine."

His hand reached for the knob and he paused. "I could join you—"

"Go!"

He chuckled and left the bathroom.

She covered her face with her hands and groaned, sinking her head beneath the surface.

When the water chilled to an intolerable degree, she sloshed out of the bathtub and dried her body, her gaze searching for her robe and not seeing it. "No…" She bit her lip.

"Is there something you need, Larissa?"

She jumped at the deep timbre of his voice on the other side of the door. "Don't come in!" Her hands jerked the damp towel over her exposed front. *Stupid. Stupid. Stupid.* She couldn't go out there in only a towel. "Would you please be so kind as to bring me my robe?"

Heavy footfalls drifted down the hall and soon returned. She waited for him to knock, but he didn't. Nor did the knob jiggle.

"Bishop?"

"Is it too much to ask that you say my name, Larissa?"

She shut her eyes, pressing her forehead to the cool wood. She would never survive eternity with this man. From the deep timbre of his voice to the stature in which he carried himself, he was too intimidating.

They were a million miles from being equals. Her mind couldn't imagine him ever being anything less than her superior.

Her fingers traced over the painted wood, and she softly whispered, "Eleazar."

She gasped and the door opened, causing her to step back quickly.

He looked at her under thick, sooty lashes. "Your robe." Holding the material open, he gestured for her to step into the garment.

She hesitated and he waited, never rushing her or appearing irritated by her internal struggle. Silus often snapped at her for hesitating when he gave her an order. Though, the bishop hadn't ordered her. He'd merely offered to help her dress.

She swallowed and stepped closer, turning to face the tub and presenting him with her back. The soft fabric covered her shoulders and her arms slid through the sleeves. His hand reached around her hip and tugged the towel free.

The graze of his knuckle along the soft flesh of her breast caused her to suck in a breath, which she held until he tied the robe shut. Pressing his palms to her shoulder, he kissed the side of her head and stepped back, leaving the billowing sleeves draped over her arms.

Dizzy and warm, she stepped away from his hold and faced him, lowering her gaze to the floor. "Th—thank you," she stuttered.

His fingers tipped up her chin. "No walls, Larissa. Now come, let us talk."

As his tall, broad form moved down the hall, she pressed a cool hand to her over-heated cheek. What was this affect he had on her? On wobbly legs, she followed him, all too aware of her nudity under the robe.

Rather than meet him in the den where he sat waiting, she detoured to the kitchen and pulled a mug down from the cabinet. Unable to forget her manners, she asked, "Would you care for a cup of tea, Bish—Eleazar?"

"Yes, tea would suit nicely."

She took her time heating the kettle and steeping the herbs, waiting for her nerves to settle. He no longer frightened her as much, but she still trembled in his presence.

"I'm also nervous around you."

She slammed a door on her thoughts and whirled around, her back to the counter. She hadn't heard him approach. "Please stay out of my head." She was still raw from sharing so much the last time she let him in.

"My apologies. Your thoughts were loud." He took the teacups and carried them into the den.

She followed with the sugar and cream, unsure how he took his.

He was taller than Silus. She preferred his scent to her husband's, as well. His darker skin showed traces of European roots and his thick, glossy hair shined black in some lights.

With shaky hands, she stirred sugar in the steaming mug. Eleazar settled into the chair across from her, setting his tea on the table to cool. He studied her and she sensed some sort of expectation that made her fidget.

"When we return to the farm, I will have

the paperwork drawn up to annul your marriage."

Her relief was so sudden, it felt as if a chair had been pulled out from under her. She sagged back in her seat and let out a stunned breath.

"Careful." He leaned forward, collecting her hot tea and wisely set it on the table. He casually occupied the space beside her. "Does that please you?"

She knew he was powerful, but to see him use his authority so unceremoniously emphasized just how extensive his influence could be. He showed no worry of complications or obstacles, only absolute certainty that he would get exactly what he wanted.

"Yes, but Silus will object."

"That's irrelevant and nothing you need to worry about."

She looked down and twisted the belt of her robe.

"He will never harm you again, Larissa. If you wish it, I'll forbid him to speak to you."

A humorless laugh filled her chest. "He'll be outraged."

"No doubt." His hand closed over hers to still her fidgeting. "Tell me something. Why did you never assert yourself more around him?"

"I beg your pardon?"

"You're no weakling. I've been on the receiving end of your power enough to know that you can protect yourself. I've read the records of each member in The Order. I know which immortals possess notable disciplines and which do not. I can't recall Silus having any special gifts. But you do."

She frowned at him. "I have no power over Silus."

"Of course, you do. I'm ten times your age and you crippled me the other day. Silus is a weakling."

She shook her head. "My gifts have always been considered basic disciplines." Compulsion, speed, agility, rapid healing. "What I did to you was a fluke. I think it came from you and I just… deflected it."

He frowned, his dark eyes moving as if he were thinking through a complicated arithmetic formula. "Try to push into my mind now."

"I can't."

"Try."

She met his stare and pushed but found no opening in his mind. "It's not possible."

He tilted his head. "I'm going to push into your mind now, but I want you to keep me out."

She adjusted herself in her seat and closed her eyes. At the first flicker of another presence in her mind, she threw up a wall.

The bishop hissed and her eyes opened. He rubbed his temple. "You're strong, Larissa."

"I don't know how I'm doing that."

"The harder I pushed, the harder you pushed back. No one in The Order can keep me out if I want into their minds." He grinned. "But you can." His smile quickly faded and he mumbled, "I don't know if that's actually a good thing."

"That can't be right. Even my little sister breaks into my thoughts at times."

"Maybe you're not as guarded around her."

Worried that might upset him, she looked down at her lap and fidgeted with the long tie of her robe again. When he didn't say anything for several minutes, she looked up and caught him watching her with a peculiar expression.

He cleared his throat and reached for his tea. "I need to know if you plan on fighting me about our situation."

"Fighting you?"

"Yes. You've had time to think about the situation, and I want to know where we stand."

It was all she could think about, but their circumstances seemed too surreal. "It's a lot to process."

"Are you accepting the calling?"

Was there another option? "What choice do I have?"

"There's always a choice. But if things proceed accordingly, we can marry as soon as the bonding is complete."

She drew back. "I…"

"We will have an eternity to grow better acquainted. It would be wise to bond as soon as possible, so the danger is behind us. We may not be able to hold off until the annulment is complete. Knowing Silus, he will try to protest the formalities."

"But you're so confident."

"Your marriage to Silus is finished. His objections can only delay the inevitable. You belong to me, Larissa."

His claim should have worried her, but it made her feel safe and cherished. But she did worry she was merely tying her life to another overbearing male. She stood and paced, putting some distance between them.

"Is it the thought of seeing Silus that has you upset? I will deal with him."

"No. Well, yes, but I trust that you will protect me." She worried her lip. "Everything's just moving faster than I expected." When she faced him, he was grinning. "Why are you looking at me like that?"

"You said you trust that I'll protect you. This pleases me."

Was it foolish of her to put trust in him so soon? It hadn't been a conscious decision, just a natural one.

She sat back down on the sofa, keeping a few feet from him. "I'm nervous about the bonding."

"Then you've accepted it?"

She wasn't going to risk losing her mind like her uncle. "We must, otherwise we put the entire species at risk of exposure."

His mouth formed a thin line. "You're accepting your fate purely due to a sense of duty?"

What was one more arranged marriage? "Yes."

He stood and carried his mug to the kitchen. She winced as he deposited it in the sink with a clatter. Bracing his hands on the lip of the sink, his shoulders bunched with tension.

She nervously followed but kept her distance. "Bishop?"

"Eleazar!"

She flinched at the sharpness in his tone and took a step back.

He pivoted and let out a harsh exhalation. "I grow tired of asking you to use my name."

"I'm sorry. Eleazar." She wrung her hands. "I'll do better."

He crossed the floor and snatched her hands, pulling them apart. "Make a fist."

"What?"

"Make a fist. Do it."

Her hands balled, and she looked up at him nervously.

"Now, put your hands at your side."

She lowered her arms, disliking how exposed the position made her. She moved to cross her arms and he pushed her hands down.

"Keep them there."

"Why?"

"Because fidgeting won't protect you. It makes you look weak, and you're not weak."

"I don't understand why you're upset."

The muscles in his jaw ticked and he looked as if he were about to say something, but instead, he turned away. "Do whatever you want with your hands."

She blinked in confusion. When her fingers laced together, she forced her hands to her side and stood straight. She didn't want to appear weak, not to him or anyone else. "It's okay."

He glanced over his shoulder.

She gave a stiff nod. "You're right. I'm too old to fidget. I'll work on it."

Something shifted in his gaze as he fully faced her.

Keeping his gaze locked with hers, he closed the distance. "Where did that little mouse go?" he whispered, lifting her hair and shifting it behind her shoulders. "Do you have any idea how beautiful you are when you wear your confidence?"

A smile trembled to her lips. "Thank you."

His gaze dipped to the lapels of her robe and his hands glided down her arms. "I ache for a time when I can touch you at will."

Her breath caught and heat gathered low in her belly, nothing like the cold chill she usually suffered at the thought of intimacy. Then, wanting to please him with another show of confidence, she reached for the robe belt and loosened the knot.

The front fell open, exposing a strip of flesh and the V of her sex. His gaze rushed to hers, questioning.

"What are you doing?"

Her chin trembled, but she lifted it anyway. "P—playing with courage. Careful. I'm delicate."

He stepped closer, his body brushing the front of hers as he swept a hand under the back of her hair and tilted her head up to face him. "You're irresistible like this."

His mouth dropped to hers, soft and warm, and she lifted onto her toes. The first slide of his hot tongue over hers pulled a moan from her throat. He deepened the kiss, his hand sliding through her hair and his mouth devouring every secret it held.

She drew back, her fingers rushing to her lips and her thighs pressing tight to relieve the building pressure he created with merely a kiss.

"Did I startle you?"

Heat gathered low in her belly and her breasts ached with need—all from a kiss. "No one's ever kissed me like that."

"That was nothing."

She considered what making love to him would be like. Judging by the way he kissed, he was a very sensual male. Curious visions flitted through her mind, but she wanted the truth. She wanted to know what he was really like and if there could be that much of a difference between immortal men.

She couldn't say the suggestion, so she opened her mind. The moment he overheard her thoughts, his gaze jerked to hers.

"You're projecting…" He frowned in question and her face heated. Her gaze jerked to the floor, and he lifted her chin. "Talk to me, little mouse. Tell me what you want."

Her heart pounded wildly in her chest. She didn't know how to say such things. "Please don't make me say it."

"Try."

"I…" Her words clogged in her throat. "I think we should complete the bond."

His mouth closed over hers, and he lifted her off the floor, guiding her legs around his hips. She tensed, but then his lips found a sensitive spot on her neck and her body relaxed. She laughed as he teased the delicate column of her throat with his nose, the gesture soft and playful and completely unexpected.

He carried her to the bedroom but left her

adrift when he deposited her on the bed. Her instincts told her to reach for him, but her body stayed stubbornly still.

Her throat tightened when he removed his shirt. She only wore a robe and wasn't ready to let it go. The mattress dipped under his weight as he climbed beside her, still dressed from the waist down. Leaning over her body, his lips found hers.

When he reached for her breast, she stiffened and he drew back. "I'll be gentle, Larissa. I won't rush you, and I'll make sure you enjoy it." He caressed her cheek and her body trembled. "Relax, sweet Larissa. I'll never hurt you."

The robe fell open, and his mouth lowered to her breast.

CHAPTER 21

The trace of Eleazar's soft lips across the sensitive tips of her breasts un-raveled something deep inside of her. He guided her hand to his hair, silently showing her that he craved her touch.

She had never touched a male while being touched herself. It was extremely intimate and liberating at the same time. Her fingers forked through his hair, and he groaned against her damp skin, pulling hard at the turgid tip of her nipple. Her lips parted on a sigh, and she arched into him, now holding him close as he suckled her flesh.

The room was cold, yet her body was burning up. Long fingers stroked over her hips, awakening her skin and putting her at ease. Her knees fell open when he pressed kisses up her throat. She arched into his exploring touch, shutting her eyes as he kissed his way to her pulse.

Everywhere he pressed those devilish lips, she heated and burned for more. Was it him or the fact that he was her called mate?

He nuzzled her hair away from her neck, and her belly pulled tight when he nibbled her ear. Chills raced down her spine as a fire burned inside of her. He tugged the lobe between his teeth and she gasped.

Exploring fingers combed through the fine hair covering her sex, teasing with gentle, unhurried strokes. His touch traveled, caressing her thighs and trailing back to her breasts.

His mouth returned to hers, kissing softly, unraveling the tension in her bones. With each stroke of his tongue on hers, the fire in her belly grew hotter.

The scent of his arousal filled the room. She was torn, wanting to kiss him back but feared he might judge her later and accuse her of having loose morals.

"You're safe with me," he whispered, and she wondered if she had accidentally projected her fears. He had her body so aroused she found it difficult to block her thoughts.

He tempted her with his tongue, dragging it up her throat and across her lips. Overwhelmed by so many arousing sensations, she whispered his name in a plea, "Eleazar…"

He growled and a low purr rumbled from his throat. "Yes, little mouse?"

"I don't know how you're doing this…"

A deep chuckle met her ear as he nibbled the sensitive flesh. "I can scent your arousal, Larissa. Your desire's beating at me."

A blush burned down to her chest. There was no hiding anything from him. They hadn't even started the bond, and this had somehow become one of the most intimate encounters of her life.

He looked into her eyes, breathing in their combined scents. "You don't have to be shy with me. Show me your lioness side. Kiss me back. Take from me what you want."

When he kissed her, she shyly teased her tongue along his. He groaned, and the weight of his arousal pressed into her. Heat spread between her thighs and she pressed her legs together. Self-conscious of her body's response, she tried to shift away from him.

"Larissa."

Screwing her eyes shut, she shook her head. It was too much. She couldn't bear such vulnerability in a male's presence.

"Larissa, look at me."

Deliberately disobeying him, she curled to her side. *I'm sorry...*

His body followed hers, stretching out behind her and pulling her back to his chest. He pressed a kiss to her shoulder and wrapped his arms around her ribs.

"Have I frightened you, little mouse?"

It wasn't him that frightened her. It was her body's reaction to him. Her breasts were full and she ached at the core. Needy. Raw. She wasn't familiar with such things and felt self-conscious of her responses.

"It's not you. It's me. I don't know how to do this."

His palm flattened over her stomach and slid lower. She sucked in a breath as his fingers teased the hair there. Her thighs pressed tight.

"Let me in."

Her insides pulled, and she forced her legs to unclench. He gently dragged a hand down her thigh and parted her knees.

"Is this what has you worried?" Long fingers traced the seam of her sex and she shut her eyes, certain he realized how wet she was. "Your body's reaction is natural, Larissa." He pressed his hardness into her. "Your preparing for your mate. Feel what you've done to me, how I prepare for you?"

He dipped a finger between her folds, pressing into her channel and her lips parted with a gasp.

"Feel how my fingers slide into you?" He teased her body open until it unfurled like the petals of a flower. "That's exactly how it should be."

But her body had never had such a response to Silus.

Warm lips trailed along her shoulder as the robe peeled away. Cool air teased her breasts as his fingers continued to toy with her. He rolled her to her back as he softly stroked her sex.

His arms bulged with swells of muscle under smooth, tanned skin with a dusting of dark hair. The same dark hair formed a line down the center of his abdomen. Unlike her soft belly, his was rigid with muscle.

He drew her arms away from her chest. "Don't hide from me, Larissa." With his fingers buried deep in her sex, he leaned over and kissed the tips of her breasts.

The fire that had burned low in her belly blazed to life. His lips burned a trail of soft caresses down her front, placing a kiss on the arch of each hip. Dragging his tongue lower, her breath hitched and her eyes widened.

The closer his mouth moved, the more uncontrollably her body trembled. She had never been so exposed in all of her life. Her heart raced as his fingers spread her nectar. Heat gathered and tugged within her belly as he teased her sensitive flesh as if he were tickling some unnamable part of her. She wanted to press against the pleasure, but it remained too elusive, solely under his control, a phantom sensation she could not catch.

Still spreading kisses along her soft stomach, she shut her eyes and luxuriated in the featherlight trace of his lips, breath, and hair teasing over her skin. Lower and lower, his mouth tormented her until his lips reached her folds.

Her spine arched and she cried out as he kissed her sex. Certain such an act was wrong, she twisted and pulled her body away from him. But he was fast and he caught her legs, wrapping a muscled arm around her thighs and holding her beneath him.

"Where are you rushing off to, little mouse?"

Her face burned as he looked up at her, eyes dilated and pupils dark, traces of her arousal glistening on his delectable lips. As if reading her thoughts, he held her stare and dragged his tongue over the plump pillow of his lower lip, sucking any trace of her flavor into his sinful mouth and grinning like a cat in the cream.

Her lips parted in curious awe.

"Every inch of you, Larissa, I plan to know every single inch. We will hide no secrets from each other. Not even here." With a firm but gentle hand, he parted her legs again. "I want you to enjoy my touch. Let yourself have this."

Jagged breath rushed in and out of her lungs as she watched him lower his mouth to her sex. One soft lick across her hungry flesh and her body collapsed into the pillows, her voice crying out in pleasure.

He teased and kissed, weaving sensations until she could hardly breathe. His soft lips woke hidden nerves as his fingers tunneled deeper, exploring her secrets but never causing her pain. Every touch, a purposeful caress, as he focused on one goal—bringing her pleasure.

His attention tightened until only she existed in his world and as all obstacles faded away, she had nowhere left to hide. Exposed, discovered, and cornered, he commanded her body to do things even she lacked the power to perform.

The physical sensations had built like a wave bound to crest, but the emotional tsunami growing inside of her shook her most. The intimacy of his touch, the completeness of his knowledge he would now have of her body, she no longer belonged to only herself.

Tears gathered in her eyes as he drove her soul into sweet ecstasy. Her limbs trembled uncontrollably and as her voice cried out, the waves crashed over her, washing away all the horror that had existed before.

Stars burst behind her eyes as heat and passion collided into a new heaven. As the tremors subsided and she fluttered back to Earth, certain her soul was forever changed, and she would never be the same. Whether there would be joy or pain, the old her was gone, and for that, she started to cry.

Eleazar kissed her and pulled her into his

arms. He rocked her as she wept, consoling her for things she couldn't understand but also telling her how beautiful she was. He held her tightly to his chest and smoothed her hair away from her face, placing gentle kisses upon her temple.

"Let it out, my lovely Larissa. You no longer need to hold it inside. I'll carry it for you. Let it out."

His caring words and gestures only made her cry more. She was not programmed for such kindness.

"I don't know why I'm crying," she confessed, curling deeper into the shelter of his chest.

"The reasons don't matter, sweet Larissa. Accept it. I'm a part of you. Hide nothing and embrace all that we are—perfect, exactly as God made us."

The weight of his words and affection crushed her in ways that left her open and afraid but also curious and tender. Should she trust his intentions, she would leave herself completely at his mercy. He would have the power to destroy her more viciously than any soul on this Earth.

But, oh, she wanted to believe he was sincere. She wanted to find the good in this world and leave all the ugly behind.

"Please don't hurt me, Eleazar," she begged softly, pressing her lips to his chest.

His heart stilled for a moment, and his hand gently cupped the back of her head. He pressed a kiss to her hair. "Never."

CHAPTER 22

He loved her. The moment she pressed that tiny kiss onto his heart, he felt himself irrevocably fall. Perhaps it was her vulnerability or the trace of her uncertain thoughts teasing his mind. But most likely it had been her sincerity. Larissa did not trust easily, so every drop she gave carried the weight of an ocean.

Her acceptance quenched his thirsty soul and he had never felt more alive. Nothing, in half a millennium, had soothed him the way that little kiss of trust had.

Love and affection crawled through him like a wave of heat, thawing the ice that surrounded his cold, hardened heart for the last five hundred years. He loved her courage. He loved her softness. He loved her vulnerability. He loved her innocence. He loved her stubborn pride. He loved everything about her. He only hoped that he could somehow earn her love in return. He silently vowed to always do right by her and protect her so she never lost the innocence she so humbly shared with him.

Holding her close, he patiently waited for her sobs to subside. The fact that she even trusted him to hold her so intimately as she lay naked in his arms, so emotionally exposed, seemed the highest honor. He was in no rush to let her go.

He suspected she was not distraught, but rather overwhelmed after falling to pieces in his arms. His body suspended in a place of agonizing need and emotional bliss. He wanted to claim her completely, make her irrevocably his, yet he needed to pace himself. She was incredibly vulnerable at the moment and he needed to bring her back to Earth slowly.

When she shivered in his arms, Eleazar reached for the sheet at the foot of the bed and carefully drew it over them. He gently sheltered her in warmth and pulled her close.

She looked up at him with diamond eyes shining in the darkness like twin silver moons. He had not been prepared to experience the mutual pleasure mates shared. Though he'd heard of this rare gift between mated souls, his mind could not fathom what the pleasure would actually feel like. Every caress, every flick of his tongue, touched his body as if happening to him. The more effort he placed into her pleasure, the more pleasure he felt himself. It was as if she somehow reflected everything he gave her right back to him.

Without coaxing, she twisted in his arms and faced him, appearing shy but curious. He gently tucked a strand of hair behind her ear and kissed her temple. Her lips trembled but slowly formed a tentative smile.

Gently placing her hand over his heart, her silent sentiment expressed more than any words could have described. "I expected every part of you to be hard as stone," she whispered. "Yet, you have tender spots, too."

His life had become so guarded and reserved, sharing those softer sides with her left him raw and shaken.

Stunned by her boldness, his breath held as she leaned closer and kissed his chest. He groaned at the sight of her little, pink tongue skimming over his flesh, and she smiled.

Looking back into his eyes, as if seeing if what she was doing was all right, she slowly moved over him and kissed a trail to his shoulder.

This eager and affectionate side of her was unexpected. She scattered kisses up his chest and to his throat.

Only a breadth away from his mouth, her lips curved into a smile against his skin and she whispered, "I've decided I enjoy kisses."

He caught her face in his hands and kissed her pouty lips with unmistakable territorial entitlement. "*My* kisses."

He plunged his tongue deep, claiming her lips and causing her to moan with pleasure.

"Say your mouth is mine, Larissa. Tell me no one else will ever touch your beautiful mouth, taste your sweet tongue, or know the softness of your lips." He bit at the plump pillow of her lower lip and possessively growled, "*Mine.*"

A delicate blush formed on her cheeks and she whispered, "Yours."

He took her mouth the only way a mate should—completely, greedily, and fervently. To his delight, she kissed him back with hunger and undisguisable need. When they pulled apart, her lips were swollen and pink.

Her fingertips slipped beneath the waistband of his pants and they both stilled, waiting to see how she would get herself out of such a predicament. Her spiking apprehension bit into him and she retracted her fingers, safely caressing his stomach once more. They both relaxed. For a female who was more modest than a virgin bride only hours ago, Larissa was proving to be an incredibly apt learner where sensuality was concerned.

His cock was incredibly hard, so hard he feared even the slightest contact with her flesh would burn right through him. Somewhere in the midst of touching him, she had draped her thigh over his. The tempting scent of her arousal hit him like a locomotive.

He gripped her wrist, stilling her exploratory touch, and she froze. "Be very sure, Larissa, because once we do this, there will be no undoing it."

His grip loosened and she hesitated only a moment. "I'm ready."

A predatory growl ripped from his throat and he tumbled her to her back, pressing the weight of his body over hers and marking her with his scent. Her eyes widened at the sight of his hard arousal. He guided her hand to his aching flesh, closing her fingers tightly around him, and showing her how he liked to be stroked.

She watched him through cat-eyes and smiled slowly, displaying sharp, little fangs as her confidence bloomed and she tugged his aching flesh between them. His vision transformed as his eyes fully dilated. His fangs extended and they purred.

He needed to get inside of her. Taking her hands in his, he forced them over her head and dragged his rock-hard cock over the apex of her thighs. She arched into him, her body suddenly electric and her desire sparking wildly with his.

His back slammed into the cold floor, and he blinked away his shock. She grinned and straddled him, her claws digging into his chest as she took control. His little mouse had vanished and, in her place, preened a proud and striking lioness.

She kissed him hungrily, taking and taunting him with her smart tongue as she rode her body over his thighs and torso, marking him with her scent as thoroughly as he had marked her.

When she tried to bite him, his fist locked in her hair, angling her mouth toward his, and he took over the kiss. Together, they were like a tornado crashing into a hurricane. Never had he expected such chemistry, such alive sensuality from his mate.

Liberated, and ready to embrace her baser desires, their animal instincts took over. He smiled and she nipped his lip, licking away a pearl of blood. He snapped at her teasing tongue. She pulled back and threw him a tempting glance, as if to say he was now the mouse of this game.

He sprang from the ground, driving her into the wall. Objects fell to the floor and shattered. She bit at his shoulder, lifting her body against his, and ground her wet sex across his flat stomach. He could take no more.

Eleazar kicked away the last of his clinging clothing and nudged her opening with his hard, weeping cock. She stilled.

Staring at him with those sharp, diamond eyes, her purr hummed louder. The significance of the moment nearly buckled his knees. This was his eternity. She was the other half of his soul.

He did not want to be so lost in a fever of passion that they missed the importance of their mating. He gentled her with a loving stroke of his finger and she softened in his arms, leaning into the caress.

Carrying her to the bed, he gently laid her in the center. Her arms extended over her head where her ebony hair spiraled across the crisp, white sheets resembling a pagan sacrifice. *His* pagan.

She was light and darkness, heaven and earth. Never before had he so completely understood the unfathomable duality of a female as he did in that moment, staring into her infinite soul and glimpsing the eternity of their future.

Her breasts heaved with anticipation as she looked up at him, body open to him, mind fully welcoming him. There had never been a more beautiful sight.

He pressed close, aligning their bodies and dragged his mouth to her ear, whispering a promise time or distance could not break, "You're mine, Larissa. For *eawichkeit,* all of eternity, I'll never let you go."

He drove his cock deep into her heat, possessing her completely. Her claws scraped over his back and they arched together.

The ferocity in which they welcomed each other's touch eddied into an explosive mating of souls. Two immortal souls, called together to form a nuclear bond as the universe had intended.

They battled to possess one another. Tumbled across the bed, falling into the floor and crashing into the walls. Glimpses of their lust sprayed like colorful rain across his mind and fantasies of their future took shape.

His seed rose within him, and his body swelled. He wanted to fill her womb and watch her belly grow thick and full with his child. The idea had his hips pounding harder against her flesh.

With a feral growl, he withdrew from her sex and flipped her to her belly. Hoisting her hips, he took her from behind.

"Mine!" he growled, plunging into her.

He rose behind her and pulled her to him. Her back pressed firmly against his front from nape to thigh. Biting into his wrist, he opened his vein and held his offering to her lips. *"Eawichkeit,* Larissa."

She licked and growled, *"Eawichkeit,* Eleazar." Her teeth bit into him as she sealed her mouth over his vein and pulled.

He plunged his fangs into her neck and claimed her. Thick, warm, life-giving blood transferred from one body to the other. Her body constricted around his as they rocked, coming together as one.

Her gripping sex milked his seed, pulling every bit of his essence into her, all of which he was honored to provide. His spine arched and his head fell back. His body shuddered in completion as her body fluttered in his grip. Her mouth still feeding from his vein as they finished together and he hissed in euphoric bliss.

She was fire in his arms. Heat and lust. Desire and satisfaction.

They fell to the bed, eyes closed, fangs still extended, panting as one. When he finally looked at her again, he did not see the timid mouse he'd come to recognize, but a powerful, confident mate watching him through diamond cat-eyes. He kissed her softly and she nestled into him, her acceptance complete and his satisfaction whole.

His powerful lioness.

CHAPTER 23

It stared at Dane, fangs dripping, shoulders heaving, claws digging into his mom's gray, lifeless flesh. He couldn't look away from her eyes. Eyes that had looked at him every day since he was born, only now they were empty, devoid of any life, as if he were staring into two dark wells.

A sharp growl jerked his gaze away from his mother's dead face, and Dane's horrified stare locked with something that was not human.

Yellow orbs, flecked with crimson where there should have been white, glared at him, glowing in the darkness. Reaching for Cybil, his hand grabbed only air.

Whirling in search of his sister, he screamed for her, "Cybil!"

The creature purred and Dane spun. It no longer held his mother's lifeless body as it now cradled Cybil in its clawed hands.

"No!"

Wakened by his own scream, Dane bolted upright in bed. The familiar scent of his grandmother's home, a mix of sweet powder and dried paint, steadied his senses as his heart hammered.

He rubbed his eyes, taking in the boxes crowding the bedroom that was now his. Boxes. Boxes of baseball cards, boxes of old clothes, and video games. Boxes of his mother's knickknacks. Boxes of crap he no longer cared about.

Pushing off the heavy blankets, still wearing his jeans, he went to check on his sister.

"Cybil," he quietly called when he found her bed empty. He knew better than to expect an answer.

Gazing out the window, a drafty chill pressing through the glass, he searched the approaching dawn for a sense of home but found none. The least he could do was find his sister.

Slipping his socked feet into his weather-beaten boots, he crept through the house, navigating the stacks of boxes and the rows of painted canvases wrapped along the walls. The tinkling of a paintbrush slushing in water told him his grandmother was already awake and in her studio.

Thirsty and still shaken from his nightmare, he went to the kitchen and grabbed a Gatorade from the fridge, chugging it down in a few gulps. His gaze scanned the shadows for Cybil.

Tossing the bottle in the recycling, he snatched his jacket from the hook on the wall. No one slept anymore. He understood. He also found himself fighting exhaustion for fear of the reoccurring nightmares that haunted him, but he couldn't stay awake the way Cybil and Gran could. They were masters of insomnia.

The screen door opened with a whine, its tight springs snapping shut behind him. The December wind cut through his clothes and he shivered, irritated that his sister had once again wandered off.

"Cybil?"

Moving past the plethora of stacked clay pots cluttering the wood-planked porch, he leaned over the spindled railing and searched for her or the dog.

Releasing a frustrated sigh, he cupped his hands around his mouth and yelled, *"Cybil!"*

Colby's bark echoed in the distance, and he headed in that direction, shoving his fists into the pockets of his jeans and bunching his shoulders against the cold.

"Cyb-illlll! Colllll-by!"

The dog barked again, and he spotted its mangy face and mismatched brindle hide racing over the hill at the edge of his grandmother's property. His sister's silhouette sat on the knoll, unmoving and staring toward the bordering woods.

She knew better than to go this far out alone.

He jogged up the hill, starting in on the same old lecture. "Cybil, how many times do I have to tell you? If you want to wander the property, get me, and I'll go with you."

She didn't move or acknowledge his presence, despite Dane's certainty that she heard him.

He caught his breath and petted the ugly, fur-covered face nudging his hip. Still in her pajamas, Cybil sat with her knees drawn up to her chest, her bare ankles shoved into sneakers caked with mud.

She'd gone too close to the woods again. "What did I tell you about the woods?"

Her arms wrapped tightly around her shins. Sounds from the Pennsylvania Turnpike whispered in the distance.

He sat beside her and scooted close, trying to steal some of her body warmth. She never took her eyes off the trees.

"You can't keep doing this, Cybil."

A strand of her long, blonde hair blew into his face and he batted it away. Her hair still held that baby-soft quality the girls his age no longer had.

"You can't keep running off like this."

He didn't expect her to answer. It had been so long since she said anything or even let a giggle slip. Dane was beginning to forget what her voice sounded like. Sometimes, she would sneeze or cough and he would try to pick up parts of her voice in that bodily function, but it was no replacement for her conversation or laughter.

A brief impression of their dog filled his mind and he scowled at her. "Colby is not the same as having a person with you."

The vision shifted from Colby's playful, panting face to a fierce protector, baring teeth and growling viciously in a way the dog never behaved. "No, Cybil. You need a grown-up out here with you or at least me."

He winced. The memory hit like a bullet through his heart, but the recollection wasn't his own.

He saw himself standing in the woods from his sister's perspective, the creature holding his mother's lifeless body in its claws. He stood in the memory, exactly as he had in reality, useless and terrified.

"Damnit, Cybil!" He shot to his feet and glared at her. "What could I have done? Stop reliving it! It's over. She's gone!"

He marched off and Colby barked. Cybil didn't follow.

His sister didn't project her memories for malicious reasons. She couldn't filter her thoughts, and he had no idea how to block the ones he didn't want to see. She was right anyway. When they had been in real danger, he proved himself to be worthless.

He had always been intuitive, but when Cybil was born, he began to understand the extent of his curse. By second grade, he had learned tricks to control it better. Not only could he see his classmates' test answers and daydreams, but he also could see the things they didn't like about him. His mind over-

flowed with unwanted opinions and disturbing secrets.

For him, there was no magic in Santa
Clause or surprises at birthdays. He overheard too much and learned things he wished
he never knew. Children were much more
perceptive than adults were comfortable admitting, and there was a world of untold secrets flitting through their heads.

Thankfully, he could only see into
younger, open minds like the minds of his
peers. He didn't know if it was an age
thing or a purity-of-thought thing. But the
more innocent a child was, the brighter
their thoughts appeared. Age, or perhaps
the bitterness of time, mutated the human
mind into an opaque shadow too murky to
read.

With the recent darkness of his sister's
thoughts, he worried he might lose this fragile
thread they still shared. But he had no way of
cheering her up, no way of absorbing her
grief on top of his own.

If their bond severed, it would be another
loss, another thing to grieve. He shivered at
the thought, hoping that, one day soon, her
silence would end.

He pushed the vision of him standing uselessly before his mother away and nudged Cybil. "Come on, it's freezing."

He saw the distant trees in her mind. First, the vision was of the woods on the opposite side of the highway, then it moved closer. Trees, branches, pine needles, and leaves, then bark. Her vision zoomed in on a single tree, and that was when he caught it. A clawed hand wrapped loosely around the bark of the trunk.

He spun and looked to the woods across the highway. His panicked gaze searching the exact place his sister just showed him, but all the trees looked the same.

His eyes scanned for any movement, but they were standing too far away. He searched for details, picking through her thoughts and staring into the distance.

Yellow leaves popped boldly against the faded brown decay and he saw the exact place the hand had been.

A chill skittered up his spine. "Come on." He grabbed her hand only to have her yank her arm free.

She glared at the tree line. Dane stared too—anxious and unsure what might be watching them.

"Do you see someone out there now?"

She opened her mind and he saw the memory. Bloodied, tattered clothing and clawed hands like the creature that killed their mom, but this one was different. He was taller with olive skin. There was something civilized about him, despite the damage to his clothing, but also something very dangerous.

Light brown hair and blue eyes. Broad shoulders bunched with muscle that didn't sway but moved with the man's confident gate. He was young and strong and, according to her memory, he saw her. Dane didn't like the determined glint in the man's eye and worried how and when it worked its way into one of his sister's memories.

"Cybil, get up," he growled. "We're getting out of here." He reached for her again and she swatted at him, pointing to the trees.

Dane's jaw fell open as the man from her vision stood in the open land before them, where there had been nothing seconds earlier.

Colby barked, and wind blew across the hill as the man strutted in their direction with determined strides. Dane's heart jolted and he glanced back at the house, noting how far they had to run.

He grabbed his sister's pajama shirt and yanked her to her feet. "Now! Let's go—"

She fought him, shoving his grip away and looking back to the woods.

"Cybil, no!" Panicked, he glared at the approaching man. His clothing wasn't tattered as it had been in her mind. And his skin was clean, his hair combed. But he still didn't belong there.

"You're trespassing on private property!" Dane yelled.

The man continued toward them, his posture casual and his steps unhurried. He even smiled, his expression friendly and non-threatening, but that meant nothing to Dane.

"God damnit, Cybil, let's go! Right now!" Dane hissed through gritted teeth.

She stretched to see around his body, side-stepping him to get to the man.

"Hello there," the man greeted, stopping only a few yards from them.

Dane slowly pivoted, standing protectively in front of his very stupid sister. "Are you deaf? I said this is private property," Dane puffed out his chest.

The man was ripped. If this guy caused any trouble, there was nothing Dane could do to stop him.

He tilted his head to the side and looked at Cybil. "What's your name, little one?"

Dane stepped forward and scowled, "Don't fucking talk to her!"

Another unwanted grin. "I'm looking for Forsythia Way."

That was the road his grandmother lived on, but there was no way Dane was helping this asshole.

A vision from his sister's mind filled his: his grandmother's house, the road, and the street sign on the corner that read Forsythia Way. He glared at his sister, silently ordering her not to point a finger or make a sound.

Then something intruded on the thought—an unwanted presence. Dane flinched, shaking his head.

"Good. I'm in the right place. I thought so." The man smiled as he somehow plucked the details right from his sister's mind.

"What the hell?" He tried to mentally shove the man out of her head but lacked the skill.

"You must be Cybil." The trespasser squatted low to the ground and plucked a blade of grass free, bringing it to his nose and breathing it in as if cataloging the scent. "I'm Cain." His gaze lifted. "And you're Dane."

"How do you know our names?"

"I'm a friend of your grandmother's."

It was a lie. Using all his energy, he shoved hard at the man's mind and caught a glimpse of their family on television.

Dane's narrowed eyes followed him accusingly. "You're a reporter."

"Hardly. I hate those vultures." The man—Cain—stood and calmly brushed off his pant legs. "I'm here to speak with your grandmother. Is she home?"

"No," Dane lied.

His sister showed a vision of their grandmother resting on the couch in her studio, and the man saw it. "Cybil!" What the hell was wrong with her?

"Thank you, sweetheart." He gestured to Cybil, "Let's go say hello."

His sister stood as if to go with the stranger.

"Cybil, don't."

She ignored him and walked beside Cain in the direction of the house. Even the damn dog pranced around the guy, acting like man's best friend to an absolute stranger and possible killer. They walked side-by-side, leaving Dane gaping on the hill, as Colby trotted after the man.

Dane searched his pockets for his phone, furious when it wasn't there, and raced after them.

"It looks like it's going to be a beautiful day," the man said, softly whistling as he strolled toward the house.

"She doesn't talk," Dane snapped, snatching his sister's hand and hauling her back a few steps. "That man is a stranger!"

The man paused and tilted his head, studying Cybil for a moment. "I see."

The screams from her memory shouted into Dane's mind. It was the last time he'd heard her voice and he couldn't stand the terror of her cries.

He jerked out of her mind, slamming a lid hard over the unwanted memories. Cybil hadn't projected that one. Neither had Dane.

The strange man continued to study her. More memories spun in a kaleidoscope view of the past few weeks until Dane sucked in a harsh breath, realizing it was the stranger fishing through his sister's thoughts.

"Hey!" He snapped, and the visions faded away.

He had never met someone with a curse like his. But this man didn't seem to view it as a curse. He appeared very competent with the skill, having much more control over it than Dane. It was almost as if this guy saw it as a gift rather than a curse. Dane had never become comfortable about possessing something that ultimately made him weird and different.

Tension marked the man's brow but quickly smoothed, replaced with an easygoing expression when he smiled at Cybil. "Do you like rainbows?"

She nodded.

"Look, just over the trees." The man pointed. In the distance arced one of the most radiant rainbows Dane had ever seen. "Sometimes, after something very bad happens, something good follows."

The breeze shifted and wind chimes tinkled in the distance. Shadows moved across the ground as clouds rolled overhead. The murky gray sky brightened to a vibrant blue, and the sun suddenly blazed above.

Cybil smiled at the man as if he was somehow due credit, and Dane scowled. He'd woken from a nightmare only to land in some twisted dream. As if someone could control the weather…

He raced after them, planning to call the police as soon as he found his phone.

CHAPTER 24

$\mathcal{A}$bilene hefted the heavy copper pot to the cellar door. The familiar scent of cool, musty earth greeting her as she carefully navigated the stairs. A strip of sunlight divided the room, chasing away shadows where unsettled dust motes danced in the air.

Opening the grate, she lit the kindling and poured soap into the cast iron tub. As bubbles formed and the water heated, she swept the cement floor and then sorted the linens.

The day was surprisingly sunny, but there was still a bite in the air. It had been an unpredictable autumn and she expected an even more unpredictable winter. They had already had a dusting of snow, and not a day later, the children were running through the fields in short sleeves and bare feet. What was becoming of the world?

The room warmed as the fire burned. Steam filled the air, laced with the fresh scent of soap. Unlatching the shutters to let more light in, she stilled when a low growl rumbled from the dim corner.

The hair at the nape of her neck rose against her bonnet. She was not alone.

Stretching her senses, she spotted the glimmer of a cobweb in the corner and the soft scurry of a mouse racing by. "Who's there?" Eyes, at a male's height, flashed from the darkness. "Jonas?"

Another growl exploded into a roaring hiss, and she screamed. Her husband charged from the shadows, fangs bared and claws drawn. He tackled her to the ground, knocking the wind from her lungs and cutting off her shrieks.

Rabid, he snarled in her face and she shoved at him, unable to escape his weight. With a sharp swipe of his talons, he clawed open her dress, cutting her flesh.

"Jonas! Please! It's me!"

Hairpins stabbed into her scalp as she fought him, but he was possessed and lost beyond reason. His claws cut into her flesh as he wrenched her skirts up to her knees. She kicked and screamed, covering her face from the horrific way he snarled at her.

"Jonas, don't! Please! You're hurting me!"

Her bare legs twisted beneath him, her skin burning with every scratch. He shoved and shook her, slamming her back into the cold ground, forcing her to be silent.

She cried, unsure what to do. The sharp bite of his claws through her dress triggered her feral instincts, unleashing a growl, she lashed out with all of her strength. She bared her fangs and snapped her jaw, fierce and formidable. Swiping her claws across his face, she kicked him off and bolted to her feet.

He snarled at her, rivulets of red streaming from his eyes and the claw marks on his face. A feral growl ripped from his throat and he launched into the air.

He came down on her smaller body with predatory speed, biting cruelly into her neck. Her scream faded to a gurgle as he dragged her to the cold floor, grinding his body over hers, his eyes delirious with bloodlust, his emotions unrecognizable to her.

He had always been stronger but never used his strength in a way that made her weak. Until now.

Shutting her eyes, she surrendered to his will and cried, no longer fighting but accepting that if she lay still, it would all be over soon.

It was not her husband that touched her but a stranger in his flesh and clothes. A predator stealing the last speck of vitality and joy from its prey. Perhaps he would drink her life away and leave her there to die. The longer it went on, the less she feared such an outcome.

Her throat was raw, too abused to swallow. She coughed and gasped, hating her body's instinct to breathe when the act cost her so much pain.

Tears seeped from her eyes, collecting grime from the dirty floor and clinging to her soiled skin. He was her husband, and she was losing him. Perhaps he was already gone.

A silent sob ripped from her heart, and she accepted this was how it would end. They would not part in kindness but in chaos. He would become such a danger to all of them, the man she loved would be long gone before he actually vanished. Had she already missed her chance to tell him goodbye?

Drowning in sorrow, she whimpered, "I love you."

He stilled, breath seething in an audible growl and eyes flickering with unrecognizable, predatory rage. But as his head cocked to the side and he looked down at her, she wondered if part of him still existed inside the beast.

"Jonas?" She spoke his name in a broken whisper, desperate for any sign that humanity still remained behind his eyes. "Can you hear me?"

He staggered off of her, hauling his body back until he crashed into the wall, a look of horror on his face.

Relief gutted her and she shuddered, her body rolling to its side and her tears falling fast. He was still in there. He wasn't fully gone to her yet.

"Thank God," she whimpered, but the damage to her throat made it difficult to speak.

The copper pot clattered to the floor in a loud crash, and light spilled down the cellar steps as the door swung wide and he fled, howling in pain as he rushed into the sunlight.

CHAPTER 25

*L*arissa stretched under the thin blanket, curling into the warm, muscled body at her side.

The low rumble of a masculine groan greeted, followed by the press of soft lips and a seductive stare from intensely inviting eyes.

"Morning." Eleazar kissed her soundly, soft lips and tongue gently seeking.

She smiled against his lips and peeked through her lashes at the window. "I believe we missed morning."

He pulled her close, seating her more firmly over him, and continued to kiss her. Her body awakened under his touch, the response as surreal as last night.

The cool air puckered her nipples into

tight points. He pulled the tip of her breast into his mouth, sending heat to her core and warming her blood. She rocked over him and he groaned, his pleasure ricocheting back to her and amplifying her own.

Grinding his hips into her, rotating beneath her, he grinned, and she gasped. Lashes lowering, she focused on the incredible awareness of him. Her senses sharpened.

Lifting her hips, he slowly entered her and they both sighed, luxuriating in the shared comfort. Head dipped back, her hair tumbled around her shoulders.

Looking down at him, she smiled. "Can all mates share such pleasure?"

He arched beneath her, stretching and pressing deeper into her core. "Some, I suppose. I've heard rumors but never imagined anything so…" His eyes closed and his lips parted, revealing twin fangs.

"Euphoric?" She craved his blood.

"Yes."

Her fangs elongated, and her breath hitched when his thumb graced the sensitive bud of her sex.

She groaned and tilted back, savoring the sensation as he glided into her heat. A fire formed in her belly as his mind pulled hers into his thoughts. She saw herself through his eyes and the vision stole her breath away.

Confident and sensual, she rode him, taking her pleasure and granting him his own. He was so strong, but his strength no longer threatened hers.

His long, trim body bunched as his muscles corded with each slow thrust. His powerful thighs filled the space between her soft feminine ones. His tapered waist pressed into her softer belly as he pulled her down for a kiss.

She bit and licked at him, finding her way to his thrumming pulse. "I hunger, Eleazar."

His hands closed around her hips, sliding lower and squeezing possessively. His body swelled inside of her. "Take what you need, my beautiful lioness."

Her body coiled around him like a hot fist. Tongue tracing below his jaw as her mouth opened, she pierced his skin and he thrust hard, burying himself inside of her. Hot, life-giving blood filled her mouth as her muscles tightened around him and his cock fluttered against the trembling walls of her sex.

His soul opened to her and love flooded in. The sensations leaving him were so intense that they became all she could feel, more powerful than her own pleasure, more valuable than her own life. The incredible bond that connected them cinched tighter until he was all she knew.

No matter what was to come, she would always need her mate. There was no existing without him after such a bond, no unraveling the threads that had sewn their souls together.

What they shared was so all-encompassing nothing else mattered. Her doubt and insecurities washed away. He saw her as a masterpiece with all of her natural imperfections, and she somehow saw him the same. They were made for one another, the other half of each other's soul.

ELEAZAR STUDIED the cars rushing by from where he stood in Larissa's apartment, holding the curtains back from the window. So many troubled thoughts below. He wanted to get her home to the farm where she would be safe.

"So, what year were you born?" his mate called from the bedroom as she plated her hair.

He laughed softly to himself. Her innocence had a way of making him incredibly self-conscious about his age. "I believe it was 1486, but time was not tracked as precisely then."

"In Spain, correct?"

"Yes, outside the kingdom of Leon, in a village called Castilla." He picked up a thin, red ribbon lying on the table and brought it to his nose. The fragrance of her hair clung to the satin band. He placed it in his pocket for safe keeping.

"Were you in Spain long?"

"No, I fled when the church changed to Catholicism."

"You left for religious reasons?"

He grinned at her endless curiosity. "Over the course of five hundred years, beliefs tend to evolve. Back then, I had no faith, and I wasn't about to have my principles forced."

"Where did you go?" The rustle of material met his ears as he sensed her dressing.

"West, to the Caribbean Isles. I then spent some time in Germany, France, and lived for several decades in Switzerland. Eventually, I grew tired of worldly matters and no longer cared for wealth or possessions. Then, when the plague infested Europe and it had become harder to feed, I no longer cared if I lived or died."

Her soft gasp made him smile. It had been a long time since anyone cared about him on a personal level. The rush of her startled worry reminded him to be more sensitive when choosing his words.

"But God had a different plan for me," he explained. "Rumors of the New World promised a fresh start. I had knowledge of agriculture, and the ground was said to be fresh and rich for planting. We traveled here on the Charming Nancy."

"We learned about that ship when we were children."

"It's an important part of The Order's history, but I doubt your teachers portrayed it honestly. It's not a memory I'd share with children."

"Why?" Drawers opened and he imagined she was gathering the last of her personal effects.

His mind went back to the early seventeen hundreds when life was much simpler, but even an immortal's life came with few guarantees. "We lost several of our group on the voyage. Rogue vampires ran wild about Europe during the plague, but our kind was not immune. There were only eleven mortal families aboard the ship for us to feed from. Once the plague broke out on the ship, even the rats below deck fell sick with the disease. The elderly and the young children were the weakest and the first to go."

Eleazar did not favor the memories of so many families forced to bury their young at sea.

"In such close quarters, infection spread like wildfire. I warned against feeding from families who had taken ill. And, sometimes, even the apparently healthy could be secretly unwell. Mothers wept over their children, risking more spread of the deadly virus, and the passenger list dwindled."

She appeared at the doorway of the bedroom, face pale and eyes wide. "That's heartbreaking."

He nodded. "Even some immortals fell ill." He looked at her, already experiencing the intrinsic way his soul tethered to hers. "There's nothing quite comparable—not even a mother's grief—to that of an immortal losing a true called mate."

Her fingers rushed to her lips as her breath hitched. The jolt of sadness stabbing into her heart chipped the ice around his own.

"The risk of death became so frightening we were all half-starved to death by the time the ship docked on the banks of Philadelphia. Untrusting of any mortal's health, we drank only from wild animals and made a pilgrimage north."

"To Lancaster."

"Yes, to the farm." Shaking away such melancholy memories, he fully looked at his mate and his heart kicked.

Dressed in an Amish gown, her white apron wrapped demurely about her and her hair braided close to her head, she made a picture of flawless beauty and made him feel every bit of his five hundred years.

"You're lovely."

She blushed, her fingers self-consciously touching her braids. "I'm afraid I misplaced my bonnet."

He crossed the room and cupped her face in his palms, gently placing a kiss on her lips. "We shall find you a new one."

Anxious to return home but also hesitant to leave the sanctuary of her apartment, he wondered how others' knowledge of their mating would change things. Silus was a minor consequence. But there was also the situation regarding whatever lurked in the wilderness. As the bishop, his attention could not solely be on his mate's comfort, but his heart and mind cared little about other pressing issues.

The moment he returned to the farm he would cease being an individual male who had just been blessed with his mate, and he'd return to exist as The Order's bishop, acting as an adviser for The Council and the members of The Order. He sighed.

"What is it?"

"I'm simply remembering my responsibilities and mentally putting my affairs in order. Are you almost ready to leave?"

She looked around her apartment. "I'm ready."

"Do you not wish to take any of your belongings with us?"

"I want a fresh start. I don't want to take anything that reminds me of my old life or what I've escaped or why I ran."

Grateful for her agreeable nature and open mind, he kissed her again. "I'll make it my life's ambition to ensure you never have the instinct to run away again."

She smiled and wrapped her arms around

him, hugging him tightly. The open show of affection startled him, and he slowly hugged his arms around her, pressing his lips into her hair.

"Our life will be happy, Larissa. I swear it."

IT WAS early morning when they reached Lancaster. The sky was still dark and birds rested in the trees. Dried leaves covered the frozen ground in a soft blanket that crunched underfoot.

A large fallen branch blocked their path. Eleazar used telekinesis to push the obstacle out of the way and called on the wind to clear the land of dried leaves.

Desiring to impress Larissa, he focused his energy on the gray sky and called upon snow flurries. White flakes sifted toward the ground in a delicate show.

She smiled and looked up, extending her arms outward beneath the wintery sky, and twirled like an angel, facing him again with a radiant smile. "You're amazing."

"Parlor tricks."

"Can you teach me?"

He'd teach her anything she wished to

know. "Of course. We can practice once we're settled at home."

"I suppose I'll live with you now."

"Yes." She'd never sleep under anyone else's roof again.

"I'm actually quite anxious to return to the farm. I miss my family."

His footsteps slowed and he wondered if she understood what was happening with her parents. If Adriel was right and Jonas Hartzler was, in fact, being called, Larissa would be devastated.

She glanced at him, already so in tune with his moods. "What is it, Eleazar?"

He drew in a breath, hating to cause her stress, when a branch snapped in the distance. His back straightened and his muscles tensed, his senses growing instantly more alert. "Shh. I hear something."

She stilled and silently waited, her eyes searching the nearby trees.

They were not alone. He scented the air, and his blood chilled. "Vampire."

When she sucked in a breath, he pressed a finger to his mouth, motioning for her to stay silent. The scent was clearly male. Her hand squeezed in his as his brows drew tight, his senses tracking the intruder and gauging its nearness. She understood, as a female, she was in greater danger than him.

I'll protect you. He sent the thought to her and her body relaxed.

Still on guard, he scanned the area. Another branch snapped and he sprung.

Don't move! The swift mental command to stay put was delivered in a hard, unmistakable order.

Eleazar chased the scent, leaping swiftly through the trees and branches, racing far away from where Larissa stood. He gave chase, abandoning his mate to find and disarm the threat, and then suffered a terrifying thought.

What if the predator was deliberately trying to draw Eleazar away from Larissa? Whatever he was chasing possessed incredible speed. Miles doubled as the distance between them stretched. He could not go any farther without leaving her dangerously unprotected.

Dropping to the earth in a crouch, his clothing torn to ribbons from racing through the trees, he growled and scanned the area through glowing eyes. "Show yourself!"

Leaves crunched and the wind screeched.

An enormous sycamore groaned and creaked, falling with an unstoppable force and rocked the earth with an explosive bang. Animals squawked and scurried to safety. The forest floor vibrated from the intense timber landing.

Eleazar? Larissa's mind reached for his.

I'm safe. Stay where you are.

His head jerked toward the crackle of crunching leaves. Dust settled beyond the scrabble of roots now protruding from the earth, and a gnarled, wild figure appeared.

As the silhouette took shape, Eleazar squinted against the approaching dawn, scenting the tinge of aged human blood in the air.

Thick, corded muscle wrapped every limb of the approaching feral male. Long, matted hair hung in snarls down its back and over its face. The stench was wild and gamy, fresh blood mixing with predatory sprays warning him that he was not welcome here. The rogue would view him as an intruder and threat, and he would not back off until one of them was destroyed.

"Who are you?"

A flash of fangs and a feral growl. The rogue let out a hungry snarl and raised its claws, curling his fingers into talons and preparing for a fight. *Vampire.*

Eleazar's focus divided between protecting his mate and surviving. It had been centuries since he was in a physical altercation, but his age gave him some advantages. However, nothing compared to the strength of a *feeish* vampire slaked on mortal blood.

Eleazar crouched low, prepared for an attack. "I intend to walk away from this, which means you will not."

Disinterested in conversation, the vampire drew in a saliva-drenched breath and lunged.

CHAPTER 26

The sudden impact threw Eleazar to the ground, his back skidding across the forest floor. The vampire snarled and snapped, swiping claws sharp enough to slit an immortal's throat, prepared to destroy.

Survival instinct kicked in, and Eleazar sprung to his feet, centuries of pent-up control exploding with one lethal thought: *nothing* would harm his mate.

The male darted at him with a snapping jaw and dog-like intent to maul. Eleazar balled up the rabid energy charging him, and with his wide-spread fingers, flung it back at its host.

A sharp grunt coughed from the rogue, the blow throwing him to the ground and driving him hard into the bark of a nearby tree. The collision shook the earth, and Eleazar growled, his claws and fangs extending as his hackles rose and he prowled closer.

The creature, a true and wild rogue, lay hunched and filthy on the soil floor. Hair matted around its face, hanging in long, dreaded hanks. Its skin was discolored from dirt, grime, and the blood of its prey. The low, purring growl that hummed from its chest was not a natural sound nor a welcoming one.

Feral and delirious, the beast needed to be put down. Eleazar approached slowly, muscles bunched, mind intent.

Eleazar, what's happening?

He slammed down a wall on his thoughts. Larissa would be safest if she stayed out of his mind—

Eleazar?

Startled once more by her stubborn and surprisingly strong cognitive skills, he gave her a firm reprimand. *Stay put and keep out of my mind!*

Her shock registered as hurt and the connection severed. Distracted by her reaction, his mind retraced their link—

The blow knocked him back, throwing

him several feet and the rogue sprung at him with shocking speed. Wild animals skittered, swarming around them. Not animals.

The imposing presence of something out there crowded his intuition. It wasn't human, and it wasn't vampire. It was something altogether *other.*

His mind sharpened with the now familiar jolt of Larissa nearing. She was on the move.

Fury spiked as he understood she deliberately disobeyed him.

Larissa! I order you to go back—

The sharp, piercing sting of his command deflected and stabbed his mind. Wincing, he gripped his head.

The distraction was enough time for the rogue to swipe a claw down Eleazar's front, cutting him open from jaw to stern.

He hissed, baring his fangs. His attention back on the wild enemy as he swept an arm out and cleared the forest floor. Sending hurricane-force winds outward, he knocked down trees and threw his enemy down as if he were as inconsequential as the fallen foliage.

The chatter of the approaching creatures grew. Their excited cackles rung like deranged voices, speaking in tongues. His mind tried to latch on to the threat, but there were too many moving in and not a single natural brain wave for him to read.

The rogue climbed to its feet, intent on Eleazar and snarling. Shadows disguised his face, but there was no mistaking the rumbling growls as a threat. Then a ban of light crossed its face and the beast hissed, pulling away from the approaching sunlight. But Eleazar saw a glimpse of the familiar and recognizable profile of the beast.

Spine stiff, Eleazar froze and tried to rationalize the sight, but there was no logical explanation. It couldn't be. It would have been impossible for such a wild threat to survive all these years. Yet, there was no mistaking those haunting eyes of his old friend, Isaiah Hartzler.

Staggered and stunned, he drew back. He'd assumed it was merely a rogue in the wild. He never actually believed Isaiah might have survived all this time. Now, this was personal.

"Hello, old friend."

Saliva clung to Isaiah's fangs as he snarled, lurching closer, drawing no nostalgia from Eleazar's presence. It was clear the male only understood that of a wild, territorial predator. Eleazar was trespassing, and Isaiah was prepared to assert his power and claim his territory.

So be it. Crouching low, Eleazar bent for battle, certain this conflict would still end in one of their deaths.

Isaiah circled and snarled, creeping closer and snapping his jaw as he swiped gruesome claws through the air. Then something in the air caught the male's attention. Isaiah sniffed and smirked, a low purr rumbling from his filthy chest.

Eleazar pulled a breeze from the south and recognized Larissa's scent right away. But Isaiah recognized it first.

"No!" Eleazar bolted after the rogue. *"Larissa, run!"*

The speed of a vampire far surpassed his own. Their kind grew unstoppably strong when they fed on pure human blood, which Isaiah clearly had been ingesting for some time.

The chatter in the trees grew louder. Whatever was following them screamed like monkeys as branches shook overhead.

Larissa! Answer me!

She blocked her mind. Eleazar doubled his speed, desperate to reach her before the rogue. Isaiah would not recognize her as his niece. Nor would he respect another male's claim. Dear God, the crazed vampire would attack her, then brutalize and kill her.

"Larissa!"

He raced after her scent that led to the perimeter of the forest. The rush of mortal vehicles crowded the road as dawn broke over the horizon. Isaiah was a hundred yards ahead of him, gaining on Larissa, and the creatures in the woods closed on Eleazar from behind.

Screams howled and cackled as branches whipped at his clothes, tearing them to tatters as he raced after his mate. He'd never forgive himself if Isaiah reached her first. He couldn't bear the thought. His mind was so distraught. He couldn't spare the focus to create obstacles, terrified that any attempt to slow down Isaiah would cost Eleazar the time he needed to find and protect his mate.

The further they raced to the edge of the forest, the louder the car traffic hissed. Sunlight filtered in as the foliage thinned. The odor of gasoline and mortals crowded the trace of Larissa's immortal scent. Then Isaiah screeched an agonizing howl and all the tree creatures screeched too as if in pain.

They fell back and Isaiah cried out like a wounded dog, wailing in pain and limping back from the interstate, retreating into the shadowed woods. Eleazar didn't turn to chase the enemy. His focus was only on reaching and rescuing his mate.

He squinted as he burst from the tree line and sunlight exploded over him. Had that been the cause of Isaiah's agonizing scream? As a rogue, it made sense that he would not be able to tolerate the sun. Perhaps Larissa thought it safer to hide in plain sight among the mortals.

Or not…

He growled, spotting his mate strolling down the center median of the busy highway in broad morning light, not a care in the world for her surroundings or the danger of the cars and trucks rushing by.

"Larissa!"

She glanced back at him but kept walking —her anger rolling off of her in waves.

Every vehicle that drove by alerted her of their passing by blaring a horn, their immense weight roaring and speed fast enough to sever a limb. "Larissa, get out of the road!"

"I will not *stay put!*" she snapped.

Exhausted, injured, and in no mood to

coddle a hostile female through a temper tantrum, he leaped through the traffic, onto the median, and raced toward her. Then, grabbing her by the upper arm, he halted her progress.

For once, he had the advantage of catching her off guard. Served her right for severing their connection.

"If you will not listen, then you will sleep." He shoved the command into her mind with acute precision and made sure his own mind was blocked in case she pulled any tricks and deflected the compulsion back at him.

Her body went limp, and Eleazar caught her safely in his arms. Sending out a short scramble for any mortals passing by, he carried her off the median, onto the highway's shoulder, but carefully stayed within the sunlight.

"We are going to talk about your attitude when you wake up." His molars locked. He needed to feed if he wanted his injuries to heal sooner rather than later, but he would not take from her while she slept. "I don't expect your submission on all things, but when I give you a direct order, I expect you to obey."

He was wasting his breath. She was out

cold and he expected her to remain unconscious until he got her safely home.

It was a long reflective walk back to the farm, one slowed by cramping hunger pangs and his fury with Larissa's disobedience. His nerves worked raw as he wondered how long it would take to find and destroy Isaiah Hartzler before the vampire hurt another soul.

As much as Eleazar wished to focus on his mate and iron out some boundaries about their communication, he had an obligation to report what he'd found to The Council.

Isaiah Hartzler, who disappeared nearly a century ago, was alive and crazed beyond redemption. There was no cure for a feral vampire, certainly not after eighty years of living in the wild surviving by mortal blood and laced adrenaline sucked raw from the veins of each victim.

It galled Eleazar that Cain Hartzler had been right. He was not fond of the young male.

Soon that male would become his brother-in-law.

The thought sank like a boulder into a placid pond, disturbing enough to alter Eleazar's peaceful view of what lay ahead. It was the only drawback to marrying Larissa, but not nearly enough to make Eleazar question his intentions. No consequence could keep him from claiming his mate in every way possible.

Cain Hartzler would be a trial he'd learn to tolerate over time. Eleazar was loath to dispense any effort toward liking the young male, but for his mate, he would try.

Today had been dangerous. If not for the scorching daylight, Isaiah would have reached her.

Eleazar's grip tightened around her subtle weight filling his arms. She was his most precious gift. His salvation. He needed to protect her before all else. He also needed to protect his flock.

Isaiah's eyes had been devoid of humanistic traits. He behaved like a cornered lion, and Eleazar suspected that whatever had been following them in the trees was the lion's pride.

The filthy, naked male was beyond feral. A true and *feeish* vampire that needed to be destroyed. Recalling the stench of mortal blood and the stains on Isaiah's skin, Cain's theories had been correct, and his uncle was most likely the animal attacking the mortal women in the woods.

He hated admitting the young male was right. He sighed, not looking forward to the conversations ahead.

Larissa's grandfather, Ezekiel, was a male Eleazar respected. He'd even go as far as to call him a friend. He was also Isaiah's brother, and confirmation of Isaiah's survival would generate a renewed and unjustified burst of hope.

There was no hope for a rogue vampire.

Eleazar did not wish to inform his mate's family that Isaiah had survived, only to sentence him to death in the next breath. There was no choice but to follow through on the execution. It had been an order decided by The Council eighty years ago, and there was no reason why such a ruling should not still stand.

This was not his expected homecoming. He was prepared to deal with the Hostetlers and Silus, but not this.

He wanted to enjoy his mate. See to her annulment and make her his wife. He had been distracted and harsh with her, and for that, he needed to explain his position, but she owed him an apology for disobeying his direct command.

He could be lenient in most things, but

he expected her to comply without question or hesitation when he required obedience. He was not Silus. If and when an order passed his lips, he would only have her best interest at heart, and she needed to trust him. She needed to obey without question. Today, her insolence could have gotten her killed.

When they reached the farm, Eleazar blocked their presence. Larissa's lashes fluttered as if she sensed them approaching their destination.

She looked up at him and grinned with groggy confusion, then quickly scowled. "What happened?"

"You disobeyed me."

Her brow pinched as she glanced to the distant buildings and neighboring fields. "How did we get here?"

His molars locked with renewed frustration as the memory of his earlier fear returned with several unwanted emotions.

She gasped, her own memories likely falling into order. "You bastard. You forced me to sleep?"

"What choice did I have? I gave you an order and you deliberately disobeyed me."

"I'm not a dog you can command!" She

squirmed in his arms and his grip tightened, his steps stretching along the frozen ground.

"Correct. You're my mate, and as such, your safety is my top priority. Do you have any idea how dangerous your actions were today?"

Her anger shifted to concern. "What happened to your throat?"

"I asked you a question," he snapped, thinking once more of how close he came to losing her.

"And I asked you one." Twisting, she forced her way out of his arms. "I can walk on my own." The moment he set her down, she took in his tattered clothing and her rage simmered. "Eleazar, what did this to you?"

"A predator in the woods."

She drew back in shock. "What was it?" It was rare for any species to cause a threat to an immortal.

His lips firmed. If he wanted her trust, he would have to give her the truth. "A vampire. Your uncle."

Her hand flew to her mouth. "That's impossible."

"Yesterday, I would have agreed with you. Today, I cannot. I saw him with my own eyes. Isaiah Hartzler is alive and out for blood."

CHAPTER 27

"I don't believe it." No longer walking, Larissa shook her head in denial. "They hunted Isaiah years ago. He's long since dead. My family has moved on."

There was no time to convince her or explain how dangerous this revelation was for their kind. A rogue vampire put them all at risk.

Capturing her hand, he yanked her into step. "We must get to my home. Once we're there, I'll show you your room and you can wait there while I address The Council about this."

Her heels dug into the cold, hard earth. "Eleazar."

Her tone demanded he stop. Frustrated with the sense that this last mile would consist of endless delays, he huffed, "Yes?"

Her fists anchored against her hips as her glare hardened. "I'm not going to wait in a room until you have time for me."

The tedious press of so many priorities left his patience clipped. "You will wait where I tell you to because until I notify The Council of your return and our union, Silus will assume he still has a right to you as his wife. My private home is the safest place for you. I need to address The Council, and you need to stop arguing with me about what is best."

Her eyes blazed. Her fury spat at him like nails. "So, you're going to lock me in a room like a cell?"

"I never said lock." However, he thought it after her recent disobedience.

Her scowl darkened and she pivoted away from him, marching in the opposite direction of his home.

"Larissa, where are you going? My house is this way."

"I've spent enough time locked in rooms. I'm not going home with you. I'm going to my parents.'"

Her stubborn pride was going to age him a hundred years. He sighed and pinched the bridge of his nose. "You can't."

"You can't tell me what I can and cannot do!"

Their laws said otherwise, but he didn't want to upset her further. "It has nothing to do with my command over you; it's everything to do with the state of your family."

Her steps halted and she spun to face him, her face suddenly unsure. "What do you mean, *the state of my family?*"

He assumed she'd been in contract with Cain and her brother might have filled her in. "Your father's not well."

Her guarded expression told him she had some details but not all.

He closed the distance between them, gently taking her hands in his. "Larissa, I'm sorry to have to tell you what will almost certainly be more bad news, but you deserve to know the truth. Your father's being called."

"No." She took a step back. "That's impossible."

"It's very possible."

"But he can't. My mother..." Her fingers fluttered to her lips. "I have to go to her."

"That wouldn't be wise—"

"She must be devastated."

"You can't navigate this for them."

When he reached for her hand, she flung his touch away and scowled. "I can't let her face this alone."

"Their marriage is not your concern. We must deal with your situation and the threat in the woods—"

"I don't care about any of that. My mother and father are being ripped apart. How can I think of anything else? I must go to them."

"Larissa, enough!" he snapped. "Your father is not well, and I forbid you to go near him."

Her head drew back. "You *forbid* me?"

"Yes, as your bishop, elder, and your mate, I command you to stay away from that house and come with me."

Her eyes narrowed and a slight shiver raced up his spine. The nearly undetectable tremor drew his attention like the whistle of a bomb sailing through the air, and he anticipated the blast a split second before detonation.

"*Command me?*" Her fury exploded with nuclear force, shoving him back several steps. "I will not be commanded or ordered or told what to do! How dare you bully me with your authority after vowing to treat me as your equal! I shouldn't have trusted you. What happened, *Bishop?* You had me in your bed, got what you needed to survive, and then you no longer needed to persuade me with silly promises?"

"My promises stand. But our situation has changed—"

"So—*in this case*—it's fine to break your promises, is that it?"

"You're being unreasonable, Larissa. I'm trying to protect you—"

"Well, you're being the same controlling, self-righteous relic you've always been. And I'm the fool who fell for your lies!"

"Larissa, I've not lied to you."

Her fury shifted into sharp pain, and he read her emotions with stabbing accuracy. His need to protect her only translated to a betrayal—another authoritative male constricting her freedom.

"If you would just trust me, you would see that my intentions are noble."

"You said it would be different." Voice small, she looked at him through glassy eyes. "You swore you wouldn't treat me the way he did."

Her sadness gutted him. "Don't label me

like him." He reached to brush his fingers along her cheek but she pulled her face out of reach. "Larissa, it *will* be different. But, for now, we must be sensible. No one knows we've mated. You are still legally wed to Silus. Your father's not himself, so your family home is not a safe place to stay. And we have a vampire that knows your scent at large. I swore to protect you and that is what I plan to do."

Her emotions flushed with vulnerability. The delicate thread of her fear was so subtle, he almost missed it, but once he felt it, there was no mistaking it. She was scared.

Approaching her slowly, he gently took her hands and kept his voice low. "This will be so much easier if you could trust me."

Trembling with worry, she stared into his eyes. "Promise you won't let him take me away from you."

A half grin curved his lips. He was glad to hear that she wanted to stay with him but then frowned. Did she honestly believe Silus might somehow get his way?

He caught her shoulders and looked into her eyes with cold certainty. "He will never touch you again, Larissa. Never."

Somewhat satisfied, she nodded and took a deep breath as she stepped back. "How long will I have to stay hidden?"

"I'm not hiding you away. I'm merely situating you close by. You can rest or read or—"

"What if I want to see my sister?"

He considered her request. The idea of her not being completely alone actually comforted him, but it was a risk. Grace Hartzler was not a likely threat to Larissa, but the female was young, which meant her thoughts were often unguarded. It wouldn't be difficult for an elder to overhear musings of her sister's return.

"As soon as I speak to The Council about our situation, I will send for your sister, but I'm afraid you should stay isolated until then."

Her disappointment was bottomless, and her acceptance brought him no satisfaction. "Fine." She stomped past him, in the direction of his home.

"Larissa, you can see her in a day or two. These are simply precautions."

"I don't want to discuss it anymore. I said it's fine."

Over the centuries, he'd heard countless jokes about mates and wives and their tempers. He was now grasping how dangerous the word *fine* could be. Nothing about his mate's mood was *fine*.

As they marched toward his home, her tension did not loosen. He reminded himself that the consequences of her first husband's actions would linger and would also be his.

Her resistance was not a complication Larissa invited willingly but an obstacle that came from abuse. Yet, in a strange way, her defiance showed signs that she was not broken as she believed, but healing and still very strong.

There would be moments when she needed to defer to him. But in those instances, he would do his best to deliver any command as gently as possible, never forgetting that she once survived a relationship with no autonomy of her own.

When they arrived at his home, entering through the offices of the safe house and traveling the empty corridors that led to Council Hall, David greeted them. The young male attempted to overlook the bishop's shredded attire and Larissa's presence, but there was no ignoring the curiosity of his thoughts.

"David, Sister Larissa will be borrowing a room for a time. No one is to know of her presence, so please guard your thoughts. In the meantime, alert The Elders that I've returned with urgent news."

"Yes, Bishop. But there is a minor situation you may want to address before I send for the others."

"What is it?"

David glanced at Larissa and hesitated. "It's, uh, private council business…"

Eleazar delved into the young male's mind and understood right away why he hesitated. Then he sighed. Another complication.

"I will first see that Sister Hartzler is situated, and then I will deal with *that* right away."

"Yes, Bishop." David stopped at the entrance to the bishop's private quarters, lingering in the office corridor.

Tension knotted in Eleazar's shoulders—a sign that he was officially home. *Only* because Larissa was, in fact, his mate would he deal with this unexpected complication first. But he would keep his new concern hidden. No need to worry her.

Larissa looked at him with uncertainty, but he blocked his thoughts, guiding her toward his private rooms.

"As soon as I show you to your room, I must see to an urgent matter."

"Fine."

He purposefully forced a calming breath into his lungs. *Another fine...*

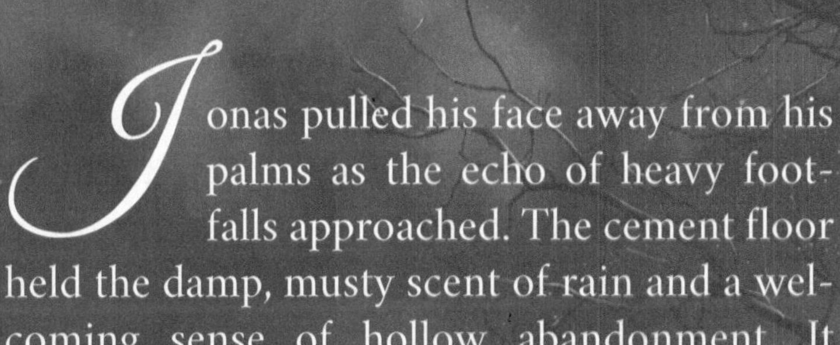

*J*onas pulled his face away from his palms as the echo of heavy foot-falls approached. The cement floor held the damp, musty scent of rain and a welcoming sense of hollow abandonment. It would only be a matter of time now.

He ached for it to be over and shoved his body off the cold floor to sit up and face his incoming visitor. He waited, staring through the barred wall. The glow of an approaching lantern grew, illuminating the long hall leading to his cell, and the impeding footsteps grew closer and louder.

He sensed the bishop's intolerant attitude before he spotted him. When the bishop's figure loomed outside the cell, the male's eyes glared and his skin wore the fresh scent of soap, but nothing smelled stronger than his irritation.

"Why are you here?" he snapped by way of greeting.

Jonas battled for the forte to speak. His hunger had become an all-consuming ache that sapped away his strength for even the weakest thought. "It's the safest place I could find."

He was no longer a danger to just himself.

"Tell me you're not here for the reason I suspect."

Jonas stood with aching joints. His muscles were weak with starvation, and his mind had not settled long enough for him to find the solutions he sought.

He met the bishop's stare. "I've come to beg for The Council's mercy, Bishop King. I wish to be executed."

The bishop swore under his breath, massaging his temples as if his head ached—an altogether strange ailment for an immortal. "I cannot kill you, Jonas."

"It's my wish. You must."

"Is it true then? You have been called to another female?"

"I only want one female. Abilene—"

"Has never been your mate! You always knew this was a possibility. You swore that you would handle the situation responsibly if a calling occurred. I'm not going to order your execution, Jonas. I'm ordering you to go find your called mate."

Fearful, if those bars opened, that he might do just that, Jonas gripped the metal door tight. "I cannot hurt my wife more than I already have!"

Bishop King dragged a hand through his hair and paced with clipped, agitated strides. "This is unbelievable," he growled.

Jonas couldn't understand why his request might trouble the bishop so. "Is it not our God-given right to decide when we've had enough?"

The bishop glared at him. "Your request invites new consequences, consequences you —should I grant your request—would not have to face. Consequences *I* do not wish to combat."

"I don't understand. What consequences?"

Ignoring his question, the bishop asked, "How bad are your symptoms?"

"Bad enough that I had your man lock me in this cell."

"Examples, Jonas. Give me examples."

Shame weighed heavily on his shoulders, crippling his spine as he hung his head. "I... I attacked Abilene. I hurt her." His throat constricted with the pain of regret.

"Is she all right?"

"She will heal—physically, at least."

The bishop forked another agitated hand through his hair, leaving the inky strands standing on end. "I order you to find your mate. I will not order your execution. That's the end of it."

"No."

"No?" He growled, but Jonas did not flinch. "It's God's will and your duty!"

"My duty is to my wife!"

"And what of your children? What duty do you have to them?"

"My children are grown—"

"You are still their father!" The bishop practically snarled. "Think of what this might do to them!"

Jonas blinked in confusion. The bishop's concern for his offspring was considerate but unexpected. "Abilene is my only concern."

He loved his children very much, but they would heal. They would take care of their mother and lean on each other.

He invited their censure, believing their

rejection might force him away and make his decision easier. At this point, he no longer trusted his will to do what was right. He trusted nothing.

"Let them hate me. Let them all hate me." He would not betray his wife and give his heart to another.

"You're being selfish."

"I'm trying to be an honorable male."

"You're behaving like a cowardice one!" The bishop's hand lashed out at the bars, striking the metal with such force the walls of the cell rattled. "I will not do it. I will not give such an order so you can escape your responsibilities!"

"*It's my right!*" Jonas bellowed, leaping at the bars.

His beast frothed from within, snapping the surface, as his control slipped out of reach. He shook the bars viciously. If the bishop would not kill him voluntarily, Jonas would attack him and force him to do the deed out of self-defense.

He would not risk his wife's safety and he could not bring himself to answer God's call.

"I granted you the right to marry Abilene. Your marriage was a privilege, and now a debt is owed in the form of duty. I will not let you endanger our kind by shirking your responsibilities, nor will you leave me to reap the blame of your demise."

"Why would anyone blame you? I've come here of my own free will while I still have rational thought. Soon I won't. I want to go before The Council and have my request heard—"

"No."

Seething, Jonas snarled, "Then let me free and see what I do!" He rattled the bars with pent-up rage, unprepared for such firm denial. "This is my dying wish! Who are you to tell me no?"

The bishop's eyes darkened with threatening malice. "You think to get your way with threats, Brother Jonas? Attack anyone in this order, and I will deliver a world of pain far worse than anything you've ever imagined. If you must die, die with the dignity of knowing you protected your family. Your request is selfish, and I refuse the matter now and every day that follows. You're going to find your mate. You're going to claim her. And this issue will be done."

"No!"

"*Yes!* I have had enough of your disobedient family challenging my authority. The discussion is over, and my decision is final!"

"I will not go to her!"

"*You will do exactly as you are told!*" Their voices climbed until every word rung off the rafters.

Neither of them heard the hallway door open or the approaching footsteps, but the soft feminine gasp stole their attention the moment it interrupted their rage.

Jonas did a doubletake as his eldest daughter appeared, white as a ghost, in the basement of the safe house where females had no place.

"Larissa?" He hadn't set eyes on her in months and worried his mind was playing tricks on him.

"Father?" Her fingers trembled to her mouth in shock. "What are you doing here—in a cell?" She rushed toward the bars.

"Stay back!" he snapped, and she stilled. His tension momentarily unraveled, replaced with concern and worries that quickly over-whelmed him. "Where have you been? Does Silus know that you are back? Your mother? Everyone has been worried."

"What am *I* doing here? What are *you* doing here?" She ignored his warning and yanked on the locked door. She glared at the bishop. "Eleazar, let him out this instant."

"Larissa," Jonas hissed, shocked by the disrespectful way she addressed their bishop. "You must go home to Silus—"

Ignoring his command, she shook the bars. "Let him out!"

"Larissa," Bishop King warned. "This does not concern you."

She glared at the bishop, then set her tear-filled gaze on Jonas. "Is it true, Father? Have you been called?"

His throat constricted with the truth, and he looked away.

Her delicate hands closed over his fingers, still gripping the bars. "Are we to lose you?"

His heart shuddered. "It will all be over soon."

"Who is she?"

"It's irrelevant." Unable to bear her empathy, he withdrew his hand from her touch, eyes pleading. "Will you go to your mother? Will you see that she has everything she needs?"

"Of course—"

"She will not."

He glared at the bishop, tired of his overbearing intrusions. "This is a family matter."

"I'm aware." The bishop's hand curled around Larissa's bicep, drawing her away from the bars and closer to his side. He reached into his pocket and withdrew a key.

The bars swung open and Jonas shuffled back, unwilling to leave. Those bars protected others from the beast he would eventually become—the monster that was already forming within his bones.

In a deceptively low voice, Bishop King, still holding Larissa close, growled, "Get out of my home. Leave this farm before nightfall, and do not return until you have answered your call and bonded with your true mate."

His arm curled protectively around Larissa's shoulders, and Jonas frowned in confusion. Though his mind had become a scrambled labyrinth of disjointed thoughts and desires, something struck him as amiss.

Bishop King's thumb brushed ever so slightly over Larissa's shoulder. Jonas's stare moved to her eyes. Her restraint went beyond simple obedience. There was something else keeping her by the bishop's side, something strong and unquivering.

Loyalty.

Jonas's head cocked. "Where is Silus?"

"Silus is an issue that does not concern

you. You have enough on your plate. Do as I command."

"I will not leave until I have my daughter's word that she will go to my wife."

"*You will do as I say!*" The bishop stormed, the force of his roar ramming Jonas's body into the wall.

Larissa gasped. "Don't! He's my father!"

"Then he should behave as such." Turning his glare back on Jonas, the bishop seethed. "Do not assume to put your wife's safety before that of my mate's."

Through the clouded puzzle of his exhausted mind, Jonas struggled to make sense of the bishop's words. "Mate?"

"Yes," he growled through clenched fangs. "Now you understand my refusal for your request. I will put her first in every decision I make, even if it means others will suffer. As her father, you should feel the same."

"Then you should understand my loyalty to Abilene—"

"She is not your mate! This is nonsense, Jonas! Enough is enough. If you want to save your family from any more pain, follow your calling. Or so help me, I will punish you in ways you've never imagined."

Larissa's eyes closed and the bishop

gripped her shoulders, pulling her face to his chest. She appeared to go willingly, and Jonas felt his paternal hold over her feather and fray.

It was starting. They were all turning their backs on him.

Head hanging low, he shuffled out of the cell, utterly alone and rejected. There was no mercy for him here.

Glancing back, he noted the protective way the bishop clenched his hand around his daughter's shaking shoulders. The bishop's refusal to execute Jonas had nothing to do with right and wrong or mercy and duty, but everything to do with a male not willing to hurt his mate unnecessarily. And there was no greater force than a male's need to protect his mate from harm.

There was no hope left for him where the bishop was concerned. No hope left that his children might aid him. Perhaps, no hope left within the farm.

No one stopped him as he exited the long hall. Nor did anyone interfere with his departure from the building. This was his end, his solitary farewell. It was a dark and lonesome exodus.

As he stepped into the light, he hissed with

renewed agony. The afternoon sun burned through his clothing and flesh, heating his skin so hot that the steaming pores scorched the fibers of his shirt.

He stumbled and lurched for shade. But the longer he searched, the worse his vision became. Crawling toward the shadows of a nearby barn, his eyes wept reflexively from the blinding pain.

He was a disgrace. Weakened by his resistance, he'd soon be helpless to protect himself from the consequences of his condition. If he didn't feed soon, find nourishment that might actually sustain him, he was going to fall victim to the powerful sun and find himself stranded in the open to burn alive. Perhaps that was exactly the fate he deserved.

He dragged himself into the cooling shade of the barn. His vision was slow to heal, leaving him with only the limited ability to see shapes of larger objects like the outline of trees and buildings.

He staggered through the shadows of the barn, waiting for the burning sun overhead to fade into night. Despite draining field mice in his desperate pain, his hunger continued to grow.

When animals came close, he hunted.

Only, his lack of agility and sight cost him accuracy. When immortals passed the barn, Jonas cowered in the shadows and reflexively bared his fangs, trusting no one and believing friends were now his foe.

For even his children had turned their backs on him—an outcome he invited if it meant they would better protect their mother, but one that pained him all the same.

He was truly and utterly alone.

Once dusk came, he stumbled out of the barn and into the darkness, letting his heart and memory act as his guide. He located his home and could sense her beyond the walls.

He did not have to call for her. The front door swung open, and he stilled before reaching the steps.

"Stay back, Jonas. Do not come any further."

His heart jerked with a cold snap against his ribs. Her rejection was a bullet into his dying soul.

"I only came to check on you, my sweet Abilene. And to tell you I'm so sorry I hurt you."

"I'll survive. For now."

Glancing up at her shadowed figure, his eyes still suffering from the sun's damage, he bathed in her distrust, wishing to revel in the pain so he might find the strength to walk away. Sorrow leaked from his eyes. "You fear me."

"I fear what you've allowed yourself to become."

"I'm still Jonas. Still your husband."

She shook her head. "Not enough. There's something else inside of you I can't contend with. I can't allow you inside this house again."

He stumbled, the bark of a nearby tree scratching his arm. "I have news of our daughter."

"What news?"

"Larissa has returned to the farm."

Her silence was unexpected. "I don't believe you."

The breath left his lungs as he stared up at her, too blinded by the earlier sun to read her expression. "Abilene, I would not lie to you about such things."

"You lied to me for months, Jonas. Your presence here is a lie. Your love for me is a—"

"*Do not!*" He drew in a harsh breath. "Do not call my love a lie. It's the greatest force in my life, and I will follow it to my death." He only had a few days left before he would no longer be able to survive the dawn. It wouldn't take much to end this on his own, the mercy of The Council be damned.

"Then so be it, Jonas. Your death is mine. If that's what you choose, I will follow you."

Furious, he growled, "I will not allow it!"

"The only choice you have is to find your mate. By sacrificing yourself, you doom us both. I will not live with the guilt of your death. I will not let you put my life before yours. I love you too much. And, once you go to her…" Her voice broke, but she quickly recovered. "You will forget all the things you felt for me."

"I could never."

In the expanse of her silence came the finality of their fate. "That's not your choice anymore." The screen door whined as it opened. "Go now, and don't you dare come back here, Jonas. Don't you dare hurt me more than destiny already has."

The door snapped shut, leaving him infinitely alone. Falling to his knees, he howled and pounded his fists into the cold earth. *"Abilene! I will not do this thing! I cannot bear it!"*

Collapsing to the hard earth as if seeking a grave, he beat his fists into the ground until his flesh bled and dirt clung to his tear-streaked cheeks.

Sobs wracked his body as hunger gnawed at him. "I love you, Abilene. There is nothing in this world more powerful than my love. Do you hear me? Do you?"

He clawed at his face, desperate to escape the prison of his soul, but there was no relief for the torture set to destroy him, no quiet space for his mind to rest. He was sentenced to an eternal hell.

CHAPTER 29

arissa was beyond distraught as Eleazar led her out of the cellar—an area she had no idea existed until today—and steered her back toward the private quarters of his house.

"You should have never come down here, Larissa."

Shaken, she wiped at more tears as they fell. "He wanted you to execute him, didn't he?"

"That doesn't matter. I refused his request, and The Council cannot grant such nonsense without my approval."

She belligerently yanked her arm out of his hold. "It matters to me, Eleazar. What's going to happen to my family?"

His jaw clamped tight. "I'm your family now. We must look forward."

Her brow knit and she staggered back. "Is that what you think? We're mated now, so all other ties will fall away?" A huff of air passed her lips. "I can't live like that, Eleazar. I've already tried."

In his gut, he wanted to hide her away and spend an eternity getting to know her. He wanted them to share an obsessive love that no other could match. Why did she not want the same?

"You're putting words in my mouth. I'm merely suggesting that we focus on our own challenges and let your family manage theirs."

Shaking her head, her gaze fell to the floor. "You don't understand because you don't have any family. You can't remember what it's like." Lifting her gaze, she looked at him through a wall of fresh tears. "He kept me away from them no matter how desperately I begged and cried. We visited on his terms, only when he needed someone to watch over me while he was preoccupied with other matters. And afterward, he'd spend hours trying to put thoughts in my head about them. He tried to poison my mind to make me believe my family didn't love me."

Her head lowered once again, and her voice nearly disappeared under the weight of her pain. "I never had the courage to tell them how awful my marriage really was."

He wrapped his arms around her with incredible gentleness and kissed the top of her head. "I'll never keep you from them, Larissa. This is only a temporary precaution. You will have your family in a few days. Once I clear our situation with The Elders and see your marriage annulled and your father has answered his calling and is no longer a danger, you can visit them as freely as you wish. I'll never stand in the way of that."

Accepting his logic despite her devastation, she sniffled and nodded. "Thank you."

He tucked a strand of hair behind her ear and kissed her brow. "I sense your exhaustion."

It was getting late and they both needed to rest. Tomorrow was going to be a draining day.

He walked her to his room and carefully removed the pins from her hair and apron. "I will find you a bonnet tomorrow."

She nodded, unraveling her braids.

He brushed the backs of his fingers down her cheek, grateful when she leaned into the caress. "I sense your hunger. Come to bed. Let me take care of you."

She followed him to the bed, wearing only her chemise, and he lifted the covers. The sight of her there undid him and his tension from the day slowly faded.

Sliding beside her, he gathered her close, tracing the curve of her shoulder to her throat with his mouth and memorizing every inch of skin. She was such a temptation, such a thrill.

"I despise every interruption that keeps me from this bed." His hands framed her ribs, and he pulled her body closer until her thighs straddled him. "I want to get lost in you, so lost, no one can find me."

Gently, he coaxed fragile responses from her body, tenderly stroking her beautiful curves and lavishing soft kisses over her skin. Her sorrow wounded him and he wanted to distract her from the sadness. Slowly, their pleasure built and echoed, climbing out of them in gasps and hungry moans.

She was his escape, an unpredicted sanctuary. Every time he pressed his lips to hers, her soft tongue greeted with fragile curiosity.

"That's it, my proud lioness, take what you need."

Her hand curled around his neck, pulling him closer as her mouth explored. Little fangs nipped at his lips and her breasts pressed into the hard wall of his chest. His hunger grew, as did his arousal, as he stroked her folds and made her purr.

She arched into his touch with beautiful need. His hunger took hold and he stripped away her clothing, dragging his mouth over every bare curve. Adjusting their position, he rolled to his back and fit her over his hard cock, entering her in one sure thrust.

Her breath hitched and her head fell back as her pleasure hit him. He cupped her hips and rose to suckle her tempting breasts, distracted by her needy pulse.

She cradled his head to her, her own mouth seeking. As she nuzzled his throat, he gave her better access. "Take what you need."

Her sharp fangs punctured his flesh and his body shuddered, hardening and rocking deeper into her heat. She fed greedily from his vein, her hips riding harder with every tug of her lips and tongue.

A hurricane of passion built inside of him and he savored every pull. There was nothing more satisfying than meeting her needs, nothing more erotic than filling her in every possible way.

His fingers trailed down her back as her spine arched and she pressed her wet sex over him. Her keening moans climbed through him, luring out his own masculine growls.

When she finished and closed the wound, he flipped her to her back and took her hard, driving into her with greedy force and claiming all that was his. Baring his fangs, he plunged his teeth into her breast and drank his fill.

Her cries of pleasure hit the rafters, echoing through the empty house. Soon those carnal cries would be a familiar song within these walls, and his house would become a home, rich with character and loud with the pitter-patter of their children's feet.

His male ego flexed at the idea and he thrust hard, urgently wanting to fill her with his seed. He fondled and teased, driving her pleasure as high as his own, and when they finished together, he saw a glimpse of heaven on Earth in her eyes.

She was his salvation in every single way a female could be.

Collapsing next to her, he tugged her body close, unwilling to let a single shadow separate them. Was this love? This need to have her close to him at his side, to know her every tell, was nothing like anything he needed before. As a matter of fact, when he had her to himself, he needed nothing else. She was his everything.

LARISSA AWOKE in an unfamiliar bed only to find Eleazar gone. Sliding her hand under the covers, she found his side of the bed cold, and she frowned. The sun had yet to rise fully and he was already gone? She'd assumed he'd at least stay and have breakfast with her, especially after reconnecting last night.

The chill filling the room brought a shiver and she snuggled deeper under the blankets. But sleep evaded her.

After several long minutes of contemplating what to do with herself, she rose. She shivered as her bare feet touched the cold wood floor. While there was a large fireplace in the bedroom, there was nothing but ash inside.

Her dress and chemise draped over the chair in the corner, but she was still without a bonnet. She quickly dressed and visited the water closet.

Once she plaited her hair, she returned to the bedroom and waited, growing more and more impatient by the hour, but no one came. She was without a kapp and, therefore, restricted to the private quarters.

She listened for sounds in the silence, her thoughts drifting to matters outside of her control. Today, Silus would learn of her return. Her father might find his mate. Her mother would be eternally heartbroken. It felt criminal to sit idle while so much went on outside of these walls.

She paced for a while, but her anxiety only grew. When she reached for Eleazar's mind, she found it completely closed off. He was likely around others and trying to keep his private business private, especially while her presence must remain a secret.

She understood why Eleazar wanted her to hide, but she didn't do well with boundaries. She spent months locked away in Silus's bedroom.

Despite all the hours she'd passed trapped inside the Hostetler house, it never welcomed her like a home. It had only ever been a prison. She didn't want the bishop's home to feel the same.

Braving the halls, she explored the old house. It was simple, more so than the typical Amish home. No needlepoint or greeting cards hung by the entry. No family birth records displayed on his walls. There was only one large mechanical clock in the kitchen and a wooden calendar that hadn't been changed in weeks.

She wondered if he'd object to her adding accents.

The second floor had plenty of bedrooms, but each one was empty and cold. The first floor had a large den that she'd visited on occasion for prayer service. Although it was within his private quarters, The Order treated it as a public space. Memories of sitting beside Silus in that room caused her to back away from the threshold before stepping inside.

Her stomach growled. Searching the pantry, she found very little fresh food. Older immortals did not rely on plants, grains, or proteins the way younger immortals did. She shut the cabinets and sat down at the table, staring at the empty kitchen in silence.

He had suggested that she rest and read,

but she wasn't tired and had yet to find a single book. In the hallway by his office door, which then led to Council Hall, she found a large poster with scribbled cursive. It was a listing of all the nearby towns and their zip codes. She spent an hour memorizing the numbers out of sheer boredom.

By midafternoon, her boredom shifted to anger. Not once had he stopped in to check on her or ask if she needed anything.

By now he had to have notified The Council of her presence and disclosed their calling. Didn't he understand how lonely it was trapped in this strange house by herself? The least he could do was send for Gracie once the news got out.

She could disregard his request and sneak out to see her sister anyway, but Gracie was most likely at her parents', which he specifically ordered her to avoid. Her heart pinched at the thought of her poor mother and she was torn. She wanted to help her, but was there truly anything anyone could do in such a situation? Maybe it was best to stay away.

If only she could talk to her siblings and find out more information. Adam was most likely working, and Larissa had only met Annalise a few times. The female might find her sudden presence intrusive and she didn't want to overstep.

Larissa wished she knew where Cain was. Of all her siblings, he was the one she held dearest to her heart. He understood what her life had been like as Silus's wife and why she left. He also understood how intimidating the bishop could be.

She had to stop calling the bishop by his title. "Eleazar…"

She foolishly looked around as if her words could conjure him. She missed him. It was a strange and difficult emotion to accept.

Crossing the room, her palm pressed to the door that led to his office. Was he in there? She listened but heard no movement or voices.

How upset would he be if she waited for him in there? She could explain that the house was too quiet and lonely, and she missed him. Surely, he would understand and be grateful that he had been on her mind.

The door clicked, and she grinned at the discovery that he'd left the door unlocked. Silus had not been so trusting.

Crossing the threshold, she sniffed the air, scenting the trace of a female. Her brow creased. Which female?

The desk was tidy and the room dim. With only one east-facing window and the sun already far overhead, there was little light seeping in.

She paused at the murmur of voices nearby.

"It will only be a matter of time. You must be patient," a male voice said. "If you dismiss The Council's orders, you'll only find yourself out of their favor, and that is not a place you want to be."

The voice was vaguely familiar but muffled. Heavy footfalls drew nearer and she pulled back into the shadows, creeping behind the open door that led to the common corridor where males often gathered after council meetings.

"He's right, my boy," another voice said. "When the time comes, you'll see it was better to obey The Council. She can't hide forever. Eventually, something or someone will bring her home, and once that happens, you'll have every right to discipline her as you see fit. Respect The Council's authority and they shall respect yours."

Larissa's heart plummeted to the pit of her stomach as she recognized the gravelly tone of Damascus Hostetler. They were speaking of her whereabouts, and it sounded like they were talking to Silus.

"When I get my hands on her, I'll beat her within an inch of her eternal life for the humiliation she's caused." Her husband's threat paralyzed her.

Three gruff chuckles rumbled. "I have no doubt you'll do everything in your power to ensure this never happens again."

A shiver raced up her spine and she held her breath, terrified to make the slightest sound.

Why hadn't Eleazar explained their situation yet? What was taking so long? If The Council understood they were mated, she would be safe from Silus. Did he know she was on the farm? Had anyone spotted them coming in last night?

"Obviously, the bishop failed," Damascus said in that deep rattle of a voice. "Of course, he wasn't invested. His mind's tied up on this Isaiah nonsense. His priorities are not our own and he's fallen out of touch."

"He claims, while in the woods, he looked into its eyes," the third, unrecognizable voice said. "He swears it was Isaiah."

"Nonsense. I was there the day we hunted Isaiah. He might have escaped us, but he didn't have long to live. Isaiah's dead. It's time we all move on."

"Bishop King won't rest until he has The Council's consent to hunt whatever's luring in the woods," Silus said.

"And we'll give it to him—as soon as he grants you the right to hunt your wife."

No comment followed, but as their footsteps and shadows passed the office door, she sensed their sneering grins. As soon as she was certain they were gone, Larissa ran back to the private quarters of the house and bolted up the steps.

Her heart pounded wildly, and no room struck her as safe. Every empty space was a cavernous corner to get caught. She fumbled through the halls, terrified someone would find her and drag her back to her husband.

She stumbled up a winding staircase to the third floor, pulling the latch of the attic door tight behind her. Hiding in the furthest crevice, by the low ceiling of the soffit where boxes and old furniture provided a decent clutter of objects to block her from view, she lowered to the floor and pulled her knees to her chest, shivering in fear.

Eleazar will not let anything happen to me.

I must trust him.

He is my mate.

Silus cannot touch me once our bond is recognized.

She caught her breath, forcing herself to repeat any calming thought she could imagine.

The large stack of boxes was draped in an old sheet that hung to the dusty, planked floor. A small dormer window facing west let in a beam of light. Dust motes danced in the golden rays, drawing her attention to a wooden chest.

"ORDER RECORDS," she read the label, noting the years were fairly recent.

The chest was unlocked and she managed to flip the latch open with little effort. Files stacked inside and she had no intention of touching any until she spotted her name.

Sliding the file free of the others, she held it in the light. A slip of paper drifted from the contents and landed on her lap.

Measurements. She lifted the paper and frowned. Not just measurements. It also contained a list of features such as dark brown hair, blue eyes, and the mention of a birthmark.

Her hand drifted to her cheek, where a

similar birthmark showed. These were *her* details.

She flipped the paper over and found a strand of her hair taped to the back and she dropped the offensive script.

She opened the file and understood. It was a manifesto, gathered by The Council, recording Silus's intent to marry her as an uncalled wife.

Every recorded statement read like a violation. Transcripts from an interview she'd given more than a year ago filled nearly ten pages. Her words appeared so painfully trusting and naive. No one had warned her what sort of male she'd be marrying.

A tear fell onto the paper, blooming into a puddle and smudging the ink. Turning the page, she found the contract she'd signed. It hadn't been just more than two years, yet it felt like a lifetime ago.

She had so much hope in her heart. She'd genuinely believed they would be happy. Her efforts alone should have granted as much. But there was no pleasing a man like Silus, and there was no erasing the memories they made as husband and wife.

Closing the file, she held it to her chest and cried as if she were holding an innocent little girl. She wished she could have saved herself from such a fate.

The sun eventually faded behind the trees, and with the darkness came the voices of males mingling below. Some went home to their mates, while others mulled about on the lawn, discussing council business in muffled voices too distant for her to overhear.

Afraid to return downstairs, she rested against the boxes until only moonlight seeped into the attic. Sometime after the stars filled the sky and the clock chimed from the kitchen below, she drifted off to sleep.

The faint creak of the door opening and footsteps approaching caused her to stir. She held her body still and squeezed her eyes tight, mentally and emotionally exhausted. Nestling closer to the draped boxes, in the silence of her worry, she drifted back to sleep.

CHAPTER 30

When Eleazar finally made it back to his office, his nerves were shot. He tried to reason with The Council about Isaiah's existence all day and made absolutely no headway. They had been just as stubborn when Cain Hartzler had pleaded with them weeks ago.

They believed he crossed a vampire in the woods, but the assumption that it might be Isaiah seemed too far of a stretch for The Elders. After hours of testimony and countless recesses, so that male members of The Order could reflect, no decision was made.

Damascus Hostetler would be the greatest obstacle of all. At one point, he even pulled

Eleazar aside to urge him to let Silus hunt his wife.

Silus no longer had a wife, he simply didn't realize it yet. As soon as the Isaiah issue was resolved and a solution decided, he would inform The Council of his new mate. At that point, her marriage to the other male would be absolved.

Depositing some items on his desk, he shut his eyes and paused. The mere thought of Larissa brought such a fresh image to mind, and it was as if he could smell her nearby.

His head angled toward the curtains and he frowned. Lifting the fabric to his face, he inhaled the familiar fragrance, notes of his mate climbed into his lungs and his gaze jerked to attention. She had been in his office.

Opening the door to his private home, he closed it behind him and yelled, "Larissa?"

The scent of fear lured him up the stairs. His mind reached for hers, but she'd closed herself off. "Larissa?"

Gripping the doorframe of his bedroom, he stared at the empty bed, his heart lurching into a gallop. Not a single lamp or candle was lit.

"Larissa!"

He raced through the house, searching for any scent of an outsider. All he could smell was his missing mate and the traces of her fear. Then, emotion sorrowfully assaulted him and he staggered, hand pressing hard to his chest.

What had she done today? Where were these feelings stirring from? And where the hell was she now?

"Larissa!"

Panicked that Silus might have found her, his steps quickened. Turning furniture on end, he sped through the house, unsure where she might have gone.

If she was, in fact, missing, he prayed she disobeyed him and went to her parents'. At least she would be mildly safe there with Jonas gone.

It filled his stomach with acid to imagine another man touching her. He should have never waited to address The Council about their union. She should have been his first priority.

His gaze fell on the attic door. It was the only room he hadn't checked, but why would she be up there? There was nothing but dusty boxes and old relics on the third floor.

The knob opened with a click and the

scent of her hair clung to the air. The steps creaked underfoot as he crept through the dark, his eyes shifting and scanning the shadows for danger.

The unfurnished attic smelled of old books and dry air. Stacks of old ledgers cluttered the corners. There was no reason for Larissa to visit such a space, yet her scent grew stronger.

"Larissa, answer me."

A pristine swatch of white caught his eye. He walked toward the back of the house, mindful of the low peaks and dormer windows that cramped the space. His heart unclenched at the sight of her sleeping on the floor.

Then he frowned. Why on God's green Earth was she sleeping on a dusty attic floor?

He ducked and pushed a large chest out of the way. Her body was tucked in front of the tiny window, draped in silver moonlight, and appearing all too childlike and innocent.

He brushed a finger down her cheek to wake her, but she hardly stirred. She must be exhausted.

Glancing out the window, he noted the view. She had probably come up here to watch when The Council members dispersed.

He should not have left her alone so long, but his long absence from the farm made it impossible to get away. Everyone had questions and concerns for him to hear and no one gave him a moment to himself.

Her pale face rested on her arms curled about the sill. His head cocked at the sight of her swollen eyes. Had she been crying?

All other concerns dissolved as he scooped her off the floor and into his arms. She mumbled something he couldn't make out and snuggled close to his chest, and something tumbled from her lap, landing on the floor with a thump.

Eleazar frowned at the spray of papers spilled around his shoes. He'd return tomorrow to tidy it. For now, he needed to see to his mate.

Holding Larissa's sleeping form firmly in his arms, he carefully carried her down the winding stairwell and back to his bedroom. When he reached his room, he pulled back the quilt and lowered her to the bed. Her face pressed against the pillow, and she sighed.

Gently lifting her shoulders, he untied the back of her apron, then removed the pins from her hair. Ebony waves rippled like a river around her face, covering the pillows and framing her beauty.

Sliding her arms from her dress, he carefully stripped her, leaving her only in a chemise, and as he folded her clothing, something crumpled in the front pocket. Fishing his fingers inside, he withdrew a creased wedge of paper and recognized his handwriting.

He unfolded the pages and bitter regret consumed him the moment he realized what he held. Moving toward the window and the silver moonlight, he read over the familiar contract, trying to imagine what Larissa felt when she found it.

It's on this third Tuesday of September, that I, Bishop Eleazar King, hereby consent to the marriage of Brother Silus Hostetler, son of Damascus Hostetler, descendant of Nicodemus Rocke, to Larissa Hartzler, daughter of Jonas Hartzler, descendant of Ezekiel Hartzler. It's in good standing that the female is in agreement with the union and has made no protests known to The Council. It's for such reason that I accept said betrothal as legal in light of The Council's divided vote, finding the union favorable seven to two, hereby overriding the call for unanimous agreement among The Elders.

*T*HE BRIDE IS *of forty-eight years. The parents of the bride have testified to being of firm belief that Larissa Hartzler's virtue remains intact and that she is healthy, with no reason to assume she shall face difficulty conceiving. It's placed upon the groom, Silus Hostetler, to fortify the link of the Hartzler and Hostetler lines.*

*S*ILUS HOSTETLER HAS TESTIFIED *to a full understanding that his bride of choice is by no means his true called mate. If, by the will of God, Silus is someday called to his true mate, his marriage to Larissa Hartzler shall be considered null and void and the female's transgressions shall be forgiven, if not overlooked. Any children conceived under the protection of this contract within the bounds of this union will be considered legitimate from here on.*

*I*N ACCORDANCE *with The Order and Family Law, upon consummation of the union, Silus Hostetler holds all rights over his wife to act as head of the* *household without question. It's within the bounds set forth by The Order's laws that the head of household should maintain any and all rights to determine what is best for his wife and family so long as he does not impede any higher laws of The Order.*

BY TAKING *vows and promising honor and obedience, Larissa Hartzler will be further known as Larissa Hostetler, wife of Silus, and as such, promises to honor and obey him in all matters. By the protection of Family Law, any male, deemed head of the household, shall preserve the final decision in matters of obedience, physical relations, and servitude. It's under the acceptance of such law, that said wife shall leave all decisions to that of her husband. The husband shall determine who may enter the home, how the wife shall serve the home, and so forth. A wife may not leave the home without the husband's arranged protection. No male shall address the wife of another male without the husband's permission. The wife shall be courteous to her husband in all matters and show gratitude for his sacrifice and protection. Furthermore, all and every possession, including that of the wife's personal effects and body shall, from here on, be under the sole protection of her husband.*

THIS CONTRACT *and union is sealed by the bishop:* Eleazar King *Witnessed by:* Damascus Hostetler
    Signed by: Silus Hostetler and his wife, Larissa Hostetler

ELEAZAR CRUMPLED the documents in his hand until his knuckles popped. He then cursed himself for being three kinds of a fool. Larissa was right. She *had* been given away like chattel.

Their laws had been created to ensure privacy. Their rigid culture, their Amish way of living, kept them isolated from the outside world. But how much were the laws protecting females like Larissa from being abused by males like Silus?

Glancing back at his mate sleeping soundly on his bed, he now understood her tears. She'd shared glimpses of her experiences with him. But he still hadn't entirely fathomed how restricted her freedom had become once she married Silus or how deep the emotional neglect had reached—no part of her remained untouched by her husband's overbearing control.

Females always had fewer privileges than the males on the farm, but the moment Larissa had tied her life to a male, her autonomy constricted to that of an infant's.

"You're back."

His shoulders tensed and he slowly faced her. "You were sleeping in the attic when I returned." He desperately wished he had good news to deliver.

Her gaze dropped to the crumpled document in his hand. "Will you burn that?"

"I can't. It's part of our official records."

She looked away and a mix of shame and anger assaulted him. Crossing to the bed, he reached for her but she leaned away from him.

Startled by her rejection, his hands dropped to his side. "You're upset with me." He was also upset with himself.

"You left me trapped in this house all day."

"I'm sorry. I tried several times to get back to you, but council business kept me tethered."

"I didn't even have a bonnet. I couldn't leave."

His mouth quirked in a half-smile. He noticed it wasn't his mandate keeping her there but rather her propriety. "Where would you have gone? No one can know you've returned until I've cleared our bonding with The Elders."

She sniffled and sat up. "I would've gone home."

"You are home."

"No, I would've gone back to my apartment. I don't want to be here anymore."

Her announcement softened his knees, and he dropped into the chair tucked in the corner. True worry choked him. "Why?"

"Because I hate it here."

"You don't mean that. This is your home."

"This is not my home. I'm no one here, just chattel on paper, traded like old goods and displaced as an orphan until others decide my fate."

"You're my mate."

"*Your* mate." Her lips formed a thin line. "Why must my identity always be tied to a male. Am I so worthless on my own?"

"Larissa, my love, you are not worthless. You're everything to me."

"How can you say that? You know nothing about me other than the fact that our souls are tied."

"So, tell me all there is to know." He edged onto the bed and took her hands in his. "I'm desperate to keep your secrets. I'm starved for every little detail. How could you think that you're nothing without a male? I'm the one who is lacking. Five hundred years on this Earth and I have nothing to show other than a lonesome existence. I have but one trusted friend. Countless acquaintances tolerate me for their own advantage and avoid me by instinct when they have no favor to ask.

"Larissa, you're warm, and giving, and so considerate of others. I watch you light up at the mere mention of your family and I'm sick with envy. I'd give half my life to have a fraction of your affection for them."

He drew her cold fingers to his lips and kissed the tips. "I can tolerate a lot of things, but I cannot tolerate you discrediting your worth. I have it on good authority that you're invaluable to my soul. How could such value attach to nothingness? You're precious—a treasure. And I'm eternally grateful that I've found you. I'd be beyond devastated if I ever lost you. Even tonight, as I searched the house for you, the crushing fear that something might have happened made me frantic with worry."

He reached for the blanket when he saw her shiver. Draping it over her shoulders, he drew the ends together at her chest. She eased her head onto the pillows and stared away.

"How can I make this better for you, Larissa? Please tell me what you need."

"I want to know where my brother is. I need to speak to Cain."

Her need for another male stung, and he wondered if she doubted his ability to protect her. Accepting that she did not want him near, he nodded and backed out of the room. "I'll send message to your siblings and ask if they know his whereabouts."

"Annalise will know."

He hesitated. Annalise was Adam Hartzler's mate. Adam was Cain's twin, and the two shared a strange bond that broke the laws of nature. He wasn't comfortable approaching Adam's mate about another male's whereabouts.

"I will speak to your brother Adam first."

She laughed without humor. "Of course, you will."

Too late. He realized what he'd done—he placed her fate in the hands of yet another male.

CHAPTER 31

Dawn crested over the horizon as the stars above faded. Jonas had fought so hard not to come to this place, knowing that once he came, he would forever surrender his heart and soul and nothing would ever be right again.

Wind chilled his skin, but his blood warmed as the beast within awoke at the scent of his mate. His soul raged for him to take what was his.

Windchimes danced and rang as gusts wove throughout the cluttered yard. The air wore the metallic fragrance of snow and the trees swayed in the whistling draft. His ears prickled at the rustle of slight movement inside the dwelling.

He bit down, forcing his jaw to lock and hardening his knees to fight the urge to storm the home. His heart was being sawed in two. Even his thinking changed with each passing moment, his everyday opinions and desires fading into distant memories until he no longer recognized his own mind.

The curse of his calling was swallowing him whole.

The dim set of the house showed before the graying horizon, and Jonas's breath hitched as a light flickered on inside. His keen hearing followed the sounds coming from within.

He took three steps forward before awareness set in. As if being pulled by a thousand lead balloons, he fought to keep his feet rooted as his honor slipped away.

Finding himself a mere ten feet from the front door of the home, his mind screamed in objection. *No!* He would move no further. He would leave.

His mind struggled to remember his wife's beautiful face. If he could just hear her voice—

A soft, feminine hum sang from within the house, stealing his focus.

His back arched as if his heart planned to rip from his chest. Animal instincts battled through the tattered shred of his humanity. Eyes wide, he watched as one foot stepped onto the rickety, old porch stairs as his other foot dragged in protest.

Sweat trickled down his spine. The overwhelming grace of surrender quickly smothered the fleeting thought of triumph, and his struggle softened as if beaten out of him. The battle was lost. His soul wanted what hid inside this home and cared about little else.

Stumbling onto the porch in clumsy, reluctant haste, Jonas tumbled into a stack of clay pots. The terracotta toppled to the planked floor, shattering across the cold ground like ice breaking over the earth.

The front door opened with a swoosh followed quickly by a snap as the screen tightly sprang back in place. His inner beast shivered at her scent, but before he could turn to face her, there was an ominous click in his ear and cold metal poking in his back.

"You stay right there, boy, and I won't shoot that pretty head of yours off your shoulders."

His body tightened at the scent of her

nearness and the crisp tone of her voice. He glanced over his shoulder, stared up the barrel of the rifle, and his heart kicked with the force of a Clydesdale.

White hair whipped across her face as a cold gust of wind cut under the porch awning. Her threadbare bathrobe fluttered open, drawing his attention to her tattered slippers.

There was no retreat left for him. The moment he stared into her eyes, he was gone—hers for all eternity.

His loyalty to all others sapped away, leaving him shaken and hollow, hungry for the female before him. She would fill every void and satisfy every ache, but a tiny shred of shame remained and he cowered like a frightened dog.

Without a bit of inflection, he held her stare. "Aim for my neck and shoot my head clear off my shoulders, and you shall be the angel of mercy I need."

Sighing, she lowered the gun, and he faced her. Her eyes crinkled and her lips pursed but kept her finger tucked neatly into the trigger guard.

"You must be Jonas."

This was no dream. Here, in the hell of his

reality, nothing was protecting her from his savage need.

"Save yourself and end this." Hooking a finger under the tip of the rifle, he lifted it until it lodged into the flesh of his throat. "I'm ready."

She lowered the gun again. "I've been expecting you. Let's get out of the cold." She reached for the door and paused. "My grandchildren are still sleeping. You misbehave and I'll blow a hole in your chest bigger than the Liberty Bell." The screen whined open, and she nodded for him to enter. "Go on."

The gun practically outweighed her petite body, yet she held it without trembling. "You're inviting me in?" Was she daft?

"I've had a visitor for the past few days who's explained matters to me. Like I said, I've been expecting you."

His jaw hardened. "Who?" Breathing deep, he scented the air, and his hackles rose. Another immortal male was inside.

His eyes dilated as a growl rumbled within his chest. There was something familiar about the scent, but his beast could only recognize the presence of another male near its mate, the presence of a threat—

"Now, don't you start growling and

snarling like some dirty dog. That man in there has been nothing but polite since he arrived. He warned me you might not recognize him." She stepped in front of him, blocking his entry and looking up at him through wise, patient eyes. "He says he's your son."

A memory of his children danced through his mind, unfamiliar yet triggering a sense of nostalgia. His mind clung to a glimpse of Abilene but the vision dissolved the harder he tried to grab hold.

He had two sons: Cain and Adam. He scented the air again. "Cain." The name passed his lips as a whispered oath. Why was Cain there?

A growl purred through clenched teeth. His son had a bad habit of getting too familiar with other males' mates.

He sneered at her. "You should not have let him inside your home."

"Oh, please, the bud's been off this rose for quite some time, and I've never been much of a fan of veal. I prefer my meat a bit more seasoned."

Did she believe she was younger than him? "What exactly has my son told you?"

"Come inside and we will discuss it. This

chill burns my lungs something fierce, and my arthritis is starting to ache."

The mention of her discomfort was enough to earn his obedience. Soon, her pain would fade and she'd enjoy the eternal health of an immortal.

She was fragile and aged but a timeless beauty. The need to please her dictated his good behavior with unexpected force. He entered her home like a docile, domesticated pet.

The scent of fresh coffee, paint, and mortal children bombarded him. Cain was there but out of sight, wisely keeping his distance.

"Sit." She pointed to the small kitchen table dominating the cramped space.

The wooden chair creaked under his weight. Resting his palms on the smooth enameled surface of the table, he watched her set the rifle in the corner.

Boxes and paintings lay stacked against almost every wall. Apothecary bottles cluttered the kitchen counter by the dozen. A collage of colored photographs decorated the ice box.

She set two steaming mugs on the table,

sliding one in front of him. He caught her hand and she stilled.

Her delicate bones were as fragile as a bird. He could snap her in half with a flick of his wrist. "You're fragile," he said almost accusingly, her brittleness concerning him.

"I'm old. It comes with the territory."

Not always, he thought.

She pulled her hand away and glared at him. "You get that one for free. Touch me again, and we'll have a problem."

His mouth twitched with the urge to smile. What exactly did she think she could do to him? His strength far outweighed hers and a bullet would be a welcomed end, so long as her aim was decent.

He did not want to be there, yet he found it impossible to leave.

"Drink your coffee."

Jonas pulled the mug to his lips and pretended to take a sip. His system no longer wanted food, and everything tasted of bitter ash.

His gaze latched onto the vital pulse at Clara's throat. There, just beneath the crepe of her pale, ivory skin, he spotted a fluttering blue vein. The thrum of her heartbeat met his ears, calling to him like a siren. *Jonas. Jonas. Jonas...*

"It's polite not to stare."

His gaze snapped to her eyes. "What has Cain told you?"

She placed her mug on the table. Flecks of paint embedded around her cuticles. "He told me to expect you. That you planned to make me an offer, but he refused to give me more details than that. He only said that it was important that I hear you out. But let me tell you, Mister Jonas, if this is some attempt to purchase my home, you can leave. This house will go to my grandchildren."

"I'm not interested in your home."

"Then what?"

His gaze drifted to the ice box. "Who is that man with his arm around you in that photograph?"

She glanced over her shoulder. "That's my late husband, Arthur. That picture was taken in Washington the year Clinton was inaugurated. My husband was a political man."

"Husband?"

"He's gone now. We lost him and my son a few years back."

"I'm sorry for your family's loss."

She gave a sad smile as her grief thickened the air. "Loss is something my family has known all too well." She took a sip of her coffee, her gaze turning away from the photographs. "Why don't you tell me why you're here?"

"Did you love your husband?"

"Very much. Are you married?"

A sharp pain knifed through his heart at the memory of his wife. He struggled to picture her face but sensed he loved her very much. He wanted—desperately—to say her name, but for reasons he didn't understand, his brain wouldn't allow it.

"I have four children."

"And a wife?"

"My wife sent me here to you." Resentment boiled in his veins with chaotic confusion.

"Well, I'm on pins and needles, Mister Jonas. What can I do for you?"

He glanced at the little orange bottles cluttered along the windowsill. "Why do you have so many medicines?"

She laughed. "I'm old. You'll get there someday."

"How old are you?"

"Tsk, tsk. Did your mother never teach you it's impolite to ask a woman her age?"

"My apologies."

She waved a hand at him with paint-dappled fingernails. "I'll forgive you. I'm twenty-nine." At his look of shock, she chuckled but her laughter faded into a rattling cough. When she regained her composure, she smiled. "I'm seventy-two."

In the corner of the kitchen, a shabbily dressed doll slouched against a worn basketball. "You're the guardian of your grandchildren."

"Yes. My daughter recently passed away. It's something I would rather not discuss if you don't mind. Still too fresh."

"How old are they?"

"Ten and sixteen."

"You worry for them." It was not a question but an observation.

"Of course. I'm all they have left. Cybil, the younger of the two, hasn't spoken a single word since her mother died. And Dane, he'll soon be a legal adult, but he's still very much a young boy. I just hope I can make it until he's eighteen, but the doctors..." She waved a hand. "It's a worry that keeps me up at night."

"Make it?"

She chuckled and coughed again. "Do you know what the difference is between doctors and God, Mister Jonas?" She raised a faded brow. "God doesn't think He's a doctor." When he didn't laugh, she looked at his shirt and suspenders. "Perhaps my attempt at humor offended you."

"No." He knew plenty about being at odds with God. "What do the doctors tell you?"

"I've refused treatment, other than pain-management drugs, at this point." She patted the pocket of her robe. "My friend Mary Jane will keep me company until the end. According to the doctors, my time's only a few months away—too soon to see my grandson turn eighteen, so you can understand my stress."

He frowned. "Treatment for what?"

"Cancer, Mister Jonas. I'm dying."

Tension coiled in his back. "You're certain?"

"We all die eventually. There's no such thing as eternal life."

"What if there was? Would you take it?"

"I'm too old to play make-believe."

"But what if you could live forever and be there for your grandchildren? Would you wish it?"

"Wishes are meant for wells." She shook her head. "The most I can do is prepare for the inevitable. My attorney added their names to the deed, and I've expressed my wishes for Dane to become Cybil's legal guardian once he's of age. I have money set aside from Arthur's life insurance policy that should keep them comfortable for a few years. Other than that, what can I do? I'm tired of fighting. I want to be with my Arthur again."

Touched by her surrender, he confessed, "I'm dying as well."

Surprise registered in her clouded eyes. "You don't look sick."

He shook his head. "When it's our time, we know. My wife knows it. My children know it. But I'm the only one prepared for it. Like you, I refuse to take the cure."

"But you're so young." She frowned. "It's strange… Cain looks your age."

"He's not."

Still frowning, she tilted her head and studied him. "How old are you?"

"Cain is thirty-seven and my eldest daughter will be fifty this winter."

Her eyes grew big. "You're fooling with me."

"Would you like to know how old I am?"

She studied him, likely taking in the glossy

sheen of his black hair and the smooth texture of his skin. "I won't believe you're a day over forty, and even then, I'm being generous."

"I can help you, Clara."

He sensed her disbelief as her lips firmed. "They warn us about people like you."

"They?"

"The speakers at the community center. They tell us how to spot frauds, people who solicit the elderly to take advantage of situations when our options run out. Well, I can promise you, Mister Jonas, you won't get a cent out of me. I don't know what game you're playing, but I don't want your help. I think it's time for you to leave."

"There is no game."

"Then what? Why are you here?" She pushed up from the table and collected the rifle, angling it in his direction. "It's time for you to go."

He stared down the barrel of the gun. "Death would be a welcomed mercy at this point."

"Well, I don't need any extra housework, so why don't you do the polite thing and see your way out of my home."

Dawn shined through the window, illuminating the many bottles of pills. He needed to seek shelter. "Imagine an eternity to protect your grandchildren and never fear death again."

"Even if that were possible, which it's not, could you offer my grandchildren the same? I've seen enough loved ones die. I don't want to see anymore. Now, get out."

"I could take the pain away."

She cocked the rifle. "You're wearing my patience thin, Mister Jonas."

He could sense her exhaustion more than anything. Where she had held the rifle steady before, she now trembled under its weight. He didn't believe she had the strength to pull the trigger and stay standing through the reverberation of a shot. But he admired her vigor and didn't want to see her weakness exposed.

He stood and stepped toward the door. Looking back at the darkened doorway leading to the rest of the house, certain his son listened to their conversation, he said, "Cain will watch over you. If you need anything, he will see to it."

He wasn't sure how his son had maneuvered his way into her trust, but he was grateful he had since Jonas had failed. Useless during the daylight hours, he fully intended to return and try again tonight. No matter what his mind or heart wanted, his soul insisted he stay by his mate.

"Lock your doors," he warned as he left. The greatest danger to Clara at the moment was him, and he had no idea what condition he'd be in when he returned.

CHAPTER 32

Larissa washed her face at the ewer, taking her time while Eleazar was gone. He'd left early that morning to speak to her family and to find Cain. She didn't expect to hear from her brother any time soon, and Eleazar was needed back in front of The Council today, so when someone knocked at the front door, she panicked.

Eleazar rarely used that entrance and she'd only ever seen him come in through the adjoining office door, so she knew right away it wasn't him entering the house.

Creeping down the steps, she pressed her back to the plaster wall and slowly peeked behind the front window's curtain. Adriel

Schrock stood on the porch, shoulders back and chin lifted in its usual proud manner.

Larissa wasn't sure what to do. She hardly knew the elder woman, and no one was supposed to know she was there.

"Larissa? It's Adriel Schrock. Eleazar sent me."

Startled that the woman knew of her presence, she questioned the sincerity of her words. Very few immortals referred to Eleazar by name. Was this woman his friend? She recognized her scent from his office.

"I know all about your situation—and your need for secrecy. You can trust me."

Biting her lip, she debated what to do.

Adriel sighed. "The longer you leave me standing here, the more suspicious it looks to anyone passing by."

Hiding behind the wood, Larissa opened the door and the female stepped inside. Her sharp green eyes sliced through the shadows. "Thank you. I brought you a bonnet and some other things Eleazar thought you might need."

When Larissa didn't take the stack of clothing, the woman huffed and set it on the chair against the wall. "You're as skittish as—"

A little mouse.

Adriel chuckled. "Is that what he calls you?

I'd sock a male for such a belittling endearment."

Larissa hadn't even felt the female in her mind.

"He'll learn, dear. There's nothing mousey about you. You're still young and discovering your strength."

Larissa blocked her thoughts and the older female flinched. "Easy." She rubbed her temple. "That's quite a jab you have." She removed her bonnet, revealing a head of spiked red hair.

Such short hair was uncommon among the Amish, and Larissa couldn't help but stare as Adriel dragged a hand over her head, further mussing the jagged mess.

"I brought you some toiletries, a new gown, which, looking at you, may be a bit too short, and a sandwich." She held up the cloth-wrapped food, and Larissa almost ripped it out of her hands.

Unraveling the material, she shoved the bread and meat into her mouth. "Thank you. I'm starving."

"I figured as much." Lifting the pile of clothes, she lowered to the chair.

Larissa hesitated and watched her, unsure if Eleazar would mind the female in his house.

"Child, I'm Eleazar's friend. You can trust me. No one else knows I'm here, and I've told no one of your presence."

Larissa took another bite of the sandwich. "Thank you for the food. And the clothing."

"Being that Eleazar and I share a long history, I expect you and I will also become companions." Leaning forward, she cupped a hand at the side of her mouth and confided, "He's overdue for a wife."

Larissa swallowed the last bite and shook her head. "I'm not his wife."

Waving her words away, Adriel rolled her emerald eyes. "Silus is a rodent. Eleazar will see your marriage to him dissolved. And the moment he does, you will become Larissa King, wife to the bishop, and a respected female among The Order."

Her lips firmed. "Only because of my marriage."

The older female studied her for a moment. "Who cares where power comes from so long as you possess the confidence to wield it. No other female will have the bishop's ear. But not only that, as his mate, you have his devotion. He's a decent male, one who, I believe, can see reason and the value of change."

She'd heard rumors of Adriel Schrock and sensed she was being recruited into some sort of campaign. "I'm not comfortable advising the bishop on issues that don't involve me."

"The *bishop*? How sweet you are to regard him as your authority still. Do not underestimate your worth, child. You are marrying the patriarch of The Order. That makes you our matriarch, the neck that supports and directs the head of our society. The females of The Order will seek audience with you, as you—more than anyone else—can impact our future. You enchant him."

Larissa laughed. "I assure you, Eleazar is quite capable of telling me no."

"Denying one's mate is a very difficult thing to do."

She studied the woman, almost certain that she lived alone in her house. From what Larissa could recall, the female had a son, but he was much older. "Are you mated?"

The intimidating woman lowered her gaze. "I chose to leave my mate."

"What? How? It's impossible to ignore the call." Larissa had agreed to bond with Eleazar because of such certainty.

"I did not ignore the call. We bonded. But then I left."

"You left your mate?" She didn't believe mates could tolerate distance.

"Cer was not an honorable male. When I fled, Eleazar helped me escape."

"Your mate's name was Sir?"

"*Cer,* as in Cerberus. He was named for the hounds of Hades, the demons of the pit, which is exactly what he was."

Larissa lowered into the other chair. "He was cruel to you?"

"Immortal males suffer a great deal when they're called to their mates. Cer resented the sense that he was indebted to a female. He always viewed females as the weaker sex. Any sense of duty or servitude sent him into a rage."

She worried her mate might also come to resent such obligation. "I don't wish to anger the bishop." Eleazar was ten times her age and far more powerful. "I want peace."

"Don't we all? That's why we must fight for equality. We need a champion, and God has chosen you."

"I think you'll be disappointed. I'm not anyone's champion. I'm just a female immortal who wants a quiet life."

"Eleazar tells me you share his passion."

Larissa blushed, memories of their intimacy rising the internal temperature of her blood.

"He also tells me you somehow managed to knock him out—twice."

"That was an accident."

"No, child. That was God's gift. I always believed if Eleazar were called, his mate would possess incredible strength. You're split from the same soul, destined to complete each other and equal by design."

Larissa shook her head. "I have no control over my abilities."

"You're a mirror of his strength. Whatever he throws at you, be it passion or power, you reflect it right back. You're a key meant to unlock his destiny and he is the key that will unlock yours."

Larissa mulled over Adriel's words in the hours after she left. She never considered herself powerful, but she was also very young. To think this other side of her existed was to think of herself as a secret left untold. She found herself curiously awaiting any clues that might prove the wise female right.

Power was something Larissa never claimed but something she envied very much.

"I see that Adriel brought you the items I requested."

Larissa spun and gasped at the sight of Eleazar. "You startled me." That's what she deserved for entertaining such self-serving thoughts. Her ego had dulled her senses and left her unguarded. She was lucky it was only Eleazar.

"My apologies." He crossed the room and pressed a kiss to the side of her mouth.

Something was wrong. "What is it?"

"The Council requests your presence in the hall."

She drew back. "They know I've returned?"

"I informed them this morning."

"And Silus?"

"He's disputing the authenticity of our bond, but I expected as much."

Females were seldom invited into the hall. "Must I go?"

"I begged The Elders to leave you be, but, due to my involvement, I had to surrender my authority to Abraham Gerig. He'll act as presiding bishop until we put all objections to rest. They require your testimony. I'll be there with you the entire time. No one will harm you, Larissa." His hand caught hers as his thumb gently traced the racing pulse within her wrist.

They stripped him of his authority. What if they gave her back to Silus?

Her body quaked with uncertainty, and Eleazar read her fear. Gripping her by the shoulders, he forced her to look up at him. "He will not touch you. I need you to trust me. I will never let anything happen to you. Ever. I'm sorry you must go through this, but once it's done, it's done forever."

She shut her eyes and nodded, trying to regain her composure, desperately wishing she possessed the power Adriel described earlier.

Eleazar ran the back of his finger down her cheek. "They're waiting for us."

CHAPTER 33

$\mathcal{E}$leazar escorted Larissa through the corridor toward Council Hall in silence. Her fear plucked on a visceral cord inside of him, and the more it intensified, the stronger he interpreted their link. By the time they reached the doors to the hall, her hands trembled in terror.

The rapid gallop of horses thundered from the east as every male approached to hear the testimony. Eleazar had no doubt Silus Hostetler already waited inside.

Adriel looked up from her sewing as she sat on her bench. The show of support registered within his mate, and Larissa lifted her chin and drew her shoulders back.

"Are you ready?"

Larissa nodded stiffly, her heart beating recklessly for all to hear.

Leaning close, he opened the door and whispered, "I'm right here. If you're afraid, just look to me or your grandfathers. You have elders on the bench who support you. And your brother, Adam, is also here."

"Cain?" It was the first word she spoke since leaving his home.

He shook his head, regretful that he had not been able to locate him for her.

He led her into the hall, and a ruckus stirred at the front. Bodies stepped aside as a wave of hostility cut through the crowd and Silus appeared, eyes glaring at Larissa, hands clenched in fists at his side.

Eleazar growled, warning the male not to come any closer as Abraham hammered the gavel and called for everyone to take a seat.

Silus's glare dropped to the bishop's hold on Larissa's arm. "How dare you touch my wife." His hateful stare stabbed at Larissa. "You will atone for your sins."

Eleazar's scent filled the air surrounding his mate until the male's nostrils flared at the repugnant claim, and he took a step back. Then, slipping an arm around her shoulders, staking an unmistakable claim, he guided her to the seats up front.

"Brother Silus, take a seat," Abraham called from the bench.

Defiantly, the male stormed toward the bench, ignoring his designated seat. "This spectacle has gone on long enough. Larissa is my wife, and this is no longer a public matter."

"The matter is not whether or not she is your wife, Brother Silus. The matter is if the bishop's calling is genuine, then there are grounds for an annulment. You have no authority over another male's mate."

"She's my wife! I have the authority of her husband until proven otherwise. I demand a word with her in private."

"Your request is denied." Abraham sat with the patience of an oak. "The sooner you cooperate, the sooner we can put this issue to rest."

Eleazar sat beside his mate and watched as Silus stomped across the hall. "Larissa, get up." When her hand tightened around Eleazar's and she did not move, Silus snapped, "I said get up!"

Her shoulders tensed, and as he grabbed for the front of her apron, a clap of thunder shook the walls. The bishop snarled, now gripping the male's offending hand and twisting it until bones crumbled.

Releasing the sack of flesh, Eleazar flashed his fangs. "Reach for her again, and I'll rip it off."

Silus staggered back, cradling his misshapen claws as the bones molded back into place.

Abraham, now irritated, hammered the gavel again. "Take your seat."

Reluctantly, Silus lowered into a chair on the other side of the aisle and stared daggers at the bishop. Eleazar was not intimidated in the least.

"It has come to The Council's attention," Abraham began, "that Sister Larissa has been called to her mate."

Silus shot up from his seat. "She's lying!"

"Sit. Down." Abraham's eyes flashed with impatience. "I will not remind you again that you have been ordered here by your elders. You will follow the laws of this council or forfeit your right to stay present. What will it be?"

Silus reluctantly sat.

Abraham released the gavel and set it aside. "As a married female, certain items must be addressed. Silus Hostetler, do you accept Larissa's calling?"

"I do not."

"Under the protest of Sister Larissa's husband, The Council shall review the testimony of all those involved in her disappearance. The Council will decide which male holds the greatest claim to her, and the matter of all other claims will dissolve once a final verdict is reached." Abraham focused on Larissa. "Sister Larissa, is your mate present?"

"Y—yes, Brother Abraham. My mate is Bishop Eleazar King."

A wave of mumbles washed through the room, and the gavel once again knocked. "Quiet."

"Bishop King, do you verify Sister Larissa's claim?"

"Yes, I, too, experienced the calling." His eyes narrowed on Silus. "We have completed the bond, and I've claimed Larissa as my eternal mate."

More gasps, and the gavel slammed harder. "If the outbursts cannot be controlled, this case will become a private matter."

"Sister Larissa, can you confirm that the bond with your mate has been completed?"

Her cheeks flushed and her gaze dropped to the hands wringing in her lap. "Yes."

"This is a conspiracy!" Silus shouted. "She's a witch! She will lie to all of you!"

"The Elders shall judge her truthfulness," Abraham barked. "And that is the last warning you get, Brother Silus." Turning back to Larissa, he lowered his voice. "My child, do you think you can come up here and answer a few questions?"

Larissa slowly nodded but kept her gaze on the floor. She moved to stand before The Council.

"Sister Larissa, how did you come to realize you were being called to Bishop King?"

"Elea—Bishop King told me so."

"Did you suffer any symptoms before he brought you this news?"

She nodded. "I hadn't been feeding well. I'd been ravenous but my appetite had been off. I assumed it was simply my nerves."

"Why would you assume it was your nerves?"

She lifted her gaze, wearing a mask of contrition. "I ran from my home. I feared I'd eventually be found and punished."

"So, you did not leave the farm to follow your calling?"

"No."

"How long have you known about the call?"

"Just this week."

"Did you dream?"

She fidgeted. "A few times. Maybe more. I wasn't sleeping much."

She told Eleazar that she had also been watching a lot of television and the fascinating machine had a way of filling her memories with stories. He believed she'd confused her earlier dreams, thinking she merely recalled something she'd watched on TV when, in fact, the memories were workings of her own imagination.

"Could you describe one of your dreams?"

Eleazar objected. "That's a private matter and irrelevant."

"Very well," Abraham said. "Are you in accordance with God's will, Sister Larissa?"

"Yes."

Relief washed through Eleazar.

"And would it satisfy you to legally wed the bishop?"

"Yes, it would."

"It's important to understand the choice you are making. You will not be permitted to carnal knowledge of any other male, including a past spouse. Should the temptation to return to Silus arise—"

"There will be no such temptation. I'm content with the mate God has chosen for me."

Silus's chair flipped to the floor as he bolted to his feet. "You filthy whore! How dare you give your body to another without my consent! I—" Closing his hands around his throat, he gasped.

The bishop's glare burned into the other male, his mind squeezing the breath from his hateful lungs as he choked for air that could not pass.

"Bishop, please refrain from abusing Brother Silus."

Silus's complexion muddled as his eyes bulged and blood vessels popped. Eleazar held him under his control for several more beats, waiting for a true sense of impotence to set in.

When he released his hold, Silus crumpled to the floor, gasping and coughing speckles of blood. Eleazar crossed the floor slowly, not stopping until the other male's fractured hand crunched under his boot.

"You will never speak of my mate in that tone again. Make no mistake, Silus, she is *mine,* by my will, her will, and the will of God. Your claim ends here and now. Do not test me on this. I may have surrendered my title today, but tomorrow, and every day after, I will be your bishop. Disobey me, and you will beg for death."

The moment he stepped off Silus's hand, he cradled it to his chest and panted. Spittle coated his chin as he stood and shouted, "This is a mockery of justice! Forget your verdict! I rescind my vows. That witch is nothing but trash that will one day incinerate in the pits of hell!" Then, glaring at The Council, he snarled, "Without discipline, a precedent has been set, and you will all pay the price."

Eleazar sheltered Larissa from such hateful speech, positioning his body directly between her and Silus. The male scurried out of the hall like the rat he was.

CHAPTER 34

$\mathcal{L}$arissa's hands trembled as the gavel hammered down. Her heart clattered against her ribs with the finality of the verdict. The Council recognized her bond with Eleazar, and her marriage to Silus would soon be annulled.

The moment Silus stormed out of the hall, she should have suffered a great relief but she remained on full display. Every male watched her as they openly discussed her most intimate relationships for all to hear.

"I want the paperwork drawn up immediately," Eleazar ordered, speaking to several elders and a few other males under his command.

Larissa tried not to listen. Hiding in plain

sight, she sat on the front pew and hardly moved a muscle, anxious to return to the privacy of the bishop's home.

Eleazar was a force of nature within these walls. Assertive and secure in his authority, he did not waver in any decision. She had discovered a softer side of the male she believed others did not know.

Her lips pressed tight, the musings of a smile taking hold as she considered that she was the only female in the world with such knowledge of Eleazar King. His comfort with her in private translated, on some level, to trust. And here, deference to him today did the same.

She had not obeyed him because he was her bishop or her mate. Instead, she accompanied him, followed his request, and trusted him to protect her. The skittishness faded, and an unbelievable connectivity had formed. She could sense her soul lacing tightly to his.

His eyes found hers, and he smiled while discussing council business with several other men. Something warm and unmistakably Eleazar touched her heart as if to say *soon.*

Soon they would leave. *Soon* they would return to the privacy of his home, where he would hold her protectively in his arms and worship her body as they met each other's needs. *Soon* this would be over and they would be wed. *Soon* the cause for sorrow would disappear.

The realization came with such welcome and acceptance, it left her shaken. Her composure threatened to slip away as tears of relief prickled her eyes.

Her affection for Eleazar grew from a slow burn, but what existed already would be impossible to extinguish. She cared for this male very much. The safety he provided filled her with such a sense of security that she hoped she found the courage to be her true self—a female both she and Eleazar grow to know together.

As the hall emptied and bodies drifted into the corridors, the volume of baritone chatter lowered. Females were not permitted in the hall unless requested and always under the escort of an honorable male. The more vacant the room became, the more the nervous energy fizzed.

Her testimony made her the focus of every male and, even as they left the hall, they did not hesitate to stare. When Eleazar finally approached, energy bubbled in her veins. Looking up at him, she silently communicated how desperately she wanted to go back to his room and be alone.

He arched a brow and grinned as if to say he looked forward to the same. "I have a few more details to discuss and then we can be on our way." Holding out a hand to help her rise, he said, "Why don't I take you to Adriel's bench and you can wait together."

The thought of passing the time with another female comforted her, and she gratefully accepted his hand. Eleazar escorted her through the groups of males still milling about. When they found Adriel occupying the bench just outside the Council Hall doors, she milled up at them with clever green eyes that always appeared rich with secrets.

"You can finally exhale," Adriel greeted with a proud grin. "You did well."

Still shaken, she whispered a quiet thank you and took a seat.

"I must finish a few things, Adriel. Can Larissa keep you company for a bit?"

"Of course."

"Thank you." Eleazar tipped Larissa's chin, pulling her mouth to his. "I know this day has been trying, but you were wonderful in there. I'm very proud of the way you kept your composure, my brave lioness." His eyes darkened as if to say he knew a brave lioness hid inside. "Later, when we're alone, I'd like to see you lose it." With a meaningful glance, he pinched her chin then walked away.

Adriel chuckled. "I'd be embarrassed for him if he didn't appear so happy. This is a new side of Eleazar."

Larissa flushed and lowered to the bench. She was coming to rely on his kindness.

"I told you he would not let you down." Adriel adjusted the material draped over her lap and expertly stitched a seam.

"Is it a quilt?" Larissa admired the detail of each swatch.

"It's for your brother and his new mate. It's a family tree." She lifted the sewn cloth and opened the folded section displaying the many branches of the Hartzler line. "The babe will be here before you know it, and your family will have much to celebrate this spring, I hope."

"It's lovely." An ache formed within her hollow womb, and she longed to someday have her own reason to celebrate.

Larissa's worries stemmed from the trials her mother faced. The thought of her mother's many miscarriages reminded her of her parent's marriage. She wondered if she would now be permitted to visit her family home.

The older woman gave her a knowing smile. "It will happen for you." She then whispered, "You must guard your thoughts, child. There are many elders about."

Not realizing that her mind had been so unprotected, she put up a barricade. Adriel gave a nod when her mind was no longer open.

"Now just think, all of this can be put behind you and you can move on with happier things."

Was it truly behind her? Silus had never been one to accept failure easily and he rarely walked away without getting the last word. He could act very entitled at times.

The unwelcome thoughts of her husband were banished by her interest in the quilt. "How do you decide the colors?"

Adriel explained her methods as she continued to sew. Males wandered through the corridors, drifting toward the front exit where several carriages waited. With so much movement and low chatter, she didn't look up when masculine footsteps shuffled nearby.

A shadow fell over her. Her hand adjusted the hair peeking from the hem of her bonnet as it tickled like a spider, and she looked up to find Silus leering at her.

Adriel's hands stilled and hissed an oath the moment she registered his presence. His oppressive arrogance paralyzed Larissa as her gaze desperately searched for Eleazar.

The corridor had emptied. Silus stared down at her with stifling arrogance. "I wanted to commend you on acquiring such a fine match, dear wife." His sneered words delivered with unmistakable sarcasm. "Wait until the bishop realizes the millstone you will be around his neck. I almost pity you. You thought I was overbearing. You won't be able to hide your inadequacies from him forever. Imagine how disappointed he will be—how *enraged*—when he discovers you're as cold and lifeless as a corpse in the marriage bed. You'll be praying to be back under me."

"That's quite enough, Mr. Hostetler." Adriel had stopped sewing and folded her hands in a nonthreatening clasp on her lap.

His glare cut to her friend. "Are you speaking to me?"

Chin high, Adriel held his cold stare. "I suggest you find your carriage and be on your way."

Silus scoffed and leaned lower to speak

directly into Adriel's face. "I suggest you learn your place and shut your mouth when a man is speaking."

A thin red brow lifted, but the rest of Adriel's face remained a mask of composure. "I see no man before me, only a boy. A small, lost boy. Go. Find your horse, loathsome boy, and be gone so we can all pity you in peace."

Larissa's eyes widened as Silus's complexion darkened. He spoke through clenched teeth. "I'm not sure who permitted you to lurk in this corridor like an unwanted mut day after day, but I'll make sure you don't return. Next time a male tells you to shut your mouth, you'd be wise to listen. Speak to me like that again, and I'll shut it for you—"

The threat was whisked out of the air as his body propelled through the corridor and slammed into the opposite wall. The impact left him gasping, and Larissa jumped. Panicked, she looked to Adriel, who still wore the same mask of composure as her dispassionate gaze latched on Silus. He choked and sputtered for air.

"Adriel, you mustn't."

The female didn't relent, her stare unbreakable. Silus's feet kicked and dangled as his body suspended a yard off the ground.

Setting her sewing basket aside, Adriel slowly stood and crossed the floor. Her skirts glided with unhurried strides and she didn't stop until she stood before him, watching him suffer through dispassionate eyes.

Hands clasped loosely behind her back, Adriel lifted her chin. "I'm Adriel Schrock, the second oldest immortal on this farm. I pinned diapers to your great-grandfather's hips when he was just a boy. I saw your great-great-grandparents perish at sea when we made our pilgrimage. Elder Abraham Gerig, the third eldest immortal on this farm, is my brother by law. Elder Christian Schrock is my son. And Bishop King is my dearest friend, and therefore, so is his mate. You, however, are as inconsequential as the flies that toil over horseshit. That is your place. I'm bound by nothing to honor you. Speak to me with anything less than reverence again, and I will snap your empty head from your neck."

His body clattered to the floor in an undignified heap. He clutched his abused throat and gasped for air as Adriel calmly returned to her bench and collected her needle and thread.

When she made eye contact with him again, she simply said, "Shoo fly. Shoo."

He scrabbled off the floor and attempted to get the final word, but his throat was too damaged for more stupidity to pass. Larissa stared, wide-eyed, as he stumbled out of the corridor, leaving them alone in the empty hall.

Adriel punched her needle through the quilt and pulled the thread in a long, determined tug. "Nothing worse than a pest. One good swat is usually all they need."

Blinking through her shock, Larissa sat back in awe and grinned. Adriel was, without a doubt, one of the most fascinating females she had ever met.

CHAPTER 35

*J*onas strained to see beyond the
cluttered clothesline. The sun blinded
him with every snap of damp fabric
that let bright rays pass between the hanging items
dancing in the breeze.

He shouldn't approach the house, but he was
desperate to set eyes on his beloved wife. If God
could offer him one glimpse, he'd be satisfied.

The heat of the day burned through his shirt.
He longed for a leather strap to tie back his hair.
His boots scuffled closer and the sun grew brighter,
forming an amber halo around the dwelling.

The soft buzzing of insects was undisturbed by
the dog barking in the distance or the children's
laughter while rolling down the hills. Without realizing he moved, Jonas found himself on the front

porch, sheltered from the heat of the fading blue sky.

A blurred figure passed the window. "Abilene!" he shouted, and the passing smudge of a body stilled as if contemplating his demand.

"Please," he whispered. "I'm running out of time."

Gone from the window, his heart raced in anticipation. Abilene. Beautiful Abilene.

The door opened, showing a gaping cavity leading to bleak nothingness inside. Snow on the hill confused him on such a hot day, and he understood he was dreaming.

Helpless to escape these moments of alternate conscience, he tipped back his head and roared at the heavens, "Why must you forsake all that I love and cherish?"

The wind howled, siphoning the heat away and leaving ice in his veins.

"Abilene!" Desperate to set eyes on her, he fell to his knees, refusing to leave.

Dreary, frostbitten squalls replaced warm, sunlit sky. The world shrouded in gray, and Jonas covered his face and cried. He needed her presence in his life. The distance seemed to be killing him faster than any curse or calling.

"I cannot willingly leave you," he wept in im-

pudent fury, "I don't know how to live without you."

"I'm right here, Jonas."

The angelic voice stilled his hysterical heart and he searched for her. Surrounded by black, the shadows washed away like circling smoke as her figure appeared.

Hope stole through his lungs like bubbling fire. He recognized her Sunday dress, but she would not face him. "Abilene, I beg you. Let me see you one last time."

She pivoted, not his wife but his mate, and Jonas stumbled backward.

Clara, appearing out of place in Abilene's clothing and kapp, stood before him. "We must finish our conversation, Jonas. Come back to me."

Jonas awoke with a start. He was not on the farm but in the woods, shivering on the frostbitten floor of leaves and twigs, shaded by branches. Close to Clara.

He sensed the nearness of his mate and his intentions pulled toward her, directing his soul to the only female that could help him. He cursed his betraying body for experiencing a thrill of excitement at the thought of Clara's proximity.

A dark need to bond with the female

coursed through his veins. His nerves frayed, at odds with the battle warring within him. His rational mind, what was left of it, craved only his Abilene. Yet his body wanted Clara, his mate.

Although she asked him to leave, he hadn't gone far. Dutybound to protect what was his, he lingered in the woods just outside of her property line. Sometimes her scent came to him through a breeze's kiss. Other times her laughter caressed his ears. In a state of constant struggle, his energy depleted with the never-ending fight to resist going to her.

He visited a nearby brook and cleaned his body in the icy water, savoring the bitter shock of the cold. His recollection of the prior days were the sketchy, jumbled musings of a drunkard, yet he hadn't swallowed a drop of alcohol.

Running a tongue over the sharp tip of his fang, he considered just how parched he'd become. Starved for blood, he thought to find something quick in the woods. But when he traveled deeper into the forest, he found a trail of animal carcasses littering the earth.

Such gluttony filled him with guilt and shame. Crouching low, he examined one of the drained woodland creatures. He'd stolen these lives in a fit of starvation and haste.

How many more would have to die before he ended this? How long would it be before his thirst grew more complex and a human suffered at his hand?

Forced to burrow deep within the earth during daylight hours, he crafted himself a shelter of broken tree limbs and leaves. Gone were the comforts of home. This was how he lived now, like an animal, a vicious predator in the woods.

But at night, when the scorching sun was set and the pain slightly subsided, he found remnants of his logic. He was not yet completely gone. Perhaps tonight was his last night and tomorrow the beast would win. Perhaps he would slip further into the darkness and when he woke, it would not only be the carcasses of small prey like rabbits, deer, and foxes that greeted him but the bodies of women. He feared becoming all the evil he kept tethered inside as the binds to his sanity gradually weakened and his mind unraveled with each passing day.

The risks had been ingrained in him since boyhood, and there would be no escaping the call. He prayed for acceptance, but his heart crumbled each time he considered never again holding his sweet Abilene.

Having not ingested actual food in weeks, his system was starved and his mind suffered. He was surviving on small game, a sad excuse for the blood his body needed, the blood that called to him now, the only blood he wanted —his mate's.

Shutting his eyes, he rose from the stream and inhaled deeply. Clara's hot, thick, rich, pumping, life-giving blood lured his mind, and all other worries disappeared. He would take her gently, aligning his body with hers as he sank his fangs deep and drank from her vein. In return, he would give her the gift of eternal life.

The happy vision cleaved apart with the sharp memory of his wife. He stumbled, unsure how he allowed the fantasy to get so far. He could not want such things. Yet, his yearning was rooted in a place with little choice.

His off-kilter steps took him on a clumsy path through the woods until he spotted Clara's house in the distance. His palms scraped against the rough tree bark and his claws gouged the surface when his need intensified.

Her scent laced the wind as if delivered to him by the grace of God. She lured him without effort or intention. And his soul recognized her as his other half, no matter how much his heart and mind objected.

He snarled as he shuffled toward the house, set on stopping only when his mouth drank from her vein. When he reached the home, the gate was locked. Sharpened claws jiggled the latch, and his senses alerted him of the scent of a nearby male. A predatory growl rumbled low and threatening from his chest.

"Well, you're a sight."

Jonas snarled in the direction of the voice, and the male held up a hand. "Settle yourself, Father. I'm here to help you."

He squinted at the male emerging from the shadows. He approached calmly and stepped into the light cast from the overhead lamps, signaling he had no interest in attacking Jonas. But, despite the male's peaceful gestures, Jonas had a duty to guard his mate against all threats, including other males, and he knew his mate was unprotected.

A vision of a child flashed in his mind. A baby nursing from Abilene's breast. Two children. Identical boys. Young men, still awkward and not quite filled out. Visions flashed through his mind until he finally recognized the male before him as his son.

"Cain?" His unused voice rasped like gravel over glass.

"Yes, Father. Remember me?"

The memories slipped in and out of his mind, frustrating Jonas at his loss of cognitive control. "Why are you here?" he snapped.

"I explained it to you yesterday and the day before that. I'm here to help you."

He searched his memory but found no recollections of such talks. The need to claim his mate loomed in his mind, distracting him from the male's point.

Cain sent out a sharp whistle. "Over here! I can't let you inside until I'm certain you'll behave."

Jonas growled. "You have no right to keep me from her—"

"Relax. I'm here to assist you."

"Assist me in what?"

"That is up to you. Have you decided how you wish to proceed?"

He would claim his mate!

His indecisive mind jerked and he looked back at his son with accusation burning his eyes. "You would betray your mother so?"

"I'm *here* for Mother. She asked me to do this."

He didn't want to choose another over his

beloved Abilene. Yet, in the battle of mind versus soul, his soul would surely win. His soul was created to outlive all of creation and time. And now, even his sweet Abilene was against him.

The realization that no one was on his side could have dropped him to his knees, but rather it allowed his fortitude to be swallowed by sorrow and he forced his outrage into indignation. "Then you betray me!"

Cain shrugged. "It appears I'm always betraying someone." He leaned against the railing of the porch and crossed his legs at the ankle as if he had not a care in the world.

Jonas found his son's arrogance unfavorable. "Leave!"

"I cannot."

"Why?" he snarled through clenched teeth.

"Because there are innocent mortals in that house, and I find myself rather fond of the little one. I won't allow you to harm them."

"I would never harm an innocent creature."

"Really? Have you not seen the massacre in your wake? Poor little bunnies. I'm not leaving."

The front door opened, and a small child

with blue eyes and hair the color of sun-bleached wheat stared at him. She did not say a word as she slowly walked to Cain's side and fit her small hand into his son's much larger one.

"Cybil, this is my father, Jonas."

The girl looked at him but did not speak.

Cain lifted her onto his hip. "Where's Colby?"

The girl pointed at the house, and Cain whistled. A scraggly dog bounded from around the back, racing to Cain and wiggling expectantly at his side. "Good boy. Let's go for a walk and see if we can find Dane."

His son, the girl, and the dog took the path. As he unlatched the gate, he looked into Jonas's eyes. "I won't be far."

Left alone with only his mate in the house, Jonas's temper calmed as he watched them trot off toward the field.

The moment he set foot on the battered porch, the front door creaked. "I'm quite tired today, Jonas, so I'd rather not have to lug this big gun around. Have you found your manners?"

Had he lost them at one point? Possibly. His memory was no longer trustworthy.

He couldn't help but smile at the sight of her. "Clara."

She cocked the gun. "Don't start."

"Start what?"

"I know that look in your eye. You're being fresh. Knock it off."

His mouth twitched with amusement. Contrary to her withered appearance, her spirit sparked like a hot fire.

He took another step only to stagger to a halt at the unwelcome fragrance of death mixing with her natural scent. He could smell it today, the stench of mortality eating at her bones and the rotting of her organs.

"You're sick." The playfulness he suffered moments ago vanished as his concern multiplied. "More than usual." Closing the distance, he approached slowly, unsure how delicate her condition had become and not fully trusting himself. "What do you need?"

"Heat. This weather isn't good for my brittle bones. Come inside."

He followed her inside, where she set the gun in the living room corner. Waving a withered hand, she invited him to sit on the upholstered settee as if they had established this routine some time ago. She settled into the chair by the end table, where tissues and stacks of paperwork mounted.

"I spoke to the doctor today. I'm running out of time. My counts are low and my kidneys are struggling to keep up."

He knew nothing of mortal medicine and very little about healing. "You could use my blood."

"No."

"It will heal you."

"I've done the transfusion. They don't last. It's my time."

She misunderstood his meaning. "Then it's time you let me help you."

"Then, perhaps, it's time you fully explain how you can help me. No more beating around the bush, Jonas. My greatest worry is keeping my grandchildren together and safe. Explain to me how you can do that."

His heart fluttered at the hint of trust in her voice. "Do you trust me?"

Her lips firmed. "The older we get, the fewer options we have. My trust for you has everything to do with my lack of options and nothing to do with affection. I'm ninety percent certain you're cracked."

He grinned. "If I were cracked, I'd heal. I'm very difficult to destroy."

"Everything dies, Jonas."

"It's unlikely. My kind can be killed, but it's not easy."

"Your kind?"

He nodded. "There are many of us. You've met my son. You can see that we stop aging once we reach our prime. We thrive with longevity."

She glanced out the window, and Jonas heard the distant voice of his son and the bark of the dog. Clara followed his gaze. She would have noticed the similarities in his and Cain's appearance. She would have questioned how a father and son could appear so close in age.

"Have we had this conversation?" he asked.

She studied him through crinkled eyelids. "You've mentioned certain things before, but I still don't believe you. Everything has a time, Jonas. Even *you* will eventually die."

"Eventually. When I'm ready."

She nodded. "I'm ready."

Clara was a unique female. Many of her cells had regenerated due to western medicine. Her soul has deteriorated and only a small part of her might recognize him as her other half. He relied on those parts to trust him.

"I dreamed of you last night. You called to me, told me to come to you."

She nodded. "I had the same dream. We were on a farm, at an old house. Is that your home?"

Yearning yawned wide in his chest. "It was."

"How is it that we share dreams?"

"It's a gift." However, sometimes he couldn't reach her. "Did you take your medicine last night?"

She glanced at the countless prescriptions stacked beside the lamp and papers. "I fell asleep and missed my evening meds."

"Your soul was lucid."

"Are you saying I don't dream when I'm medicated?"

He wasn't sure. "I know little of such things, but it's a theory." He wanted to go to her. He wanted an invitation to hold and comfort her.

"How can you be killed?"

Her pivot into much darker topics jolted him. "Do you wish to wound me, Clara?"

She rolled her eyes. "I wish to understand

how someone who believes they are immortal dies."

He adjusted his posture, suddenly uncomfortable seated on the settee. "All right. If we're mortally wounded and trapped in a fire, we will die. On very rare occasions, the sun can burn us alive if shelter isn't available. Decapitation is unfixable. As is having our heart ripped out. Seldomly, a blood disorder can be transmitted to us. If ignored, some disorders can become fatal. To my knowledge, those are the only ways."

"That's why I only see you in the evenings."

He nodded. "My *condition* limits me."

"Will it always be that way?"

He chose his words carefully. "If I don't accept the cure, yes."

"And the cure is?"

He held her stare. "You."

Keeping her expression unreadable, she looked to the window again. "You know, my grandson can read minds. I'm not sure how he does it. My daughter never believed he could because he could only hear other children's thoughts. Whenever we would test him and think of a number or color, he would usually get it wrong. But, over the years, I've seen enough proof to believe he can actually do it. Cybil hasn't spoken a word since their mother died, but Dane knows what she's thinking most of the time. We believe in God but not in Santa Clause. Our government steadily searches for signs of life in outer space, yet we arrogantly assume we are top of the food chain here on Earth." Her eyes narrowed as she returned her sharp stare to him. "Are humans the most advanced species, Jonas?"

"No."

"And what, exactly, do you call yourself and your son?"

"Immortal."

Her lips firmed, her stare holding him prisoner as she studied him. "And your main diet?"

"Blood."

She kept her expression blank, but her eyes moved as she appeared to process his claim. "Like Dracula?"

Jonas once read of the fictional creature. "Only when our humanity is forsaken. We live peacefully, removed from society, and devoted to a gentle set of values."

Her glance moved over his stained attire

of a simple shirt, black trousers, and suspenders. "Amish?"

"Yes."

"Clever."

"We do it for our protection."

"I imagine you do it for ours, as well. I've seen you lose your temper."

He dropped his gaze. "I apologize." He had no memory of any such outburst. "My condition leaves me especially irritable. I'm not always in control of my actions."

"So Cain has explained. He says you won't intentionally hurt me, that it would hurt you to cause me any suffering. Is that true?"

"When I'm in command of myself, yes."

She noticeably relaxed with a deep breath that stirred a brisk cough. "Tell me more about your condition."

"I've been called. God has decided it's my time to mate."

Her brows lifted. "Your kind doesn't usually mate?"

"This is different. The calling is a sacrament among our kind. The bond goes beyond intercourse."

She held up a hand. "And your claiming God called you to me?"

"Yes. Once called, a clock starts. My time

is running out. Every day I will get worse until my humanity disappears. The only cure is claiming my mate."

"I assume this bond you speak of is a little more involved than a secret handshake."

The side of his mouth quirked up in amusement. "Yes."

She stared at a stack of papers and bills on the table. "There's no other cure?"

"No."

Her intuitive gaze returned to him and narrowed. "You don't want this?"

He couldn't agree or disagree. "My soul recognizes you as my salvation, and my instincts have lured me here like an addict. But my heart…"

"Belongs to someone else." When he nodded, she said, "And my heart will always belong to Arthur."

He growled at the thought of another male touching her.

"Do I need to get the gun?"

Seething, he curled his hands into fists and forced his temper to calm.

"What's really happening here, Jonas? You don't wish this. I'm an old lady. I'm dying. You, from what your son tells me, are very much in love with your wife. Why do this?"

"I have no choice. To ignore the call is to choose death and damnation over eternal salvation."

"And if we *bond,* as you say is required, I'll be like you? Immortal?"

"Yes."

"That's how you think to take my cancer away?"

He nodded but worried about the regenerated cells born of western therapy. Would they recognize him? He supposed he only needed the conformity of whatever remained of her soul.

"You would be young again. Ageless. And your suffering would end."

She held up a withered finger. "Not so fast. Let's assume this is actually possible. My grandchildren would age right before my eyes, their lives only a flash of my eternity. I've lost so many people I've loved. Sometimes, death is a natural and peaceful end where survival seems a burden and curse."

"Yes," he agreed painfully.

"If we did this, you would no longer belong to your wife?"

His throat constricted. "Correct."

She took a moment to process the information then rested her hands on the arms of her chair and looked out the window. "Seems quite the curse. Can you give my grandchildren the same immortality you think to give me?"

"No. It only works on called mates."

"Then I'm afraid I can't help you. As much as I want to protect my grandchildren, I can't bear the thought of watching them die. It's right that my time comes before theirs. And now, it's my time to die."

"Then it's my time to die as well."

Appearing startled by his acceptance and statement, she frowned. "That's not fair."

"No one claimed any of this was fair."

"You can't pin your survival on me—"

"I haven't. None of this was my choice. It's God's will."

Her scowl hardened. "*He's* really starting to piss me off."

Jonas had always found such comfort in his faith, but recently he'd been adrift as if the compass he'd come to rely on no longer defined right and wrong. He was lost, having to choose a direction when his heart wanted to go one way and his soul another.

"I'm ready to die beside you, Clara, if that's your will."

"That's not my will," she snapped. "None

of this is my fucking will, Jonas. If my will meant anything, my daughter would be alive, her husband would be alive, and I'd be sitting here with Arthur instead of you."

He flinched at her scorn.

"I'm sorry," she quickly apologized. "I'm sure you understand the frustration of being powerless in the face of destiny."

He kept his gaze on the floor and quietly confessed. "They've all turned against me. Abilene has threatened to follow me into death if I don't finish this and bond with you. If I leave this world, she will die, and my four children will be orphans."

"Are your children all grown?"

"Gracie, the youngest, is in her twenties, but they are still very young for our kind."

"And your wife would rather die herself than survive your death? She'd prefer to see you with someone else?"

"She loves me. This situation has broken her heart, but she still loves me and wants to see me happy."

"Well, you don't look very happy, Jonas."

Lifting his gaze, he looked at her through a pained stare. "We would be. It's not our place to know what the future holds. But called mates are predisposed to share a harmonious and happy life. It would be a natural consequence of the calling."

"And what would happen to your wife?"

Too much emotion made any prediction impossible to swallow. "I don't know. I imagine she would eventually move…"

"Well," she said when it was clear he wouldn't be able to finish the thought. "No need to torture you beyond what you're already suffering. I get the picture." She reached for a piece of paper. "This is from my attorney. Dane is still too young to act as the executor of my will, and I'm afraid the state will divide them the moment I'm gone. If Cybil doesn't start talking soon, she'll be especially vulnerable where bad people are concerned. So, I want her to stay with Dane so he can protect her."

"You might be able to hear her thoughts if you transitioned."

"That's not what I'm suggesting. When the time comes, I want you to take my grandchildren away from here. Hide them on your Amish farm until Dane's of legal age and can take custody of Cybil. He will have this house and whatever's left of my estate once the government is through with taking their cut."

"I... Without bonding, my return is unlikely."

"Then get your son to do it. Cybil's quite fond of him. Dane's coming around. And I'm sure there wouldn't be an issue with a dog like Colby on a farm."

"Cain's path is not mine to decide. He isn't a male who easily follows directions. And he's hardly on the farm anymore."

"But you have three other kids. If you do this for me, if you give me your word that my grandchildren will be looked after until they're of age and able to look after themselves, I will bond with you."

His heart jolted in his chest. "Clara, if you bonded with me, you would be there to raise them too."

"I'm not finished. I have one more condition."

He drew back, terrified of what that final condition might be.

"You must promise to look after them, and I'll do whatever you need to complete the bond. But then you must end my life. I don't want eternity. I only want the pain to end."

He bolted to his feet. "I cannot!"

She glanced at the gun but did not make an effort to reach for it. Her eyes wore the exhaustion of too many sleepless nights and years of endless grief. "Then I'm sorry."

"A mate cannot harm a mate. It's unheard of! Besides, I'm a man of faith. I cannot commit murder. You're a child of God. I would be murdering *His* child. You would be damning my soul."

She waved a finger. "But first, you would have to die, and you've already explained how unlikely that is. These are my conditions, Jonas. I'm giving you what you need and giving you my blessing to live out eternity with your Abilene. What are you afraid of?"

So much…

He didn't believe he could commit such a crime. Legends of countless mates told of an unbreakable bond. It simply wasn't possible.

But if he could remedy this curse and return to his sweet Abilene…

He considered the duality of nature, heaven to hell, a countering good for every evil. There would undoubtedly be a price to pay for such trickery. What if he agreed to such horror only to pay with his soul anyway? There was too much unknown.

"I don't think it's possible."

She sighed and pushed herself up from the chair. He could sense her exhaustion. "Then

I'm sorry. That's my only offer. You see, just as you long to return to Abilene, I long to be with Arthur again. But he's no longer here. I can't give you my eternity when it costs us ours. We had a plan, and I'm going to keep my word to my husband."

He stood. "Clara, it's simply not possible—"

"How do you know? There are things I can do to ensure I go. Before I do, I'm willing to give you what you need to survive and go back to your family, so long as you promise to look after mine. What do we have to lose, Jonas? If we're both prepared to die anyway, why not give it a try?" She gripped the hallway wall leading to her bedroom. "Think it over. You can see yourself out."

CHAPTER 36

The following morning Eleazar woke to find Larissa absent from their bed. He found her standing near the window, her form silhouetted by the gray light seeping through it as a cold winter dawn approached. Enraptured by her breathtaking presence, he silently watched her for several minutes.

"I can sense your mind waking," she murmured, her breath forming a small cloud of vapor on the glass of the window.

"I could watch you for an eternity."

Glancing over her bare shoulder, she smiled at him.

Last night, he had planned to let her rest but when he finally finished all council business, Larissa rushed into his arms and her relief had been jarring. Adriel quickly informed him of the incident with Silus to save Larissa the chore, and Eleazar had been hard-pressed to find the bastard, but his mate proved a distraction he was too weak to ignore.

They made love the moment they entered his private home. Her mind was a wild and welcoming place to play, and he spent hours satisfying his ravenous mate. Every time he touched her, she surprised him with a response more beautiful than the last.

"Come back to bed, Larissa. You'll catch a chill."

She tossed him another playful smirk and gathered the white sheet higher to her chest. "Immortals cannot catch a chill."

He drew the covers back, inviting her to bed. "Humor me."

She took a step then stilled. "Eleazar?"

A guarded expression stole over his face. "Yes?"

"I like who I am with you." She padded softly toward the bed and sat on the edge of the mattress. "I mean, I like the way you encourage me to speak my mind and be myself."

It was difficult to imagine anything else. A censored version of Larissa seemed a crime.

He reached for her hand and gently laced his fingers with hers. "I'm not interested in imitations. I will always want the real you."

Her smile stole the morning, outdoing the spectacular dawn and filling him with gratitude for the day and their life ahead. Leaning into him, she brushed a kiss to his lips.

Looking into her vibrant eyes, he teased her lips open and pulled her beneath him. All theories of his mate being a cold female were officially put to rest. His little mouse hid a lioness inside, and she possessed a deep hunger for touch and affection that he would gladly spend an eternity satisfying.

When he tried to enter her mind, she pushed him out and he frowned. Drawing back, he studied her. "Are you keeping secrets from me?"

"Adriel told me to practice guarding my thoughts better since I'll be spending more time with…" She had the good grace to blush. "Elders."

He rolled to his back, pressing a hand to his heart as if she'd mortally wounded him. "Ouch."

She laughed and crawled over him, pulling his hand away from his heart and pressing a kiss in its place. "But she's right. I'm used to blocking my sister. Gracie's abilities are nothing compared to The Elders' and Adriel's."

He was aware of Grace Hartzler's abilities. "Your sister has a remarkable gift."

"Yes, but Gracie's skills are more of a reflex, like superior hearing. The Elders are nosey."

He laughed. "Is that so?"

"Yes." Looking down at him with a teasing smile, her face framed in a halo of silken, dark hair, she was perhaps the most beautiful creature he ever set eyes on.

He tucked a thick strand behind her ears. "Perhaps you're right. I want to know your every thought, Larissa. I want your desires so I can meet them for you and share moments when we're both lost in rapture. You don't have to hide your mind when we're alone. You're safe here."

To prove his point, he opened his mind to her. She inhaled sharply, glimpsing a memory of their bodies entwined the night before. He unveiled his hunger and her body softened, her lips returning to his.

The heady scent of her lust intoxicated his mind and his pulse raced as he slid inside of her. Like waves crashing into the banks of the shore, they molded to each other with every motion, changing and shaping to fit perfectly like nothing else in this world could.

As he held her to him, he sought her throat. She tipped her head invitingly, offering him the sustenance he needed while she took her pleasure.

"How is it that I feel like we've done this a thousand times?"

Her arms wreathed around his shoulders as her body rocked slowly. "I feel it, too. You're so familiar to me, and I'm not sure how that's possible."

He pulled her closer, nibbling along her jaw. When he sank his fangs into her flesh, she tensed in a wash of pleasure that ricocheted into him, multiplying in a repetitive echo of ecstasy that pushed them both over the edge. Their bond was so succinct, the rightness of their union nearly put tears in his eyes.

Falling to the bed in a tumble of limbs and satisfaction, they caught their breath. He never believed such peace could exist.

"I'd like to visit my mother today."

And then the peaceful aura was gone.

"Larissa, you cannot interfere with an-

other immortal's calling. Your father is oblig-
ated by law to do this thing. It's God's will."

She pulled her arm out of his grasp and sat
up. "I know it is. And, if what we're experiencing is normal, I know he won't be able to
resist it."

He didn't like the idea that their bond
might be ordinary. "Your situation's
different."

"How so?"

"You were called to a superior. A well-en-
dowed male with insatiable appetites."

Realizing he was making a joke, she rolled
her eyes. "Eleazar, I need to go to her."

He sighed, not liking the idea but unable
to find a decent excuse to deny her now that
The Council had been alerted to their situation. "I will take you."

"Thank you."

Her evident joy was a reward in itself. "I'll
have the evening free—"

"Oh." She frowned and flushed. "I had
hoped I might visit alone. This is a difficult
time for my family, and I don't want to add
more stress."

She had, once again, blocked her thoughts
and he questioned her sincerity. "Larissa,

your family will need to adjust to my presence in your life."

"They will. But, with my father and Cain away, they only know what Adam reports, and he's a very private male. Let me have this day to be with them while you're preoccupied with council business. I want to tell them, in my own words, what has happened so they have time to adjust."

Disgruntled that his presence would be such a shock and adjustment, he hardened his jaw and rose from the bed. "If that's what is needed."

"Eleazar, you must understand, to me, you are my mate and I'm beyond happy with God's choice, but to them, you are their bishop." Her words stung more than they should have. "My mother is a prideful woman. She will have a difficult time even speaking to me about private matters in your presence. Please understand, I'm asking this for her, not for me."

Eased by her genuine explanation, he compromised. "All right, Larissa. But I do not want you walking alone. I'll take you."

"Thank you!" She hugged him and delivered a kiss mixed with gratitude and invitation. When he grasped the sheet veiling her body, she shifted out of reach.

"I'll dress and we can go."

Plans to have her again washed away with the morning dew, and they were soon readying a buggy.

As the sun crested the horizon, Eleazar looked east and suffered a melancholy sense of foreboding. The bitter cold blanketed the earth in a crisp frost as magenta hues fought for the sky and clouds rolled overhead.

The horses huffed and kicked as steam rose off their bodies and misted from their nostrils. They rode in silence, nothing but the click-clack of hooves on the ground accompanied by the rattling of their rig.

Larissa shivered and he pulled her closer to his body. "You need a cloak."

"I'd rather make new ones than have to ask Silus for my things."

"Of course." The less she asked of Silus, the better. "I'll send for the materials you need."

When they pulled in front of the Hartzler house, he said a silent prayer that the day would not be too difficult for his mate. The door of the house opened, and he sensed Abilene's presence before he spotted her.

As he handed Larissa down, her mother gasped. "Larissa? Is it really you?"

Eleazar gave a polite nod, regretting the site of the woman's gaunt cheeks and the fact that her appearance would no doubt trouble his mate. "Good morning, Sister Abilene."

"B—Bishop King." Her startled gaze searched her daughter's composed expression then returned to him. Her desperate fear pierced him like a thousand needles. "Is Jonas…?"

"I have no news of Jonas's whereabouts. I'm only here to deliver your daughter."

He could see she wanted to embrace her daughter but would not do so in his presence. Saving Larissa the need for an urgent explanation, he casually grasped her hand and gave her an affectionate squeeze. *Call for me when you are ready to be picked up.*

She nodded. "I will."

Tipping his hat toward Abilene, he circled the carriage and collected the reins. It was difficult to willingly leave Larissa behind, and he counted the moments until she would return to his side again.

"How long have you been home, Larissa? And why is the bishop escorting you?"

"May we go inside and talk? I'm freezing."

Leading her mother into her childhood home, she immediately noted the unusual sense of emptiness compared to the fullness it once was with six of them living under its roof.

A squeal pierced the vacant silence and Larissa was thrown off balance as her younger sister Gracie catapulted into her arms. "You're back! I knew you would come back! Oh, how I've missed you, sister!"

Larissa laughed joyfully and hugged Gracie's smaller form. "Oh, Grace, I have missed you dreadfully. You look exactly the same."

"Did you expect me to change?"

"No, I just… I guess I've just been away for so long, I assumed something should look different."

She turned her concern back to her mother. She had lost weight. Her cheeks were gaunt and her eyes heavily shadowed.

The momentary sense of joy attached to their reunion crumbled under the press of reality. She collected her mother's cold hands in hers and looked into her eyes.

"I'm so sorry I haven't been here for you, Mother. If there's anything I can do—"

"There's nothing to be done." Her mother withdrew her hands and busied herself at the counter, where a loaf of raw dough needed to be worked. "Your father belongs to her now."

The sharp certainty of her statement sliced like a knife. "Mother…" She wanted to say that she would always have a part of him, but in light of all she has lost, any attempt to beautify the pain seemed trite and insincere. "I hate that this is happening to you."

Hate was not a word their kind often used, but its potency fit at the moment.

Her mother's eyes closed and she exhaled. "I hate it too." When she opened her eyes, she stared at Larissa through a wall of unshed tears and worked her fingers into the dough. "But I love your father, and we all must make our sacrifices."

Her stoic words were made of strength and grit, but her voice crumbled under their weight. Larissa took a step to comfort her mother, only to have Gracie catch her sleeve and hold her back. With a shake of her sister's head, she understood that their mother did not wish to be coddled.

It broke Larissa to think of the pain she

had to bear on her own. But her mother was a woman of pride, and she would likely do her best to fall apart in private and save others the empathetic ache. It was no wonder Adam was not around. Her brother, a gifted empath, would suffer every ounce of their mother's agony.

They each had their ways of coping, but this was happening to *her* family, and Larissa had so much regret for the months Silus had kept her away. She ached to hug her mother. "Let go of me, Grace."

Sweeping across the floor, she pulled her mother's needing hands from the dough and wrapped her arms tightly around her. The press of her bones through her gown silently confessed that her mother was not taking care of herself.

Blinking back her own tears, Larissa found the basket of eggs and lit the stove. "Let me help with the morning meal while we catch up. I'm sure there's plenty of happy news to discuss. How is Adam's new wife?"

Larissa busied herself at the cook stove while Gracie chattered about Annalise and Adam's marriage, their expected son, and how well Annalise was adapting to Amish life. Her mother set the dough to rise in the covered trough but didn't contribute much to the conversation.

Larissa was overjoyed at the thought of having a nephew. Gracie was certain the baby was a male. She imagined he would have silver-blue eyes just like Adam.

They broke their fast while chatting about the chilly weather, the price of fabric, and, again, what items they could make for Adam's son. Annalise wasn't expected to deliver until early spring, so Larissa had plenty of time to stitch something special.

Her mother barely touched her food, though she did manage a few meager bites. Larissa could only console her worry by reminding herself that had she not prepared breakfast, her mother might not have eaten at all.

"Tell me about Bishop King," her mother requested, her gaze downcast as if to avoid making an unnecessary assumption.

Larissa's chest warmed at the thought of her mate, but before she could announce her news, Gracie blurted, "Ugh, must we speak of that old codger?"

"Grace!"

At Larissa's sharp reprimand, her sister shrugged. "What? You know he's an old goat."

"Eleazar is not an old goat!"

"*Eleazar?* If he hears you call him by his Christian name—and I have no doubt that old fossil can hear an acorn fall from a million miles away—you will find yourself in trouble."

"Stop that, Gracie! You have no idea what you're talking about."

"Wow, he must have chastised you at some length when he found you."

"He did not *chastise* me!"

Gracie fought a smirk and held her hands up in surrender. "My apologies. I had no idea you were so fond of antiques."

"For someone so fearful of him overhearing, you sure have a loose tongue," Larissa snapped. "Do be quiet."

Her sister cocked her head, and Larissa sensed the delicate brush of her mind trying to intrude on her thoughts, which she only met with a scowl.

"What's gotten into you? He's a grumpy old rooster. Since when do you care what we say about him?"

"He is not as grumpy as everyone thinks. And stop trying to read my thoughts."

"Something's different," Gracie finally said. "You're different."

Her mother also studied her. Their twin stares caused Larissa to fidget with uncertainty.

"Larissa, where is Silus?" her mother asked.

She screwed her lips together then mumbled, "The Council has agreed to give me an annulment."

"I see," her mother said as Gracie drew back in shock.

"No…" Her sister shook her head. "Who is it?"

Her news, after all the name calling, no longer carried the same level of excitement. "What does it matter so long as I'm rid of Silus."

Her mother reached for her hand. "So, it's true then? Your father has claimed as much, but I didn't believe him. Have you been called?"

She couldn't deny her smile. "Yes. I'm bonded."

Her mother's smile was perhaps the greatest mating gift anyone could have offered. "I'm so very happy for you, Larissa."

"Wait. Who is it?" Gracie demanded.

Apparently, Larissa was getting very good

at hiding her thoughts. She smirked. "It's the bishop."

She laughed as her sister's jaw appeared to unhinge. She sputtered and, for once, words failed her.

"Are you happy?" her mother asked.

She met her curious stare with a genuine smile. "I'm very, *very* happy."

"Then I'm happy for you."

Gracie finally recovered. "Why can I not have one fun brother-in-law?"

"Grace, hush," Abilene chided. "I imagine he's quite different when you two are alone."

Blood rushed to her cheeks. "He is. He's decent and honorable. I know he can be rigid, but he protects me. He's gentle and kind when I need him to be."

Gracie frowned. "He must be overbearing and difficult. "

"He's complex, but I find him refreshingly flexible in a way Silus never was. Eleazar cares about my comforts and wants to see me happy." Hearing herself come to his defense only proved how much she had come to care for him in such a short time. "We make sense together. He's helping me repair my confidence."

It needed no explanation that her marriage to Silus had changed her in ways that were not good. Like a beaten down dog, she had learned to cower and hide quietly rather than make any sort of fuss. Eleazar didn't want a silent mate. He wanted to hear her voice and know every desire.

"I think I can make him happy, too."

"Has Silus been informed?" Abilene asked, her concern clear.

"Yes. We returned a few days ago. Yesterday, I had to sit on trial before the Elder's Council. Oh, Mother, it was so frightening being in there with only males. I hope I never have to walk into that room again. But I did, and Eleazar told The Council what had happened. Silus became very agitated and made a scene, but The Elders chastised him. They asked me questions and I was so nervous I can barely recall answering them. Before I realized what was happening, The Council granted me the right to an annulment."

"I would be frightened Silus might retaliate. Do be careful, Larissa," Gracie said, all traces of humor gone.

"Oh, he tried to approach me after the trial, but Adriel Schrock—Do you know her, Mother? She's a fascinating female. Anyway, she put Silus in his place, and I don't think he'll bother me again. He was quite humiliated."

"I wish I could have witnessed that." Her sister's grin was almost maniacal.

"Once the paperwork is signed, Eleazar and I can be married, and I never have to deal with that rotten male again."

Her mother's lips trembled under the strain of her smile. "Well then, I suppose I had better begin sewing you a new dress. In this weather, I'll never be able to grow celery in time—"

"Oh, no, Mother. I don't wish for another wedding. I only want to say my vows to my husband with my family and God as our witnesses, and perhaps Adriel Schrock, since she's one of Eleazar's closest friends. He's a very private male, and I do not wish to burden him with an overdone ceremony and celebration. I simply want to marry him so we can begin our life."

Gracie, who had been quiet for some time, appeared troubled. Larissa took her hand. "Grace, what is it?"

Frowning, her sister first looked at their mother then her. "You're the fourth. How is it possible that in my twenty-one years on this Earth, not a single member of The Order was called, and no one from the Hartzler line has been called since Uncle Isaiah's disappearance until Adam and Cain, yet in the past four months, four of my kin have been?"

The unwelcome thought that their callings might somehow be linked to her uncle's return troubled her and she shook the thought away, trusting that God had simply decided it was her time.

Larissa wanted to label the callings a miracle, but her mother would disagree, surely viewing their father's fate as a curse. The three of them wondered in silence, unsure how so many callings could happen all at once. And Larissa suffered a bite of uncertainty, worried that the outbreak might be some sort of glitch and her happiness could get snatched away at any moment.

A shiver of apprehension skated up her spine and she suddenly wanted her mate. "I should call for Eleazar. It's getting late."

She sensed her mother's exhaustion and worried when she last fed. It was tempting to offer her vein, but such an act was forbidden.

Gracie's pout disappeared the moment Annalise arrived with a gust of bone-chilling wind slipping in behind her.

Her new sister-in-law glowed with life as

she greeted Larissa with surprise and excitement.

"I thought Adam would've told you I was home," Larissa said, encasing Anna's swollen belly in loving hands. "I had hoped you could help me reach Cain."

At Anna's surprise, Larissa realized no one had delivered her request. "Did you speak to Adam?"

Larissa frowned. "The bishop did." Why hadn't her brother given Annalise her request?

Anna's mouth twisted in apology. "He doesn't want me contacting Cain until I deliver the baby."

"Why? He must know that your heart is his."

"It has nothing to do with loyalty. There are some new concerns about my shared link with Cain. The other day I had…an episode."

Larissa scanned the room and sensed the universal concern. "What happened?"

"Cain was injured, and I somehow suffered his pain and injuries."

"But you're okay? And has anyone spoken to Cain?"

"Cain is fine," Gracie said. "But it was quite traumatic for Annalise and the baby.

It's best that their link remains severed for now."

Regretful that they lost their only connection to their brother while he was away from the farm, Larissa accepted that it was for the best. In her sister-in-law's delicate condition, she wouldn't want to take any risks. "Well, hopefully he returns soon."

Her mind reached for Eleazar, only to be greeted by a vacant block. He must be with The Elders and guarding his thoughts.

She sat a while longer, making small talk with Anna and asking about her plans for their new home. But the longer she waited, the more restless she became to return to her mate. Again and again, she mentally reached for Eleazar only to find his thoughts blocked. They needed to come up with a more effective way of communicating.

So much discussion about Adam and Anna's baby filled Larissa with envy. She was delighted for them but curious why she had never conceived once married. She understood conception didn't always happen right away, but more than a year of marriage with no results struck her as troublesome.

Although she was grateful she didn't carry Silus's young, she hoped there was no reason for concern. Her mother suffered several miscarriages. Larissa secretly wondered if their infertility was somehow linked to them being bedded by males who were not their true mates. She would ask the bishop if he knew of any such issues in the past.

As the sun set, she grew impatient. It had been gloomy and cold for most of the sunlight hours, but she could manage the walk. "Mother, do you have a cloak I can borrow?"

"Of course, but should you not wait for the bishop."

"He's still with The Council. I think I'd like to surprise him."

She made her goodbyes and promised to visit again soon. It had been a lovely day and more than a year since she enjoyed her family without the pressure or worry that Silus would punish her when she returned.

Bundled in her mother's cloak, she drew the fabric closed and walked briskly toward her mate, excited to return to the shelter of his body—and anxious to have him warm hers.

The wet air chilled her to the bone. Clouds shrouded the sky as the sun faded behind the trees, and the wind whistled through the naked branches. There was nary a soul about in such dreadful weather.

The scent of burning wood seeped from chimneys and filled the air. Shutters clattered, whipping against the distant houses with each hard gust of wind. Icy rain drizzled against her face, and she was grateful her mother had lent her a cloak. Relief washed over her when the safe house came into sight.

The Council doors were shut when she entered the hall, and Adriel's bench was empty. She could hear the murmur of masculine voices from within, and once more, she tried to notify Eleazar of her return, but his mind was still blocked.

The corridor leading to Eleazar's office was dark and empty. She walked quickly and grinned when she found a fire lit and an ottoman sitting temptingly before the hearth. Stepping into the room, she removed her damp cloak and bonnet and rushed toward the fire, chafing her hands and eager to get warm.

Her skin burned and tingled as warm blood circulated through her fingertips. She settled onto the ottoman, her joints stiff from the frigid walk, eager to be close to the crackling blaze.

The door slammed shut and she jolted back from the flames, startled by the bang. Her eyes searched the shadows. Her spine stiffened, the hair on the back of her neck tickling like a spider's tiptoes.

Silus stepped from the dark shadow, and her breath left in a woosh. "Hello, wife."

Dane glared at the man standing in his doorway, certain something wasn't right. His grandmother had been lying that evening when she left. He could sense it in the finality of her goodbye as the cab arrived to take her to a new facility to run some tests.

She had gone with the man, Jonas, and left him and Cybil alone in the house with Cain. Now, they were being told to pack a bag.

Dane had a terrible feeling about whatever was to come. His grandmother left with teary eyes after kissing both him and Cybil and making them promise to do as Cain said. But he didn't trust the man and had no clue why his grandmother would trust them to his care.

This sudden change of plans made no sense to Dane since his grandmother had been adamant that she no longer wanted to undergo treatment. He demanded she give him more information, but she was firm in only telling him that she loved him and he should look after his sister.

As the cab drove away, he watched her look back and suffered the cold fear that he might never see her again.

"Are you guys about ready?"

Dane's glare narrowed on Cain. "What's the rush?"

The man shrugged. "No rush."

Cybil packed her suitcase in silence. Nothing had been right since Cain arrived, and he didn't understand his sister's fascination with the strange man. Every time Cain was around, Cybil's mind filled with warm orange, pink, and red colors. Dane wondered with repulsion if she had a crush on the man.

His reluctance to leave with this stranger gnawed at him. "I don't understand why we have to leave. How long do a few tests take? And who has a lab open at this time of night? You aren't telling us something, and I don't want to leave. Why can't we just stay here? I'm old enough to watch Cybil."

His sister shot him a withering look, embarrassed by his insinuation that she needed a babysitter.

"We have no idea how long the tests will take," Cain explained, and Dane resented that a stranger had more information than him about his grandmother's situation. "Your grandmother wants you to come with me for the time being." He playfully yanked on Cybil's blonde ponytail. "Have you ever been on a farm?"

She looked up at him with big eyes and smiled as she shook her head. Dane rolled his eyes at such blind adoration.

"You're going to love it. There are all kinds of animals and plenty of other kids your age."

Her grin stretched and Dane scoffed. Why was everyone simply accepting this guy's presence? And the other one, Jonas, was even weirder. "We have to bring Colby, you know."

"That's fine. Colby will love the farm."

Dane packed in silence and seethed at his lack of control over the situation. He might just be a kid but he suspected something wasn't right.

Cain carried Cybil's bag to the door and she followed him like a stray. Dane looked around the bedroom, fearful he might never see it again. It wasn't even his room, yet it held the only keepsakes they had left from his parents.

He paused from zipping his bag and went to the pile of cardboard boxes stacked in the corner. Digging through worthless baseball cards and forgotten video games, he fished around the bottom, his fingers sifting through loose LEGO pieces until his hand closed around the smooth photo album.

The first page opened with the creak of dry, rotted plastic. There, in a faded picture, was his mother in a hospital gown holding him the day he was born. He ran his finger over the vellum covering.

She looked like she just battled on the front lines of a war, but her smile was victorious. He always loved this picture. His mother was strong, and he could see it in the way she slouched with exhaustion but still held him protectively in her arms. He could also see her softness in her eyes.

He flipped the next few pages and found pictures of himself blowing out candles on his first birthday cake, his first day of kindergarten, him smiling proudly with his missing tooth. He continued to turn pages until he reached the empty ones. There was so much space left to fill, but hardly any family left.

Emptiness occupied him in a familiar ache that might never leave. He shut the book and stashed it securely in his backpack before zipping it tight.

He suffered the same intuitive nausea he'd experienced the day his father died and again on the night they searched the woods for his mom. His grandmother's health was in rapid decline. No matter what tests they ran, there wasn't much hope. They assumed they had months, but now he wondered if they even had days.

"Dane?"

He faced the man with a distrustful glare but found himself at the stranger's mercy. "She's going to die, isn't she?"

Cain sighed. "No one knows how this night will end or what tomorrow will bring. We can only hope that things work out for the best."

Resentment weighed heavily on his shoulders as he lifted his backpack and shut out the light. He didn't want to go to some farm and he didn't want to stay with people he didn't know. He wanted his mother back and to hear his sister's voice again, but those dreams would never be answered. So, he did the only thing he could and, holding his sister's hand, followed the strange man.

CHAPTER 38

arissa's heart raced as Silus's rough hand covered her mouth with crushing force and silenced her scream.

"You must be pretty satisfied with yourself. Vainly parading about as if you've been given your due. Well, what about me, Larissa? Where is my due? What do I get for the time I wasted on you?"

Her mind screamed for Eleazar, but all thoughts scattered as Silus smashed her against the wall, pressing his body hard against hers and hissing in her ear. "Do you know the shame you've brought to my family name?"

The frantic breath pumping from her nose

beat against his clenched fingers and her jaw throbbed beneath his punishing grip. His arm banded around her waist, cinching painfully against her ribs and causing the bone to splinter against her lungs. She gurgled and struggled to break free as he tried to suffocate her—his strength had always been greater.

His fury exploded as he slammed her head into the wall. "You're an abomination, no better than the Whore of Babylon. Tell me, Larissa, is it as Ezekiel says in the Bible? Did the bishop touch you with the flesh lengthened to that of a mule? Were his emissions like those of a horse as he rutted into you, a married woman who vowed her life to another male?"

His fist locked in her hair, ripping her head back from the wall only to slam it forward again. Blinding pain exploded behind her eyes.

"Did you allow him to fill you with quantities that rival the flooding of the Nile?"

She trembled, knowing from experience, the more fanatical Silus grew, the more he quoted scripture, the fouler his moods darkened and the more dangerous he became.

"Silus, please…"

"Please, what? Go ahead, Larissa, beg me

for forgiveness, and I shall help you atone for the disgrace you brought to my home."

She whimpered, and tears reflexively flooded her eyes as he jammed his knee hard into her thigh. Her legs buckled and he tackled her to the ground. Her eyes bulged as his weight knocked the wind out of her, and his hands closed around her throat.

"Stupid female, you belonged to me first." His grip tightened and her lungs seized. His eyes dilated, and she feared he wouldn't stop until he ripped her head off.

She clawed at his face only to have him jerk her by the throat and slam her head hard against the floor.

"You're not so proud now, are you? *The Lord shall cut off all flattering lips and the tongue that speaketh proud things.*" Spittle rained from his lips as blood vessels ruptured in her eyes and clouded her vision.

"How do you think your bishop will like you without your whore mouth and serpent's tongue?"

She wrenched his hand away and sucked in a crippling gasp. Her windpipe was crushed and hardly any air could pass. Her punctured lungs frantically tried to breathe.

His fist slammed into her cheek and heat

bathed her face as blood poured from her nose. She choked on the flood of metallic pain as it closed the small opening in her throat.

"For it's the blood that makes atonement for the soul, faithless witch! Nothing but a bitch in heat!" His fangs extended and his jaw gaped wide. *"I come to do thy will of God!"*

His fangs punctured her ravaged throat, burning her flesh with gnawing force, and she silently screamed through the pain. He drank violently from her, spilling her vein as he tore at her throat, as if intent to drain her dry. Her strength waned and her heart fluttered with each fading beat.

Her blurred vision darkened to shadows as her senses feathered away. The delicate trace of memories grazed her mind and she clung to the feeling of happiness she'd momentarily known with Eleazar, certain this was her end.

An explosion vibrated the walls, like the thunder of a grandfather oak crashing through the house. Excruciating pain ripped through her as the flesh of her throat tore open, and Silus's crushing weight vanished.

Vicious growls and snapping bones collided with the scent of ripping flesh as agonizing screams bellowed over her gasping coughs. She rolled to her side, wheezing and gasping for air, but it was not enough.

Strength depleted and anemic beyond measure, she surrendered to the numbing darkness and let go.

CHAPTER 39

"Drink," Eleazar's command rasped past his lips in a broken plea as he cradled his mate's lifeless body in his arms. "Please. You must drink."

He pressed his open wrist to her mouth, tipping back her ravaged throat, as he shook with uncontainable rage. Her throat was crushed and ripped open and her head lulled in an unnatural manner.

Blinking hard against the uncertainty that threatened to break him, he swallowed against the lump in his throat and reopened his vein. Without her feeding, the wounds would be slow to heal and her suffering unbearable. Only her immortality kept her tethered to this world when her ravaged body so clearly wanted to stop functioning. She needed blood.

Jaw clenched, he coaxed her mouth open and let the healing blood trickle in. "Just a little swallow."

He worried that the slightest touch might cause more damage. He should have never left her alone. He should have kept his mind open. He assumed she would have waited for him, but he'd been wrong.

Mouth pressed tight, he fought back tears. "Why did you leave without an escort? I told you to wait for me." He shook his head, unable to accept that this was it. "Stubborn female, I order you to drink!"

Her lashes fluttered, and a weak sigh breathed over his flesh. Her brow tightened as she attempted to swallow.

"That's it, my brave and beautiful lion, try to swallow. You're so strong…so strong." His throat closed around his voice as his eyes took measure of the damage. He'd never dreamed of seeing her so weak, and he'd give anything to restore her strength. "You're not a mouse," he whispered. "You're my brave Larissa and I need you to fight, now. I need you to come back to me."

Once a few drops made it into her system,

her strength improved, but she was still incredibly weak and battered. Her skin took time to mend. He helped things along by using his tongue to heal what he could. The gaping wound at her throat was wide enough to expose the bone of her clavicle and the gnarled pink pulp of torn tissue and shredded muscle.

He never experienced such a dark and unstoppable rage as he now suffered when thinking of Silus Hostetler. The moment Eleazar detained him in a cell in the crypt, he decided that letting him rot there for an eternity would be too generous a fate. His first concern was Larissa. But as soon as she was out of danger, he would see to the other.

The door creaked and Adriel stepped in, not seeing him from his seat on the floor, draped in shadows, where he cradled his mate.

"Eleazar—" She gasped, no doubt scenting the blood. "What's happened?"

He opened his mind, and Adriel rushed to kneel beside him. She understood there was a problem when he mentally ordered her to come to him.

"Silus did this?"

He nodded, slightly off balance from the amount of blood Larissa had already taken.

"Let me help you." Adriel collected a pewter cup from the desk and opened her vein.

"I can't—"

"Don't be a fool." She filled the cup and shoved it below his nose and his refusal vanished.

He needed his strength if he wanted to heal Larissa. When he drained the cup, she refilled it again.

"You know you cannot let this stand, Eleazar."

He glared at her. "As if I would let anyone do this to my mate and walk away un-punished."

Adriel's brow pinched as she examined the visible injuries. "You know, it's been almost three-hundred years and I still flinch from time to time, fearful that *he* watches me."

It was clear that she spoke of her mate, Cerberus.

"It will take centuries for her to heal from this. The greatest wounds are always on the inside."

He couldn't debate such a claim from a female who had lived a similar hell. "He will pay."

"Where is he?"

"Downstairs, in a cell."

"Not good enough."

He stared at the jagged skin of his mate as it struggled to seal shut. "He won't be there long."

Like Larissa, his friend had suffered many nights of unthinkable cruelty. In the end, when they rescued Adriel, pregnant with her son and weakened to a state that only time could heal, she joined them on their pilgrimage to America.

No matter how strong of an immortal Cerberus was, justice eventually found him. For nearly three hundred years, the monster atoned, awaiting the regeneration of his limbs as the rest of his body atrophied from starvation and neglect. By now, his flesh would have rotted off the bone and muscle would have withered to dust. Once an immortal's remains scattered to the wind, they were irreparable.

"Do not hesitate, Eleazar. As her mate, you must do everything in your power to protect her."

His jaw remained clenched. "First, I will

see her marriage annulled. I'll need you to watch over her. I want no one else near her."

"I'll get some rags and a basin of warm water so we can clean her up."

As soon as her wounds fully healed, he would carry her to their bed to rest. But he didn't expect her eyes to open any time soon.

CHAPTER 40

ane's shoulders bunched against the cold, his numb fingers curling tightly around Colby's leash, as he followed the man holding his sister. Once again, he wondered why they hadn't called an Uber or a cab. "How far are we walking?"

The weather was cold, dark, and miserable. Cybil slept soundly in Cain's arms, her head resting on his shoulder and her eyes staying closed for long bouts. He had no idea how she could sleep like that.

"There's a rest stop up ahead. We can call for a taxi when we get there."

Dane scoffed. "It would have been helpful to have one pick us up at the house."

"I wasn't expecting the distance to be this hard on you."

Dane shook his head and sneered, "You make it sound like there is something wrong with *us*. We're wandering around in the pitch-black night in the freezing cold. We must have gone six miles by now!"

"Try two."

"Whatever. Cybil will probably have the flu by the time we get wherever we're going."

"I told you, we're going to my farm."

"Right. How many other children have you lured there?"

Cain shot him a withering glare. "Watch it."

"*You* watch it." His jaw locked, and his soaked feet refused to take another step. Colby whined, tugging to follow Cain and angering Dane all the more. "That's it! I'm not going any farther. I want to talk to my grandmother."

Cain tightened the blanket around Cybil's shoulders. "Stop being a baby."

"Screw you! I'm sick of following along with no information. Where's my grandmother and where the hell are we going?"

Cain took a menacing step toward him and hissed, "I said *move*."

"I don't have to do crap. You're not my dad, and you're not my brother. You're not even a friend. I'm tired of just following along while everyone else acts crazy. I'm going back. Cybil—"

"Shut your mouth," Cain hissed, placing a hand over Cybil's ear. "Stop thinking only of yourself."

"Myself? I haven't done anything for myself in so long I can't even remember what it feels like to do something selfish and normal for a kid my age! I'm taking my sister and we're going back."

"Back to what? You're not a stupid kid. You know what's happening here. I promise I'm not out to hurt you or your sister. I only want to help you."

"Help us what? You and Jonas show up out of *nowhere* and everyone starts acting like it's perfectly normal to have strangers as house-guests. You're right. I'm not stupid. I know when something's wrong. Cybil, wake up—"

Cain caught his hand in an unbreakable grip and Colby growled. "And who is going to protect your sister when your grandmother's gone? You?"

"Yeah, me!" Dane jerked his hand but couldn't break his hold. "Get off." He swallowed gulps of air, his shoulders rising and falling with each seething breath.

Cain chuckled and released his arm as if proving his point. "You're just a kid."

If he weren't holding his sister, Dane would have lunged at him. He wanted to punch that arrogant smirk off his face.

As if reading his thoughts, Cain lifted a brow in challenge. The wind whipped at their clothes as they faced off. "That's what I thought. Let's go."

Cain continued walking, and Dane stood his ground. "Cybil, wake up!"

His sister stirred, and something vicious flashed in the man's eyes, catching the moonlight in an unnatural way. "Enough. Let her sleep."

"She's not going with you. Cybil, I said wake up!"

Cain crossed the distance in two strides and gripped Dane by the front of the shirt. "What's the matter with you? I said leave her be. She doesn't need you upsetting her. For Christ's sake, be a man and quit your bellyaching."

Anger became a living thing that seethed within Dane's heart. He shoved him with both hands but the man didn't budge.

With pitying eyes, he chuckled. "Let's not do that again."

Dane's jaw quivered as an all too familiar helplessness paralyzed him. "Why are you doing this?"

Cain released his shirt. "Look, I know you are confused and upset, but I'm not the guy to help you with that kind of stuff. I'm just here to take you to the farm."

"We're not going to your goddamn farm!"

"Don't you get it, kid? Your grandmother's dying. There is nothing you can do about it. And once she's gone, you and Cybil will be all alone."

"We'll have each other."

"For how long? She has eight years before she's a legal adult. Do you have any clue what could happen to her in that time? You won't be able to go with her once you're of age and, I'm sorry, but I don't think you're ready to take care of her by yourself."

"That's not your decision!"

"Fine," he snapped. "Let's just assume you two are kept together. You'll be an adult soon but you aren't in a position to be anyone's legal guardian. She'll stay in the system and you'll both be on your own until you get your life together. Do you understand that there are bad people out there, people who would love to get their hands on a beautiful little girl like her, who doesn't talk and can't tell?"

Ice formed in Dane's veins. "There are good people out there, too."

"Okay, but come on, Dane, I know you're different. You've seen what's in people's minds."

He swallowed, not wanting to admit that his telepathy had limits and he could only overhear the thoughts of children.

"Ah," Cain said with understanding. "I didn't realize."

Certain he hadn't said anything, he snapped, "What are you talking about?"

"You can only read the thoughts of innocents. Once a person becomes jaded, they're blocked to you."

Shaken, he looked up at him, mouth agape. "How…"

Cain tapped the side of his head. "We have some things in common."

Dane had suspected, but now his suspicions were confirmed. "How long have you been that way?"

"It varies, depending on who I'm around. You're easy."

He scowled. "Because I'm a kid?"

"Sure, we can say that's the reason." He started walking and Dane rushed after him.

"What other reason would there be?"

"Plenty. I could probably teach you how to control it better."

"You can?"

"Sure, when we get to the farm."

He started walking again when Cain did. Dane wasn't giving in, but it was too cold to stand still on the side of an icy road. "We're never gonna see her again, are we?"

This time, when Cain looked at him, he read empathy in his eyes as if he understood such loss. "I don't know. I can only tell you that my father has your grandmother's best interest at heart."

"Why? He doesn't even know her."

"Let's call it a mission from God."

"If the treatment works, will they meet us at the farm?"

He didn't need a verbal answer to understand that his grandmother would not be coming to the farm. He read the truth in Cain's eyes.

"How could she just leave us? She's supposed to take care of us."

"She left the house to you and Cybil. That's her way of taking care of you."

"Will I see her again?"

Something bleak and sad flashed in Cain's eyes. "I don't know if we'll ever see them again."

He frowned at the way he included his father in his grandmother's fate. "Is your dad some sort of doctor?"

"Let's just say he has access to things the average person doesn't. You'll understand more once we get to the farm."

Exhausted, he debated what to do. "Are you going to hurt us?"

Cain scowled. "No. You'll be looked after. You're old enough to learn a trade and there are plenty of males around to teach you."

"Where will you be?"

"I probably won't stay. But you can work and Cybil can go to school and play with the other females. She needs a place where she can feel safe again."

Colby whined, pulling on the leash as if urging him to move faster. Dane hesitated. "What if we hate it?"

"Give me one month. If in one month, you decide to leave, we'll figure out something else."

By then, they would have to know if the treatment worked or not. "Fine. One month."

CHAPTER 41

$\mathcal{A}$ weak sigh broke the silence and Larissa's lashes fluttered. She resembled an angel. Eleazar swallowed hard, recalling Adriel's warning of the internal damage that still would remain.

Larissa's ivory flesh had mended and healed. Her skin was clean and the external bruises had faded. Shadows formed in purple crescents on her cheeks, and her color was still more pale than it should be.

"Larissa?" He slowly traced the back of his knuckle gently down her cheek. "Can you hear me, love?"

Her eyelids twitched but did not open.

Laying a hand over hers, he whispered, "Rest. You're safe now."

A floorboard creaked, alerting him of an audience. Adriel hovered by the threshold to the bedroom, holding another pewter cup. "I brought you this."

He breathed in, prepared to let out an objection, but her stern look deflated any protest. Waving her into the room, he accepted the cup and drank gratefully.

Adriel's blood was aged and potent. It would replenish him several times faster than that of a young immortal or a mammal. Finishing the offering, he sat the cup carefully on the bedside table. "We're breaking the law."

"I imagine many laws will be broken tonight, *Bishop*."

He glanced at her, hearing the pointed way she used his title, but not exactly sure why.

"You'll need one more dose before you see him. He has immortal blood in his system."

His jaw locked. He didn't need the reminder. "Larissa's blood is young."

"It's still immortal, Eleazar. Don't be foolish. This time you won't have other males there to aid you."

He recalled the night they put an end to Cerberus. There had been several of them against one, and it had been quite a battle. "I'm older now. Stronger."

"And your mate depends on you, so do everything in your power to return safely."

He laughed without humor. His friend had discovered his Achille's heel. Larissa would forever be his greatest vulnerability, and loving her would drive him to rethink every move he made in his eternal life. He would do nothing to jeopardize her safety and everything to ensure it.

"No one can ever know," he said quietly, his gaze studying his motionless wife.

His friend rested a hand on his shoulder. "I shall take it to my grave."

He believed she would. If not for his intervention, Adriel would likely have been dead by now, or worse, tortured for centuries. An immortal's ability to heal was sometimes a curse when their existence was filled with such misery.

But Adriel's loyalty wasn't born of debt. It was reciprocated by his own. He covered the hand resting on his shoulder with his own. "Thank you."

"It's not necessary—"

"It is. You were there with her the other day when he approached her and you were here for me tonight. You are a true friend, Adriel, one I'm grateful to know."

Her hand slipped away and he took no offense, understanding that she could not tolerate a masculine touch for too long.

"I'll see about preparing a kettle for when Larissa awakes, and I'll bring you another." She collected the cup from the table and left the room.

Silus had his own injuries to tend to and no one waiting at his bedside as he atoned in a cell. Eleazar dropped the stack of planks and tools onto the cement floor with a loud clatter, and the bastard stirred from where he rested in the shadowed corner.

A moment of silence passed as Eleazar lit the torch and mounted it on the wall, casting an amber glow throughout the cellar.

"You can't keep me in here," Silus growled, pain evident in his voice. Without additional blood, his wounds would be slow to heal.

Eleazar reached for a folded sawhorse and opened it, situating the stand on level ground. He did the same with the other, then set several long boards across the top, forming a table—roughly the length of one male.

"Come dawn, my family will realize I'm missing. You will have to answer to The Council, Bishop, and I plan to tell them you imprisoned me without the right to speak my peace."

Eleazar untied the string of a small leather sack and poured nails onto the table. He counted to make sure he had enough.

"Once they find out what you did, you'll face consequences."

Lifting the hand saw, Eleazar pointed it at his prisoner. "You always say too much, Brother Silus." He crossed a two-by-four over the wood planks and cut it to length, eye-balling it to fit perfectly along the width of the four planks.

Once he sawed it, he cut two more, nailing one two-by-four to the head of the table, one to the foot, and one to the center. He lifted the flat surface to inspect that all pieces were secure. Then he set it against the wall and started the entire process over again.

Silus rested one forearm through the bars and watched him while his other arm hung uselessly at his side. "You'll see what she's like. Eventually, you'll know how infuriating—"

Before he could speak another blasphemous word about his mate, Eleazar had him by the jaw, a pair of pliers wedged in his mouth, locked on his tongue, and a look of sheer murder in his eyes.

"Speak one more ill word of her, and I swear to all that is holy that I will break every tooth in your head and cut out your tongue."

Sweat gathered on Silus's battered face.

"Nod if you understand."

He mumbled an incoherent word and nodded. Eleazar released him and returned to his woodworking.

Silus watched him through bloodshot eyes. The longer Eleazar worked, the tighter the male's tension coiled.

Once Eleazar had two flat surfaces constructed, he started on the sides—cutting wood to the length of the other piece's width. All four would have to be roughly two feet high.

Silus grew impatient with watching the process and paced the cell. Dry blood clotted on his torn shirt, and he moved with a slight limp. His skin bore the remaining claw marks from Eleazar's fists, and his hair was in complete disarray. His arm still appeared broken as it hung lifelessly at his side, loose from the socket.

Setting each constructed piece aside, Eleazar kept his gaze on his work. "I warned you what would happen if you ever laid a finger on her again. It's forbidden to touch another male's mate. You've broken one of our most sacred laws."

His words cut away as he took several moments to seethe through his rage, remembering the filthy condition in which he found her: throat ripped open, body drained of her divine blood, her precious life sustained by a thread. It had been clear that Silus meant to end her.

Hardly calm, he pushed out a jagged breath and asked, "What would you have told The Elders if she had died?"

Their eyes met, and it was clear he had not thought that far ahead.

Elazar slammed a fist into the cement wall, sending cracks bursting outward like tributaries. *"What would your excuse have been?"* He shouted. Bearing his fangs, he spoke through clenched teeth. "What justification did you have to touch my mate?"

"She's still my wife."

His breathing stopped as he glared at Silus

with pure hatred. Eleazar reached behind him, removing a sheath of papers from the waste of his trousers and marched to the cell.

"Sign them," he growled, shoving the contract through the bars as the papers fluttered to the dusty floor.

Silus glanced dispassionately at the annulment papers and made no move to collect them.

"Pick them up and sign them!"

They locked glares. Eleazar would not budge. If he had to open a vein on the male to seal the contract in blood, he would. He would see that it was signed.

"If you want any mercy for your crimes, you will sign the annulment. There's no winning her back. She's mine. Not a single elder on The Council will overlook your crimes tonight. You've been ordered by them to sign. Now *pick up the papers and sign!"*

With a deep huff of distaste, he bent and collected the papers. "I'll need a pen."

Eleazar flung one into the cell and Silus grunted when it embedded in his arm. He yanked the pen free with a grunt and used the wall as a flat surface, scribbling his name in black ink and blood. He fed the papers through the bars and Eleazar collected them from the floor, rolling the contract into a scroll and storing it safely in the waistband of his pants once more.

"Will you let me out now?"

"Not yet." He returned to his wood-working.

"Tomorrow, my father, my grandfather, and my great-grandfather will demand I be released. You may be the bishop, but you're not The Council."

The corner of Eleazar's mouth kicked up in a sardonic grin. "Your ignorance baffles me. What a fool you are to think you will just walk away from this."

"You said if I signed—"

"I said I would be merciful, which is more than you deserve. Come dawn, you'll still be breathing. Consider that my show of mercy." He lifted the handsaw and examined the blade. "I heard you had a run-in with Ms. Schrock."

"Who?"

Certain he was well aware of his friend's name and existence, he glared at him. "Adriel Schrock." Eleazar set down the saw and gripped the handle of the planer. "Not many people know the story of Adriel's mate."

He shaved a long coil of wood off a jagged

plank. Shavings gathered on the floor. He examined each edge for splinters and roughness, set on smoothing his work until it appeared flawless.

"Cerberus was a cruel bastard. He never had a kind word to say to his mate. Some males are simply that way, entitled and suffering from a god complex. After too much time left to their own devices, they cannot be fixed."

Eleazar replaced the section of wood with another and continued to shave down the edges. Each shift of his booted feet sifted through the collection of shavings gathered on the floor and the scent of wood mixed with the putrid odor of dry, rotting blood.

"Aside from The Elders and those who traveled here on the Charming Nancy, no one remembers Cerberus. They call Christian Schrock a bastard because they assume Adriel had him out of wedlock. But that's simply not true. Christian is the son of mated parents. His mother is a female of honor and his sire, well… Suffice it to say, Christian's genealogy speaks for itself, and that is why he holds a seat on The Council."

Appearing to grow tired of Eleazar's story, Silus prowled the cell from dark corner to dark corner. His agitation showed like that of a caged animal.

Eleazar continued to sand down the pieces of wood until every edge and side was smooth. He wasn't a monster, after all.

He used a drill press to carve twin holes into one short side and fed a rope through the holes, knotting the braid so it wouldn't slide free. He tested the handle, satisfied with its sturdiness.

Retrieving his satchel of nails, he selected several strong ones. He aligned two planks and nailed them to a supportive piece, edge to edge, forming a perfect right angle. He secured the inner seam with another two-by-four.

"I did not know Cerberus, and back then, Adriel was a stranger to me. Today, she's one of my closest friends." He met Silus's stare with a punishing glare. "I'm very protective of those who have earned my favor and loyalty."

He removed more nails and hammered another section to the foot of the larger piece, forming another ninety-degree angle.

"Cerberus was a problem. He could not be taught to do right and there was no un-training his mind from its defiant patterns. He would have beaten and raped Adriel until he killed her, or at least eviscerated her soul and left nothing more than a hunk of flesh and bone.

"Rabid immortals must be put down when *feeish,* but when they're not *feeish,* lines are blurred. Evil must be contained."

After hammering the fourth side to the base, he now had a cavernous box. Admiring his work, he lifted it by the roped handle and leaned it carefully against the wall, facing the cell. He glanced up, noting it was certainly long enough to fit a man but not wide enough for shifting or twisting."

He lifted the last long piece and sanded the edges. "Tonight, when you attacked my mate, you nearly drained her of blood. They say immortals have eternal life, and we claim only an unanswered immortal risks the chance of turning."

Eleazar stared through the dark cell with glistening, dilated eyes. "But I've been around long enough to know that inside every immortal lurks the one thing we all fear." His tongue traced over his long fangs and his claws distended. "We're all just trying to deny our nature but, deep down, we're all susceptible to our basic instincts." A low growl rumbled from Eleazar's chest. "We all hide a vicious vampire inside."

Silus stopped prowling about the cell. Now, he had his full attention.

"As immortals, we require blood. It's the one key to our eternal salvation. Without it, we are weak. Our strength wanes and our bodies atrophy. Madness sets in as the hunger for blood wholly possesses our every desire. You see, Brother Silus, life is full of duality. Heaven requires a hell, good is balanced by evil. And when a species' only guarantee is the gift of eternal life, it can quickly flip into a curse. As immortals, our bodies naturally refuse to die, even when our souls beg for a merciful death. Our flesh can waste away and organs can painfully decline, slowing our healing, but we will heal. That is our gift, God's intended promise to us. Our species can regenerate limbs and graft skin, but without the nourishment of blood, the process is long and painful."

He lifted the final piece of wood off the sawhorses and fit it carefully over the box. Proud of his fine craftsmanship, he grinned at Silus.

The male tensed and took a step back. "I

want to speak to my father. I demand to face The Elders!"

Eleazar chuckled and swatted the sawdust from his pants. "I'm afraid your chance to make demands has passed."

He swept the wood shavings toward the wall with the side of his boot and closed the sawhorses. Once his materials were stacked neatly out of the way, he reached into the tool box and withdrew a long machete, wrapped in cloth. Unraveling the fabric, he revealed the freshly sharpened metal that caught the glint of the torch in its polished blade and spine. He flexed his fingers around the handle, fitting the bolster comfortably at the base of a tight fist.

The blade sliced through the air with a quick practice swing, and the flame flickered on the torch. He grinned at Silus.

"We buried Cerberus in a box about that size, and that is where he remains today, starved, alone, and trapped for the rest of his eternal existence. Nothing to do but think about what he's done."

The bishop's flat mouth flexed into a quick smirk that didn't reach his eyes. "Like I said, I had no real attachment to Adriel back then. Imagine if I had shared the friendship we share today. I wonder how much worse I would have made Cerberus's atonement then."

Eleazar glanced at the crumbling ceiling where cobwebs gathered and centipedes crawled. "I'm in love with the female sleeping in my bed. You'll never grasp how all-encompassing such an emotion can be, but I can sum it up for you. I would gladly die a thousand deaths to save her one moment of pain. I would forsake my God and all my laws to protect her, not because it's my duty, but because we share an unbreakable bond akin to nothing I've ever experienced before."

He kicked the box and it slid loudly down the wall, clattering to the floor.

"Tonight, you tried to kill her."

"Bishop—"

He launched at the bars and snarled, *"You put your hands on my mate and tried to drain her dry! I could hear her screams!"*

He shivered. The only thing worse than the sounds of Larissa's screams was the silence that followed in the time it took to get to her when her screams had stopped.

Seething, he glared through the cell bars. "Now, it's your turn to scream."

Silus staggered back as the bishop revealed a key. The bars creaked open. And before he could escape, Eleazar was on him, snarling and slicing through limbs, biting and drinking back his mate's stolen blood. Eventually, his screams stopped too.

It was still dark outside when Eleazar emerged from the safe house, dragging the heavy box behind him. His clothes were soiled with blood and adrenaline thrummed through his veins.

He dragged the box far into the woods, to an area crawling with poisonous oak that most would avoid. It took only a short time to dig the hole. He inspected the box one last time, making sure the lid was nailed tight, when he noted some blood had seeped through the wood, staining the corner.

He knocked on the top. "Rest well, Brother Silus. Should we be here when you heal, I may consider your apology then. But no promises." With a booted foot, he shoved the hand-crafted coffin into the ground.

CHAPTER 42

ain held up a hand and they stopped moving. "Quiet. Something's out there."

Dane stilled and placed a hand on Colby's head, calming the dog. Since losing his mother, he didn't like being in the woods after dark. He wanted to ask why the cab had dropped them off so far from the house but he was too afraid to make a sound, unsure what was out there.

"Take your sister." Cain deposited Cybil's sleeping body into Dane's arms and pressed a finger to his lips. "Don't move."

He disappeared beyond the trees and Dane's breath hitched. Anger battled with his worry as he quickly spiraled into a frenzied panic. How could he have just left him there?

Tears of frustration formed a boulder in his throat as he wanted to yell for Cain to come back, but screaming might alert whatever was hiding in the woods. Should he wake up Cybil?

His body trembled, unsure what to do and Colby pulled on the leash. Suddenly, Cain reappeared, strutting out from the trees with a smirk.

"What was it?" Dane hissed.

Cain grinned and examined his hand. "None of our business. Damn, I think I touched poison oak." He collected Cybil and they continued walking.

Bitter, cold and exhausted, Dane snapped, "Next time, don't leave us like that."

Cain glanced over his shoulder. "You'll be safe here."

He rolled his eyes. As if the Amish had any sort of security system to protect him. They didn't even own guns.

"We own guns."

"Hey! Stay out of my head."

"You need to learn to guard your thoughts. And we have guns for hunting. However, using weapons for self-defense is frowned upon."

"Great," Dane said dryly.

Cain chuckled. "Don't worry. We protect ourselves in other ways."

It had started to snow and the ground was quickly covered in a blanket of white, blotting out their footsteps and turning the earth silver under the bright moonlight. Glancing back, Dane wondered if anyone would ever know they had come this way. No one, aside from his grandmother, knew they were here. Maybe she didn't even know.

"Do you guys have phones?"

"There's a call box on the road, not far from here."

It was a small but comforting relief. He would see how the day played out, but chances were, he and Cybil would be sneaking back this way later tonight.

"One month," Cain called from several steps ahead. "You agreed you'd tough it out for one month."

Dane scowled and focused on blocking his thoughts, clueless how one did that. The most he could do was picture Colby and thought of nothing else.

"That'll work."

"Shut up," he snapped, soaked feet crunching over the snow.

ABILENE STARED through the frosted glass as snow sifted like sugar from the sky. Winter was upon them.

She gazed at her reflection in the glass, mouth slackened by sorrow and eyes weary. Her hair hung loosely about her shoulders.

Her fingers reached for her reflection and touched the sad eyes staring back. Her warm fingertips melted the cool frost into moisture, and twin tears slipped through the condensation, mirroring the tears on her face.

It had been days with no word from him. Her head hung as she worried if he was even still alive. Without a bond, she had no way of reaching him, no way of knowing if he'd mated or found his end.

She was alone. This winter marked the death of her marriage and all that she knew as a young female and, from here on, she would be wiser. The Bible spoke of seasons, and this was clearly a time for sorrow. She did not know if she had the strength to grow when so much of her wanted only to lie down and die.

Jonas held his head in his palms and prayed, *Dear Lord, give me the grace to endure this which you have so tested my love. For love bears all things, believes all things, hopes all things, and endures all things. Let my love and the love of my Abilene endure this task you have charged me with and forgive me for the wrong I'm about to do.*

The door to the bathroom opened, spilling light into the dim motel room that they had checked into some time ago. His stomach cramped with the encroaching expectations, and he glanced up as his mate came into view.

A pale, pink bathrobe encased her body and her silver hair hung in thin strands around her face. Everything she was, her entire being, called to him, and he found himself rising and crossing the room, desperate to get to her.

She held up a hand. "Have you signed the papers?"

He glanced at the small table against the wall and nodded.

"Good." She went to the table and picked up the pen. With a deep breath that ended in a fast exhale, she scribbled her name on the last page. Facing him, she folded the sheath of papers and handed it back to him. "This is everything you should need if anyone ever asks."

He shook his head, unable to accept the paperwork. "Let's not do this, Clara. We could be happy. I'm an honorable male and—"

"Jonas, we've already agreed."

He pivoted and ran a hand through his hair in frustration. "I can't!"

She coughed and crossed the room to where his jacket hung. Stuffing the paperwork into the sleeve, she went to her bag and selected several pills from a bottle. "It's not your choice, it's mine." She swallowed back the many blue pills. "It's already begun."

Sucking in a harsh breath, he raced to her side and caught her wrist. "What have you done?"

"Nothing I hadn't warned you I'd do. You're a nice man, Jonas, but I plan to spend my eternity with my husband." She lifted her wrist. "Should we get started?"

Everything about their contaminated bargain struck him as unholy—a loophole. Mating was a sacrament. Surely there would be a consequence for any attempt to manipulate God's plan.

And why didn't she want him? Infuriated

that she could be so indifferent and callous, he looked away and snapped, "How is it you feel nothing for me?"

"That's not true. I just signed away the custody of my grandchildren to you. Clearly, I feel something."

"And what if I'm to die? What will come of your grandchildren then?"

"Cain will protect them."

"Cain," he sneered. "My son is too self-serving to do what you ask."

"I think you're wrong. He and Cybil share a connection."

Snarling with frustration, he got in her face and sneered, "My son is more likely to drain that little girl dry than spare a moment of his own comfort to see to hers."

She blinked and her eyes unfocused. "Your anger can't undo what's been done, Jonas. I'm getting tired and I need to rest now."

She went to the bed and coughed. His anger morphed into concern and he found himself by her side. Her body was warm, but she shivered. He helped her recline into a comfortable position.

"You had better start soon. I'm falling asleep."

His heart raced, and he hesitated. "Can… Can I hold you?"

"I think that would be nice."

He slowly eased onto the bed, taking up the space behind her and curling a gentle arm around her waist. She shut her eyes and sighed.

"It's been a long time since a man held me like this."

The scent of her blood called to him and his eyes focused on her pulse, following every darkened vein under the translucent covering of her skin.

"Will it hurt, Jonas?"

He swallowed. "No. I will make it pleasurable for you."

Eyes still closed, she smiled. "Well, there's something to look forward to. Go ahead then, I'm ready."

Her pulse slowed and her body cooled. He drew back the opening of her robe, exposing her narrow shoulder. Sweeping away her hair, he breathed her in and pressed a kiss over her pulse.

A soft sigh met his ears and his body hardened. He pulled her closer, holding her tight in his hungering, aching need, and sank his teeth into her vein.

She stiffened then instantly relaxed. Hot, nourishing blood met his tongue and he groaned, pulling greedily from the source. His body rocked into her, hungry and wanting for more. Her breathy sighs were short and labored.

His grip tightened and he tasted her panic but sent a calming command out and she relaxed. The darkness inside of him retreated and his body purred at the relief, his soul sewing to hers and a new hope stitching his heart together again.

The tinge of something synthetic met his tongue and he pulled away, licking his lips at the bitter taste of western medicine. He rolled her to her back and smiled down at her, biting into his wrist and opening his vein.

"Now, you must drink, sweet Clara."

She watched him through silver lashes, her gaze barely sneaking through the slits of her eyes as she slowly shook her head.

"No, Jonas." Her hand weakly covered his. "Now I'm done."

His body trembled, the scent of her anemia strong and alarming. "You must. I've taken too much blood and we have to complete the transition."

"We discussed this," she murmured, her words slow and slurred.

"Forget what we discussed!" he snapped. "You must drink!"

Her hand slipped away and her head lulled deeper into the pillow.

"Clara! I command you to drink." He cradled her shoulders, dragging her body over his, and pressed his wrist to her thin, cold lips. "Clara! Open your eyes!"

He sent out a mental command, but her mind hid under a fog of muscle relaxers and sleeping aids.

"Clara!"

His heart thundered and he shook her violently, panic choking him as sure as sleep suffocated his mate. "Clara, please," he begged, a gasped sob ripping through his constricting throat. "I need you."

Crimson smeared across her lips and her mouth slackened. Her pulse slowed to an untraceable flutter and he rocked her in impotent desperation, weeping and cradling her frail body close to his heart.

The agony he suffered in the hours that followed was beyond any pain he'd ever known. Part of his soul amputated as her heart slowed and no longer beat. He wept over her, cradling her lifeless body in his arms. He would never be whole again.

Laying out her still, lifeless body, he righted her robe and curled his arms around her. His tear-chapped face pressing into her hair and skin as he wept for what would never be. He waited for the dawn to come, welcoming its scorching rays and eager to die beside her.

CHAPTER 43

White, snow-covered fields stretched as far as his eyes could see. Cybil had finally woken and walked beside him in palpable awe.

As the sun crested the horizon, painting the sky in fiery shades of pink, the temperature warmed. Dane's feet were numb and soaked through, and he desperately wanted to collapse.

Colby raced up the hill, leaving pawprints in the snow and barking at something in the distance.

"We're almost there," Cain said, grinning down at Cybil.

"You said that two hours ago," Dane grumbled.

"Hey, I can't help it if you're slow."

His knees screamed for rest as they marched up the steep hill, the snow now several inches thick. The sun shined brightly against the white hills, making it difficult to see what waited on the other side of the steep knoll.

Cybil ran ahead and gasped. Colby barked and disappeared.

"Don't go any further," he yelled, hurrying his tired, frozen legs to catch up. "Jeans were definitely the wrong choice."

All the breath left his lungs in a whoosh. Set deep in a valley of the mountains was an enormous spread of well-worked countryside. Stone walls and farmhouses dotted the picturesque view. Red barns popped against the white earth, and animals left a speckled trail of footprints like Colby's.

The dog raced forward, chasing several clucking hens and sending a goat romping in the other direction. It was something out of a storybook.

He glanced down at his sister and laughed. Her smile meant everything to him. When he reached for her hand, she curled her small, cold fingers around his.

"Let's go," he said, pulling her down the hill toward the winter majesty.

As they traveled downhill, animals bleated. The warm, welcoming scent of smoke plumed from chimneys, and he ached to warm his body beside a fire. He could smell various foods cooking nearby and envisioned crispy fried bacon and fluffy eggs.

Boys in black, brimmed hats and girls in layered dresses and cloaks glided down the hillside on toboggans, and Cybil stilled to watch them from afar. Dane sensed her curiosity and grinned at the thought of her participating in such a normal childhood activity.

Only then did he realize how encased in grief their lives had become. An unexpected stab of hope wedged between his ribs and he frowned. Maybe this place wouldn't be so bad after all.

Cybil giggled as one child took a tumble at the foot of the snowy hill, and Dane stared in shock. It was the first time he had heard her laugh since their mom died.

Sensing Cain watching him, he looked up. Awash with vulnerable emotions, he looked for Colby and thought only of the dog. *Colby, Colby, Colby,* he mentally repeated, hiding any other thoughts.

He wasn't ready to concede and admit that coming to the farm might have been a wise decision for Cybil after all.

"Let's keep moving," Cain said, directing them west. "We're going to that house over there."

"Whose house is that?" Dane marched after him.

"My grandparents'. It's where you guys are going to stay."

A wooden fence boxed in the old colonial, and the front door opened the moment Cain unlatched the gate. A slender woman dressed in a plain bonnet and maroon gown smiled at them, and Cybil stopped walking.

"Cain," she greeted with a smile. Colby rushed ahead to sniff the woman's hand and she laughed. "And who is this?"

Cain looked back, giving no command that they follow. "That's Colby, and this is Cybil and Dane." He took the stairs and crossed the porch, pressing a kiss on the woman's cheek. "Guys, this is Nanna Faith."

She frowned, studying Cain with a confused look. Cain nodded with a solemn look in his eyes, then her smile reappeared but didn't reach her eyes. "You must be freezing. Come in, come in. I'm sure your grandfather will have many questions about your journey," Nanna Faith said softly as she held the door.

Dane towed Cybil along the path and told Colby to stay outside.

The house was bare and simple. The furniture was mostly made of wood and the wood floor was worn in spots. Braided rugs added a minimal splash of color.

"Cain." A man, appearing about Cain's age, filled a doorway. He had long black hair, as shiny as a crow's feather, with a silver streak down the side. "You're back."

Cain removed his hat and held it in both hands, appearing more humble than Dane believed him to be. "Hello, Grandfather."

Dane did a doubletake. Surely this guy wasn't Cain's grandpa. It was physically impossible, genetically preposterous. Yet, he had introduced the woman as Nanna Faith.

A moment passed when no one spoke a word, but Dane had the suspicious sense that plenty was said.

The man lowered his gaze, a grief-stricken look crossing his face. "So, you are certain it was Isaiah?"

Cain nodded solemnly. "I think the chances are extremely high."

"Very well. Come inside, children."

The men walked deeper into the house, and Dane halted Cybil from following. "Take off your shoes."

They stomped out of the wet shoes, leaving chunks of slushy ice melting into the hardwood floor. Dane leaned down and using the sleeve of his sweatshirt he tried to mop up the mess before anyone saw it. When he looked up and found Nanna Faith watching him, he flushed. "Sorry."

She smiled. "It's only water."

On socked feet, they followed her into the kitchen. He knew Amish people didn't do cars or electricity, but actually seeing such primitive appliances in use was like traveling back in time.

Nanna Faith stood behind a wooden side table and sifted flour into a wide bowl. Other cooking powder cluttered the surface, and everything was jarred rather than packaged.

"You can warm your hands by the woodstove," Faith said as she dug her hands into the bowl and kneaded the contents.

Dane led Cybil to the boxy woodstove with a smokestack that shot right through the kitchen roof. "Careful." They held out their hands and divine heat warmed their frigid fingers.

"Cain, why don't you come to my study where we can talk."

"Don't be long, Ezekiel," Faith said, rolling out a thick wad of dough on the surface of the table.

Dane's stomach growled with hunger. "Sorry."

Faith laughed. "Help yourself to the sausage on the table."

He gradually worked his way to the table but hesitated to help himself to their food. Cybil wasn't so shy. She bit into a fat link and grinned at Faith.

"Do you like it?"

"She doesn't talk," he told the woman.

"Oh. Well, have as much as you like. We have plenty more."

He stole a link and took a bite. The warm, fatty flavor of freshly grilled meat met his tongue, savory and more delicious than anything he'd eaten in weeks. "Wow."

She grinned. "We make everything fresh here. No markets or pre-processed additives."

He wondered why the rest of the world settled for anything less. He helped himself to another sausage.

"Nanna?" A female voice called from the front of the house and he stiffened, self-conscious of their presence once more.

"In the kitchen, Grace."

A woman appeared and stilled the moment she spotted them. "Oh, I didn't realize you had company." She gave them the same strange look Faith had given them when they arrived. "Are they…English."

"They arrived with your brother a few minutes ago."

"Cain's back?"

This beautiful woman was Cain's sister?

She wore an identical bonnet to Faith's, only her hair wasn't tucked under the lace as neatly. A wisp of long, chestnut hair swept over her neck, and he wondered if she realized it had escaped.

He frowned at the sight of her bare feet. Weren't her toes cold?

She giggled. "I said, 'Hi, I'm Gracie.'"

Oh shit, she was talking to him? "Uh…"

Her smile was enchanting and her eyes were the prettiest shade of blueish silver he'd ever seen. "Do you have a name?"

"Um, yeah…" He swallowed and his sister frowned at him, jamming an elbow in his side. "Uh, Dane. I'm Dane. And this is Cybil."

"Dane and Cybil will be staying with us," Faith explained. "Why don't you make them some tea, Grace. They've had quite a journey."

"Sure." She set a kettle on the woodstove and continued to study them. It was clear she had a few questions.

A few? More like a hundred—like where did they come from.

Dane's back pressed to the chair and his mouth stopped chewing. He could hear her thoughts. How old was she?

Twenty-one. How old do I look?

The girl stiffened, her hand releasing the wooden handle of the kettle as she abruptly faced him. "Did you say something?"

Eyes unblinking, he pressed his lips shut and swallowed. "No."

"Oh," *I swore I heard him.*

I can hear you!

"How are you doing that?" Grace snapped. "You can hear me?"

"Yes!" Her hands rushed to her temples, and she staggered away from the woodstove.

What am I thinking? Colby, Colby, Colby...

"A dog, but that's not the point." *How are you getting into my head?*

He frowned. *Same way you're getting into mine. I don't know how it works.*

"Well, get out," she snapped.

"Grace!" Faith chastised.

"He's in my head!"

"You were in mine!"

"I'm in everyone's," Grace argued. "I'm allowed. You're different." *You're just some kid.*

And you're just some girl.

"Stop that!" she snapped. "Make your own tea." She stomped out of the kitchen, and Faith shook her head.

"I have no idea what's gotten into her."

CHAPTER 44

Larissa's mind came awake with the life-affirming warmth of a new dawn, and she drew in an audible breath as her eyes found his. She frowned at his position on the chair. "Why are you over there?"

Eleazar leaned forward and collected her hand in a delicate grip. "How do you feel?"

"I feel fine—" Her frown deepened and her breath hitched.

He gave her a moment to recall the evening before.

Her eyes shimmered with a wash of fresh tears. "Where is he?"

"Gone."

Her panic was palpable. "Eleazar, what did you do?"

He forced a smile, but his face wore the worry and exhaustion of the previous night's events. "Nothing that you need to worry about. You're safe. That's all that matters."

She pushed herself to sit up, not a single wince of soreness and her motions were agile once more. "I don't believe you."

He blocked his mind and stared into her eyes. "Do you trust that I will always protect you?"

She nodded, though her gaze pinched under the heavy concern that knit her brow.

"Then trust that I resolved the issue, and let's never speak of it again."

"His family…"

"I'll handle it." He reached behind him and withdrew the annulment. "He left you a parting gift."

She accepted the sheath of papers with an unsteady hand and brought it to her nose. "Blood."

"Yes. A mix of yours and his."

The papers fluttered to the floor, and the wall of tears spilled from her eyes. "I'm sorry."

"None of this was your fault."

"I should have waited for you to come get me from my parents'."

His lips firmed. The last few hours had been so terrifying, he vowed not to chastise her for such foolishness, but he had to ask. "Why didn't you wait for me?"

A sad smile trembled to her lips. "I missed you."

The simple confession rained over him like a cleansing baptism. He laughed with relief. "I missed you too."

She scooted over and waved for him to join her on the bed. He could deny her nothing. Sliding beside her, he pulled her close and she nestled into his side.

"I saw my sister-in-law. She's quite pregnant and beautiful. It got me to thinking that I might like to…" She looked up at him with a shy smile. "It would be nice to have children close in age to my brother's."

A possessive need to kiss her crawled through him. Nothing would please him more than to see her body flourish with life and his line continued. "Last night was horrific. Let me at least hold you in one piece before we put your body through any sort of trauma again."

Her smile wilted. "Oh, Eleazar, I'm so

sorry to have put you through that. You must have been terrified."

"Only of losing you."

Her arms tightened around him. "Well, I'm here now. Safe with my mate."

He pressed a kiss to her hair. "Mine."

She glanced up at him and smiled. "Yours."

His mouth found hers and traced a slow kiss. Her body softened beneath his touch as he caressed her luscious curves. She nipped at his lips and he growled hungrily. "Frisky little lioness."

Her nipples puckered as he removed the sheet and kissed a trail down her front. The scent of her arousal called to him, and he groaned with dark desire. "Ah, what you do to me," he whispered, scooting lower as he licked her curves, sending goosebumps across her belly.

His fingers teased and her body arched, a look of pure temptation on her face. Gone was the skittish little mouse—in its place, the female he loved.

Larissa's eyes widened, and she shifted into a seated position. "What was that?"

He pressed his lips tight, but it was no use. Her body was a distraction that left his mind vulnerable, but he no longer felt the need to hide his true feelings from her. He trusted her to care for him as endlessly as he would care for her. "I love you, Larissa."

She blinked rapidly, tears rushing to her eyes as she smiled. "I love you, too."

He pressed a kiss to her shoulder and nuzzled her throat. "Let me make love to you."

She shut her eyes and eased back into the pillows. Her entire essence radiated peace and contentment. He kissed lower and smiled against her honeyed flesh as she moaned.

He teased her for some time, licking over her most sensitive peaks and delving his tongue into every secret she hid. There wasn't a single part of her she could keep from him.

She whimpered, drenched with need and pleading for him to fill her. Dragging his rigid body over hers, he aligned his hard cock with her soft and welcoming sex.

"Please, Eleazar. You're torturing me."

His scent filled the room, strong, rich, and heady. Daylight filtered through the windows, bathing them in morning light. Her tapered legs curled around him, pulling him close, and their tongues danced in a fiery kiss of passion that quickly heated to demanding.

He plunged into her heat, burying himself to the hilt. Her body arched, angling him deeper. He thrust hard and, together, they cried out in ecstasy.

Claws scraped over flesh and mouths bit and pulled. Her moans of pleasure echoed his as, together, they wove a tapestry of passion and desire. They reveled in the absolute freedom of their love and he never wanted to let her go—even an eternity would not be enough.

Her body was heaven, and her mind was an endless maze of provocative opinions he could never imagine on his own. His soul entwined so intricately with hers, they would never untangle from each other.

Lacing his fingers with hers, he pushed her hands over her head and buried himself deeply, thrusting hard. He wanted to possess every inch of her being and then some. He wanted to give her all that he was and would ever be.

Looking into her dilated eyes, his vision changed and his fangs extended. She desired a family and he would give her one. Anything she wished for, he would provide.

Her bite punctured his skin and she drank from his vein. His body shuddered with euphoric satisfaction and his seed spilled deep within her womb. Her body clenched around his, milking every ounce of pleasure from his soul.

But he would never run out of joy to share with her. As sure as the sun recreated the dawn for all of eternity, his love would forever grow for his mate.

$\mathcal{A}$ knock disrupted the solitude of the house and Larissa frowned, fearful that the day's interruptions would continue long after dark, and she might spend another day alone.

"Go away," Eleazar grumbled toward the intrusive knock, pulling her close.

She nestled into his side and smiled. "What if it's someone with council business?"

"The Council can wait. I'm taking the day off."

Beyond pleased, she trailed her fingers over his thighs and stroked him. "The whole day?"

"Yes. And tonight, when we make love again, you will be Larissa King."

Her heart jolted with excitement. "I think I will make a good wife to you."

"Oh, I agree." The knock rattled again, this time pounding with more insistence.

"Maybe you should see who it is."

He glanced toward the window and frowned. "It's your brother."

"Adam?"

He was already climbing out of bed. "No, the other one."

"Cain!" She untangled her body from the sheets and quickly searched for clothes. "Where's my dress?"

"Wear this." He tossed her trousers and a male-cut shirt.

She laughed. "I can't wear this."

He arched a brow. "Two weeks ago, you were wearing much less."

Her eyes narrowed. "That's not nice."

"Are we really going to lecture each other—"

"No. Forget it." She shook out the attire. "I'll look ridiculous."

Another knock pounded. "I'll meet you down there."

She quickly finished dressing and raced after him, anxious to see Cain. As she took the stairs, she heard her brother's familiar voice.

"I have important business to—Larissa? What are you doing here, and what on God's green Earth are you wearing?"

She rushed to her brother and hugged him tightly. "Oh, Cain, I have so much to tell you!"

He wore a comical look of confusion as she released him and hooked her arm around Eleazar. Her brother's face paled.

"No."

Eleazar grinned. "It's an interesting twist, don't you agree?"

Cain continued to shake his head. "How…? When…? *What?*"

Taking pity on him, Larissa laughed and took his hand, pulling him into the den. "It's a long story, but we're both very happy about our situation."

"Larissa," Cain whispered. "The guy's older than dirt."

Eleazar cleared his throat and pulled her to his side. "Watch it."

Cain did watch him with a look of disbelief in his eyes. "I, uh, have some important matters to discuss. Council business."

She curled her arms tighter around Eleazar's. "Is it about Father?"

Cain's lips firmed into a flat line. "Yes and no. It's really a private matter among males—"

"Anything you tell me, Larissa will eventually learn, so speak freely."

Her brother hesitated and took a seat. "Fine, I'll just come out and say it. I killed an immortal."

When she gasped, Eleazar sent a calming stroke along her mind and she settled her emotions. His eyebrows lifted, but his voice remained flat. "Who?"

"I don't know her name."

"You killed a female?"

"Before you condemn me, let me explain. She wasn't like us. She was a transition, but not like any kind I'd met before. She was…undercooked."

"Excuse me?"

"She wasn't fully transformed. She still had mortal tattoos, and there was something severely off in her brain."

Larissa looked up at Eleazar, who wore a frown that matched her own. "Someone tried to mate with her."

"Is that possible?" Larissa asked.

"Anything's possible. But if an immortal attempts to bond with a mortal that is not their called mate, the transition gets…disrupted. I haven't seen it happen in centuries, but it's not unheard of."

"She was dangerous."

Eleazar nodded. "The blood exchange leaves them deranged and they must be destroyed just as a rabid animal must. Do you think that is what's been killing the English women in the woods?"

"No, I still believe that's my uncle. Before I ended that thing, she mentioned his name."

Eleazar stiffened. "Then it's true. He's still alive. I also had a run-in with an immortal in the woods. He was deeply *feeish* and looked very much like your uncle. I've informed The Council. This incident confirms our suspicions."

Cain scowled. "More women have died. If they would have listened to me weeks ago—"

Eleazar held up a silencing hand. "What's passed has passed and we need to focus on the future. The creature in the woods possesses incredible strength and speed but is also limited by its condition. However, we do not know how many *others* it has created. I believe I heard them in the woods the day I saw Isaiah. There were many."

Larissa's hand curled around her throat. "They were all mortals? He killed them?"

"He changed them," Eleazar explained. "Who knows why he murders some and attempts to transition others, but he has to be stopped."

"I can stop him."

Larissa's heart sputtered in her chest. "Cain, no. It's too dangerous."

He ignored her objection. "I'm perfect for the job. I have no ties here, and I never will. Annalise and Adam are expecting their first child, and I'm certain they will have many more. There's nothing left for me here. Let me do this, Bishop. Let me take the risk so others don't have to."

Her body quaked with worry. Such decisions should not be rushed into.

"You could be hurt. Gravely injured. Without other immortals there to assist you—"

"I won't get hurt. I can't." Cain shifted and glanced away, his face riddled with shame. "My pain is what links me to Annalise."

"Then why risk it?"

"Because I'm certain I can take the time to hunt him and return in one piece. I won't allow anything bad to happen to me. I won't jeopardize Annalise and the baby."

Eleazar pinched the bridge of his nose. "I do not pretend to understand this connection you share with a claimed mate. It's unheard of."

"These are tumultuous times."

"I think it's a bad idea," Larissa blurted, unable to hold her tongue a moment longer. "Not only could you get hurt, but you could hurt Anna and the baby." She blinked back unexpected tears. "What would I do if something happened to you, Cain?"

He grinned. "You have a mate now. Bishop King would protect you."

She scoffed. "You two are suddenly friends?"

Cain laughed. "We're a far cry from friends, but I trust he will take care of you. Where is Silus, by the way? Have you seen him, Bishop?" He paused and scowled at his wrist. "I stumbled across a patch of poison oak last night. Still itches…"

Eleazar's eyes narrowed. "I can only permit you to hunt Isaiah if you give me your word that you will stay out of harm."

"Done."

"If at any time you doubt your success, return to the farm at once."

"Fair enough."

"And I expect you to return in one month with an update on your progress."

"Fine."

"Then we're in agreement. Now, tell me what news you have of your father and why you stink of mortal children."

Larissa's anger faded as she listened to the trials Cain had faced over the past few weeks. As she learned what he'd done to help their father and how he vowed to protect the children of the murdered woman in the woods.

Eleazar went to his office to retrieve some extra cash for Cain's journey, and while they were alone, she took her brother's arm and smiled. "You used to be my hero. Now, I'll have to share you with many."

"I'm hardly a hero, Larissa."

"Don't do that, Cain. Don't let the assumptions others make about you alter the perception you keep of yourself. You're a male of honor and worth. And, as much as I hate to think of you in any sort of danger, you're doing a brave and selfless thing." She gave him a moment to process her words, then asked, "Are you scared?"

When he didn't make a sarcastic comment or deny his fear, she understood he suffered some hesitation about the task ahead.

"A little." He gathered her hands in his much larger ones and lowered his voice. "Promise you'll check in on the children. I can't help but think they're our responsibility after our uncle killed their mother and father took away their grandmother. They have no one left."

She would check on them often. "Do you think Father will return?"

Her brother swallowed and looked away. "He either bonded with his mate and will make a life with her, apart from his past, or he failed. All I know is that Clara was adamant that it was her time to die. She was very sick when they left, very close to death."

Her jaw trembled as a tear fell from her lashes. She quickly swept it away. "Mother will be devastated."

"No more than she already has been."

"I will look in on her when I look in on the children. Perhaps there's a reason for so much heartache, and we will all be surprised in the end."

He pinched her chin and smiled. "You've always had a romantic mind, sister." Cain studied her for a moment. "Are you truly happy with the match God has chosen for you?"

"Happy would be an understatement."

"Then I'm happy for you." He stood, and Eleazar returned with a thick envelope.

Eleazar slipped an arm around her and pressed a kiss to her hair. "That should be enough for anything you need." There was a mutual distrust between the two, yet they seemed to form a momentary truce, perhaps on her behalf. "Be careful, and try to return as soon as you can."

"Wait!" Larissa wasn't ready to see him go. "Perhaps a vile of Cain's blood would be wise. Then you could track him if he doesn't return."

Both men nodded in agreement, appearing relieved to have the additional sense of security. Eleazar owned a case with glass tubes, needles, and a tunicate. Cain sat patiently as he withdrew a sample of his blood and capped it off.

"I'll keep this safe."

They walked Cain to the front door, and she was surprised to see so much snow outside. "Be safe, Cain."

Her brother nodded and hugged her tightly. "You do the same."

The finality of watching her brother walk away left her shaken. In the past, whenever Cain had visited her home with Silus, she always feared her husband's mood might change. Sometimes it did and sometimes it didn't. That was the problem with Silus; he never followed any one set of rules.

Eleazar's hands rested gently on her shoulders and she instinctively leaned back into his strength.

"You care for your brother very much." It wasn't a question but an obvious statement.

"My family has suffered so much. I don't think we can survive any more trauma."

Eleazar pressed a kiss to the top of her head. "Cain will be back in a few weeks, safe and well."

He couldn't make the same promise about her father.

She hugged him tightly. "This is different."

"Different?"

She rested her cheek against his chest, drawing comfort from the steady beat of his heart. "I've never been with someone who soothes me when I'm troubled. I think I might become addicted to being by your side."

His arms closed around her. "I think I might like that."

He closed the door and lit a fire in the woodstove. Then, together, they put on a kettle and waited for the coffee to brew. It was such an ordinary, beautiful way to spend a snowy morning. It was a perfect start to their ever after.

CHAPTER 46

$\mathcal{T}$he thud of the Bible falling to the floor awoke Abilene with a start. Her eyes adjusted to the daylight and her ears caught the laughter of children in the distance.

Retrieving the book from the floor, she stood from the chair where she'd slept. Through the frosted window, she found a masterpiece of white as if the earth had been freshly baptized by snow.

Children sledded down wintery slopes and tractors slept under drifts. Trees drooped under the weight of ice, showing like crystals as the branches caught the morning sun.

A mantle of white shouldered the hills and fields. It was as if the world she had known yesterday had washed away. More certain than ever before, she sensed her husband's soul now belonged to someone else.

Like the ground, encased in ice and hidden away, Abilene's heart had been buried. A protective hand drifted to the front of her apron, dropping low on her abdomen, where she hid her secret well. The other female might have gotten Jonas, but she didn't take all of him. Pray God, she not lose this one.

Her strength wavered and she needed to feed. Though her desire to keep living had faltered over the passing months, her devotion to her unborn babe gave her purpose again.

After adding wood to the stove and setting a fresh pot of water on the burner, she went upstairs to dress for the day. The house was cold and her bare feet chilled to the bone, but she couldn't recall where she'd left her boots and stockings.

A draft caught her ankles that made her pause just outside of Cain's bedroom. Her son had been gone for some time and she wondered if he returned.

Knocking softly, the door whined open. "Cain?" She frowned when she spotted the window open wide, snow dusting over the wood floor. "Cain?"

The room was empty and as cold as a tomb. She shut the glass and chafed her hands to warm her skin. As she passed Grace's room, she found it empty and her daughter already gone for the day, likely off to feed the animals at dawn as she always did.

Weak with hunger and anxious for a warm cup of tea and a comforting bowl of hot oats, she hurried to her room, but as soon as she opened the door, she sensed she was not alone.

Her hackles rose as she scented another presence. She stilled and scanned the shadows. "Who's in here?"

A jagged breath caught her ear. She rushed around the bed only to stagger to a halt at the sight of her husband crouched in the corner, tears of devastation in his eyes.

"Jonas?" His name was a ghost passing through her lips. How had she not recognized his scent? "Why are you hiding in the shadows?"

He opened his mouth to speak, but all that came out of his was a silent cry. Her heart broke and she fell to her knees, pulling him into her arms.

"Tell me what's happened. How have you come here?"

Every grim exhalation spoke of the trauma he'd suffered, but he appeared incapable of speaking a word.

"It's all right. You don't have to say anything." She pushed the hair from his eyes and cupped his face. "Are you hurt?"

He shook his head and sucked in a stuttering breath. His hand covered his chest and he shut his eyes, leaning his head into the wall. His suffering had such a poignant hold on her, she needed to help him.

"Come off the floor, Jonas. Let me help you to bed."

He allowed her to guide him and docilely laid down when she pulled back the quilt. She rubbed a soothing hand down his back as he sobbed. It was a horrible sight, nearly unbearable to her heart. She comforted him for hours, waiting silently for his tears to dry.

When he finally quieted, his stare focused on the blank wall across from the bed, she gently asked, "Jonas, where is your mate?"

"Gone."

Her blood ran cold. Gone how? Gone where?

Afraid for his soul, she sucked in a sharp breath. "Is it too late?"

He looked up at her, his gaze aged a hundred years. "I don't know. I hardly recall coming here last night. I only knew that I wanted to reach you before…" His hand squeezed over hers. "Abilene, what does this mean for me? What does it mean for us?"

Tears burned her throat. She swiped at her eyes with irritation. "I can't lose you another time."

Too many burdens of late pressed into the creases of his eyes. "Let me stay here. I'll never leave again."

There was no veiling the sorrow in his eyes. Jealousy knifed through her, carving unchangeable scars into her heart.

His hand traveled up her arm as he clung to her. "I have never known another female as I have known you, sweet Abilene. I swear it."

She couldn't breathe. Before she could organize her thoughts, he spoke again.

"I took her blood, but that is all." His gaze turned away and his voice strained. "She didn't survive the transition."

Swallowing back a sob, she pulled his gaze back to hers. "You didn't break our vows?"

"Never."

She doubled over with relief, hugging him tightly to her. "I'm never letting you go. Do you hear me? Your soul is mine, Jonas. I cannot share you."

He held her tight, his lips pressing a soft kiss into her hair. Tears of happiness choked her when he once again looked into her eyes. "No more tears, my love. I'm home where I belong."

She pulled her gown open and climbed into the bed beside him, desperate to be in his arms again. Their bodies came together like a masterpiece written by God.

His mouth kissed and tasted her, and when his palms spread over her womb, he stilled. Then, eyes filled with wonder, he looked at her. "You are with child."

It was her first genuine smile in a very long time. "This one's going to live," she vowed.

He worshipped her body, anointing her body with kisses as they celebrated the sacrament that was their marriage. And when they finished, he held her close to him as if never wanting to let her go.

What they shared could not be replicated by strangers or destined souls. Their love was pure and formed over time. They shared the endless devotion of two hearts, and no matter what threatened them, be it time, distance, or even death, a love so pure would never fade.

"I love you, Jonas."

"I love you more, Sweet Abilene," he rasped, then let out a rattling cough.

CHAPTER 47

*D*estiny shivered and cursed herself for the hundredth time for thinking Uggs were appropriate footwear while hunting a killer in the snowy mountains of Pennsylvania. After a *disagreement* with her crew, she told them to go back to the rest stop. Now, she was wandering through the woods, completely turned around, with an *assassino* on the loose—not her best moment.

Another victim was discovered this week. Another female drained of blood, traces of sexual assault, and fang marks at her carotid artery.

Destiny stomped her wet feet and marched in circles, trying to find a cell signal. Her gloved hands fisted against the cold as the wind whistled eerily through the trees. With each pivot, she held up her phone and cursed her provider when the signal failed.

"Come on," she snapped. Her low battery warning appeared and she growled.

Just then, Adele's muffled voice belted out the first verse of "Rolling in the Deep" and her brother's name flashed on the phone. "Oh, thank God!"

She bit the fingertip of her glove and yanked her hand free. "Vito?"

"Destiny, were you at my place?"

She pressed her lips together. "Uh, no. Why?" Such a lie.

"Liar. All my shit's moved around, and *why* is my gun cabinet open?"

She cleared her throat. "I, uh, needed to borrow something."

"From my hunting cabinet? What the hell did you take?" The rifling and sorting of heavy artillery clattered through the phone. He growled. "Destiny, where the fuck is my crossbow?"

"Look, don't get mad, but I needed it."

"*For what?* That shit's dangerous. And you don't have a clue how to use it. Bring it back right now!"

"I sort of can't."

She could actually picture him clenching his teeth the way he always did when she annoyed him. "Why not?"

"I'm sort of stranded."

"Stranded where?"

"In the woods, but it's fine—"

"Where the hell's your crew?"

She winced. "They went back to the Jim Thorpe rest stop."

"Goddamn it, Destiny! What the fuck did I tell you about hanging out in those woods? Why would your crew leave you there?"

They hadn't wanted to. They tried to get her to leave with them, but she persisted in staying and everyone got fed up. "I don't know. It was the weirdest thing. They all just left."

He growled again and let out a stream of Portuguese curse words. A door slammed and the engine of his car cranked to life. "Send me your location so I can kick your dumb ass when I get there."

"Calm down, Vito. That's why I have the crossbow."

"Are you insane? There's a fucking killer in those woods! Why can't you have a normal job?"

"Like what? All the strippers you work with?"

"At least they're safe! You, on the other hand, have a death wish."

Her phone beeped in her ear. "Look, V, I gotta go. My phone's about to die."

"Of course, it is. Send me your fucking loca—"

The phone powered down. *"Merda!"*

Her eyes widened as soon as she realized how much light the glow of her screen had been giving. It was dark as fuck in the woods now that the sun had set.

Fear teased her stomach and she pocketed the useless device. Maybe this *was* a bad idea.

She could yell for help, but what if the killer heard her?

Fingers freezing, she shoved them into her gloves and crossed her arms, bouncing in place for warmth. Pine needles and crunchy dead leaves peeked from the snow on the forest floor.

A low squawk came from above. Could have been an owl or chipmunk or maybe a bat. Did bats squawk?

Searching the shadows, she debated which direction would lead to the bottom of the mountain. That would be the safest place to wait for her brother.

Leaves crunched behind her, way too loud to be a small animal, and she spun around. *"Who's there?"*

She lifted the crossbow with gloved hands, fumbling to find the trigger in the dark. "Don't come any closer!"

Spindly trees cast black shadows over blue puddles of moonlight. Branches and vines resembled legs, giant hands, and long, gnarled fingers. Her mind was playing tricks on her.

Lifting the crossbow at her chest, she pointed the loaded tip ahead of her. So long as the arrow wasn't aimed at her, she figured she was safe.

Her hands trembled under the weight of the weapon after a few minutes. She hadn't moved, but anxiety left her breathless.

Another branch snapped and something crunched behind her. Her body did an about-face so fast she got dizzy.

"I'll shoot anything that comes closer!"

Wind whined above, followed by a creak. She gasped as a large, dry limb whipped through the branches and hit the ground with a loud thud, and her finger clenched over the trigger, sending the arrow whizzing into the darkness. She yipped and continued to search her surroundings.

If a tree falls in the woods and no one's around… "I guess it does make a sound," she muttered, trying to calm her nerves with lame humor.

She could not shake the sense that she was being watched. With trembling hands, she pulled out her last arrow. It took forever to load the sophisticated bow in the dark. She just prayed she didn't lose an eye.

Once she heard it click into place, she searched the ground. "Where the hell is my glove?"

Sweeping her hands over the covered earth, she rummaged around the leaves and snow for her missing glove and hissed when her fingers swept over something sharp. She pressed her finger to her lips and tasted a warm trickle of blood.

Great. She didn't have a first aid kit on her because she was seriously the stupidest woman alive in Jim Thorpe tonight. She sucked her finger into her mouth and froze as something let out an ominous growl behind her.

Paralyzed by fear and certain it was no

chipmunk, she gripped the bow and stared straight ahead.

Something big jumped from the trees—maybe a mountain lion or a bear—she didn't fucking care. It landed close and she screamed, bolting into a dead run and plowing headfirst into a tree.

Red eyes flashed, and she was sure this was the thing that had been killing the girls in the woods. She screamed as loud as her lungs would allow and scrambled to her feet, running as fast as her legs could carry her.

It was incredibly fast and she failed gym class in high school, but she kept going, panic pumping her legs as every breath burned through her like fire.

It grabbed for her, claws scratching down her back and shredding her coat into ribbons. It fucking cut her and the intense searing pain upset her stomach. She couldn't take it. A stubbed toe was basically her threshold for pain, and her back burned as if acid ate away her skin. She was going to pass out, and whatever that was, it was going to fucking eat her!

She stumbled, tripping over her bulky boots and whacking her knee on something hard. "Don't hurt me!"

She flipped to her back and covered her

face, peeking through her fingers as she hyperventilated with fear. What the hell was it? Tall, with long hair and human features. It wasn't a wild animal—or was it?

Fangs. The motherfucker had fangs.

"*Vampiro*," she breathed, certain she was about to breathe her last breath.

It drew back a clawed hand as if to strike her, and she scrambled for the crossbow when something that could only be a jungle cat leaped at the thing and tackled it to the ground. Her screams kept coming as she scurried to her feet, crossbow in hand, and bolted away as the two predators fought in a scramble of violent hisses and howls.

A disgusting snap, and one of them cried out and fled. The tussle stopped and she threw her open, bleeding back against the tree, searching for whichever one remained. She lifted the bow and tried to listen for any sound.

A twig snapped and she pointed the arrow toward the quiet crack. Gray-camo fatigues tucked into heavy black boots stepped into view. Was it the National Guard?

Her gaze traveled upward to a tapered waist and black fabric stretched tight over a muscled chest. Maybe she hit her head and was dreaming. It was freezing and steam rose off his bare skin. He stepped fully out of the shadows and planted his treelike limbs firmly in a streak of moonlight.

"You've got to be kidding me." Beyond that well-worked chest and thickly corded neck was a face she recognized all too well. "What are you doing here?"

He scowled. "What am I doing here?"

"I'm working!"

"Stay down!" He launched into the trees and a horrible growl sent birds scattering overhead. A split second later, he scared the crap out of her, jumping out of nowhere and landing right in front of her. "Where's your van? Where's your lights and equipment? You clearly have a death wish." He took a menacing step forward, a look of pure distaste on his face.

She raised the crossbow. "Stay back!" Why was this guy always in the woods? The last time she saw him, another body had been discovered, just a few feet from where they were.

He laughed. "What do you plan to do with that?"

"Don't come near me! I'll shoot." There were only two explanations for his presence. He was either hunting the killer in the woods or he *was* the killer in the woods. "I mean it! Back up!"

"Put the weapon down, Destiny."

When she didn't obey his command, there was a faint tingling along her scalp. She adjusted the bow and pointed it directly at his heart. "Not one more step!"

He frowned. "I said, *put it down*."

"Did you kill those women?"

"Put the bow down!" When she ignored the command again, he lost his temper and shouted, "Why won't you do as I say?"

"Answer the question!"

His jaw twitched in frustration, and he spoke slowly. "You will drop the weapon and follow me to the bottom of the mountain. You will forget everything you saw here tonight—"

"Are you crazy? I'm not going anywhere with you!"

He growled and stomped toward her, menacing impatience flashing in his eyes.

Shit, shit, shit! Her finger squeezed as she screwed her eyes shut, and the arrow released with her clipped scream. Then everything went silent.

She gasped and opened her eyes as he dropped to his knees with a grunt, the arrow protruding from his chest where a stain of blood bloomed. He looked up at her from the wound in shock, his mouth opening in a gasp for breath as he wheezed. "Anna…"

To Be Continued…

Want more edgy romance from Lydia Michaels?
Read Prodigal Son (Order of Vampires 3) Now!

Claim your FREE book when you subscribe to Lydia's newsletter!
Click here to sign up for Lydia Michaels' Newsletter.

Are you follow Lydia Michaels?
Stalk her on TikTok, Instagram, Facebook, Goodreads, and BookBub!
TikTok @LydiaMichaels
Instagram @lydia_michaels_books
Facebook @LydiaMichaels
Goodreads
BookBub

Show Your LOVE

If you enjoyed this book, please don't forget to leave a review.

LYDIA MICHAELS' READING ORDER

MCCULLOUGH MOUNTAIN
Almost Priest
Beautiful Distraction
Irish Rogue
British Professor
Broken Man
Controlled Chaos
Hard Fix
Intentional Risk

JASPER FALLS
Wake My Heart
The Best Man
Love Me Nots
Pining For You
My Funny Valentine
Side Squeeze

CALAMITY RAYNE
Calamity Rayne Gets a Life
Calamity Rayne Back Again

THE SURRENDER TRILOGY
Falling In
Breaking Out
Coming Home

SURRENDER GAMES
Sacrifice of the Pawn
Queen of the Knight

MASTERMIND
Blind
Untied

NEW CASTLE
First Comes Love
If I Fall
Something Borrowed

ADDICTED TO YOU
Crush
Bang
Throb

THE ORDER OF VAMPIRES
Original Sin
Dark Exodus
Prodigal Son

STAND ALONES
<u>La Vie en Rose</u>
<u>Simple Man</u>
<u>Sugar</u>
<u>Breaking Perfect</u>
<u>Hurt</u>
<u>Protege</u>

About Lydia Michaels

Lydia Michaels is the award winning and bestselling author of more than forty titles, a certified life coach, and transformational speaker. She is the consecutive winner of the 2018 & 2019 *Author of the Year Award* from *Happenings Media,* as well as the recipient of the 2014 *Best Author Award* from the *Courier Times*. She has been featured in *USA Today, Romantic Times Magazine, Love & Lace*, and more. As the host and founder of the *East Coast Author Convention*, the *Behind the Keys Author Retreat*, and *Read Between the Wines*, she continues to celebrate her growing love for readers and romance novels around the world.

In 2021, Michaels released the groundbreaking, non-fiction series, ***Write***

10K in a Day, to commemorate her career in the publishing industry. She looks forward to many more years of exploring both fiction and non-fiction writing, teaching about the craft, and learning from the others in the author community.

Lydia is happily married to her childhood sweetheart. Some of her favorite things include the scent of paperback books, listening to her husband play piano, escaping to her coastal home at the Jersey Shore, cheap wine, *Game of Thrones*, coffee, and kilts. She hopes to meet you soon at one of her many upcoming events.

You can follow Lydia at www.Facebook.com/LydiaMichaels or on Instagram @lydia_michaels_books

Read By Mood
Billionaire Romance
Falling In | Sacrifice Of The Pawn | Calamity Rayne | Blind

Contemporary Romance
Wake My Heart | The Best Man | Love Me Nots | Pining For You |Almost Priest| My

<u>Funny Valentine</u> | <u>Side Squeeze</u> | <u>Almost Priest</u> | <u>Beautiful Distraction</u> | <u>Irish Rogue</u> | <u>British Professor</u> | <u>Broken Man</u> (LGBTQ) | <u>Controlled Chaos</u> | <u>Hard Fix</u>|<u>Intentional Risk</u>

Emotional Favorites
<u>La Vie en Rose</u> | <u>Simple Man</u> | <u>Wake My Heart</u> | <u>Sacrifice of the Pawn</u> | <u>Crush</u>
Romantic Comedy
<u>Calamity Rayne</u>

Erotic Romance
<u>Breaking Perfect</u> | <u>Protégé</u> | <u>Falling In</u> | <u>Sugar</u>

First in Series
<u>Almost Priest</u> | <u>Falling In</u> | <u>First Comes Love</u> | <u>Wake My Heart</u> | <u>Crush</u> | <u>Original Sin</u>

Paranormal Vampire Romance
<u>Original Sin</u> | <u>Dark Exodus</u> | <u>Prodigal Son</u>

LGBTQ+ & Menage Romance
<u>Broken Man</u> (MM) | <u>Breaking Perfect</u> (MMF) | <u>Crush</u> (MMF) | <u>Hurt</u> (Non-Consensual) | <u>Protege</u>

Sexy Nerds & Second Chances
Blind | <u>Untied</u>

Teacher Student, Workplace, and Age-Gap Love Affairs... Oh my!
<u>British Professor</u> | <u>Pining For You</u> |<u>Breaking Perfect</u> | <u>Falling In</u> | <u>Sacrifice of the Pawn</u>

Single Dads & Single Moms
<u>Simple Man</u> | <u>Pining For You</u> | <u>First Comes Love</u> | <u>Controlled Chaos</u> | <u>Intentional Risk</u>

-

Dark Tortured Hero Romance
<u>Hurt</u>

Non-Fiction Books for Writers
<u>Write 10K in a Day</u>: Avoid Burnout